THE PRICE OF DARKNESS

DC Paul Winter is working undercover to infiltrate the inner circle of the city's premier drug baron, Bazza Mackenzie. Adrift in a brutal world of hard-won respect and easy money, Winter appears to be in his element. Worryingly so . . . But headquarters' concerns about Winter become supplanted by two high profile Portsmouth murders: a visiting property developer is shot dead with clinical efficiency, and a government minister visiting the city is assassinated by two helmeted motorcyclists. DI Faraday, Winter's erstwhile boss, is involved in both enquiries and finds that there is evidence which implicates the beleaguered Paul Winter. The relationship between the two men has never been easy, but now the time has come to bury their differences . . .

Books by Graham Hurley
Published by The House of Ulverscroft:

THE PERFECT SOLDIER
ANGELS PASSING
DEADLIGHT
BLOOD AND HONEY
ONE UNDER

GRAHAM HURLEY

THE PRICE OF DARKNESS

Complete and Unabridged

CHARNWOOD
Leicester

First published in Great Britain in 2008 by
Orion
an imprint of the Orion Publishing Group
London

First Charnwood Edition
published 2008
by arrangement with
the Orion Publishing Group
London

British Library CIP Data

Hurley, Graham
    The price of darkness.—Large print ed.—
    Charnwood library series
    1. Faraday, Joe (Fictitious character)—Fiction
    2. Police—England—Portsmouth—Fiction
    3. Detective and mystery stories
    4. Large type books
    I. Title
    823.9'14 [F]

    ISBN 978–1–84782–347–2

Published by
F. A. Thorpe (Publishing)
Anstey, Leicestershire
Set by Words & Graphics Ltd.
Anstey, Leicestershire
Printed and bound in Great Britain by
T. J. International Ltd., Padstow, Cornwall

This book is printed on acid-free paper

To Peggy Hurley
1916–2007
Cherished and Missed

Acknowledgements

My thanks to the following for their time and advice: John Ashworth, Martin Chudley, Laura Caton, Roly Dumont, Martin Evans, Neil Farnham-Smith, Pat Forsyth, Diana Franklin, Lyn Hoptrough, Richard John, Andrew McCall, Mike Mortimer, Phil Parkinson, Tim Pepper, Brett Rennolds, Dave Sackman, Jonathan Sands, Danielle Stoakes, Barry Walker, Tara Walker. My editor, Simon Spanton, beat the editorial drum with his usual flair, while Gillian Redfearn kept us magnificently in step. To my wife, Lin, a promise: the rest of the journey starts here.

When we are not sure, we are alive.

Graham Greene

Prelude

Uncomfortable in the heat, Winter followed the funeral cortège as it wound up the path towards the cemetery. From here, high on the rocky hillside, he could sense what had drawn the dead man to Cambados. Not simply the lure of Colombian cocaine, delivered wholesale across the Atlantic. Not just the prospect of ever-swelling profits as he helped the laughing powder towards the exploding UK marketplace. But the chance to settle somewhere remote, somewhere real, to make a life for himself amongst these tough, nut-brown Galician peasants.

The cortège came to a halt while the priest fumbled with the gate of the cemetery and Winter paused, glad to catch his breath. The view was sensational. Immediately below, a tumble of houses crowding towards the water-front. Further out, beyond the estuary, the aching blueness of the open sea.

Last night, after an emotional tour of his brother's favourite bars, Bazza had ended up locked in an embrace with Mark's girlfriend's mother. Her name was Teresa. She was a plump, handsome woman who walked with the aid of a stick and, as far as Winter understood, the

1

funeral arrangements had been entirely her doing.

The priest had accepted her assurances that Mark had been a practising Catholic. The friends he'd made had secured a plot in the cemetery. God had doubtless had a hand in the jet ski accident, and Mark's death doubtless served some greater purpose, but the only thing she understood just now was that her daughter's life would never be the same. Bebe had been only months away from becoming Mark's wife. There would have been children, lots of children. God gives, and God takes away, she'd muttered, burying her face in a fold of Bazza's linen jacket.

The mourners began to shuffle upward again, and Winter caught a whiff of something sweet, carried on the wind. Beside him, still hungover, was a lifelong friend of Bazza's, a survivor from the glory days of the eighties. The last time Winter had seen him was in court, a couple of years back. He'd been up on a supply charge, coupled with accusations of GBH, and had walked free after a key witness had changed his mind about giving evidence. Last night, by barely ten, he'd been legless.

'What's that, mush?' He had his nose in the air.

'Incense.' Winter paused again, mopping his face. 'Gets rid of bad smells.'

★　★　★

Late evening, the same day, Winter was drinking alone at an empty table outside a bar on the

2

waterfront. The bar belonged to Teresa. According to Bazza, she'd won it as part of a divorce settlement from her husband, an ex-pro footballer, and for old times sake it was still called the Bar El Portero, the keeper's bar. Winter had been here a lot over the last couple of days, enjoying the swirl of fishermen and high-season tourists, conscious of the black-draped photos of Mark amongst the gallery of faces from the goalie's past.

Tonight, though, was different. Bazza and his entourage had disappeared to a restaurant, and to be honest Winter was glad of an hour or two on his own.

The first he knew about company was a hand on his shoulder, the lightest touch. He looked up to find a tall, slim Latino helping himself to the other chair. He was older than he looked. He had the hands of a man in his forties, and there were threads of grey in his plaited hair. The white T-shirt carried a faded image of Jimi Hendrix.

'You're a cop,' he said.

'Yeah?'

'*Sí.*'

'Who says?'

'Me. I know cops. I know cops all my life. You tell me it's not true?'

'I'm telling you nothing. Except it's none of your fucking business.'

There was a long silence. The Latino produced a mobile and checked for messages. Then he returned the mobile to his jeans pocket, tipped his head back against the chair, and

3

stared up into the night sky.

'We're wasting time, you and me, Señor Winter. I know who you are. I know where you come from. I know . . . ' He shrugged, leaving the sentence unfinished.

Winter leaned forward, irritated, pushing his glass to one side.

'So why bother checking? Why all this drama?'

'Because we need to talk.'

'About what?'

'About you.'

'Yeah?'

'*Sí* . . . you want to tell me what you're doing here? In Cambados?'

'Not especially.'

'You're a friend of Señor Mackenzie.'

'That's right.'

'And you've come over because of his brother.'

'Yeah.'

'Because you and Señor Mackenzie are . . . ' he frowned, ' . . . friends.'

'Spot on, son. Bazza and me go back a while. And it happens you're right. I am a cop. Or was. I'm also a mate of Bazza's. A family friend. Here to support the lad. Here to help. Here to do my bit.'

'But cops never stop being cops. And that could be a problem.'

'Yeah?'

'*Sí.*' His gaze had settled on Winter's face. 'I have a question for you, Mr Winter. It's a very simple question. As it happens, I know about your friends, about Señor Mackenzie, and I know about you. This man is a cop, I tell them.

4

It's all over his face, the way he talks, the way he moves, his eyes, who he watches, how he watches, everything. Sure, they tell me. The man's a cop. And a good cop. A good cop turned bad. But clever. Useful. Me? I tell them they're crazy. *Loco*. And wrong, too. Why? Because like I say cops never stop being cops. Never. *Nunca*. Not here, in Spain. Not in my country. Not in yours. *Nunca*. Whatever they say. *Nunca*.'

'And the question?'

'Tell me why you're really here.'

'You'd never believe me.'

'I might.'

'OK. And if you don't?'

'It will be bad, very bad. For you. And maybe for us, also.'

'How bad is very bad?'

'The worst.' He smiled. '*Lo peor*.'

Winter took his time digesting the news. Bazza had pointed out this man twice in the last couple of days. His name was Riquelme, though everyone seemed to called him Rikki. He was Colombian. He was said to hold court in a four-star hotel along the coast. Not a gram of cocaine came into Cambados without his say-so.

Rikki was still waiting for an answer to his question. Winter swallowed a mouthful of lukewarm lager and glanced at his watch. Conversations like this he didn't need.

'I'm fifty in a year or two . . . ' he looked up ' . . . and you know the present I've always promised myself? Retirement. No more fannying around. No more working my arse off for people trying to stitch me up. No more chasing brain-dead junkies around. But you know something about my line of work? It doesn't pay. Not the kind of money I'm going to need. So what do I do? I look for someone who might take me seriously for once. And for someone who might understand what I'm really worth. Happens I've found that someone. And that someone, just now, needs a bit of support. *Comprende?*'

Winter waited for some kind of response. The Columbian studied him for a moment or two, then produced a thin cheroot.

'Bullshit,' he said softly.

1

TUESDAY, 5 SEPTEMBER 2006.
PORTSMOUTH, ENGLAND

There are no post-mortem clues for last impressions. Was this body on the slab really asleep when it happened? Was he dreaming? Or did some faint scrape jolt him into wakefulness? Did he half-discern a strange shape — mysterious, uninvited, inexplicable — beside the bedroom door? Did he hear the lightest of breaths? A footfall on the carpet? Was he aware of a looming shadow in the darkness? And maybe the soft rustle of clothing as an arm was slowly raised beside the bed?

Faraday, watching the pathologist lift the glistening brain from the cuplike remnants of the shattered skull, could only wonder. Soon, he thought, they'll be developing a test for all this, some kind of clever biochemical method for reproducing a man's last thoughts imprinted before the neurones shut down for ever. The process would doubtless be both lengthy and expensive but days later investigators would find themselves looking at a multicoloured printout, admissible in court, a digital snapshot of this man's final seconds of life. What had gone on inside his brain. What he'd seen. What he'd felt. The green line for apprehension. The red for disbelief. The black one, the thickest, for terror.

7

Looking up, the pathologist caught Faraday's eye. Earlier, before peeling back the face, he'd indicated the powder burns on the pale skin of the man's forehead. Now he pointed out the pulpy blancmange of the frontal tissue, pinked with blood and tiny fragments of bone, where the bullet had tumbled into the deep brain, destroying everything in its path.

'Single shot,' he murmured, reaching for the scalpel, 'Unusual, eh?'

It was. Driving back to the Major Crimes suite at Kingston Crescent, Faraday pondered the investigative consequences of the pathologist's remark. The post-mortem he'd just attended was a coda to the day's events, a painstaking dismemberment of flesh, bone and connective tissue that normally yielded a modest helping of clues. Killings were usually ill-planned, spontaneous explosions of violence, sparked by rage or alcohol, or a simple desire to get even, and that kind of retribution left a telltale spoor of all too familiar wounds. In this case, though, it had been evident from the start that the Major Crime Team were dealing with something very different.

A single bullet at point-blank range was the mark of a professional hit, a calling card rarely left at Pompey scenes of crime. The news had found its way to the duty D/C at Major Crimes at 07.56. An agency cleaner, failing to raise the tenant at a leased house in Port Solent, had let herself in. In the master bedroom lay the body of the man she knew as Mr Mallinder. At first she'd assumed he'd overslept. Only when she saw the

8

blood on the sheet beneath his head did she take a proper look at his face. She'd never seen an entry wound before and the statement she'd volunteered that afternoon had recorded the faintest disappointment. So small. So neat. So different to what you might have expected.

Faraday had driven up from the Bargemaster's House, pushing north against the incoming rush-hour traffic, summoned by the Duty D/S at Kingston Crescent. Port Solent was a marina development tucked into the topmost corner of Portsmouth Harbour. No. 97 Bryher Island was an end unit in a tightly packed close of executive houses, and uniforms had taped off the scene within minutes of their arrival. By the time Faraday added his ageing Mondeo to the line of cars in the central parking bay, an investigator from Scenes of Crime was already sorting out a pile of silver boxes from the back of his van.

'Beautiful job.' He nodded towards the open front door. 'Nice to have a bit of quality for once.'

*　*　*

Back at Kingston Crescent, early evening by now, the car park was beginning to empty. Faraday slotted his Mondeo into a bay beside the rear entrance and spent a moment or two leafing through the post-mortem notes he'd left on the passenger seat. Amongst them was a reminder to phone home and tell Gabrielle that their planned expedition to the Farlington bird reserve would have to wait.

9

He peered out through the open window. After another glorious September day, it was still warm, the air thick with midges. Shame, he thought. There would have been swallows everywhere, a manic scribble of scimitar wings overhead, and later a chance for Gabrielle to pit her camera skills against a classic Pompey sunset.

He took the stairs two at a time, with a steely resolution that lasted until the first landing. A minute or so later, still out of breath, he put his head round the door of the office that housed the Intelligence Cell. D/C Jimmy Suttle occupied one of the three desks.

'So what've you got for me?'

Suttle abandoned a packet of crisps, wiped his fingers on the chair, and reached for his notepad. Still on light duties after a serious run-in with a Southsea drug dealer, the young D/C had surprised even himself with his talent for coaxing some kind of picture from a multitude of databases and carefully placed phone calls.

'You want the story so far?'

'Yeah.'

'The guy was a property developer. Jonathan Daniel Mallinder. The firm's called Benskin, Mallinder. His oppo's name is Stephen Benskin. They work out of a suite of offices in Croydon. The stuff they do is residential mostly, town-centre developments, mainly in the south. I talked to the FIU and belled a couple of contacts they gave me. Seems that the blokes themselves, Benskin and Mallinder, are a bit of a legend in the business. Came from nowhere but put

10

together some really shrewd deals. Class operators. Staked out some territory of their own. Real respect.'

Faraday nodded. The Financial Investigation Unit was an obvious port of call in a case like this.

'You've talked to Benskin?'

'Yeah, this morning. I assumed the news would have got through but it turned out it hadn't. The bloke couldn't believe it. He was sitting in Heathrow waiting for a flight to Barcelona. He'll come back after the meeting and says he'll be down here first thing tomorrow.'

Suttle glanced up, his finger anchored in the pencilled scribble on his notepad. According to Benskin, Mallinder had been shuttling down to Portsmouth for a while in a bid to sort out a major project. Lately, he'd been staying over for nights on end. Hence the three-month lease on the house in Port Solent.

'Project?'

'The Tipner site. You know when you come in on the motorway? The greyhound stadium? The scrapyard? All that? The land's zoned for development. It's complicated as hell but it seems that our Mr Mallinder had become a player. There was nothing signed and sealed but it seems that he was keen to have the whole lot off the people who own it. Benskin says that Mallinder was looking for a result before Christmas.'

Faraday sank into the chair across the desk. Tipner was a muddle of terraced houses, light industrial sites and acres of scrapyard littered with the bones of dismembered military kit. The spur motorway straddled the scrapyard and on the harbour side, for years, incoming motorists had enjoyed a fine view of a rusting submarine alongside the tiny quay. The sight had often brought a smile to Faraday's face. It buttonholed you. It made no apologies for the mess. It was chaotic, deeply martial and spoke of the perpetual struggle to make money out of half-forgotten wars. As an introduction to the rest of the city, it couldn't have been more perfect.

'What are they going to do with the site?'

'Develop it. There's some kind of plan already. Basically, we're talking offices, a bit of retail, plus a load of apartments. That's where the real money is. Secured parking, poncy kitchen, balcony you can sit out on, nice view of Portchester Castle, three hundred grand a shot, easy.' Suttle glanced up. 'That's according to an estate agent mate of mine. Put in a couple of hundred units and you're looking at serious money. No wonder Mallinder was up for it.'

'What else have you got on him?'

'Married, Wimbledon address, two kids, both school age.'

'Anyone been in contact with the wife yet? Apart from the local uniforms?'

'Me, boss. She's coming down tomorrow with Benskin first thing. Jessie's going to find somewhere up near Port Solent for her to use as a base. The scene won't be released for a while yet.'

'Jessie's FLO?'

'Yeah.'

Jessie Williams was a long-serving D/C, new to Major Crimes, with a smile that could warm an entire room. As Family Liaison Officer, she'd be doing her best to buffer Mallinder's widow from the pressures of the coming days.

Faraday sat back in the chair, turning his gaze towards the window. Try as he might, he couldn't rid his mind of the sight of Mallinder's brain, lying in a big stainless steel bowl, swimming in a thin broth of pinkish fluids. How many enemies might a man like this have acquired? Who had he upset?

'Form?'

'Nothing to get excited about. Got himself involved with a traffic stop a couple of months back. Some kind of dodgy manoeuvre on the A3 running north towards Petersfield. The woollies let him off with a caution.'

'But nothing on PNC?'

'Zilch.'

'Shame.'

The Police National Computer listed all known offenders. A conviction for fraud or money laundering would have been nice, thought Faraday. In these situations you were always looking for short cuts, the first hint of debts unsettled, just a single tiny straw poking out through the toppling haystack of a man's life.

'Timeline?'

'He came down from London yesterday morning. His wife said he left after breakfast. His diary had a couple of meetings in the afternoon,

13

one with a council bloke, the other with a planning consultant. That last meeting went on a bit and they had a drink afterwards.'

'Where?'

'Gunwharf.' Suttle named a pub, the Customs House. 'The guy he was with says Mallinder was on good form. In fact this guy would have stayed for a meal with him but he had to get home.'

'So Mallinder ate alone? At the Customs House?'

'As far as we know, though the girl at the food bar couldn't put a face to the check and card slip. His next-door neighbour in Port Solent says he was back at the house around half nine. It all seems to fit.'

'And was he alone then?'

'No idea. She just heard the car pull in.'

'Did she say anything else? Anything . . . ' Faraday frowned ' . . . about regular visitors, for instance?'

'Yeah. Seems Mallinder had a girlfriend.'

'Description?'

'Asian girl. Medium height. On the young side. Nicely dressed. Called by three or four times that the woman knew about, mostly around ten. Stayed an hour or so, then left.' Suttle was grinning. 'Not rocket science, is it?'

'A tom?'

'Has to be. The guy's married. He has kids, a career, a reputation, all that bollocks. Plus he's probably minted. A proper relationship, a girlfriend, she's liable to have stayed the night. No . . . ' He shook his head. 'A tenner says

14

Mallinder was buying it. Makes every kind of sense.'

'She came by car?'

'On foot, according to the neighbour. Need we enquire further?'

Faraday nodded. Suttle was probably right. Currently Port Solent supported two escort agencies, both catering for the higher end of the market. For someone in Mallinder's position, company was a phone call away.

'We've actioned it?'

'Tomorrow, first thing. We didn't get to the neighbour until close of play. She works at IBM. Gets home at five thirty. The description's pretty detailed. Piece of piss, boss. Should be.'

'Excellent. What have we got in the way of seizures?'

'Just a laptop and a digital camera. Plus Mallinder's briefcase. There's an address book in the briefcase and some paperwork, but according to Benskin most of the real stuff will be on the laptop. Bloke came over from Netley to sort it out.'

Faraday nodded. In evidential terms, PCs and laptops needed careful handling. The process was time-consuming and the Hi-Tech Unit was overwhelmed with jobs. The last time he'd checked, there was a three-month wait for hard-disk analysis.

'We may need to fast-track it,' he said. 'Is there anything else?'

Suttle shook his head, then bent to his notepad to make sure. Faraday was on his feet, tidying his own notes, when there came a knock

15

at the door. It opened to reveal a woman in her early thirties. She was wearing jeans and a pair of battered Reeboks. A rumpled off-white linen jacket hung loosely over a bleached pink T-shirt and the tan suggested a recent vacation. She was looking at Faraday. Lightly freckled face. A hint of caution in the green eyes.

'D/C Suttle?'

Faraday shook his head, nodded at the figure behind the desk. Suttle clearly hadn't a clue who this woman was.

'D/I Hamilton.' She smiled. 'Gina. We talked on the phone.'

'Yeah, of course we did.' Suttle pushed his chair back and shook the outstretched hand. 'Shit, I'm sorry. This is D/I Faraday.'

Faraday, too, recognised the name. Gina Hamilton was a Devon and Cornwall Detective Inspector attached to the Major Crime Incident Team at Exeter. A long-term drugs inquiry had brought her to Portsmouth, though Faraday was vague about the details. A phone call from HQ earlier in the week had asked him to sort out a D/C to give Hamilton whatever assistance she required, and Jimmy Suttle — still largely office-bound — had been the first name in the frame.

Suttle was indicating the spare chair across the desk. In a couple of minutes he'd be through for the day. She could use the phone, read the paper, whatever. Then, if she fancied it, he'd take her to the bar upstairs for a drink. Hamilton was watching him, amused.

'A phone would be good,' she said.

16

Detective Superintendent Martin Barrie headed the Pompey Major Crime Team. He was thin to the point of near-invisibility, chain-smoked whenever the opportunity offered itself, and had never bothered to scrub the flat Essex vowels from the throaty whisper that passed for his voice. In the early days, barely a year ago, a couple of the younger detectives on the MCT had found it difficult to take him seriously as a boss — no obvious presence, none of the bullish leadership qualities of their former leader — a mistake Barrie hadn't allowed them to repeat. One was now back in uniform, teaching road safety awareness to class after class of stroppy Pompey kids. The other had binned the job completely.

Now, finding Faraday at his door, Barrie nodded at an empty chair. As Senior Investigating Officer, he was in formal charge of the Mallinder inquiry but a year under Barrie's command on other jobs had taught Faraday to expect the lightest of touches on the investigative tiller. If you'd won this man's trust, then he gave you plenty of leeway. Better still, if you got into trouble, there was no one better to watch your back. And for Faraday, as Deputy SIO, that was no small comfort.

'The PM?' Barrie ripped a page from his notepad and reached for a pencil.

'Exactly as we assumed, sir. Single bullet, point-blank range. According to the cleaner, Mallinder slept with two pillows. Both were missing, so we're assuming the bullet got no further than the bottom one. Remove it from the scene, and we're left with nothing.'

'How about the shell case?'

'Same MO. The pathologist recovered tiny shreds of fabric from the entry wound. That tells me the killer had the gun in a cloth bag of some kind to contain the expended case. This is a guy heading for sainthood. The anti-litter people would love him.'

'Any other keyholders? Apart from Mallinder and the cleaner?'

'Only the agency. We're checking on keys.'

'OK.'

Barrie was scribbling himself a note. Faraday watched the bony, yellowing fingers racing across the notepad. At length the Detective Superintendent looked up. Less than an hour earlier, he'd chaired the first Operation *Billhook* squad meet. The size of the investigative team — twenty-three and counting — was testimony to the importance he attached to an early result. People like Mallinder were Pompey's guarantee of a decent future. The fact that somebody had killed him did little for the city's reputation.

'So forensically, we're nowhere,' Barrie muttered. 'No bullet, no shell case, no reports of a gunshot from neighbours. Scenes of Crime have found entry damage around the front door but nothing we can positively ID. We've got prints everywhere but I'm betting most of them are Mallinder's or the cleaner's or this bloody girlfriend of his. Is the pathologist sticking with three to four in the morning?'

'Yes. I think he'd like a bit of wriggle room either side but basically . . . yes.'

'Terrific. So here's a guy turns up in the middle of the night. No one sees him arrive, no one hears him at work, no one has a clue how or when he goes. He wears gloves, he uses an automatic and presumably a silencer, and he leaves sod all behind. He isn't pissed, he isn't forgetful, in fact he's Mr Tidy. These people don't exist in Portsmouth . . . ' he shot Faraday a bleak smile ' . . . do they?'

'Prima facie, sir, you'd say not.'

'Fine. So where next?'

'We need to take a good look at his laptop. It's over at Netley at the moment but we ought to fast-track it. Do you want me to talk to Wowser?'

Wowser Productions was a Southsea consultancy security-cleared to analyse seized computer equipment. They normally turned jobs round within a working week but charged the earth.

'I'll give them a ring.' Barrie was wincing. 'What else?'

The two men quickly ran through the tick-list of actions generated by a major incident like this. Checks on CCTV footage were already under way, with two D/Cs trawling through videotapes at the Civic Centre control room. Suttle was pressing the force Telephone Intelligence Department for billings on Mallinder's mobile and landlines, and had drawn up an application for a Production Order to access the dead man's bank accounts. The D/S in charge of Outside Enquiries had detailed two D/Cs to locate and interview Mallinder's lady friend, and Barrie seemed confident that further actions would follow.

Within days *Billhook* should be a great deal wiser about the small print of Mallinder's private life, but in the meantime Barrie could do little but steadily extend the reach of the house-to-house teams in the hope that someone in Port Solent might have noticed a tiny blip in the steady pulse of marina life. A strange car. A new face. Maybe even a visiting boat that no one had seen before. Anything, in short, that might flag a pathway forward.

Faraday mentioned Benskin, Mallinder's partner. Barrie nodded.

'He's down tomorrow, first thing. According to Suttle, he's cleared his diary. You need to talk to him, Joe, find out what the firm's been into. These developer guys are canny, keep their cards well hidden, but a class job like this might concentrate the man's mind. Unless . . . ' he frowned ' . . . he knows more than we think.'

Faraday nodded. Barrie had a point. Business partnerships could be as volatile as a marriage. According to Suttle, Mallinder and Benskin had come from nowhere, piling deal on deal, taking established developers by surprise. The closer the relationship and the higher the stakes, the greater the possibility of events running suddenly out of control.

'You're suggesting Benskin might have something to do with this?'

'It's possible, Joe.' Barrie smiled thinly. 'Either that or Mallinder's pissed a rival off. We have to start somewhere.'

He produced a packet of Rizlas from the desk

drawer and got to his feet. The pouch of Golden Virginia lay on the sill beside the open window. He slipped off the elastic band and began to roll himself a cigarette, gazing down at the near-empty car park. At length came the scrape of a match and a long sigh as he expelled a thin plume of smoke through the open window. Then he turned as Faraday asked whether there was anything else he needed to know.

'Yes. Willard's been on a couple of times.' He nodded at the phone. 'It seems the Chief's taking a personal interest. I gather the emphasis is on an early breakthrough. Quicker the better, Joe, eh . . . ?'

★   ★   ★

Returning to his own office, Faraday sorted quickly through his e-mails, tapped a reply or two, and then put through a call to the Bargemaster's House. As he'd half-expected, there was no response. Gabrielle loathed answering the phone. Her years as an anthropologist in various remote corners of the planet had taught her very different ways to measure the world's pulse and he pictured her now, out in the garden enjoying the last of the sunshine, content for the caller to leave a message under this electronic stone.

'Me,' he announced. 'Sorry about the birds. Back soon. À *bientôt*.'

He put the phone down and eyed it for a moment. Accounting for his every move was something new in his life and he wasn't quite sure what to make of it. Gabrielle was on holiday from her apartment in Chartres, a month at the very most, but even so he'd found it odd to be fitting the rough contours of a copper's life into someone else's routine. Not that Gabrielle had burdened him with demands. Far from it. In fact he'd never met anyone who was so cheerfully self-sufficient. But in a relationship that was getting deeper by the day, he felt he owed her an honest account of himself. This is who I really am, he wanted to say. And this is the life that has made me this way.

He found Suttle upstairs in the social club. The young D/C had commandeered a couple of stools at the far end of the bar and was locked in conversation with Gina Hamilton. The moment Faraday appeared, he was on his feet.

'What are you having, boss? My shout.'

Faraday settled for a pint of Guinness and found himself a stool. Gina made room for him at the bar. The spareness of her frame and the steadiness in her eyes spoke of an appetite for regular exercise. She'd barely touched the glass of lager beside her battered leather bag.

'You're here for a while?'

'Couple of days. Max.'

'Drugs job?'

'Yeah.' She nodded. 'Big time. At least in our neck of the woods.'

Without going into details, she outlined an operation she'd obviously been nurturing for a while. A distribution network centred in Plymouth. Cocaine mostly, with special offers on crack and smack when the Scouse dealers could be arsed to get out of bed. A supply chain running into Devon and Cornwall from sources upcountry. Dozens of outlets around the coast. Kick down a few doors, she said, and you'd spoil the party for a couple of weeks. But nail a truly major supplier and the damage might be a little more permanent.

'So why Pompey?' Faraday didn't bother to hide his interest.

Gina hesitated a moment. She looked on the young side to be an experienced D/I, and she was plainly worried about sharing too much intelligence. Faraday was about to put the question a different way when Suttle helped him out.

'Terry Byrne.' He handed Faraday a brimming glass of Guinness. 'Who'd have believed it, eh?'

Terry Byrne was a young Scouser who dealt from a chaotic terraced house barely a mile from Kingston Crescent and had won himself a city-wide reputation for ultra-violence. Lately he'd been settling heroin debts with a kettle full of boiling water tipped over the lower body, a process known as jugging.

Suttle resumed his seat beside the West Country D/I. Faraday could sense already that he was determined to make the most of his social responsibilities.

'Cheers, boss.' Suttle turned to touch glasses with Gina. 'And here's to some decent scalps, yeah?'

Faraday was still thinking about Byrne. The city's cocaine trade was largely controlled by a prominent local criminal, Bazza Mackenzie.

Recently, he'd been setting up a series of arms-length franchise operations, minimising his own risk while still enjoying huge profits, which he washed through his ever-expanding business empire. Dealers staked by Mackenzie were all Pompey boys, people he'd known most of his life, and collectively they'd made it very plain indeed that they intended to keep things local. A toerag Scouser like Terry Byrne could flog as much smack as he liked. But the moment he moved into something respectable like cocaine he'd be looking at a serious turf war.

'Byrne's really the target?' Faraday needed to be clear.

'Yes.' Gina nodded. 'He is.'

'And you're sure about the intel?'

'Yes. I gather our Force Intelligence blokes have been talking to yours. I don't know whether you're in the loop or not but he's expecting a delivery. Wholesale. Industrial quantities. Tomorrow, if we're lucky.'

'Cocaine?'

'Yes.'

'With some of it heading your way?'

'That's the story.'

'How much?'

'Between one and two kilos.'

'Shit.' It was Suttle. He looked impressed.

Faraday was still watching Gina. That weight of cocaine in the lock-up would be the making of a young D/I.

'You're serious? *Two kilos?*'

'Yes.'

'And you've got Byrne plotted up? Pennington

24

Road? Surveillance? The whole nine yards?'

'Absolutely. And tomorrow, if it all pans out, we'll be on the road back west with him.'

'So who orders the strike?'

'Exeter makes the decision. Then I handle the tactical end. That kind of weight, I imagine we'll settle for a traffic stop once we're close to home. There's no way my bosses would let it run. We'd have the media all over us if we fucked up.'

'Sure.' Faraday nodded. 'So you'll be relying on interview for further arrests?'

'That's the plan. The bloke at the wheel will be looking at five to six years. That's a big incentive to come up with a few names.'

'And this guy's known to you? The courier?'

'We've had dealings, yes. Bloke's an animal but he's just hooked up with a Ukrainian lady, a real stunner, and she's another reason he might come across. Who knows?' She reached for her drink, took a tiny sip, then checked her watch. 'Shit. I'd no idea it was so late.'

Faraday ignored the hint. He still wanted to know how Byrne had laid hands on a couple of kilos of cocaine. In Pompey.

'I've no idea. Force Intelligence are talking some kind of deal in Manchester but that's something I can't vouch for. Me? I'll be happy with that kind of seizure and a day or two in the interview suite. Fingers crossed, we'll end up with both. Plus a handful of arrests down the line. You want the rest of this?'

She handed Suttle her glass, still two thirds full. Suttle looked at it a moment, then poured the contents into his own glass.

25

'You know who'd cream themselves over a conversation like this?' He was looking at Faraday. 'Paul Winter. Two kilos of the laughing powder? Plus someone to work over in the interview room? Shit. A couple of days and you'd start running out of holding cells. Shame, eh?'

'Shame, what?' Gina had slipped off the stool, slipping her jacket over her shoulders.

'Shame Paul's not around any more. You're driving?'

'Yeah.'

'No wonder.' Suttle gestured at her empty glass. 'If only he'd been as cluey as you.'

2

Paul Winter had always hated Gatwick Airport. Now he edged the luggage trolley through the scrum of waiting relatives and friends on the Arrivals concourse at the South Terminal, following the couple ahead of him. For reasons he didn't fully understand, he seemed to have acquired three sets of bags. A dodgy wheel gave the overloaded trolley a mind of its own, and two hours of business-class hospitality on the flight from Santiago de Compostela didn't help. When the short, stocky figure in the tan chinos came to a sudden halt, Winter caught him squarely in the left thigh.

'Shit, mush, what the fuck are you about?' Mackenzie hopped around, rubbing his leg.

Winter muttered an apology. Mackenzie was with his daughter, Esme. Esme's husband had been waiting for the best part of an hour. The three of them walked across the concourse towards the exit to the car park, Winter in pursuit. No one bothered with introductions, and it wasn't until Winter was sitting in the back of the big Volvo estate, mopping the sweat from his face, that he was any the wiser. Mackenzie had disappeared.

'My name's Stuart.' Esme's husband was a tall, bulky man, in jeans and a new-looking suede

27

jacket. He half-turned in the driving seat, offering a perfunctory handshake. 'My wife says you're a mate of her dad's.'

'That's right. Me and Bazza go back a while.'

'Behave himself, did he?'

'Good as gold.' Winter's attention had been caught by an African family trying to wrestle a fridge into the back of a rusting Mondeo. Christ knows where the seven kids would go. 'You know something?' He said to Stuart. 'This country's fucked.'

Stuart ignored the comment. By now, he was talking to Esme. He wanted to know more about some incident they'd already discussed over the phone. Last night, Winter thought. In the restaurant.

'Did you manage to square it with the management in the end?' Stuart was looking for the parking ticket.

'Yes.' She nodded. 'I thought it was just a question of money at first. I went round this morning and gave them a couple of thousand, but then I realised it was more than that. They wanted an apology. I suppose it's pride. Dad sussed that at once.'

'And?'

'*No problema*. He said he was sorry, really sorry, and they said they understood — difficult time and all that — and they ended up having a couple of brandies on it, which is ironic really because that's pretty much where it all kicked off last night.' She laughed, reaching for her seat belt. 'They even gave me half the money back, said two grand was way over the top for that

28

amount of damage. Bit of a result really . . . ' She glanced behind her. 'Eh Paul?'

Winter grunted. He hadn't been there in the restaurant himself but one of Mackenzie's younger lieutenants had given him chapter and verse over breakfast this morning. Bazza, he said, had taken offence at something a bloke at another table had apparently said. This was a bit of a mystery because the guy was a local and Bazza didn't speak a word of Spanish, but nothing got in Bazza's way in that kind of mood and in the end, when everyone else piled in, it had all got out of hand. Later, back at the hotel, Bazza had dismissed the whole incident. The restaurant had been dead, he'd said, and he'd had more than enough of death for one day. What the place needed was a spot of entertainment and he'd been happy to oblige. Shame these people had no sense of humour.

'Where's he off to now?' Winter wanted to know.

'London. That's why he left his car here.'

'Business?'

'Haven't a clue.'

They left the airport and joined the motorway. As the Volvo headed south, Winter took advantage of the empty back seat, his legs stretched out, his eyes closed, listening to the murmur of conversation in the front.

Esme was Mackenzie's only daughter. Winter had known of her existence since the early eighties. By then Bazza had become a target for the city's Drug Squad, dealing recreational narcotics with enough success to catch a sniff or two of the serious money. He'd binned his job in an estate agency and set about turning the city's appetite for amphetamines, ecstasy and quality marijuana into the beginnings of a properly organised business. In this enterprise, he'd had the enthusiastic support of a bunch of mates from the legendary 6.57 crew, Pompey's army of soccer hooligans, and being Bazza he'd felt the need to add a bit of social tone in the shape of a leggy, well-connected high school dropout called Marie.

Esme had appeared within a year, by which time Bazza had moved on, but over the following decade Pompey's apprentice drug baron had warmed to the notion of fatherhood and Esme had celebrated her fourteenth birthday by attending a raucous gathering at the local Register Office where her parents pledged each other their undying love.

By now, thanks to the cocaine trade, Bazza was a wealthy man, and by the time Esme herself got married — barely three years ago — he'd acquired a circle of friends from every corner of the city's establishment. The wedding had taken place at the Cathedral in Old Portsmouth and a handful of the photos taken afterwards had found their way onto the noticeboard in the upstairs bar at the Kingston Crescent nick.

Give or take minor convictions for assault and affray, no detective had ever managed to lay a hand on Mackenzie, and by now — especially amongst the older hands — there was a rueful acceptance that he'd become too successful, too armour-clad, to take down. Criminals as wealthy as Bazza could afford to hire the very best advice from white-collar professionals who'd keep him at arm's length from the law, and there in the Kingston Crescent bar was the living proof of the immunity he'd so cannily bought himself.

Winter smiled at the memory. The line of beaming faces had included three solicitors, a couple of accountants, two members of the Pompey Premiership team, an architect who'd made a fortune in Dubai, a prominent local journalist, a handful of minor TV celebs, as well as an assortment of builders, publicans and shaven-headed men of leisure who couldn't wait to get stuck into Bazza's limitless supply of Krug. Coupled with the reception at the Royal Trafalgar, Bazza's own seafront hotel, the day had been a kind of coronation. After twenty busy years, he'd become the undisputed king of the city.

An hour into the journey, Winter felt a tap on his knee. It was Esme. Stuart had asked him a question.

'What about?' Winter struggled upright, rubbing his face. He wasn't certain but he thought he sensed a headache coming on.

'Bazza. Tonight. Back at the airport. He just seemed different, that's all.'

'Yeah?'

'Yes. Definitely. My wife here tells me he's taken it pretty badly.'

'About Mark, you mean?'

Winter's eyes found the rear-view mirror. Stuart was watching him carefully.

'Of course. It's not every day you lose

31

someone you grew up with. Not at that age.'

'Sure, Stu, but you've got to be realistic. The two of them were virtual strangers, totally different personalities, chalk and cheese. OK, they shared the same surname, but Mark found it hard sometimes, having to play the elder brother.'

'Really?' Stuart sounded surprised.

'Yeah. Mark and Bazza were always falling out. Back in the early days they shared a dossy old flat in Southsea, just off Goldsmith Avenue, up near the football ground. In fact there were four of them in there — Mark, two of his mates, and Bazza. Mark was on the building sites, earning good money, and his mates were in the same game. Baz had binned school and was flogging crap houses for some toerag estate agent at that point, brilliant at it he was. In fact that's how he met Marie. Her dad was an architect, had some connection to the business.'

'Is that right?' Esme had turned in her seat. She sounded slightly shocked.

'Yeah. Baz never fancied the tools. Getting pissed on in the rain was never his idea of a good day out. Job for inbreds, he used to say. That was the thing about Baz though, even then. Number one, he was absolutely sure he was always in the right. Number two, he never kept his opinions to himself. It used to drive Mark mad. 'Titch' he used to call him.'

'Who?'

'Bazza. Your dad. The short-arse. He ignored it, of course, like he ignores more or less everything else in life unless it turns a profit.

That's why he's been so successful. But that's the secret, isn't it? It was the same in my game. The bloke who kept his eye on the ball was the bloke who got on the scoresheet. Regardless of what everyone else might be saying.'

Stuart's soft laughter brought the conversation to a halt for a moment. He glanced across at Esme, then up at the mirror again.

'So how come you know all this? About the flat and everything?'

'Because we busted them. Bazza was ambitious, even then. Plus he'd upset people. In that kind of situation it's easy to squeeze people for a cough or two. One Sunday morning I had three blokes in the holding cells on possession charges, *three* of them, and they were all dying to stitch Baz up. We had an auction in the end and the scrote I was silly enough to believe put Bazza alongside a couple of thousand Ecstasy tabs. The bloke said he'd bought them in Amsterdam, then shipped them home on the ferry. That kind of weight, we were bound to knock a few doors down.'

'You did Mark's flat?'

'Yeah.'

'And?'

'Nothing. Or not much, anyway. A bit of weed, a couple of tabs of speed, but all of it recreational. We tore the place apart, trying to stand the intelligence up. Shame really. Mark had just redecorated.'

'You pulled them all in?'

'Of course. Mark was outraged and his two mates weren't too happy, either.'

'What about Bazza?'

'He was clever. The rest of them used the duty brief but he phoned for another solicitor, someone he'd met through the estate agency. This guy was shit hot, ran rings round us. Mid-twenties, he was, mad on football, used to guest in Bazza's team when they were so far ahead of the rest of the league they could afford to drop a point or two. Fact was, we had nothing on Bazza except the whisper from the shitbag grass, and this brief knew it. It all came down to the passport in the end. Bazza had stuffed the ferry tickets and an Amsterdam hotel receipt in the back, and there was a Dover entry stamp bang on the date we got off the bloke in the holding cell. Naturally we challenged him and you know what he said? He swore blind he'd gone to Holland to buy tulips for his new girl-friend.'

'Was that my mum?' It was Esme.

'Yeah. Before you were born.'

'She hates tulips.'

'Exactly. Baz was winding us up. Not just us, but Mark too. They threw Baz out after that little episode, made him find a place of his own. Wise bloody move, says me.'

'And this solicitor?' Stuart again. 'He's still around?'

'No. He went to London and made his fortune. You'll see his name in the crime reports sometimes, exactly the same MO. Get alongside the quality criminals and help them to a bigger fortune. Down here he'd have got the same result with Bazza but it would have taken a bit longer. A young bloke like that, he was impatient. And who can blame him, eh? In the end it's just money, whichever way you cut it.'

Winter chuckled, gazing out at the blackness of the night, waiting for a response that never came. Finally, he caught a murmur from Esme. She wanted her husband to drop her at home before he ran Winter back to Portsmouth. She was tired. She'd had enough of travelling and she needed to check that the live-in nanny hadn't done anything vile while they'd been away.

★ ★ ★

Bazza's daughter lived on a seven-acre spread on a flank of the Meon Valley. Winter caught a glimpse of a sprawling Hacienda-style confection in white stucco and black wrought iron as the Volvo purred up the drive. Two double garages formed a right angle at one end, and there was a line of trellis around a swimming pool at the other. A child's red and yellow tractor lay abandoned outside the front door and there were lights on in three rooms upstairs.

'Slut.' Esme got out. Without a backward glance, she walked to the door, unlocked it and disappeared inside. Moments later the lights upstairs went out. Then the front door slammed shut, leaving Stuart and Winter alone in the darkness.

'She's knackered,' Stuart said. 'You can always tell.'

They set off again. For miles, as they sped down the Meon Valley, Winter was glad of the silence in the car. Then, as the lights of the city appeared, he stirred. He wanted to know why Esme had never used her law qualifications. Bazza had put her through years of university, followed by a pupillage at a leading barristers' chambers just off the Strand, but to Winter's knowledge Esme had never set foot in court to plead a case of her own. So what had happened?

'Me.' Stuart didn't elaborate.

'And the kids?'

'Yeah. She still wants four. I say three's plenty.'

'And she's no regrets . . . you know . . . about a career?'

'Not in the way you'd expect, no. The kids were a handful, and I think that surprised her, but we've got the nanny now, and the horses, and that seems to have done the trick. Most days she's like a pig in shit, can't get enough of all that country air. She might be a bit arsey tonight, but that'll pass.'

'And you?'

'I earn the money.'

'I meant liking the countryside.'

'It's fine. Buy that amount of land and no one really bothers you.' Winter nodded. He felt like a taxi fare in the back. No harm in that.

'You're in the City, right?'

'Canary Wharf. But it's the same thing.'

'Investment banking?'

'Yes.'

'Like it?'

'Love it. Most days.'

'American firm?'

'Yes.' He nodded, his eyes still on the road.

36

'Tell me something . . . a guy like you, given what you've done with most of your life, all this must be pretty strange, musn't it?'

'All what exactly?'

'Coming in with Mackenzie. Turning your back on the rest of it.'

'It wasn't me who turned my back. They sacked me.'

'Sure, but we're talking a driving offence, aren't we?'

'I was three times over the limit. The people I worked for didn't even give me a hearing. Sometimes I think they were just waiting for the right excuse.'

'You sound bitter.'

'I am. Or I was. But you learn pretty fast that there's no percentage in all that bitterness bollocks. You've got to get on with it. You've got to get up in the morning. You've got to earn a living, for fuck's sake. If you want the truth, Stuart, I now regard it as a career decision. Why? Because there comes a time in your life when you know you're due for a change.'

'Yes but . . . ' He frowned, struggling to find the right word. 'Change? Is that all it is? You're telling me you spend years and years trying to put the likes of Esme's dad away and then suddenly, bang, you're working for him? That's just a bit of a change?'

Winter took his time answering. Finally he said the two jobs weren't as wildly different, as totally incompatible, as most people might think. The best thief-takers could have made equally blinding careers as quality criminals. You needed focus. You needed cunning. You needed to dream up all kinds of ways of getting people into the deepest shit. Above all, you needed not to care about the human consequences of the job you did.

'What you were *really* after,' he said, 'was a decent war record. You need to be putting blokes away on a regular basis. I took lots of scalps, hundreds of the fuckers. And you know how? By making friends with these people. You do that in pubs, in low-life caffs, in holding cells, and then — when the time is right — in interview. By then, if you know what you're about, these people think you're their best mate. Most of them are seriously fucked up. Either that or they're plain inadequate. They like you. They trust you. They're absolutely fucking positive you've got their very best interests at heart. And you know what you do next? You put an extra big smile on your face. And then you screw them.'

'You make it sound like acting.'

'That's right. You play a part. It *is* acting. And the better you are, the more blokes you pot. I've done it most of my life. I'm an expert. Believe me.'

'I do.' Stuart fell silent for a moment. Then he glanced up at the mirror again. 'Have you had this conversation with my father-in-law?'

'Bazza, you mean?' Winter met the eyes in the rear-view mirror, then lay back against the seat, staring up at the vanity light, letting the question settle in his aching head. 'Yeah, several times. But you know what it is with Bazza? The bloke just never fucking listens.'

'Should he?'

'I'm not with you.'

'*Should* he listen? Should he understand what a great actor you are? I mean let's not piss around here. You're family now. He's let you close. I'm in the risk business. I do it every day of my working life. I know how to calibrate these things. For my money, Mackenzie's wildly exposed.'

'Thanks to me, you mean?'

'Yes.'

Winter shrugged, fingered the stitching on the cold leather, admitted how odd the situation must seem to anyone with half a brain. But in truth, he said, the invitation had been Bazza's. He'd made the running. He'd offered the deal, negotiated the terms, made an improvement here and there on Winter's prompting. And now, for a sum approaching twice his annual CID salary, plus a windfall bonus or two, ex-D/C Paul Winter was on a trial contract. Depending on results, the arrangement might continue. If it fell apart, the consequences could be awkward.

'How awkward?'

'Very.'

'We're talking violence?'

'We're talking serious damage.'

'To you?'

'Oh yes. Big time.'

'That sounds like blackmail.'

'That's your word, not mine.'

'But am I close?'

Winter smiled, refusing to answer. They were back in the city by now, closing on the forest of cranes that badged the final stages of the new development at Gunwharf Quays.

'Drop me at the gate here,' Winter said suddenly. 'I could do with the walk.'

★   ★   ★

After the warmth of Cambados, the night air felt chill. Winter trailed through Gunwharf, hauling his bag behind him, avoiding clusters of Portsea youth loudly debating which waterside bar to hit next. At the prices they charged here, he was amazed they could afford to drink midweek. No wonder volume crime was on the up again.

Winter lived in a third-floor apartment in Blake House, one of two waterside blocks that put a shine on the residential side of the Gunwharf development. For £550,000 he'd bought a view of the harbour, two en-suite bedrooms, a video entryphone and a state-of-the-art kitchen that still defied his attempts to make sense of the instruction manuals. Eighteen months after moving in, he'd yet to risk using the oven.

He dumped his bag in the master bedroom and wandered through to the living room. He'd left the big picture windows curtained against the sunshine, and now he drew them back with a flourish. If anything brightened his glummer moments it was this: the lights of Gosport across the water, the shadow of a big yacht ghosting through the harbour narrows, the faintest tootle of a trad jazz band aboard one of the charter boats that offered evenings afloat for anyone with lots of friends and a couple of grand to spare.

All his working life Winter had dreamed of a view like this. Every day it changed. Every day it offered something new, something different. He'd always regarded Pompey as theatre — the faces, the mischief, the ever-thicker tangle of plots and subplots — and now, thanks to the move into Gunwharf, he'd found himself a seat in the front row. This was a city with a pulse. From here you could almost reach out and touch it.

He stood by the window for a moment or two, waiting for the view to work its usual magic, but nothing happened. Four days on the Galician coast had been his second taste of life inside the bubble that was Bazza Mackenzie's world. These were people he'd known for most of his professional career. As a working detective, he'd held their files on various jobs. He knew what they drank. The kind of women they fancied. The kind of madcap expeditions they still organised to the more remote Pompey away games. But this time he'd had to become one of them.

A couple of weeks back, once he'd agreed terms with Bazza, they'd insisted on including him on a weekend expedition to Middlesbrough. They'd flown up there on a chartered jet, half a dozen of them. Bazza had arranged transportation at the other end. Expecting a couple of hired Mercedes, Winter had stepped off the Learjet at Newcastle Airport to find himself looking at a Hummer, desert brown, tinted windows and a mounting for a heavy machine gun on the roof above the cabin. Bazza had insisted on driving the thing himself, tying Pompey colours to the whiplash aerial and ploughing the widest of furrows through the bank holiday traffic on the way to the ground.

Inside the Riverside stadium, they'd trooped upstairs to the hospitality box and settled in. By half-time, with Kanu on fire and Pompey ahead, they were calling for more Moët. By the end of the match, celebrating with a toot or two, they were arguing over which escort agency to call. Winter had ended up with a pale nineteen-year-old from Lithuania. She'd done her best under the circumstances but in the end he'd felt sorry for her. She'd shown him photos of her nipper back in Vilnius. She was a nice kid.

Winter turned away from the window. He'd never realised how useless money could be, how little — in the end — it really bought you. The trip up north had been a laugh, no expense spared, but flying back next day with a planeload of hungover middle-aged criminals, he'd started to wonder how you could ever survive a life like this. Limitless Moët. As much cocaine as you could handle. The girl of your choice. The finest restaurants. Plus the best seats in the casino afterwards. But who, in the end, cared a fuck about any of that?

Bazza, he now realised, didn't. Winter had watched him carefully over those couple of days. He'd footed most of the bills and clearly enjoyed the chance to buy huge helpings of showboat anarchy, but when the Moët came round he barely touched it, and he'd even shaken his head at a second line of coke. No, what had really mattered was the fact that he could do it, that he could flaunt his wealth, because wealth was power and power was the currency that Bazza enjoyed spending most of all. In that sense, thought Winter, the entire trip, doubtless like others, had been yet another billboard for Bazza's achievements, for the journey he'd made, for the distance he'd come since the 6.57 days. Not that he'd ever, for a second, forget about the football. The fact that Pompey had ended up screwing Middlesbrough 4–0 had put the biggest smile on his face.

Winter drifted into the kitchen in search of a couple of paracetamol, still faintly depressed, thinking again about what he'd heard about last night's scene in the Spanish restaurant. Getting that pissed, that out of control, just wasn't Bazza's game, not any more. So maybe Stuart was right. Maybe Mark's death really had shaken him. Winter found the tablets, then caught sight of the answerphone winking through the open door. Returning to the lounge, he bent to the machine. Bazza's throaty rasp. What a surprise.

'I need you up here first thing.' He sounded impatient. 'There's a train at half six, gets to Waterloo around eight. I'll be at Costa Coffee. OK?'

★   ★   ★

Faraday pushed the remains of his pasta aside to look at the photos again. Gabrielle had just printed them out.

'You managed to find it OK?' He recognised the distinctive shimmer of the mudflats beside Langstone Millpond. Gabrielle must have taken this first shot an hour or so before sunset. In the rich yellow light the mud had the consistency of warm chocolate.

'*Bien sûr*. I found a map. Upstairs.'

'But how did you know where to go?'

'I looked on the Internet. I found a site. The man who makes this site, he was there yesterday and again this evening. He counted. I counted. Me? I won.' She laughed, nodding at the photo. Against the sun, the birds had lost their whiteness but their sheer number was deeply impressive. Faraday began to count but quickly gave up.

'You know what these are?'

'*Oui*. In French we say *aigrettes*.'

'Little egrets.'

'The same, *d'accord*. So maybe *petites aigrettes*.'

'So how many?'

'I count two hundred and thirty-one. The man, he says two hundred and nine. He has the website. He has to write the figure. I say that makes him . . . ' she frowned. ' . . . *prudent?*'

'Cautious.'

'*Oui. Mais c'est spectaculaire, n'est-ce-pas?*'

Faraday wasn't sure whether she meant the photo or the birds themselves but either way it made no difference. Egrets were one of his all-time favourites, a slim, elegant, china-white bird, a member of the heron family. In twos and threes they could freeze him in mid-step. En

44

masse, like this, and he wouldn't have moved for hours.

'You were lucky,' he said. 'And I'm bloody jealous.'

The last time he'd seen little egrets in these numbers was five or six years ago, on nearby Thorney Island. A colony of them had found a roost in a clump of trees behind the sea wall, and Faraday remembered the evening he'd ventured slowly closer, hugging the cover of the dyke until the dazzling whiteness of the trees had resolved itself into hundreds of individual birds. He described it now, the shuffle and mutter of the birds in the branches overhead, the way they made space for each other, the way that more and more of the colony returned from a day on the mudflats until every tree was *complet*. Later, he said, J-J had drawn a picture of the scene, each bird suspended like a Japanese paper lantern, impossibly decorative.

'Your son? He saw them too?'

'Of course. He was there with me.'

'But the noise they make. Tonight . . . ' She gave a little bark, a small hard sound, then followed it with a *gulla-gulla-gulla*. '*C'est commeça?*'

'*Oui, absolument.*' He was laughing.

'You think it's OK? *Authentique?*'

'Definitely.'

'*Et* J-J?' She pronounced the J with a softness Faraday had always loved.

'He's deaf. I told you.'

'I know. But the sound, the calls they make.

45

He can't ever hear this thing. *C'est dommage . . . non?*'

She was right. It was a very big pity. For the benefit of his deaf son Faraday had spent years and years trying to figure out ways of translating sound, rather than meaning, into sign language but had finally given up. J-J was simply missing one of the senses that gave depth and dimension to the world around him and there seemed no way to compensate for this loss. How do you describe the colour red to a blind man? It was impossible.

'Here . . . ' Gabrielle had another shot, a close-up, four egrets pegged to a branch, each bird gazing out in a different direction. 'Funny, *n'est-ce-pas?*'

Faraday reached for his plate. In his experience some individuals took to birding with an acuity that appeared to be entirely natural. They knew what to look for, taught themselves to remember details of plumage and flight, quickly absorbed the kind of knowledge that put a blur of movement through the binoculars or a perfectly framed moment of stillness into a wider context. How a sudden irruption of waxwings would indicate a failure of the berry crop in Scandinavia. How the presence of an exotic American visitor, like a yellow-billed cuckoo, might signal the presence of powerful frontal system over the Atlantic on which the bird had hitched a lift.

Gabrielle was like this. To her, Faraday thought, birds were simply one more key to understanding the way that everything else hung together, a quest that appeared to have occupied most of her adult life. Maybe this gift of hers for catching and classifying the tiniest detail, something seasoned birders called jizz, had grown out of her career as an anthropologist. Maybe the study of man — his origins, his social habits, the way he organised for peace and war — led inexorably to the biggest picture of all.

'You remember the Vendée?' He stabbed at an olive.

'*Oui.*'

'Purple herons? Marsh harriers? Blue-headed yellow wagtails?'

'*Oui*. And the *gentilhomme* in white.' She pushed her chair back, stood briefly on one leg, her arms held out in front of her, her finger-tips touching, in imitation of the white stork they'd seen. There were several breeding pairs supplied with specially-built nesting platforms in the marshland south of Brouage, and they'd spent the best part of an afternoon watching this single specimen, utterly motionless, half-curtained by reeds, waiting to snap at a passing grasshopper with its magnificent bill.

That was the afternoon, Faraday had often told himself, when he'd realised that this relationship of theirs might just survive the fate of others that had come and gone over the last few years. They'd spent a week or so in the Languedoc in her old VW camper van and the decision to detour west, on the long trek back to Chartres, had been hers. Not because the rumour of extraordinary birdlife might have pleased her new friend. But because she was genuinely interested.

He tidied the last of the pasta onto his fork and drained his glass. Tonight Gabrielle was wearing a pair of khaki jungle shorts and an old T-shirt of his she must have found in the chest of drawers upstairs. The T-shirt was several sizes too big and the shorts were patched to death, but nothing could mask her vitality, a constant sense that every conversation was simply another unlocked door in her life, just waiting for a gentle push.

Gabrielle masked this nosiness of hers with a deftness that was itself a rare talent but Faraday had spotted her insatiable appetite for finding out, for *knowledge*, very early on. He'd met her on a bus in Thailand and fallen into conversation. The journey had gone on for hours, up and down the lush green hills near the Burmese border, and he'd recognised at once the sheer force of her curiosity.

She needed to understand the way things were. She needed to figure out how they'd ended up that way, and how they might relate to everything else. Then she revelled in making the necessary connections, some of them obvious, some of them not. In another life, Faraday thought, she'd have made a great detective. As it was, with her mass of auburn curls, her slim, hard body and the brilliance of her sudden grin, he was rather glad she'd stuck to anthropology.

'*Et demain?*' Faraday was curious to know what she had planned for tomorrow.

'I go to Heathrow.'
'Why?'
'To meet someone.'
'Who?'
'Your son.' That softness again. 'J-J.'

3

The train was late. Winter joined the press of commuters streaming off the platform, glad he didn't have to endure this pantomime every working day. How perfectly sane people ever put up with it was beyond him. Even the younger ones, if they managed to find a seat, were asleep within seconds, slack-mouthed, dead-looking, dribbling peacefully onto their laps as the train clattered towards Waterloo.

He found Bazza occupying a corner table in the Costa Coffee shop. With him was a fit-looking youth in motorcycle leathers. He'd unzipped the jacket to reveal a tiger tattoo on his pale chest and he had a red bandanna knotted around his throat. Beside him, on the spare chair, was a full-face helmet.

'This is Deano.' Bazza was evidently on his second cappuccino. 'He's big into jet skis. Semi-pro, so he says.'

The youth nodded. For the time being, he said, he was still doing shifts as a motorcycle courier. It was good money but the way things were going he'd be full-time on the circuit within months. He had a soft West Country accent and savagely bitten nails. Winter wondered what had brought him to Bazza's attention. Bazza had anticipated the question.

50

'I got Deano's name from the QHM before we all went out to Spain. This bloke will mark your card, he said. What Deano doesn't know isn't worth ratshit.'

'QHM?' Winter was lost.

'Queen's Harbour Master. Bosses the Pompey water. The Harbour, Spithead, the lot. Nothing moves without his say-so.'

Winter was eyeing the ever-lengthening queue at the counter. At this rate, coffee would be a prelude to lunch.

'Know him socially do you, Baz? This QHM?' He asked dryly.

'Yeah. And that's how I know he copped it big time over all those jet skiers. You know something, son?' He was talking to Deano now. 'QHM hates bloody jet skiers. Or used to, anyway. Just a bunch of blokes who fancied something big between their legs. That was his description, not mine, but he's right as it happens. Some afternoons you can go down to the beach at Hot Walls, bang by the Harbour mouth, and this monster ferry comes in, P&O job, and you know what these arseholes are doing? Only riding the bow wave, the *bow* wave, right there, right under the fucking nose of the boat.' His hand chopped across the table. 'Can you believe that?'

Deano said he could. Stuff like that happened everywhere. Gave the sport a bad name.

'Too right. And you know something else? QHM could do bugger all about it. Except it got serious, really serious.'

'How?' Even Winter was interested.

51

'Can't say.'

'Why not?'

Bazza looked coy for a moment, shook his head, touched the side of his nose with his finger.

'State secret, Baz?' Mackenzie didn't do coy.

'Yeah.'

'OK, so tell us.'

'All right, then.' He leaned forward, gesturing the two heads closer. 'They call it asymmetrical warfare. Out in the Gulf the navy guys are bricking it. Aircraft carrier, battleship, it doesn't matter what you're sitting on. A couple of dozen blokes on jet skis can see you off. Rocket launchers, kamikaze attacks, it doesn't matter how they do it. *Dagger-dagger . . . boof . . .* and you're history. A million quids worth of guided missiles and there's still fuck all you can do about it. Sweet, eh?'

Winter began to wonder where this conversation was leading. Bazza never did anything without writing the script beforehand. What part did he have in mind for Deano?

Deano was equally curious.

'I don't get it,' he said.

'Of course you don't, son. All I'm trying to say is the QHM, my mate, he's got a very big problem with blokes on jet skis. Leave out all the macho bollocks about the ferries and bow waves and there's the real stuff underneath. Week one the ragheads are blowing themselves up on Tube trains. Next thing you know they're strapping themselves to a load of Semtex and hopping on a jet ski. *Comprende?*'

52

'No.' At least this youth was honest.

'OK. Here's how it works. The QHM has got himself in a bit of a state. He thinks he's staring disaster in the face. Fuckwits on jet skis. Everywhere. Plus something much worse down the road. So what does he do? He does the clever thing. He makes some phone calls. He sorts out the blokes who take jet skis seriously. He gets them onside. He asks them to put on a little show, out there in the harbour. And you know what? They do it. They plan it. It all happens. Sixty-odd blokes on jet skis back around May time. All day. Off the naval dockyard. And you know something else? The punters turn up in droves and they just love it. Fancy displays from blokes like you. Free rides if they're lucky. Brilliant. But you know the best thing of all? The QHM thinks it's Christmas. From now on, he *loves* jet skis, can't get enough of them, and pretty soon someone's on the phone to Yamaha, and you know what they do? Give him three free ones, three kosher jet skis, so he can add them to the Harbour Patrol. And you know what happens then? The bloke he's talked to first, the bloke who's organised the gala day out, all those jollies for the punters, he volunteers to organise a rota for weekends, guys from the club he's in, so suddenly the QHM finds himself with full cover at weekends, all year round. Sweet, eh? Problem solved.'

Deano was still having trouble with the small print.

'These blokes are taking on the terrorists?'

'No, son. They're sorting out the dickheads

who've been making life on the Harbour misery. The ragheads are something else. But that's the whole point, see. It's the same whatever game you're in. You set a thief to catch a thief.' He leant back, shooting a grin at Winter. 'Ain't that right, Paul?'

Winter ignored the dig. He'd spotted a break in the queue but when he got to his feet Mackenzie told him to sit down again.

'The boy's up against the clock.' He nodded at Deano. 'You need to hear this next bit.'

He turned back to the youth, explained about his brother. Mark had fallen in love with jet-skiing out in Spain. He was no great shakes at it, would never hold a candle to blokes in Deano's class, but it was a good buzz and a bit of laugh, plus Mark had ended up on a knockout stretch of coast. The best way of seeing that coast was on a jet ski and Mark had been out on the water whenever he got the chance.

'So what happened?'

'He hit a rock. Submerged, it was. Not his fault.'

'And?'

'He died. The doctor I talked to said he was knocked unconscious, swallowed a lungful of water, ended up drowning. Bloke said he wouldn't have known a thing about it but he was probably being kind. Either way, it's the same result. We buried him a couple of days ago.'

'Bummer.'

'You're right.' Bazza nodded, looked away for a second or two. Winter was watching his eyes carefully but there was no sign of emotion.

Bazza, typically, had moved on. 'So, son . . . ' he turned back ' . . . question is, what do we do about it?'

'Do about what?'

'My brother. Mark. We need some kind of memorial. There's no way we're going to forget him.'

Deano frowned. Dimly, like Winter, he was beginning to fathom what Bazza had in mind.

'Are we talking jet skis?'

'Yeah.'

'What, exactly?'

'I dunno. That's why I belled you. That's why you're here.'

He bent into the conversation again, mulling over the possibilities. At first, he said, he'd thought about some kind of parade of jet skis, like a waterborne funeral procession, *loads* of blokes, loads of people watching, pictures in the paper, flags at half mast, maybe even coverage on TV.

'Where?' It was Winter this time.

'Pompey.'

'But no one knows Mark there. Not amongst the jet skiers.'

'Exactly. Wank idea. The QHM would stop shipping for a bit while the blokes did the business, I know he would, but you're right — it doesn't cut it, we'd be pissing in the wind.'

'So what else do you fancy?'

'Well, then I thought about some kind of statue, Mark in his skiing suit. There's a launching ramp over at Lee-on-Solent. You could put it there.'

55

'Same problem, Baz.' Winter shook his head. 'No one would have a clue who he was.'

'You're right. So then I came up with something else. Listen. The Mackenzie *Trophy*. How does that sound?'

'Trophy?' Deano had just looked at his watch. 'Like in Cup?'

'Yeah. A race. A Grand Prix race. The biggest jet-ski race in the country. In Europe. In any-fucking-where. Mega prize money. Sponsorship. Telly. Lots of fanny in little bikinis. Loads of celebs. Huge crowds. Plus people like *you*, Deano, the top blokes, the cream of the fucking cream, all fighting for the Mackenzie Trophy.'

'Where?'

'Pompey. Spithead. Every year.' Bazza spread his hands wide, the sorcerer, the showman, the guy who makes things happen. 'Genius, eh? And you know something else?'

'What?'

'The QHM loves it.'

★   ★   ★

It was nearly half past nine before the officer at the front desk rang to say that Stephen Benskin had arrived. Faraday grunted an acknowledgement and went next door to fetch an extra chair. D/C Tracy Barber was on standby to join him for the interview. When she put her head round his office door he asked her to sort out some coffees while he fetched the property developer from downstairs.

Benskin was a squat, powerfully built man in

his early forties. His closely razored hair had left a blueish shadow on his pale skull and he wore his lightly striped grey suit with the restless impatience of a nightclub bouncer.

'Mr Benskin?'

Benskin turned to face Faraday, tossing the copy of the Force newssheet he'd been reading onto the counter. His eyes were hard, more black than brown, and the lines on his face, deeply etched, spoke of a sense of almost permanent irritation. Here was a man unused to being kept waiting.

'And you are . . . ?'

'D/I Faraday. You'll have talked to my colleague, D/C Suttle.'

Benskin's handshake was firm. He looked Faraday in the eye a second or two longer than was necessary, watched him punch the numbers into the door lock, then followed him upstairs.

Tracy Barber was already unloading the coffees onto Faraday's desk. Benskin caught her eye before Faraday had a chance to do the introductions.

'You do tea as well?'

'Whatever.'

'If you don't mind, love. Earl Grey if you've got it.'

The word 'love' brought Barber to a halt beside the door. She might have been a year or two younger than this man but she always stood her ground.

'The name's D/C Barber,' she said, 'next time you want to ask a favour.'

Benskin watched her leave, his thin mouth

57

curled in what might have been a smile.

'Stroppy,' he said softly. 'We like that.'

Faraday ignored the comment. By the time Barber returned with the tea, he'd established that Benskin had been in his apartment in Limehouse on Monday night. He'd spent the evening working on his laptop in preparation for yesterday's meeting in Barcelona. This morning he'd driven across to Wimbledon to pick up Sally and bring her down to Portsmouth. To be frank, he said, he thought she was still in shock.

'She's a strong woman, Sally.' Benskin was watching Barber. 'But no one can really handle something like this.'

'I'm sure you're right. How well did you know them? As a couple?'

'As well as I know anyone. Better probably. People say there's no sentiment in my game. That's a lie.' He threw the phrase out like a challenge.

'You've been together how long? You and Mr Mallinder?'

'Eight years. Give or take.'

'You knew him before?'

'Before when?'

'Before you went into business together.'

'Yeah, by reputation I did. He was with another firm, much bigger. He put together some bits of land in Slough. I liked the way he did it. Land assembly in a place like that can easily turn into a nightmare. He did it brilliantly. No drama. Everyone still mates at the end.'

'The name of this firm?' The question came from Barber. Benskin was looking at the

58

notebook open on her lap.

'What's the form here?' He addressed the question to Faraday.

'It's an interview, Mr Benskin. We ask the questions; you tell us about your partner. You'll appreciate our need to know. At this stage in the inquiry, to be frank, we're pretty much in the dark about what your firm's been up to. Pretend we know nothing. Just make that assumption.'

'I never make assumptions. Is this on the record?'

'D/C Barber keeps notes but you're not under caution so none of this is admissible.'

'In court, you mean?'

'Of course.' Faraday offered him a cold smile. He wanted to know more about Benskin, Mallinder. Had Benskin been operating on his own before Mallinder's arrival?

'No. I was with another company. Not Mallinder's outfit.'

'So the business started with the pair of you?'

'That's right.'

'Equal shares?'

'Down the middle. Jonno bought one kind of expertise to the table, me another. We were a perfect fit. That's the way I saw it from the off and that's the way it played out.'

'What was Mallinder's . . . ' Faraday frowned ' . . . special talent?'

'Negotiation. Face to face, he was awesome. He could strip the flesh from your bones and you'd still be smiling when they carted you off. To be frank, I never quite worked out how he did it. Maybe it's a Jewish thing. Maybe it's in the blood. When he needed to be, he was ruthless as hell. But you still loved the guy, regardless.'

'And your special talent?'

'Pretty much everything else. Sorting out the money side. The legal side. The contracts. Jonno was the guy for the big picture, the headline coup. That stuff, it's all vision and timing. Some people love it. Jonno adored it. It's like the Lord Mayor's Show. He needed to be in the golden carriage, he needed the attention. Me? I swept up afterwards.'

'Was that ever a problem?'

'I don't know what you mean.'

'Mallinder grabbing the limelight?'

'Christ, no. At the end of the day it's about profit, and like I say we carved the turkey fifty-fifty. Jonno was a class operator, don't get me wrong, but most of these deals turn to ratshit unless you get the small print right.'

'And that was your job?'

'Exactly.'

Faraday nodded, waiting for Barber's racing pencil to catch up. He'd stationed a cassette recorder on his desk and cued it before the interview, but psychologically there were advantages to writing the key facts down. Benskin was on the record and he knew it.

'Talk me through those first few years,' Faraday said.

'Why?'

'Because it may help. Unless, of course, you've got a problem with any of that . . . ' The smile again, even chillier.

Benskin shook his head, said it didn't matter.

Once they'd got the business up and running, he and Jonno had cut their teeth on small brownfield sites in prime commuting country around London. Already it was obvious that New Labour had a big problem with the lack of new housing starts and a business opportunity was staring them in the face.

'It all boils down to votes,' he said. 'The punters who've moved out to the country don't want some bloody great new estate spoiling their view. But the people left behind in the cities can't find anywhere to live. So what can politicians do without pissing anyone off? Easy. First off, they commission a survey. The survey finds all kinds of wasted space in what us lot call the urban environment. Derelict land, old warehousing, knackered shops, whatever. Each of these little bits of land could support half a dozen starter homes or a smallish block of flats so next they pass a bunch of laws that force local authorities to start taking this kind of shit seriously. They *have* to find room to house people. So they start looking round for likely sites and — hey — guess who's got there before them?'

'You.'

'Exactly.'

Benskin was beginning to relax now. This was his story, the narrative that had shaped his professional life, and it wasn't hard to sense a boastful pride in the way Benskin, Mallinder had set about turning a housing crisis into a personal fortune.

'What kind of scale are we talking here?'

'We started with a couple of punts in Enfield. Horrible area but they worked a treat. We assembled four parcels of land, sold them on to a builder or another property developer, and made money on the turn. This wasn't rocket science but pretty quickly we realised where we were going wrong.'

Their mistake, he said, was selling for cash. On a slowly rising market that would have made sense. But post-9/II, once the world had settled down, house prices had gone barmy. On average a competent builder could throw a block of six flats up in under a year. But within that time, you might have been looking at a 15 per cent rise in the market.

'So what did you do?'

'We started selling for cash plus.'

'Plus what?'

'Plus a slice of the proceeds of sale. Gross, of course.'

'How big a slice?'

Benskin looked at Faraday, disbelieving, then shook his head.

'That's commercial. In confidence. I'm here to help you out with Jonno. Why would you need to know this kind of detail?'

'Because it might help.'

'With what?'

'The bigger picture.'

'Really?' He thought about the proposition then shook his head. 'No way. Sorry, guys.'

'OK.' Faraday shrugged. 'But it made you money?'

'Of course it did. That's what businessmen do.'

'A lot of money?'

'Yes.'

'So what did you do next? More of the same?'

'Of course. Because the situation, deep down, hadn't really changed. People still needed somewhere to live. Plus we were getting swamped with immigrants, especially round London. They were pouring in. More heads. More roofs. Most politicians live in la-la land. They haven't a clue what's going on out there, they're a complete waste of space. People like us were different. Jonno and I lived and breathed it every day of our working lives. We'd developed a business model you wouldn't believe. We couldn't stop making money. Still can't, actually.'

Tracy Barber had put her notebook aside for a moment. Faraday gave her a nod.

'I'm not quite clear about this business model of yours,' she said. 'What exactly was so special about you two?'

'We travelled light.'

'What does that mean?'

'It means we never got suckered into full-blown development. We didn't have huge offices. We kept staffing levels incredibly low, just a handful of the kind of people we really needed. Businessmen talk a lot about vertical integration. That means land purchase, outline planning permission, full-spec drawings, sorting out a builder, advertising for punters, the whole kaboodle until the moment Mister and Missus step into their nice new house. There are loads of people in that game, loads of them, and we always thought they were carrying too much fat. The truth is, vertical integration can be a pain in the arse. Every day you're looking at another hassle — builders, planners, the utilities people, punters, you name it. Jonno and me? We spotted opportunities, assembled land, got outline planning permission, cast a fly or two and then moved on. You know what they started calling us in the business? The Ghost Squad. Brilliant. Jonno loved it.'

Tracy nodded and reached for her pad. Faraday's turn.

'And it's stayed that way? Land assembly? Selling on?'

'Basically, yes. Though naturally we became more ambitious.'

Three years ago, he said, they'd got wind of a town-centre parcel of land in Farnham in Surrey. Not a huge site but absolutely prime commuting country. Within a month or two some neighbouring land came on to the market. Put the two bits of land together and they were tantalisingly close to a fourteen-townhouse development.

'That's significant? Fourteen houses?'

'Very. Put up more than fourteen houses and you had to make provision for social housing. Nowadays it's worse. Nowadays it's only ten houses. But either way, that means getting the scrotes in, and *that* means lowering the tone. In a fourteen-unit development in the middle of Farnham we were talking 450K a pop, easy. Ask people to live alongside families on benefit, and you'd be lucky to see 300K. Aggregate the difference and you're talking over two million quid. We can all do the maths. It's simple. It's just a fact of life.'

'So what happened? In Farnham?'

'Jonno went back to take another look. It turned out there was a shop exactly where we needed the land, a hardware store, an old family business. Jonno asked around a bit, like you do, and pretty quickly he discovered that this shop was in the shit. The big out-of-town operations were crucifying them. Why would you buy white gloss at twenty pounds a tin when B&Q are knocking it out at twelve ninety-nine?'

'So what did you do?'

'We bought the place.'

'As a going concern?'

'Yeah. Except it wasn't.'

'And then?'

'We tacked it on to the other bits of land and got planning permission.'

'For fourteen houses?'

'Of course. Within a week we had two developers and three builders on the phone. It was an auction. You couldn't go wrong.'

Faraday nodded. Benskin, Mallinder, he'd concluded, were a pair of commercial magicians, conjuring huge money from little more than a handful of phone calls and a great deal of conversation.

'And Mallinder? He was the one who negotiated all these deals?'

'Yes.'

'So how many people did he upset?'

'None.'

'I don't believe you.'

'Fine.' Benskin shrugged. 'That's your privilege. But like I told you before, Jonno never left a meeting without making a friend. The guy was a genius at it. He should have gone into social work. Or the Church.'

Faraday glanced over at Tracy Barber. The brief history of Benskin, Mallinder seemed, on the face of it, all too plain. They sniffed the wind. They stalked their target. They pounced at a time of their choosing. No wonder, in the development game, they'd become such big beasts.

'Competitors? Rivals?'

'Everywhere.' Benskin conceded the point with a smile. 'When the other guys start bitching, that's when you know you've got it right.'

'What does bitching mean?'

'It means snidey articles in the trade press. It means blokes turning their backs in the pub or at some poncy do. It means loads of badmouthing and innuendo. Some of the braver ones even do it to your face.'

'Names?'

'You'd be wasting your time.'

'Why?'

'Because these people are all talk.'

'Isn't that a judgement we should be making?'

'Of course, and I'm sure you will, but if you're looking for me to grass these people up then I'm afraid the answer's no.'

'Grass up?'

'Sure. Believe it or not, there's a kind of protocol here, a code if you like. We fight tooth and nail, of course we do, but at the end of the day it's just a game. If I thought there was a real problem with any of these guys, then I'd sort it. But there isn't. Believe me.'

Tracy Barber stirred.

'I thought you said Mallinder didn't make enemies?'

'He didn't. Not amongst the people he was dealing with. Your mate here was asking about rivals. But even then enemies is too strong. It's envy. And you know why? Because most of them can't be arsed to put the effort in. Talent is cheaper than table salt. It's hard work that makes the difference. You reap what you sow. That's the secret of getting rich.'

'Or ending up dead?'

'Very funny.'

A perceptible chill had settled on the interview. At length, Faraday mentioned the Tipner project. He wanted to know the strength of Benskin, Mallinder's interest.

'Tipner was a one-off for us. I never liked it from the start. It was Jonno's baby, to tell you the truth.'

'So why the reservation? On your part?'

'The place is a dump. Literally. It's been used and abused for years. Horrible stuff, asbestos, heavy metals, you name it. You know the bill for the clean-up? Fifty-three million quid. And that's before you pour a foot of concrete. And there's something else, too. We're off the pace.'

'What does that mean?'

'It means we've been beaten to it. There's already a preferred developer in place. They've

67

done the heavy lifting. And the fact that they might be in the market for a buyer tells me there can't be that much profit in it.'

'So why was Mallinder so keen?'

'Good question.'

'You must have asked him.'

'Of course I did. In fact it became a kind of running joke.'

'And?'

'He said it was partly about the city itself. I've never been able to pick it up but he said the vibe down here was really good, really promising. Gunwharf. The new Northern Quarter development. The university. The history of the place. The Trafalgar celebrations. All those sexy events on the harbour. Some days, to tell you the truth, I thought he was working for the council.'

'So there was more to his interest than Tipner? Is that what you're telling me?'

'Yes. I think maybe there was.'

'Are we talking other sites? Or other people?' It was Barber.

'Both, probably. But I just don't know.'

'But you were close, *really* close. Or at least that's what you said.'

'Sure. And he'd come back with stuff — one or two development possibilities, bits and pieces of MoD land. It all made sense, I'm not blaming him, but compared to the returns you can make around London, the sums just didn't stack up.'

'So it must have been something else, musn't it? To make him that interested in Portsmouth?' Barber wouldn't let go.

'I don't know.'

'Really?'

'Yes.'

Faraday was watching him carefully. 'The lease he took on the house in Port Solent,' he said. 'That tells me he was down here a good deal.'

'He was. And renting was much cheaper than hotels.'

'So how often did he come down?'

'A couple of times a week. Some weeks less, some weeks more.'

'And you always compared notes afterwards? You were in the loop? You knew what was going on?'

'Yeah, more or less. I was never his keeper. That wasn't the way it worked. But yes, he kept me up to speed.'

'So why so much time down here?'

'Tipner, mainly.'

'Which you couldn't understand.'

'Which I didn't fancy. It's a judgement call. We had a difference of professional opinion, that's all.'

'But I still don't get it, Mr Benskin. Here's a guy whose judgement you really respect. He doesn't make mistakes, not big mistakes. So there has to be a reason, doesn't there? About the strength of his interest in the Tipner site?'

With some reluctance, Benskin nodded. Tracy Barber cleared her throat. Her voice was low.

'The man's dead, Mr Benskin. The least you owe him is an answer.'

'OK.' He frowned, taking his time. 'Jonno believed he was on the verge of some kind of breakthrough. He believed he could turn the deal around. Frankly, I thought he was talking bollocks.'

'What kind of breakthrough?'

'All the serious profit in the Tipner site is residential. As it is, there's a big problem. Partly social housing again, partly the way the planners have zoned the place. But there's a big piece of land next door, acres and acres of it, right by the harbour. At the moment it's used as a firing range. If the MoD were to release it, you're looking at a prime, prime site.'

'And the Ministry of Defence?'

'They've always said no. They'd barely even discuss it.'

'But Mallinder?'

'Jonno thought otherwise. He said they could be convinced. And he said he was the guy to do it.'

'Having acquired the site from the current developers?'

'We hadn't got that far, nowhere near. But yes, you're right, that was the plan, that's the way it would have to go.'

'And you'd benefit from this sudden windfall?'

'Obviously. And Jonno was right. It would have meant a lot of money.'

Faraday asked about paperwork, about files Mallinder would have kept on the Tipner project, about names and contacts and detailed records of meetings he'd attended. Benskin said he'd organise it, send the stuff down.

By now, mid-morning, he was plainly anxious to leave, but Faraday hadn't finished. He wanted to know about the last couple of weeks, about any signs of stress or tension he might have noticed in his partner, about possible pressures in Mallinder's private life — in short, about any tiny clue that might explain the small black-smudged hole in his forehead.

At each question Benskin shook his head. Jonno lived for his work and his family. He was about to move house to a bigger place in Wentworth. He was looking forward to their planned expansion into foreign markets, chiefly Spain. At this Faraday pressed for more detail, but Benskin was unforthcoming. Plans were still at an early stage. They were looking at a number of possibilities in terms of partnership but even an outline contract was at least six months away.

At length, after nearly two hours, Faraday called a halt. Should the need arise, he'd be back for more detail, perhaps another interview. Benskin, on his feet now, said nothing. Tracy Barber escorted him back downstairs to the front desk, returning minutes later to find Faraday gazing out of the window. A pair of distant rooks over the motorway were mobbing a bird she could barely see.

'It's a kestrel.' Faraday turned round. 'Punchy, wasn't he?'

4

WEDNESDAY, 6 SEPTEMBER 2006, 12.23

Winter went back to Portsmouth on the train. Mackenzie had offered him a lift but a couple of hours of headbanging after Deano got on his bike and roared off had left Winter with a yearning for a bit of peace and quiet. In these moods Bazza was out of control.

Winter, to his alarm, had been saddled with the task of making the Mackenzie Trophy come true. At first, listening to his new boss back at the station, he'd wrongly assumed that this wild idea was nothing more than a particularly violent blast of wind in the hurricane that was Bazza's life. He'd probably been thinking about Mark. Someone had mentioned Pompey's appetite for staging big events. Someone else had been talking about jet skis. And suddenly, hey presto, there it was: the Mackenzie Trophy. Immortality for Mark, poor bastard, lots of profile for Bazza and a big leg-up for the family name.

In the way of things, Winter would have expected nothing less. Mackenzie had a brain like a firework display, forever sending up volley after volley of fizzing little schemes, and people who knew him well simply closed their eyes, put their hands over their ears, and waited for the rocket sticks to fall to earth. Once in a while, to be fair, he'd see to it that one of these wheezes actually came to something. The Royal Trafalgar Hotel, now the showpiece of the Mackenzie empire, had started life as a gleam in Bazza's eye. As had a couple of café-bars, a chain of tanning salons, an estate agency, a taxi firm, a double-glazing outfit and even a North End pet shop that specialised in exotic reptiles. But the Mackenzie Trophy?

Winter shook his head, watching the blur of stations as London's outer suburbs slowly thinned. Maybe it was down to Mark, he thought. Maybe Baz genuinely wanted to somehow commemorate his brother's death. Or maybe it was something more complex, Bazza's way of coping with all that grief. Dream up a monster stunt like this, push it hard, make it happen, and there'd be precious little time left for feeling sorry for himself.

Whatever the truth, Winter was well and truly kippered. With Deano gone, Bazza had got down to business. To Winter's horror, he'd produced a checklist of steps he wanted actioned. This in itself was evidence that the Mackenzie Trophy was something more than a passing fantasy, and Winter's heart sank as Bazza led him through the unfolding plan.

First off, he wanted the locals on board. Given ample support from the QHM, Winter was to sort out the RNLI, the SSA, the RYA and the PHE. Faced with this nonsense, Winter had briefly perked up. Bazza was taking the piss. He knew about the life Winter had just left. He knew that coppers battled daily against a blizzard of initials. This was his little joke, a touch on the

73

elbow, a matey way of making him feel comfortable in his new role.

Far from it. The Royal National Lifeboat Institution, the Solent Skiers Association, the Royal Yachting Association and an outfit called Portsmouth Harbour Events all needed a call. One by one, Winter was to recruit them for the cause. That done, he was to talk to the city council. These people loved publicity, especially free publicity. A big stunt like this would bring thousands of punters flooding in, especially once Winter had explained about the media coverage.

Media coverage? He'd tried to bring Bazza back to earth. There and then, over his second hot chocolate, he'd tried to bring this madness to a halt. He knew bugger all about the media. He had no contacts in television and precious few anywhere else. Even in Pompey his knowledge of local journalism didn't extend beyond a couple of pretty young *News* reporters whom he'd occasionally tapped up for favours.

Bazza had dismissed him out of hand.

'Bollocks, mush,' he'd said. 'This is like pyramid selling. You start with the QHM, with the guys on the water. Then you rope in the council. Once you've done that, it sells itself. The boys at Sky will be *throwing* money at you. Then you talk to Eurosport, Channel Four, ITV, whoever. You get an auction going. You start thinking international rights, airline rights, video streaming. You know what, mush? Play it right, and we're looking at a fucking great *profit*. Every cloud eh?'

Winter was appalled. By the time Bazza got to

74

the end of his must-do list, he knew that he was staring disaster in the face. He was an ex-copper, for Christ's sake, not some Pompey hustler trying to turn a fatal accident into a huge media event. He'd joined forces with Bazza on the promise that there'd be room for his special skills, his contacts, his experience. Not this pantomime.

Bazza, of course, had seen the expression on his face.

'You think you're not up to it?'

'I know I'm not up to it.'

'You're wrong. You think it's a crap idea?'

'I think it's bizarre.'

'You're right. But so was *Big Brother* and look what happened to that.'

The link between *Big Brother* and Bazza's latest baby was lost on Winter but as Mackenzie slid the list across the table, he knew they'd got to a point of no return. If he didn't pick up this piece of paper, his brief relationship with the Bazza Mackenzie organisation was over. With untold consequences.

'This is crazy,' he'd muttered, folding the list and slipping it into his jacket pocket.

Now, sitting on the half-empty train, he tried hard not to visualise what lay ahead. Endless phone calls, e-mails, meetings. Arms to be twisted. Ears to be bent. With luck and a generous helping of bullshit, he could cope with the Pompey end of things. But what would happen when he took on the bigger boys in London? The TV people? The media agents? All those savvy guys who held the keys to

75

sponsorship? How on earth could he set about shafting them when he didn't have a clue what language they spoke?

He sat back and closed his eyes. A situation like this, it paid to have a mate or two, someone you could drag out for a drink to share your troubles. In the job for most of his adult life, he'd done without friends, glorying in his canteen reputation as the loner, the maverick, the bloke who scored result after result without all that teamwork bollocks and broke most of the rules in the process. The knowledge that most of his colleagues found him deeply irritating had never failed to please him, and on his last day he'd left the force without even considering a farewell pint or two, but now — after a couple of hours of Bazza at full throttle — he began to regret his lack of mates.

He thought some more about it, about the absence of good-luck cards, phone calls, text messages, about the sheer thickness of the wall that had so abruptly sealed him off from his previous life, and as the train slowed for the stop at Guildford, he fumbled for his mobile. Jimmy Suttle's number was stored on the SIM card. This time of day the boy would be up to his eyes. When the recorded voice cut in, telling him to leave a message, he wondered whether he shouldn't just forget it. Then he changed his mind.

'It's me — Paul,' he muttered. 'You free tonight?'

* * *

76

D/C Jimmy Suttle was a couple of hours late by the time he finally made it to Port Solent. Scenes of Crime were still ripping No. 97 Bryher Island apart and so the Family Liaison Officer had made arrangements to rent a room at the nearby Tulip Hotel for the day. The room was on the fourth floor and the door opened at once to Suttle's knock. The last time he'd seen D/C Jessie Williams, she'd been throwing up over the back of a chartered cruise boat on a CID night out.

'Everything OK?' Suttle could hear a low mumble of conversation from the bedroom behind her.

'She's got the telly on. Do you mind if I push off for a break?'

'Not at all. How is she?'

'Fine.' Jessie shot him a look.

Suttle stayed in the corridor while Jessie went into the bedroom, explained about her colleague and asked whether she needed anything from downstairs. Then he stepped inside and closed the door behind him.

Sally Mallinder was sitting on the bed with her back against the headboard, watching three people discussing a carriage clock. She was a striking woman, middle-aged, blonde. She'd kicked off her shoes and made herself comfortable, her bare feet tucked beneath her. She was wearing a loose cotton shirt outside a pair of blue culottes and was very obviously pregnant.

'*Cash in the Attic.*' She nodded at the screen. 'I never miss it.'

Suttle, for a brief moment, was nonplussed.

He'd come to inquire about a murder, not watch daytime TV.

'Do you mind?' He bent to the set and turned it off.

Before she had a chance to protest, he pulled up a chair and sat down. Half an hour ago he'd debriefed the D/C who'd managed to establish a name for Mallinder's regular visitor. She was a Bengali prostitute called Aliyah, and with luck she'd be volunteering herself for interview at Kingston Crescent at some point this afternoon. For now, though, Suttle needed a domestic angle on the dead man.

'Can I just say, Mrs Mallinder — '

'How sorry you are? Sure. Of course. Thank you.' She was still looking at the blankness of the screen. At length she glanced across at Suttle. 'So what do you want to know?'

'It's about your husband, obviously. In cases like these we try and establish a sequence of events leading up to what happened. It's just a start, that's all.'

She said she understood. Jonathan had left home around half eight on Monday morning. He'd dropped the kids at school and given her a ring from his mobile around lunchtime. Everything had seemed perfectly normal. He was cheerful about the meeting he'd just had and said he'd probably be back some time late tomorrow afternoon.

'That's *yesterday* afternoon,' she added.

'Of course.' Suttle had his notepad on his lap. 'Did he say anything else about the meeting?'

'No. But then he never went into details.

78

Jonathan was a man who lived his life in boxes. Business was box one. We were box two.'

'Second best?'

'Alphabetical order.' She looked away. 'Though sometimes, I admit, it was hard to tell.'

Suttle scribbled himself a note. Bitterness was like a bad smell, he thought. You couldn't miss it.

'You're telling me you knew very little about your husband's business life?'

'I'm telling you he spared us the details. I knew broadly what he got up to — the deals he was doing, what might happen at the end of it — but if you've come here to ask me about his diary, about who he met, where they fitted, what happened, I'm afraid I can't help you.'

'Was it always like that?'

'Yes. In many respects he was a very private man.'

'And family life? Do you mind me asking?'

'Not in the least. Family life was wonderful. He was active, he *did* stuff, he was funny, he'd stayed young at heart, the kids adored him. What else would a woman want?'

What else indeed. Suttle made another note. Then he looked up.

'No problems, then?'

'Domestically, you mean?'

'Yes.'

'None. We led a very full life, always have done. Jonathan worked hard and played hard. I respected that, gave him space if you like.'

'Space for what?'

'Space for this . . . ' She nodded vaguely towards the window. 'I don't know what it is with

79

Portsmouth but my husband just loved it. Given half a chance, I'm sure he'd have moved us all down.'

'And you?'

'I never got it, never understood the charm of the place. We had a weekend down here once, the whole family. The dockyard was OK, the kids loved the old boats, but the city itself . . . ' She pulled a face, leaving the sentence unfinished.

'What about business pressures? Can you think of anything recently? Anything that might have upset him?'

'No.' She shook her head, emphatic. 'As I told you, Jonathan kept his business affairs to himself. But why would anyone want to kill him? Especially like that?'

'Like what?'

'Like . . . so professionally? So *coldly*? It makes me shudder even thinking about it. Someone like Jonathan, he's canny, he's clever, he just doesn't get into situations like that. He knows the boundaries, he knows how far to push. He might take the odd liberty — we all do — but there are limits and he'd be the first to respect them.'

'The odd liberty?'

'Yes.' She frowned, and Suttle became suddenly aware of the shapeliness of her hands, cradling the swell of her belly. 'He takes a risk or two sometimes. But that's fine. That's what makes him fun.'

Suttle was wondering about her use of the present tense. Mallinder was clearly going to leave a very large hole in her life.

'Was the call you mentioned the last time you heard from him?'

'Yes. Sometimes he'd phone in the evening to talk to the kids, but on Monday he didn't.'

'No late-night call?'

'No. But then I didn't expect it. I go to bed early. He knew that.'

'And no indication that something might have upset him? No calls to the house you might have been aware of? E-mails? Anything like that?'

'Nothing. I don't make a habit of looking at his e-mails but if there was anything wrong, really wrong, I'd be able to tell, believe me. No, Jonathan had the lowest blood pressure of any man I've ever known. Nothing got to him.' For the first time she smiled. 'We're moving next week, can you believe that? Much bigger place over in Wentworth. Me? I've been tearing my hair out for weeks. Jonathan? He just gets on with it. Take this last weekend. Boxes to pack? Arrangements to make? Little details you can't afford to forget? It's just never a problem. He copes. He keeps a little mental list. And come six o'clock, with the kids still rushing round, you know what? It's all sorted. Amazing. I kept meaning to ask him. What's the secret? Just how do you always manage to stay so calm? So cheerful?' She sniffed, then turned her head away. Suttle found a box of tissues on the carpet beside the sofa. She dabbed at her eyes then blew her nose. 'Shit,' she said quietly. 'I swore I'd never do this.'

'It's completely understandable.'

'Yeah?' She looked at him. 'You'd know, would you?'

The interview came to an end shortly afterwards. Suttle gave her a phone number and told her to call if she thought of anything else he ought to know. She nodded, getting heavily to her feet. Benskin was going to drop by the hotel at some point and take her back to London. If she never saw Portsmouth again, she said, she wouldn't be the least bit sorry.

Out in the corridor Suttle asked if there was anything else she needed.

'Yes.' She nodded. 'The keys to my husband's car.'

Suttle remembered a line from the preliminary SOC report. No one had been able to get inside the Mercedes parked in the drive.

'You don't have a spare set?'

'No. I phoned the garage in the end. They're dropping some off. Tomorrow.'

'So what will you do?'

'Do?' She looked vacant for a moment then stepped back into the room. 'Christ knows.'

* * *

Faraday took the call on his mobile as he stepped into Barrie's office. He hesitated a moment, backed into the corridor, then returned seconds later. Barrie turned from his PC. Faraday rarely grinned.

'Good news?'

'Very.'

82

'*Billhook?*'

'My son. He's just stepped off the plane at Heathrow.'

Barrie took a moment to absorb this news. 'But I thought he was deaf?' he said at last. 'I thought he couldn't talk?'

'He can't. That was a friend of mine on the phone. She's up there to meet him.'

'Great . . . ' He stared at Faraday then frowned. 'So where are we with *Billhook?*'

Faraday took a seat beside the desk, still trying to picture Gabrielle's efforts to cope with his windmill of a son. J-J's brand of sign language was never less than theatrical but if she could survive six months with Vietnamese hill tribes, he thought, then conducting a conversation with his deaf son should be a breeze.

'Joe . . . ?' Barrie was running out of patience.

Faraday apologised. He'd just had a call from Glen Thatcher, the D/S in charge of Outside Enquiries.

'And?'

'We might have a hit on CCTV.'

Number-plate recognition cameras on the M27, he said, had picked up a stolen car heading west at 03.47 on Tuesday morning, a black Ford Escort registered to a twenty-three-year-old from Southampton. The car had been nicked earlier on in the day from a car park in the New Forest and now the team at the CCTV control room had established further sightings.

'Where?'

'On the approach road to Port Solent, around half past nine, Monday night.'

'Details?'

'None, I'm afraid. All we got was a rear shot but the blokes are pretty sure it's the same car.'

'And later, on the motorway?'

'Two up. A guy behind the wheel and a bloke beside him. They've both got the visors down so I'm afraid there's no detail but the passenger was much smaller. He was wearing a grey hoodie so we can't really see his face. There could be other people in the back, of course.'

'And you think these sightings might be significant?'

'Very.'

'Why?'

'The visors, for one thing. That tells me these guys are aware.'

'Anything else?'

'Yes. The car was found this morning, back in the New Forest. Burned out.'

Barrie permitted himself a smile. He was itching for a roll-up, Faraday could tell.

'Witnesses?' he asked.

'We're talking a different car park in the forest, quite remote. The fire was called in by a passing motorist at five in the morning. It was windy last night and by that time the fire had spread a bit. According to Outside Enquiries, it took three appliances to put it out.'

'What kind of state was the car in?'

'Totally burned out. The fire investigators have been on site for about an hour. The way I see it, sir, we need more than that.'

'You want to put Scenes of Crime in?'

'Yes. But we've got to get a move on. Once the

fire people have finished they'll want to clean up.'

Barrie glanced at his watch. Three appliances meant a small army of firemen. Surely any worthwhile evidence would have been trampled to death by now?

'Maybe, but in my view it's still worth it. I'm not talking a major operation. Just a single CSI would do it. I was going to drive out and take a look myself.'

CSI meant Crime Scene Investigator. Faraday waited for a decision. Like every Detective-Superintendent, Barrie hated wasting resources.

'You're sure we can tie this vehicle to Port Solent?'

'Definitely. Like I say, we caught it on the approach road.'

'And then what?'

'We don't know. There are cameras at the main car park. It's a different control room. The guys are still looking at the footage.'

'How about leaving Port Solent?'

'That's a definite, too. The same camera on the approach road caught the Escort leaving.'

'What time?'

'At three thirty-eight. That ties in exactly with the ANPR sighting on the motorway.'

'How many people?'

'Two for sure in the front. Both visors are down, exactly the way they are on the motorway, and the smaller guy is wearing a grey hoodie.'

'OK.' Barrie scribbled himself a note. 'Go for it.'

Faraday got to his feet but Barrie motioned him to stay put. He wanted an update on other developments, starting with Benskin.

'You think he might be a runner?'

'Possibly.'

Faraday quickly summarised the morning's interview. Benskin and Mallinder had been close working partners, as they'd suspected. In deal after deal, they'd seen absolutely eye to eye, agreed on everything, and as a result they seemed to have come from nowhere to a position of some prominence in double-quick time. Only when they were getting towards the end of the interview had Faraday detected the slightest hint of daylight between them.

'With respect to what?'

'The Tipner project. Benskin was pretty frank. He thought Mallinder had got it all wrong for once.' He gave Barrie the details.

'We need someone to talk to the current developers.'

'Of course. Outside Enquiries have got it down as a priority action.'

'When?'

'This afternoon. We should have something in the pot by close of play.'

Barrie nodded. The regular *Billhook* squad meet was scheduled for *18.15*. He'd be at HQ in Winchester for a meeting so he wanted Faraday to chair it. Any major developments, he expected a phone call.

'No problem.'

'Excellent.' Barrie scribbled himself another note. 'And the rest?'

'We've got a name for the escort Mallinder's been using, the Asian girl. We're expecting her sometime this afternoon. She's volunteered to come in.'

'And the wife?'

'Suttle says he drew a blank. The woman was a bit pissed off to be second best to his business interests but he thinks she loved him to bits. Apparently he was great with the kids, great with her, no obvious tensions, about to move house, everything apple pie.'

'Except he's using a prostitute.'

'Yes, sir.'

'And got himself killed.'

'Exactly.'

★ ★ ★

Faraday was out in the New Forest within the hour. He'd had a brief phone conversation with the fire investigator who was already on site and had warned him that Scenes of Crime personnel were en route from Fareham. Faraday recognised the white Peugeot van as he pulled into the car park from the road that wound through this corner of the forest. Barrie, as Faraday had suggested, had asked for a single Crime Scene Investigator.

His name was Tim Riddick. Faraday found him on the other side of the van pulling on a grey one-piece forensic suit. The last time they'd met was a couple of months back on a rape in woodland near Waterlooville.

'What's the story, boss?' Riddick zipped up the suit, looking across at the blackened remains of the Escort.

Faraday explained about the CCTV sightings. There was a possibility the Escort might be tied to the Port Solent hit.

'How many blokes are we talking?'

'Two.'

Riddick nodded The fire brigade investigator was still at work on the shell of the burned-out car, bagging samples from the charred debris beneath the front seats. The seats were nothing more than a framework of metal and springs twisted into grotesque shapes by the heat of the fire, and Faraday studied them a moment, imagining this tableau in some cutting-edge London gallery. Then he stepped back, gazing around. The acrid stench of the fire still hung in the air. The car park was surrounded by trees and shrubs, and the vegetation on one side of the site was blackened. At least an acre, he thought. Maybe more.

The fire investigator was writing labels for his sample bags. When Faraday asked whether it was too early to draw conclusions, he shook his head.

'Peach of a job,' he said. 'Just look at that.'

'What?'

The investigator was pointing at the window frames. Faraday assumed the windows themselves had disintegrated in the heat but evidently he was wrong.

'They're all wound down. Whoever did this knew exactly what they were about. A wind like last night's, you park exactly on this line, broadside on. Then you wind the windows down, lift the tailgate, empty a load of accelerant inside, put a match to it and run like fuck. Loads of draught, burned a treat. Lovely job.'

Faraday watched Riddick. He was moving carefully across the sodden ash around the car park, scanning the ground. Everywhere there were footprints, tyre tracks, indisputable evidence of a couple of dozen firemen. Normally, Faraday wouldn't dream of disturbing a crime scene but on this occasion there was nothing left to contaminate. Barrie had been right: putting in Scenes of Crime was a waste of time.

Faraday turned to the fire investigator again.

'What happens to the car?'

'We'll take it back to the depot. I'll need some more photos. The recovery truck's due any time now.'

'We'll grab a couple of shots before it leaves.'

'Sure. Help yourself.'

Faraday waited for Riddick to return. As he'd expected, there was little value in extending the search any further. There might have been another vehicle here that the guys in the Escort had used to leave the scene but the fire and its aftermath had destroyed any surviving shred of evidence. Of course he'd pop off some shots for the file but the fire investigator had it about right. Class act.

'Yeah.' Faraday nodded. 'Just like Mallinder.'

★   ★   ★

Winter was on the Gosport ferry when Suttle returned his call. It was hot for early September, and Winter had made himself comfortable in a seat on the top deck, enjoying the sun on his face.

'The answer's yes.' Suttle was obviously in a hurry. 'Round eight? Somewhere quiet? I'll give you a bell.'

The line went dead and Winter struggled to his feet, a broad smile on his face. Standing at the rail, he watched as the ferry manoeuvred alongside, nudging the Gosport pontoon.

Jimmy Suttle, over the last couple of years, had virtually become the son that he and Joannie had never had. Unlike many of the younger D/Cs these days, the lad had a real appetite for the job. He'd always been happy to listen to Winter's war stories, picking up tips wherever he could, and when Winter had found himself fighting a brain tumour, young Jimmy had made it his business to help out. At the time Winter had been involved with a part-time call girl with an unlikely name, and between them she and Jimmy Suttle had kept the demons at bay. An American neurosurgeon had finally saved Winter's life but in truth he'd been inclined to give the proper credit to Maddox and to Suttle. Only the prospect of near-certain death, he thought now, had made him realise the importance of real friendship.

Winter joined the queue of passengers disembarking. Minutes later he was knocking on an office door in a new development overlooking the biggest of the harbourside marinas. The name on the door read 'Harbour Events'.

He'd talked to Andrew McCall an hour or so earlier on the phone. In the flesh he was older than Winter had expected, a tall, slightly piratical figure with mischievous eyes and the faintest suggestion of a limp.

'What can I do for you?'

Winter introduced himself. He'd decided on the word 'consultant'.

'Consultant to whom?'

'Beaver UK.' He used the name of one of Bazza's many companies.

McCall roared with laughter. 'Mackenzie? You're in with him?'

'He's my client,' Winter said stiffly.

'And he *pays* you? Christ, that's a first.'

Winter ignored the dig. He wanted to know what lay behind Harbour Events. McCall was happy to oblige.

'I'm a facilitator,' he explained, ' . . . a midwife if you like. People come to me with ideas. I put them in touch with other people who might be able to help. I give their little boat a push, and once they're all set up and shipshape, they sail away.'

He mentioned the Whitbread Round-the-World Race. Back in 1997 he'd organised the departure from Southampton. On that occasion he'd been working directly for Whitbread and he'd been rather more hands-on.

'But why did you give it to the Scummers?'

'Because they were up for it. Ocean Village was perfect. Terrific backdrop. The event went like a dream. It's all turned to ratshit since, of course, which is why we brought the Global Challenge here last year.'

He waved a languid hand towards the window.

91

Beyond the forest of masts in the marina Winter caught a glimpse of the ferry returning to the Pompey side of the harbour.

'Brilliant. So you ended up stuffing the bastards?'

'The Scummers? Big time.'

McCall shot Winter a grin. Scummers was Pompey-speak for anyone who'd had the misfortune to be born in Southampton, and the very word was enough to start a riot in certain Pompey pubs. On the football pitch, and elsewhere, no victory was ever sweeter.

Winter began to talk about Bazza's determination to organise some kind of jet ski race. To his amazement, McCall appeared to take him seriously.

'It's a good idea,' he said. 'In fact it's a corker.'

'You're serious?'

'Absolutely. And you're right about QHM. In fact he's become a bit of a convert.'

'So you think it's do-able?'

'Of course.' He gazed at Winter, puzzled. 'Don't you?'

★   ★   ★

Aliyah Begum turned up at Kingston Crescent in the late afternoon. She gave her name and asked for D/C Yates. Yates, who'd visited the escort agency earlier, was out on another action and so the call from the front desk finally made its way to Faraday. En route to fetch her from downstairs, he put his head round Suttle's door.

'Join me in my office,' he said. 'Give me a couple of minutes.'

Aliyah Begum was even younger than Faraday had expected. Under the lip gloss and the Western-style trouser suit she could easily have passed as Mallinder's daughter. She accompanied him back upstairs. She had a flat Midlands accent and a nervous habit of playing with the gold bangles on her wrist. Suttle joined them.

By now Faraday had realised that no one had told her about Mallinder. He broke the news with a woodenness that took Suttle by surprise. Aliyah stared at them, aghast, her eyes going from one face to the other.

'Why?' she managed at last.

'It's a good question,' Faraday conceded. 'We don't know.'

'But . . . ' She was still trying to understand, still trying to make sense of this appalling news.

'He was shot,' Faraday said, 'the night before last. We think it probably happened around three, four o'clock in the morning.' He paused, letting the implications sink in. Suttle reached for his pad. 'How long have you known Mr Mallinder?'

'A month. Maybe longer. Say six weeks.'

'And how did that come about?'

'He phoned the agency. They sent a book of photos round. He chose me.' She said it with a hint of pride.

'And you went to see him?'

'Yes, that same night. He wanted full service. We had sex. He was nice. I liked him.'

'And you went back? Regularly?'

'Yes.'

'Did you ever stay the night?'

'No. I could have done but it would have cost a lot more money.'

'Did he ever ask you to stay the night?'

'No. Usually I stayed for about an hour. That was all he wanted.'

'And he never asked for anyone else?'

'No.' She shook her head, failing to hide the flash of anger in her eyes. Faraday saw it. So did Suttle.

'Did he ever give you a key?'

'Never.'

'Did you become friends?'

'No.' She was playing with the bangles again. 'You think sometimes you could be friends. Maybe you'd like to be friends. But no, not in that situation.'

'But you talked?'

'Of course we talked. We're not animals.'

'What did you talk about?'

'His family. Mine sometimes.'

'And did you get the impression he was happy? At home?'

'Very. He showed me photos of them all. He had lovely kids. A lovely wife, too. He was a lucky man.'

'And yet . . . ' Faraday shrugged ' . . . he needed you.'

'Of course. It happens a lot. Especially with men like him away from home.'

'And business? Did you ever talk about that?'

She glanced at Suttle. Then her eyes found Faraday again.

'Why do you ask?'

'Because it might be important.' Faraday paused, waiting for an answer, then carried on. 'Did you know what he did for a living?'

'A little. He bought and sold land, I think.'

'That's right. So let me ask you the question again. Did you ever talk about any of that?'

Her head went down. She knotted her fingers.

'Yes,' she said at last.

'In what respect?'

'He wanted to know about a couple of places in Southsea. One was a kind of grocery. The other was a restaurant. He thought I might be able to help.'

'Why? Why you?'

'Because they were both Bengali, these places.'

'And did you help?'

This time she was determined not to answer. Faraday let the silence stretch and stretch. Finally, with a glance at Suttle, he ran out of patience.

'Mr Mallinder is dead,' he said softly. 'Somebody killed him. We need to find that somebody and to do that we need people like you to help us. We've got a choice here. We can all go down to another police station. We call it the Bridewell. We can arrest you. Caution you. Get you a lawyer. Or we can just carry on here, just as we are. It's your choice.'

'Arrest me for what?' She was looking alarmed.

'Obstructing the course of justice. It's a serious offence. Think about it.'

She nodded, studied her nails for a moment or

95

two. Her nails were purple, embellished with tiny silver stars. Finally, her head came up.

'I told him that I'd ask around, make some enquiries.'

'What did he want to know?'

'He wanted to find out whether, you know, the business was good at these places.'

'You mean successful?'

'Yes.'

'Why?'

'I don't know. He never said.'

'And what did you find out?'

'I found out . . . ' she ran her tongue over her lips then swallowed hard ' . . . that business wasn't good.'

'And you told him?'

'Yes.'

'But he still didn't explain why?'

'No.'

Faraday shot a look at Suttle. The next question was obvious.

'Did you get the impression he'd asked you to do this because you were Asian yourself?' asked Suttle. 'Because you'd have contacts? Family ties?'

'Of course.'

'And do you think that's why he chose you? From all the other girls?'

'Maybe.'

'Were there other Asian girls in the book?'

'No. I'm the only one.'

'So how did that make you feel?'

'It made no difference.' She shrugged. 'He paid the money. I think I made him happy.'

Suttle nodded. He didn't doubt that for a moment. Faraday took over again.

'The background you come from . . . here in Portsmouth . . . it's pretty tight, isn't it? People are pretty close? People know each other? Families worship together? Get together in the mosque?'

'Yes, of course.'

'So word would get around?'

'About what?'

'About what you do for a living.'

'Maybe.'

'Surely not maybe. Definitely.'

'Whatever.' She shrugged again.

There was a long silence. Then Suttle stirred.

'So what do your parents think about what you do for a living?'

'My parents are in Leicester.'

'So where do you live?'

'In a flat in Southsea. With some other girls.'

'Asian girls?'

'No, English.'

'So you've *no* family here? Is that what you're saying?'

She looked at Suttle for a long time. Then she shook her head.

'Of course I've got family here. Extended family. Distant cousins. Aunts. Uncles. That's how it is in our culture. We have family everywhere.'

Faraday bent forward in his chair. They were close to an admission this girl was clearly dreading.

'So they'd be upset . . . ' he suggested ' . . . if

97

they found out about you . . . about what you do. Am I right?'

She nodded. Her voice was low. 'Yes.'

'And if they saw this man, this white businessman, come calling? At the grocery store? At the restaurant? And if they realised that he was your client? And that you'd been nosing around, asking questions on his account? How would they feel then?'

'They wouldn't like it.'

'Wouldn't *like* it? Surely it's stronger than that. Surely they'd hate it. They'd hate what you do. And they'd hate all the other liberties this man was taking. Am I right?'

She nodded, said nothing. Faraday asked for the addresses of the two properties and with some reluctance she obliged. She also supplied her own address and mobile number. Finally, when it was plain that the interview was over, she stood up.

'The man at the agency was right,' she said in the same small voice. 'He told me I was mad to come here.'

Faraday studied her for a moment. Then he shrugged.

'We'd have found you anyway.' He said.

5

WEDNESDAY, 6 SEPTEMBER 2006. 20.27

Winter had settled on the Duke of Buckingham for his meet with Jimmy Suttle. It was a decent, well-run pub in Old Portsmouth, attracting an evening crowd of young professionals, the occasional teacher from the grammar school across the road and quietly spoken retired couples taking advantage of the midweek supper offers. No one from Bazza's entourage would dream of setting foot in there.

Winter bought a pint of Stella and made himself comfortable at a table at the back of the bar. He'd acquired a paper from the shop up the road and a major report on one of the inside pages tallied developments in the city's latest murder hunt. Winter was still admiring a grainy shot of Faraday hurrying into the nick at Kingston Crescent when he felt a tap on the shoulder.

'Top up?' Jimmy Suttle was looking at his half-empty glass.

'Why not.' Winter showed him the paper. 'This one of yours?' Suttle glanced at the article. 'Yeah.'

He fetched the drinks from the bar and settled into the spare chair. He looks older, Winter thought. More settled. More confident. More cautious.

'Go on then . . . ' Winter nodded at the newspaper.

Suttle ignored the invitation to share the secrets of *Billhook*. He reached for his drink and swallowed a mouthful. To Winter it looked like shandy. Bad sign.

'So how have you been?' Suttle wiped his mouth with the back of his hand. 'How's life on the Dark Side?'

'I'm not with you, son.'

'You're working with Mackenzie, the way I hear it. Am I right?'

'Yeah . . . ' Winter nodded, ' . . . In a manner of speaking, I suppose I am.'

'He pays you? You take his money?'

'Yeah.'

'So they're true then, these rumours?'

'Yeah. Except . . . ' Winter paused, frowned, looking for another word.

'Except what?'

'Except nothing. You're right. It's true. I run the odd errand. I make the odd suggestion. It's what you do in my situation, unless you want to sit at home all day and climb the walls.'

'What about a real job? What about working for some brief? Delivering writs? Making notes in court? Just like every other excopper?'

'I didn't fancy it, son. And the pay's crap.'

'He pays well, then? Mackenzie?'

'Well enough.' Winter had barely touched his glass since Suttle had arrived. 'You sound pissed off, son.'

'Not pissed off. Just disappointed.'

'*Disappointed?* How does that work?'

'Easy. It's about Mackenzie. The man's a scumbag. So are the people who run with him. Take the bastard out and this would be a decent city to live in.'

'That's bollocks, son,' Winter said mildly. 'Take Mackenzie out and we'd be back to the days when the place looked like Beirut. Where do you think the money for all these flash refurbs comes from? The café-bars? The seafront hotels? You think all that money comes from the government? From the Good Fairy? Mackenzie's a suit these days. He's a face, a player. He spends money. He invests. He turns half-arsed businesses around. He creates jobs for young kids. He makes life in this shithole just a little bit more pleasant.'

'So we're lucky to have him? Is that it? Only I remember the days when you couldn't wait to put him away.'

'That was then. This is now. And now, son, is too late.'

'How come?'

'Because the guy's made it. Because he's king of the castle. Because there isn't a solicitor or an accountant or a councillor or anyone else with a bit of clout in this city who'd say a bad word against him. Bazza's home safe, son. He's out of reach. We've lost him.'

'That's pathetic.'

'Who says?'

'Me. And you know why? Because the day we chuck the towel in over Bazza is the day we might as well chuck the towel in for good. The bloke's bent. He'll always be bent. And the way it is now we're sending a fucking great message to every toerag kid in this city. You know what that message is? Forget school. Forget exams. Bent pays.'

'I'm afraid it does.' Winter nodded. 'It's a fact of life, son.'

'*Fact of life?* What happened to you, Paul? What happened in that head of yours? Maybe it was that surgeon over in Phoenix. Maybe he took out more than he should have done. Maybe it's not your fault, not your doing. Maybe I should tell all the blokes at work that you're not the lying devious scumbag who sold out to Bazza Mackenzie. You know what they're saying now? They're saying it's no surprise, what you're up to. They're saying you've been at it for years.'

'With Mackenzie?'

'Of course.'

'And you? What do you think?'

'I'm going with the surgeon theory. I think he made a mistake. I think you're clinically deranged.' He suddenly bent forward and touched glasses. 'Cheers, you bent old bastard.'

Winter, with some relief, swallowed a couple of mouthfuls of Stella. He wanted to know about the Port Solent job, about life on Major Crimes, about Faraday. Suttle looked at him, amused now, no longer angry.

'You sound like you miss it.'

'I do. Of course I do. Not all of it. Not all the PC bollocks about risk assessments and approach strategies. But this . . . ' He tapped the newspaper. 'Yeah, of course I miss it.'

Suttle told him a little about Mallinder's

death. Professional job. Middle of the night. Single shot to the head. Couple of promising lines of enquiry.

'Like what?'

'Can't say, mate.' He shook his head, changing the subject. 'You remember Terry Byrne? Scouse headcase?'

'Pennington Road? Couple of pit bulls? Wraps of smack at a fiver each?'

'That's him. Except it's not smack any more, or not just smack. The bloke's into the laughing powder, big time. We had a D/I down from Devon and Cornwall, a real looker. They'd got intel on Byrne, fuck knows where from, but they'd put him alongside a couple of kilos headed for the West Country. She's after nicking the courier on the way home, got the whole thing plotted up, but that's not really the point, is it? What's your new boss doing? Letting psychos like Byrne get away with that kind of weight?'

'Two kilos?' Winter began to laugh. Then he reached across and gave Suttle a pat on the arm. 'This is kosher?'

'So she said.'

'And is that why you've come? You want to send Bazza a message?'

'Not at all. I'm just curious. I thought you might be in a position to know.'

'I know nothing. If you want the truth, he's put me in charge of some wank idea involving jet skis. You know what the bloke's like. He chucks you a bone, tells you to get on with it. Except this bone's fucking enormous.'

'*Jet skis?*'

103

'Yeah.'

He told Suttle about Mark's accident, the trip out to Cambados for the funeral and Bazza's absolute determination to come up with some kind of memorial. At first he'd assumed the Mackenzie Trophy was a joke. Now he knew different.

Suttle was fascinated. He wanted to know more about the trip to Spain.

'So you're socialising with all these guys, Bazza's lot — drinking with them, eating with them, partying with them . . . how does that work?'

'It doesn't. They know who I am. They still take the piss. And I do, back. Bazza would like us all to be mates, I can see him trying to work on that, but it'll never happen. You're right, son. Do what I've done all those years and you're lumbered.'

'Once a copper always a copper?'

'Yeah, I suppose.'

'Must be hard then? Lonely even? Socially?'

'Sure. You're right. But then it was before. In the job.'

Winter's head went down a moment, then he looked up again. Suttle was watching him carefully.

'You know what happened at the end? When they nicked me for DUI? You know what *really* happened?'

'Yeah. You were three times over the limit.'

'Exactly. But they knew exactly where I was drinking, what time I'd be there, the lot, and they'd got the whole place plotted up. Maybe

104

someone fitted me up. Maybe someone made a phone call. Either way it doesn't matter. The minute I'd turned the key in the motor, the moment I'd started to pull out from that little cut across the road from the pub, they had me. And you know something else? They were fucking loving it, every minute of it, back of the traffic car, down to the Bridewell, book me in, arrange a sample, the whole nine yards.'

'It had been a long time coming. You'd been winding them up for years.'

'Sure. And maybe that made it all the sweeter. But it doesn't change anything, does it? Twenty-plus years in the job. More scalps than any other fucker. And they end up pulling a stroke like that.' He shook his head, reaching for his glass again, then caught Suttle's eye. 'Don't give me that look, son. I'm on foot tonight. Not that I have much choice any more.'

★   ★   ★

Faraday was back in his Mondeo, en route home, when his mobile began to trill. He glanced in the mirror then reached for the cradle.

'Yes?'

It was Barrie. He'd finished the last of his meetings at HQ and wanted an update. Faraday slowed for the next queue of traffic, wondering where to start. The *Billhook* squad meet, to be frank, had been a disappointment. There comes a moment in most inquiries when the optimism and zip of the first forty-eight hours begins to

105

evaporate, leaving the slow, measured plod towards some kind of result. Not that the team had returned entirely empty-handed.

'CCTV have come up with a hit on the Port Solent car park camera, boss. The black Escort was there from around ten onwards. Two blokes picked it up at half twelve.'

'Where did they go?'

'They didn't.'

'I'm not with you.'

'They just sat there. Until four minutes past three. Then they drove off.'

'Description?' Barrie was sounding almost cheerful.

'One guy was much bigger than the other. The smaller bloke is the one wearing the grey hoodie. The guys tried the zoom and everything, but the grain on screen gets horrible.'

'What about the place in the New Forest? The car park?'

'I'm afraid we drew a blank. You were right, boss. Everything was trampled.'

'Shame.' Barrie was obviously thinking hard. 'We need bodies back into the marina, any place that was open Monday night, pubs, restaurants, fitness clubs, the lot. These two blokes must have been in there somewhere. The hoodie might ring a bell or two.'

'Done, boss. It's actioned for tonight.'

'Excellent. This car park in the New Forest. Wasn't that where the Escort was nicked in the first place?'

'The New Forest, yes. But a different car park.'

'No witnesses in the first car park? Where the car got nicked?'

'Not so far. I've arranged for posters at the site but I wouldn't hold your breath.'

'Where was the owner?'

'Out running. He ended up taking a cab home.'

Faraday eased forward. The traffic lights a couple of hundred metres ahead had just gone red again. Barrie wanted to know about the development company handling the Tipner site.

'Outside Enquiries put a couple of blokes in this afternoon. They did an interview with the guys who run it.'

'And what did they say?'

'Bit of a mystery, sir. Mallinder's interest turns out to be a lot more casual than we thought. They've had a couple of conversations with him, sure, and I gather Mallinder was up to speed on the latest financial projections. Apparently the scheme's very tight. Don't hold me to these figures but I gather they're looking at around three hundred million pounds overall costs which leaves a nominal profit of around forty million.'

'That's *tight*? Forty million quid?'

'So they say. Forty million is around twelve per cent. Most developers won't get out of bed unless they're looking at fifteen per cent plus. The real money's in residential. At the moment the council are holding out for thirty per cent affordable housing. If they can get that down to fifteen per cent, it starts looking more attractive.'

'What about the Tipner ranges?'

'They say the MoD won't budge. And they swear blind they'll be the first to know if they ever do. This lot are the council's preferred developers. They've got the thing pretty much stitched up.'

'So what's Mallinder been up to?'

'Pass, sir. The more we know about Tipner, the less it fits his MO. Mallinder, Benskin have never done anything this complicated. It's full of aggravation and to make things worse there are rumours of a new football stadium on the site. No wonder Benskin didn't fancy it.'

'You're going to talk to him again?'

'In the end, yes. And there's another line of enquiry he might be able to help us with.'

'What's that?'

Faraday described the interview with Aliyah Begum. In his view, they were looking at a possible motive.

'Revenge, you mean?' Barrie got there first. 'Teaching our friend a lesson?'

'Something like that.'

There was silence on the line. Barrie was thinking. Then he came back.

'A single bullet? No clues? No forensic? Don't get me wrong, Joe, but our Asian friends wouldn't bother with a hit man, would they? Supposing you're on the right lines? Odds on they'd use a knife, blood up the walls, real horror show. It's a nice idea of yours but I can't see it somehow.'

'I've still asked Outside Enquiries to action it, sir.' Faraday said. 'They're doing a couple of visits tomorrow. The grocery store and the

108

restaurant. Can't do any harm.'

'Of course not. Anything else?'

' 'Afraid not.'

'How about that vagrant son of yours?'

'Ah . . . ' Faraday smiled ' . . . now you're talking.'

★ ★ ★

The Bargemaster's House lay beside Langstone Harbour, on the city's eastern shore. Thanks to a large cheque from Janna's American parents weeks after her death, the sturdy Victorian red-brick dwelling had become home for Faraday and his infant son. And over the intervening years, as the implications of J-J's deafness became more and more obvious, Faraday's love for the place had deepened to the point where he couldn't imagine life without it.

He had a love-hate relationship with gardening and never quite managed to keep up with repairs to the timber cladding on the upper storey, but the view in the early morning from his first-floor study — the rich yellow spill of dawn sunlight over the water, the incessant comings and goings of Langstone birdlife — never failed to put a smile on his face. In an often troubled world, he knew he owed the Bargemaster's House a great deal. It served, above all, as a kind of sanctuary.

Gabrielle's camper was parked in the road outside. J-J hadn't bothered to unload the mountain of bags in the back. *Plus ça change.*

Faraday eased the Mondeo onto the hard-standing at the rear of the house, realising with something of a shock that he hadn't seen his son for nearly two years. After a grounding in video production in Portsmouth and London, J-J had somehow organised himself an attachment to an editing outfit in Moscow. Faraday had never quite grasped exactly what he was doing out there but his occasional emails were bursting with even more enthusiasm than usual and the gaunt young face in the handful of photos he'd sent had even put on a little weight.

Faraday pushed in through the front door. Already he could hear laughter from upstairs. Gabrielle, he thought. He made his way up to the top landing. His study door was half open. J-J and Gabrielle were sitting in front of Faraday's PC, sorting through a sequence of photos. Most of the faces looked Russian — badly shaved old men huddled in threadbare anoraks, sleek middle-aged women laden with shopping bags — and the photos must have been taken in winter because the streets and rooftops behind were crusted with snow.

A shot of a child reaching for an icicle made Gabrielle laugh again. Faraday recognised the onion domes of the Kremlin in the background. He tiptoed across the study, then paused behind his son. He could smell the tang of cheap tobacco in his hair. Faraday let his hand fall briefly on J-J's shoulder. J-J glanced up, taken by surprise. For a split second, still absorbed by the photos, he hadn't a clue what was going on. Then he was on his feet, pushing back his chair, giving Faraday a hug. In moments of high excitement J-J always balled his fists either side of his head, a gesture of triumph, as if he'd just scored a goal. He was doing it now, stepping back, beaming at his father.

Faraday held him at arm's length, just looking. The boy had grown a beard. It changed his face, his manner, completely. The vulnerabilty he'd always worn, that ever-willing sense of openness that had sometimes made Faraday fear for this son of his, had gone. He looked older, stronger, somehow *bigger*, and Faraday found himself wondering quite what had worked this transformation.

'Long time,' he signed. 'I've missed you.'

★ ★ ★

Gabrielle cooked a ratatouille of vegetables from the garden. After Faraday had finished helping J-J in with his bags, the sitting room next door looked like a kasbah, and they demolished the ratatouille around the wooden table in the kitchen. Amongst the heap of presents J-J had brought back was a huge flask of Georgian wine. It was empty by the time J-J was demanding second helpings from the saucepan on the stove and Faraday fetched a bottle of decent Merlot from the rack that served as his cellar.

It was obvious at once that J-J and Gabrielle had become friends. A single day together seemed to have bred an easy intimacy and J-J included her in his bubbling torrent of conversation without a thought for her signing skills. Catching the expression on her face from time to time as J-J described the highlights of his

111

life in Moscow, Faraday marvelled at the speed with which she seemed to have penetrated the blur of hands and fingers. This wasn't something she'd confected to help the evening along. She actually seemed to understand the boy.

J-J, it transpired, had finally parted company with the video production company who'd flown him out to Russia in the first place. They were making a series about the oil boom and J-J's job had been largely technical, setting up an editing suite, then logging hours and hours of video rushes as the location work got under way. The job had been really boring, he explained, and in his spare time, with his mother's treasured Leica, he'd haunted the big spaces of the city, putting together a photo essay on the world he found around him.

A handful of these shots had attracted the attention of a woman from one of the state TV channels who occasionally dropped into the editing suite, and she'd passed them on to a girlfriend who was looking for material for a leading magazine. Within weeks, much to his delight, J-J had found himself with a full-time commission. The people at the magazine, he said, had approved of his take on Moscow street life. They liked his filmy eyes and bony Slav faces. They loved what he'd made of an alley, three dustbins, a priest and an urban fox. Pretty soon he'd signed a deal with an entrepreneur specialising in posters and arty postcards. Then had come the invitation to appear on a TV show devoted to the outer reaches of Russian cultural life.

The fact that J-J was a deaf mute had, it seemed, been an enormous advantage. Not because he'd been an object of curiosity but because the sight of him explaining in sign his passion for the single image had touched something in the Russian soul. For them, real life had always been theatre. These people, he signed expansively, gave you *room*. They were generous. They loved the way he used his hands to shape meaning and nuance. They seemed to understand instinctively what he had to offer. And as a result, as sales of his cards and posters soared, he'd ended up with quite a lot of money.

'How much?' Faraday couldn't resist the question.

'Seventy thousand.'

'Roubles?'

'US dollars.' J-J grinned at him, nodding. 'With more to come.'

The money, he said, was still in a bank account in Moscow but under the new regime there'd be no problem transferring it to the UK. He wanted to put down a deposit on a place of his own, maybe in Portsmouth, maybe somewhere else along the coast. He wanted a base to call home, a launching pad for more expeditions to more countries. He wanted to use his Russian contacts and his Russian earnings to build a career in photo art.

Listening to J-J's description of the world waiting for his viewfinder, Faraday could think only of Janna, his long-dead wife. She, too, had been a photographer, carving out the beginnings of a reputation for herself in Seattle galleries.

113

She, too, had the eye, the talent, the inner conviction that would stop a passing browser in mid-step and bring them back to a certain shot, to the play of light on the bones of an old shipwreck, to the boil of summer thunderheads caught in stark black and white over the northern Rockies. She'd never had her son's taste for the surreal, for composing bizarre metaphors from the most unlikely ingredients, but the vision was there, and the appetite to share it with anyone who'd spare her the time.

He'd barely mentioned Janna to Gabrielle, but now, at J-J's suggestion, she demanded to see some of her work. Faraday had lived with these photos for the best part of two decades, hanging personal favourites around the house, but J-J's departure for Russia had prompted a rethink in his life, and he'd carefully wrapped and boxed the shots before storing them up in the attic.

J-J helped him to retrieve them. They carried armfuls back downstairs, spread them amongst the Kazakh rugs and painted wooden icons that still littered the floor. Then J-J took Gabrielle by the elbow, nudging her on from shot to shot, signing his admiration for his mother's composition, or the way she'd taken a risk with the exposure in a particular shot, or her happy knack of teasing a mood from the play of shadows on various surfaces, and watching him Faraday became aware of a sense of mystery as well as pride in the way that this expressive gift had so seamlessly passed from mother to son.

Later, once J-J had finished the last of the wine and abandoned the living room for a bed upstairs, Gabrielle lay full length on the sofa, her head on Faraday's lap. Any sense that he might have burdened her with this boy of his had long gone, and when he tried to put this thought into words she reached up and sealed his lips with a single moistened fingertip.

'Not a boy at all,' she murmured. 'A man.'

6

The news about the Mercedes came first to Jimmy Suttle. He'd taken a call from Sally Mallinder. She was back in London at the family home, waiting for the Mercedes garage to return her husband's car. As a favour to a valued client, in these difficult circumstances they'd volunteered to send a couple of members of staff down with a replacement set of keys. The guys had set off early. By half eight they were parked outside the Port Solent house. Only one problem. The car had gone.

'Gone?' Faraday was trying to make sense of a sheaf of overtime figures.

'Disappeared, boss. Borrowed. Vaporised. Maybe even nicked. The blokes are still up there. They're not quite sure what to do.'

'We've got the vehicle's details?'

'Of course.'

'Then circulate them.' He looked up at last. The implications of this latest bit of news were beginning to sink in. Scenes of Crime had released the Port Solent house late yesterday afternoon. The overnight uniformed watch had been withdrawn. 'The Mercedes' keys were missing?'

'That's right, boss.'

'So you're telling me this guy's come back? For the *car*?'

* * *

The city's CCTV control room lay in the basement of the Civic Centre. Over the last couple of days search shifts had been divided between two sets of D/Cs. D/C Dawn Ellis had been part of the team that had scored a hit on the black Ford Escort. Now Faraday told her to meet him in the control room.

Ellis had driven up from Southsea. She was a slim, attractive vegetarian with a fall of jet-black hair who lived alone in a Portchester semi. Faraday had always had a soft spot for her, not least because she was one of the few detectives who could cope with Paul Winter, but lately he'd become aware that two years on Major Crimes had blunted her appetite for the job. Too many interviews with hysterical fourteen-year-olds who couldn't make up their minds whether they'd been raped or not. Too many late-night calls to Southsea nightclubs, inter-viewing a line-up of pissed Somerstown boys about a slapping that had got seriously out of hand. She'd confided to a close friend that she'd had enough of slag adolescents and homicidal kids, and when rumours began to circulate that she was considering a new career in alternative therapy, Faraday was inclined to believe them.

Now, in the control room, she knew exactly which camera tapes to list for review.

117

'This one on the approach road to Port Solent, the same camera we scored a hit with on Monday. What time do you fancy starting?'

Faraday said midnight. It seemed a fair enough guess. Any earlier, and the neighbours might still have been up.

Dawn began to spool through last night's footage. Between midnight and half past one they counted maybe three dozen cars leaving the marina complex. After that, for a longish period, nothing happened. Then, in the distance, the flare of a pair of headlights. Dawn toggled the fast forward control, slowing the oncoming blur. Finally it resolved itself into the low, elegant shape of a Mercedes sports coupé. It was white. Right colour.

'Can you read the plate?'

Dawn shook her head, inching forward a frame at a time. The camera was old, the resolution poor.

'We had this same problem with the Escort,' she said. 'Crap lens. You think they'd do something about that, wouldn't you?'

She used another control to zoom in on the figure behind the wheel, but the bigger the image the grainier the detail.

'Has to be,' Faraday said softly. 'Has to be.'

Dawn returned the image to full frame, inched forward again. Sitting beside her at the tiny review console, Faraday was aware of how physically tense she'd become. This hunt for a tiny particle of evidence, a shape behind the wheel, even a face, had begun to matter.

'There,' she said at last. 'He's the small one

from the Escort, I'd swear it. Might even be a kid.'

Faraday peered at the screen. All he could make out was the grey outline of the driver, the pale disc of his face shadowed by a hoodie.

'You think so?' Faraday was trying to remember the detail on the photo she'd printed off in this same room last night. Dawn spared him the effort; she had a copy in her briefcase.

'Look.' She laid it on the desk in front of Faraday. 'See for your-self.'

Faraday compared the two images. There was nothing to disprove the similarity but equally he could see no clinching evidence that would survive the attentions of defence counsel in court.

'People wear hoodies all the time,' he pointed out.

'Yeah, boss.' Dawn began to spool forward again. 'Especially kids.'

'But we're not looking for a kid. We're looking for a contract killer, someone who knew exactly what they were doing.' He nodded at the screen. 'And if this guy was so careful at the house, what's he doing coming back for the car?'

'You tell me, boss.' The Mercedes was slipping out of frame. 'I'm just here to sort the pictures.'

She chose another tape, gambling that the Mercedes had headed west on the motorway. Sure enough, eight minutes later a camera on a gantry beneath the Paulsgrove estate recorded the same car. This time the resolution was better, good enough to read the number plate. Faraday consulted the Mercedes' registration details in his file. Bingo.

Dawn had frozen the sequence again. This stretch of motorway was lit throughout the hours of darkness and it was possible to make out the driver's hands on the wheel.

'He's wearing gloves,' she said. 'And he's pulled down the visor again so we won't get a clear shot of his face. What does that tell you?'

'He's aware. Obviously.'

'Exactly.'

Dawn explained that Pompey coverage on the motorway ended at Junction 9. After that, cameras fed pictures to the control room in Southampton. She made a note of the time readout on the tape and glanced at her watch. She could be in Southampton within forty minutes or so. Did Faraday want to come?

Faraday shook his head. He had a thousand things to do.

'Give me a ring.' He got to his feet. 'I'll be back in the office.'

★   ★   ★

Winter got up late. Part of him that resented Mackenzie's call on his time was determined to make this small private point. My life is still my own.

He wandered through to the bathroom and splashed his face with cold water, all too aware that Mackenzie wouldn't have the slightest interest in the hours he kept. The only currency that mattered in Bazza's busy life was results.

He struggled into the silk dressing gown he'd inherited from Maddox and fired up the kettle in

120

the kitchen. For a brief moment he toyed with making proper coffee but then he caught sight of the percolator, still full of yesterday's grounds, and he settled for instant instead. Next door were the notes he'd brought back from Gosport. Andrew McCall had been more than helpful.

He began to leaf through them, trying to imagine the conversations he'd be obliged to have over the next couple of days. Key to the Mackenzie Trophy, in McCall's view, was the support of the council. This chimed exactly with what Bazza had been saying but McCall had a couple of names to add to Mackenzie's must-do list. One of them was a key player in the directorate responsible for tourism, leisure and sports. He'd dealt with her a number of times and promised she'd jump at a proposal like this.

'Just tell her it's world class,' he'd said, 'and she'll sign up for anything.'

Winter looked at the phone, wondering whether he was really ready for this next step of the journey. Last night's session with Suttle had been cut short by a call from Jimmy's current shag but an hour or so back in the company of a working copper had upset Winter more than he'd thought. The boy was right. Burying the job, leaving it behind you, was bloody hard.

He rang the council number on his notes and finally got through to a secretary. Ms Hammond, she said, was in conference. She'd be available to talk on the phone in about an hour. After that she was off to London.

Winter gave the secretary his name and

number. When the woman asked which organisation she represented, he stared blankly at the wall.

'Beaver UK,' he said at last.

'And you specialise in what, Mr Winter?'

Winter tried hard to come up with something plausible. Then he caught sight of himself in the mirror at the end of the lounge. Maddox's scarlet gown brought back all kinds of memories.

'Adult entertainment,' he said, feeling instantly better.

★   ★   ★

The phone began to trill less than twenty minutes later. Winter was soaping himself in the bath. He reached out for the portable, demanded to know who it was.

'Celia Hammond. You called.'

'Ah . . . ' He struggled upright in the bath, wiped the suds from his eyes. 'Andrew McCall gave me your name. I've got a proposal I think might interest you. I thought I might pop over for a chat.'

'What is it? This proposal?'

Winter gazed at the phone for a moment. He wasn't used to being bossed like this. He liked things nice and casual. That way he could make the running.

'It's about jet skis . . . '

He shut his eyes, lay back in the bath, tried to imagine this woman's office, the view from her window, the size of her desk, the crescent of sofa she'd keep for special guests. The key to the next ten minutes, he'd decided, was bullshit. He told her that clients of his had approached him with a view to organising the first in a series of annual jet ski Grand Prix. They had access to major sponsorship funding. Comprehensive television coverage was virtually guaranteed though negotiations were at a critical stage and he couldn't reveal details. An international list of top riders had already expressed interest. Various commercial spin-offs were in development. And the best news of all was the preferred location.

'Which is?'

'Here. In Portsmouth. My clients have looked at venues all over the UK. They've even been out to Spain and Portugal. But nothing — *nothing* — in their view can compare to Spithead. They're mad for it. And so, if you take my advice, should you be.'

'So when you anticipate this happening?'

'Next summer.'

'You mentioned sponsorship. Are we talking prize money? Or is this event *entirely* self-funding?'

'It pays for itself. It won't cost you a bean.'

'And your clients can deliver? You're confident about that?'

'Absolutely. I trust them with my life.'

There was a brief silence. Winter gave his plastic duck a poke with his big toe. Then Ms Hammond came back on the phone, no less businesslike.

'And what's your role in this, Mr Winter?'

'Me?' Winter was enjoying himself now. 'I'm a facilitator. I put people together. Get the chemistry right and the most amazing things can happen. I've lived in this city all my life and, believe me, I recognise potential when I see it. We're talking world class here. Anything less, my love, and I wouldn't be wasting your time.'

★ ★ ★

Faraday was in conference with Detective Superintendent Barrie when Suttle knocked on the door. He apologised for the interruption but he had Dawn Ellis on the phone.

'And?' It was Barrie.

'She's got a couple more hits on the Mercedes, sir. It came off the motorway at . . . ' he glanced down at his pocketbook ' . . . Junction 7. A camera at West End tracked it at 04.23. After that it disappeared. She thinks we're probably looking at somewhere in Thornhill or Bitterne. She seems to know the area pretty well.'

So did Barrie. He'd been a D/I there on division. He offered a nod of thanks to Suttle and waited for him to shut the door. Then he asked Faraday for his assessment.

'I think it's extremely significant, boss. Force Intelligence have circulated details but Southampton should be blitzing this.'

'I agree. There's a dodgy estate in Thornhill. Kids round there get into all kinds of mischief. I'll give the Duty Inspector at Bitterne a ring for starters.'

Faraday was wrestling with the word 'kids'. Try as he might, he still had difficulty tying a hit as efficient as the Port Solent job to some toerag tearaway from the wrong side of the tracks. No kid he'd ever met was this organised, this careful. They always made mistakes, left a calling card or two. And part of their MO was they never seemed to care.

Barrie wanted to know about last night's enquiries around the marina. Outside Enquiries had put a team of D/Cs into every café, bar and pub that would have been open on Monday evening. The fact that CCTV had caught two men returning to the Escort at 00.28 should have been an enormous help.

'That time of night, the stragglers tend to stand out. They'd be noticed. Am I right?'

Faraday shook his head. In all, the Outside Enquiry team had visited nine premises, mainly bars and restaurants, and on every occasion they'd drawn a blank. Only in the multiplex had there been any prospect of a sighting.

'They were having a late-night showing at Screen One,' he explained. 'The movie had drawn a pretty thin crowd and one of the attendants thought he'd seen a couple of blokes who might fit.'

'Descriptions?'

'He said one was much older, middle-aged. Fit-looking guy. Wore jeans and some kind of jacket.'

'And the other?'

'A kid. That's what drew his attention. They looked odd together.'

'What did he mean by kid?'

'Fourteen, max. Skinny. On the small side.

Wore a hoodie. Bit of a shrimp.'

'And the colour of the hoodie?'

'Grey.'

'So where does that take us? Assuming it's the same couple?'

'I've no idea, sir, but we're not exactly spoiled for leads, are we?'

★   ★   ★

Too right. Back in his office Faraday stared glumly at the notes he'd made earlier, debriefing the D/Cs who'd paid a visit to the Halal Grocery and the Taj Mahal restaurant. On both occasions they'd had some difficulty locating the owners of the respective businesses. When they'd finally nailed down a name and a phone number for the Bengali entrepreneur behind the Taj Mahal operation, he'd been less than helpful. Yes, he'd had some dealings with a Mr Mallinder. Yes, he'd even consented to give the man half an hour of his time. But when he'd been patient enough to listen to what the man had to say, he'd had no hesitation in showing him the door.

Pressed by the detectives for details, he'd refused to discuss figures. This man, he said, had wanted to steal his business from under him. Of course he owned the freehold of the premises. He had legal documents to prove it. But nothing in the world would persuade him to sell up for the figure mentioned in their extremely brief discussion.

One of the D/Cs had enquired why Mallinder would have been interested in the restaurant.

Was he moving into the curry business? At this the Bengali had roared with laughter. Of course not, he'd said. These people come down from London. They buy my place. The place next door. And the place next door to that. Come back in a year and you're looking at a block of flats. Who gets the profit? Who makes the money? Not me, my friend.

Before they left, the D/Cs had asked about Aliyah Begum. The Bengali, according to the detective debriefed by Faraday, had looked genuinely perplexed. He knew plenty of Aliyahs, and hundreds of Begums, but he knew no girls answering to the description they'd given him. If such a girl existed, she should answer to her family and to the Prophet. In a society as faithless and debased as this one, she was just another speck of dirt. She was worth nothing.

Faraday was still wondering quite how far to pursue this line of enquiry when his phone began to ring. It took him several seconds to place the name. Gina Hamilton? A fellow D/I?

'Devon and Cornwall.' She was laughing. 'You've forgotten, haven't you?'

Faraday bent to the phone, trying to hide his embarrassment. The woman who turned up earlier in the week, he told himself. The out-of-town surveillance team who were sitting on Terry Byrne.

'How did it go?' he asked.

'Brilliant. Total result. I'm just phoning to say thanks.'

Her team had tracked the courier back along the coast, crossing the Devon border just west of

127

Lyme Regis. They'd followed the target as far as Honiton and HQ had taken the decision to call the strike minutes later. Three traffic cars had penned him in a lay-by, and he'd been singing like a birdie ever since.

'Names?'

'Plenty.'

'Arrests?'

'Half a dozen.' She laughed again. 'And counting.'

She thanked him for the second time and brought the conversation to a close. Moments later, Faraday was looking ruefully at the phone. Half a dozen bodies in the holding cells? Two kilos of cocaine in the lock-up? No wonder she'd made D/I so young.

★ ★ ★

It was early afternoon when Bazza Mackenzie arrived at Blake House. He'd phoned a couple of hours earlier, telling Winter to expect him, but he hadn't mentioned company.

Now, Winter stood in the hall, eyeing the videophone. Esme was wearing a T-shirt she must have picked up in the Caribbean. *Treasure the Virgins* read the logo across her ample chest. Behind her, dwarfing his boss, stood Brett West.

Winter triggered the door release downstairs. Westie was the most inventive of Bazza's heavies. He'd put on a bit of weight since his days as a young pro on Aston Villa's books, and he had a huge appetite for the laughing powder, but his poise and dress sense had never left him and he still turned heads in the pricier Gunwharf café-bars. For a black guy, he was readier than most to take a joke but blokes who knew him well never underestimated the pleasure he took in dishing out serious violence. Mackenzie kept him on a retainer for use in extreme situations and Winter was inclined to believe the stories he'd heard about Westie's collection of trophy snaps. Before the ambulance was called, he evidently liked to take a photo or two.

The four of them gathered in the big living room. Mackenzie helped himself to a seat on the sofa and patted the cushion beside him. Esme ignored the invitation, making herself comfortable at the table by the window. She was wearing a shortish skirt with high leather boots. She had a tan suede briefcase with a Virgin Atlantic tag on the handle. It looked brand new.

'Ezzie's going to be driving this little project,' Bazza announced. 'I've put her in charge because we're going to get ourselves involved in all kinds of legal bollocks. You OK with that, Paul?'

Winter signalled his agreement with a nod. He didn't care where the buck stopped, as long as it wasn't with him.

'*No problema*,' he said. 'Very wise.'

Esme was looking more sour by the minute. In Cambados Winter had sensed that she didn't much like him.

'We'll need to sort out a new company, a stand-alone job. Ezzie's got it in hand.'

'Not Beaver UK, then?'

'No.'

'Thank Christ for that.' Winter thought briefly about describing this morning's exchange with the city council but decided against it. Esme, for one, wouldn't see the joke.

'Go on then.' Bazza was looking at his daughter. 'Show him.'

Esme unzipped her briefcase and slipped out a folder. Winter wandered across and picked it up. It was shiny and white, good quality card, and embossed on the front were the words *The Mackenzie Trophy*. Inside, nicely framed on the left-hand page, was a small head and shoulders photo of a middle-aged man, heavily tanned, with a loop of red beads round his neck. He was grinning at the camera. Behind him, beyond a line of moored boats, the blueness of the sea.

'What do you think?'

Winter was still looking at the photo. Beneath it, the simple legend *Mark Mackenzie, 1961–2006*. For Bazza, he thought, the design showed signs of serious restraint.

'It's class,' he said. 'But what's it for?'

'You put stuff in it. Press releases, invites, cuttings, schedules, whatever. It's *branding*, Paul. We do it with the hotel. With bits of the property business. It sets a tone. Tells people to watch their manners. That's just a mock-up. I thought I'd run it past you first.'

Winter nodded. Was this the moment to be picky? To argue for silver embossing rather than gold? Esme saved him the trouble.

'It's fine,' she said briskly. 'I've told the printer to go ahead.'

She took out a leather-bound notebook,

silencing her father's protests with a look, and then began to go through the next steps that she and Winter would need to take. This was a carbon copy of Bazza's master plan but she dressed it up in management-speak. There was talk of time-sensitive delivery dates and the probable need for an environmental impact audit but Winter wasn't fooled for a moment. She was staking out her territory, establishing her role. Winter was the lamp post. She was the dog.

The list complete, she looked up.

'We need to get on with this,' she said. 'Nine months might sound a long time but believe me we're pushing the envelope already. The council are obviously key, Paul. You and I need to formulate an approach strategy. Like now.'

'Done.'

'What?'

'I sorted it this morning. A woman by the name of Hammond. She runs pretty much everything. Loves the idea to death.'

There was a long silence, broken finally by Brett West. He was standing at the window, gazing out. His low chuckle filled the room.

'Fuck me,' he said softly, 'Not just an arsehole copper then?'

★ ★ ★

Faraday had heard of Gibbon, Prentiss, Verne. Estate agents, he thought. Down in Old Portsmouth. The call had just been routed through to him by one of the squad's management assistants.

131

'Who am I speaking to?'

'My name's Fraser, Fraser Gibbon.'

'And what can I do for you, Mr Gibbon?'

'It's in connection with this business in Port Solent. The murder. I've been meaning to call you all week.'

'Why?'

'Because I think we ought to talk.'

'About what?'

'About Mr Mallinder.'

'You knew him?'

'Yes.'

Faraday glanced at his watch. In a couple of hours he was due at the regular *Billhook* squad meeting. In the meantime everything else could wait.

'I'm at Kingston Crescent police station. Do you want to come in?'

'I'd prefer not. We're down in Broad Street. Do you know the Camber Dock?'

★ ★ ★

The Camber lay at the heart of Old Portsmouth. The city had grown up around this ancient harbour, and it still served as home for a clutter of fishing boats, pilot launches and assorted leisure craft. Faraday loved the area. A thousand years of history had worked into the bones of the place and even now the developers hadn't quite ruined its scruffy charm.

Gibbon, Prentiss, Verne had premises on the seaward side of the dock. Faraday paused outside for a moment, his attention caught by the properties in the window. A great deal of money had settled in this corner of the city and he briefly wondered what J-J's Russian windfall would really buy him. A one-bedroom waterside apartment was up for sale at £210,000. How many postcards would his son have to sell to find that kind of sum?

Fraser Gibbon occupied an office at the back of the agency. He was a tall, sallow-faced man with thinning hair and a clammy hand-shake. He apologised at once for dragging Faraday away from his desk.

'Not at all.' Faraday took the offered seat. 'I assume it's important.'

'It may be. I suspect that's for you to judge. It's just that I thought it best . . . you know . . . to volunteer myself before you came knocking at my door.'

'Why would we want to do that?'

'Because you'll be going into Mallinder's affairs. Or at least that's my assumption. Am I right?'

Faraday said nothing. Gibbon looked uncertain for a moment. Then he tried to warm the atmosphere with a smile. The silence stretched and stretched.

'You told me you knew Mr Mallinder,' Faraday said at length. 'Exactly how did that come about?'

'He called in here one morning, back in the spring, April, I think. He said he was looking for a property.'

'What kind of property?'

'A house. It had to have at least five bedrooms

and one of them had to be en suite. He wanted off-road parking and if possible a sea view. He was very specific.'

'Did you know what he did for a living?'

'No.'

'Did you get the impression that this was some kind of business investment?'

'On the contrary, he wanted to live in it. It was to be his family home. He said he had children. And he said his wife was pregnant.'

'He wanted to move down here? You're sure about that?'

'Absolutely certain. Finding a property that size isn't easy round here. They exist, of course, but they very rarely come up for sale. As it happens, Mr Mallinder was in luck.'

He explained that a very pretty Georgian house round the corner from the cathedral had suddenly come on to the market. The sea view was limited to a glimpse of the harbour from a dormer window in the roof and it lacked parking, but the accommodation was perfect and the owner was including an option on a lock-up garage round the corner.

'Mr Mallinder went to see the property the following weekend. He spent no more than half an hour looking round but I could tell he fell in love with it. He put an offer in the following week, which I thought was strange.'

'Why?'

'Because his wife hadn't had sight of the place. He seemed to be making all the decisions himself. When I made a little joke of it, he just said he knew his wife's taste inside out. That may be true, of course, but moving house is a big decision. Especially at that kind of price.'

'How much was it on for?'

'£545,000.'

'And his offer? Do you mind telling me?'

'Not at all. He opened at £400,000. That was a marker, of course, to test the water. He would have gone much higher.'

'So what happened?'

'Nothing. Absolutely nothing. The owner turned down his offer, which I must say was no surprise, and Mallinder simply withdrew.'

'Do you know why?'

'Not then I didn't, no.'

'But now?'

'Now . . . ' He nodded. 'Yes, I do.'

Mallinder, he said, had reappeared in Old Portsmouth in late June. This time he had something much smaller in mind. Character was important, and a sea view would have been nice, but the key driver was price. He had £270,000 to spend, not a penny more. For that kind of money, said Gibbon, he was struggling already.

'He still wanted all those bedrooms?'

'Not at all. Three would have been ample. I asked him whether he'd thought about an apartment but he wasn't keen.'

Mallinder returned the following week, late in the day. After discussing a handful of properties, he suggested a drink in one of the pubs round the corner. Over a glass or two of wine the two men became friends.

'I'd no idea, of course, that he was in the property game himself but he was pretty hard-nosed when it came to negotiation and I remember not being surprised when he told me what he did for a living.'

'What did he say, as a matter of interest?'

'He said that he was in partnership with another developer, a man called Benskin. Basically they assembled land and then sold on with planning permission. It doesn't sound like rocket science but to make decent money you have to be extremely choosy where you buy in the first place. Either that or bloody lucky. Mallinder, Benskin were a bit of a legend, real players in the land-assembly game. It was slow of me not to make the connection earlier.'

'So you did know him?'

'*Of* him, certainly.'

After the pub they'd shared a meal in a fish restaurant up beyond the cathedral.

'To be frank, I liked him. I'm not married myself and he was incredibly charming, in fact excellent company. This is an old family firm and I pretty much run the show single-handed. Charlie Verne died years ago, Edgar Prentiss is in a nursing home, and my father has retired to the Costa del Sol. That leaves little me. After twenty years in the navy it can get pretty lonely, take my word for it.'

The friendship deepened. By now Mallinder had confessed that his original bid for a big family house had been in the nature of a gamble. His wife had wanted a larger house to cope with a new baby and he'd tried to bounce her into moving down to Portsmouth. By this time, though, she'd set her heart on a property in

Wentworth and wouldn't hear of leaving London.

'So where did the smaller place fit?'

'I'm not entirely sure. I think he was a bit reluctant to admit it but I sensed that the relationship might have been in trouble. On a number of occasions he told me he was fed up with living in London and by that I think he meant more than the location. Plus he seemed to have fallen in love with this place.'

'You mean Old Portsmouth?'

'Yes. But in a wider sense too. He could see the potential in the city. He could see the possibilities for *growth*. I know a lot of people bang on about the history of the place, and the up-and-coming university, and all the big sporting events and so forth, but Jonathan was different. He was prepared to put his money where his mouth was. He really *believed* it.'

'What kind of money?'

'Hundreds of thousands, on a fifty-fifty split.'

'You were going into partnership?'

'It was mooted, certainly. In fact in principle we had the makings of an outline agreement. My father played a very modest role in this business — he made all his money in the motor trade — but he's always been more than generous when it comes to a sensible investment and he was certainly interested in this one.'

'So what was it?'

'Essentially, as far as he was concerned, it boiled down to more of the same. Jonathan and I were going to set up a limited company. With my local knowledge and his development expertise,

137

the prospects looked extremely promising. Jonathan was right. This city is on the up. Chose the right targets and you can't fail to make decent money.'

He quickly tallied a list of possible development opportunities. They ranged from a sprawling Victorian fort on the city's south-eastern tip to a handful of more modest inner-city sites just begging for the wrecker's ball. The Taj Mahal, thought Faraday. And the Halal Grocery Store.

'What about his current work?' Faraday said carefully. 'What about Benskin, Mallinder?'

'He'd cut and run.'

'Are you sure?'

'Absolutely.'

'He told you that?'

'On several occasions.'

'And had he discussed that with his partner? Stephen Benskin?'

'I've no idea. Given the kind of man Jonathan was, the answer's probably no. The more I got to know him, the more I realised the degree to which he relied on bluff. His life was one long poker game. But he was bloody good at it.'

'Did he bluff you?'

'I'm sure he did in some respects but that's because it was so much part of his nature. Deep down I'm positive he meant it about coming down here and setting up a business together.'

'You've got paperwork?'

'Of course. That's why I phoned you in the first place. I assumed you were bound to find his end of it. My copies are in here.' He nodded down at the desk drawer.

'May I see them?'

'Be my guest.'

He unlocked the drawer and brought out a thinnish file. Faraday flicked quickly through. As well as a draft partnership agreement, heavily amended in pencil, there was a series of reports on prospective development targets.

Faraday looked up.

'There's no mention of the Gateway project. Up at Tipner.'

'Why should there be?'

'I understood Mallinder had an interest.'

'He certainly never mentioned it to me. And if he had I'd have been astonished. Getting involved in something like that would run counter to everything he believed. The scheme's far too complicated, for one thing. And, to be frank, the profit's not there, certainly not on a scale to justify the effort you'd have to expend.'

Faraday returned to the file. In all, he counted a dozen development targets.

'So what was the time frame here? When was it all going to happen?'

'That was dependent on funding.'

'His or yours?'

'His. I have a line of credit I can call on from my father. With the balance from Jonathan, it would have been more than enough for our purposes. Jonathan needed to release funds from Benskin, Mallinder. He was very loath to go to the banks.'

'You're sure about that?'

'Absolutely. Not only did he say so but it's

entirely in keeping with the kind of man he was. He hated the very idea of mortgaging himself to some third party if there was the prospect of the loan rolling on and on. Benskin, Mallinder were always very inventive in the way they financed their deals. With short-term money, Jonathan never had a problem. With an immature business, on the other hand, something like this . . . ' Gibbon nodded at the file, ' . . . there had to be another way.'

'Which meant pulling his share out of Benskin, Mallinder?'

'Inevitably.'

'I see.'

Faraday sat back a moment, trying to get this new development into perspective. For one thing, he now understood why Mallinder had gone to the lengths of leasing a house in Port Solent. He wasn't down on the south coast to invest in fifty-three acres of Pompey scrapyard at all. He was down here to change the course of his entire life, with untold consequences for both his family and his business partner. Whether or not either of them had got wind of this latest project of his remained to be seen. What mattered now was turning this conversation into solid evidence.

'I'll need to get someone to take a statement.' Faraday glanced at his watch. 'Will that be a problem?'

7

Winter was asleep when the buzzer rang. He struggled upright on the sofa, gazed at the television, fumbled for the remote to mute the volume. He'd had a bath earlier and the belt on Maddox's dressing gown had somehow loosened. Parcelling himself up again, he padded into the hall, peering at the videophone. Bazza again. Second time in one day.

He buzzed the entry, unlocked his own front door and returned to the lounge. On screen a pair of mangy lions were disembowelling an antelope. The animal's eyes were wide open, its long neck arched back, and Winter was trying to work out whether it was still alive when he heard a footfall behind him. Reflected in the big picture window was Bazza's short, squat silhouette. Winter was about to suggest a nightcap when another figure, much bigger, stepped in from the hall. Brett West was wearing a light raincoat, beautifully cut, ankle length, unbelted. The sight of Winter in a woman's dressing gown failed to put a smile on his face.

Bazza studied Winter a moment, then gave West a nod. West strode across to the window and pulled the curtains shut. Moments later he was back in the hall. Winter heard the double turn of the mortise lock. Not a good sign.

141

'What's this about then?' Winter was still looking at Mackenzie.

'Sit down.'

'Why? What the fuck's going on?'

West was back in the room. When Winter refused to move, he took a step towards him. Mackenzie lifted a cautionary finger. West stopped, then shrugged.

'Just tell me when, boss.'

'When what?' Winter was still looking at Mackenzie.

'When *what*?' Mackenzie seemed to have paled under his summer tan. 'You're telling me you don't know how these things work? You think this is some kind of game? You're trying to tell me you're fucking *surprised*?'

West had shed his coat. He folded it very carefully over the back of a chair. Winter watched him, aware of a small, cold pebble of fear at the very pit of his stomach.

'Baz, I haven't a clue what you're talking about. Last time we had a conversation, we were business partners. Now you barge in here like it was Dodge fucking City. This isn't what you do, not if we're going to make this thing work.'

'Business partners?' Mackenzie bent to the low coffee table beside the sofa. Winter had been re-inspecting the Trophy folder earlier. Now, Mackenzie stabbed a finger at the photo on the inside page. 'That's my brother, in case you hadn't realised. My *brother*. Kith and kin. Blood. Family. *Comprende?* He does something silly. He dies. We're devastated, all of us. Tell you the truth, we're fucking broken in half. The bloke's only forty-five, for fuck's sake. So what do we do? We give him a decent send-off. We fly half a planeload of his mates down there. We spend a bit of money. Because we all knew him. Because we're all family. That's about trust . . . yeah? And missing the bugger . . . yeah? But do you know what else I do? In spite of everyone telling me I'm off my head? I get you down, too. Why? Because I trusted you. Because you were on board. Or so I thought.'

'So what's changed?'

Mackenzie stared at him.

'What's *changed*? Fuck me, do you think we're *really* stupid? Do you think we're thick? Is that it?' He took a step closer. Winter could see the madness in his eyes. 'Any more of this, mush, and I'm not going to waste my breath. I'll just tell Westie to get on with it. Is there a room in this khazi needs redecorating? Only it'd be a shame to mess your carpet up.'

Winter stood his ground.

'Just tell me, Baz.'

'Tell you what?'

'Tell me what I'm supposed to have done here.'

Mackenzie shook his head and shot a glance at West and for a moment Winter thought he'd blown it, gone too far, but then the cropped blond head swung back towards him. Anger had given way to something else. Disbelief.

'I get a call this evening, right? Bloke from Cambados. Bloke we met a couple of times. His name's Rikki. He's Colombian. He's a big player, the main man, and he's laughing fit to

143

fucking bust. Why? Because it turns out someone's been grassing.'

'About what?'

'About a fucking great load of cocaine he's just sent here, yeah *here*, to fucking Pompey. You're telling me you don't know anything about this?'

'Nothing.'

'You're off your head.'

'Bollocks, I'm off my head. I'm just telling you, Baz, I haven't the first fucking clue what you're on about. I remember this bloke . . . Rikki, whatever his name is. Tall guy? Ponytail?' Mackenzie nodded. 'So what's he saying then? And how come it leads to this fucking pantomime?'

Mackenzie couldn't believe his ears. At length he began to laugh. Then he looked at West.

'Fuck me, you have to hand it to him, don't you? They always said he was good, never lost his nerve, but shit . . . ' He turned back to Winter. 'You know something, mush? You're wasted here. You should be in Hollywood, performance like this.'

West took a step forward. For the second time Mackenzie motioned him to stay put. Winter wanted to know about the cocaine. Was this a wholesale deal? With Bazza's name on the label?

'You have to be fucking joking.'

'What are we talking about then?'

'We're talking about a scumbag Scouser called Terry Byrne. You'll know young Terry. Terry's an ambitious kid. He's got the balls for the business but he's stupid too. In fact he's so stupid he puts down a whack of money for a couple of kilos from Cambados and never realises he's got the Filth all over him. They obviously tracked the stuff to Bilbao. They were probably on the fucking ferry. They certainly knew it was coming because they pulled a guy on the road down the west somewhere and had the lot off him. Now our Rikki doesn't care because he's already been paid but he's a nice man, Rikki, and when he gets a phone call this morning about a load of numpty dealers getting themselves lifted in Plymouth or some fucking place he starts putting two and two together. And you know the conclusion he comes to? You know where the finger points? At you, my old mate. *Eez a cop, that man. I tell you already. I tell you before. Ee comes down here. Ee asks the questions. Ee talks to people. And then ee knows . . .* '

Winter shook his head wearily. Bazza's Spanish accent was crap. So was the conclusion he'd come to.

'You're way out of line, Baz. This would be a joke if it wasn't so sad.'

'*Sad?* I don't believe this.'

'Well you'd better start trying, my son. Do you know what I've given up for you? For this charade? I've given up the best years of my life. I've given up a job I loved. I've given up a job I did better than any other cunt in this city. And for what? For this? To get myself in Westie's fucking *scrapbook*?'

West started to growl. Mackenzie told him to shut up. Then he turned back to Winter.

'You were thrown out, mush. You were in the

145

fucking gutter. You told me yourself. They couldn't wait to get rid of you.'

'Sure, of course I was thrown out. But you know what they're doing now? They're re-employing civvys, ex-coppers, on CID. Why? Because no one wants to be a detective any more.'

'You're telling me you wanted to go back to the job?'

'No, I'm telling you I *could* have done. In time they'd have had me back. Not in uniform. Not with a warrant card. But as a civvy. I could have done that. It would have been possible. But not any longer. Not after I signed up with your lot. Once that got around I was dead in the fucking water. That's one reason you're just plain wrong, Baz.'

'You want to tell me another?'

'Yeah. You really think I'd be silly enough to blow a load of cocaine from *Cambados*? When I've talked to this Rikki? When I know he doesn't trust a word I say? When I know he's just itching to drop me in it? That tells me a lot, Baz. And one of the things it tells me is you should have looked harder at the goods before you bought.'

'What goods?'

'Me, Baz. I don't know what game you were playing but if this is really the kind of bloke you think I am than it doesn't say much for your fucking judgement, does it?'

Mackenzie took a tiny step back. There was just a hint of confusion in his eyes.

'You're a disgrace,' he said. 'And you're a fucking grass.'

'You're right, Baz, I *am* a disgrace. I'm a bent copper. And I was silly enough to believe all those promises you made.'

'*Me?*'

'Yeah. All the stuff about coming on board, about going legit, about the stuff we could do together, about *opportunities*. But it's not about that at all, is it? It's about you being as bent and paranoid as ever. Me? I should never have got involved. Not if I wanted to avoid drivel like this.'

Winter tightened the belt on his dressing gown. He hadn't taken his eyes off Mackenzie for a second. By the window, West stirred.

'The cunt's lying,' he said.

Mackenzie wasn't so sure. Winter could sense his uncertainty.

'If you've got this right,' he said to Mackenzie, 'then you're talking big-time U/C, covert operations, the lot. I can see why you might think that. I can see where this phone call you got from Rikki might have led. You think I've stitched you up. You think I'm part of some monster fucking plan to worm my way into the organisation, to nose around, to find out where the bodies are buried. If all that was true, then one of the things I've got to maintain is my cover. Right?'

Mackenzie nodded, said nothing.

'So if that's true, if that's the case, if that's the way it happens in real life, then what the fuck am I doing pulling a stroke like Cambados? Knowing full well you'll find out? Is that some clever double bluff? Or might you just be looking at the wrong bloke? Go on, Baz, do yourself a favour, work it out. Of course I'm bent. I wouldn't be here if I wasn't. But I'm not stupid. Or at least not *that* stupid.'

Mackenzie was frowning now. He looked away for a moment, avoiding Westie's glare.

'You're a clever fucker,' he said softly. 'I grant you that.'

'Thanks, Baz. But that's not the issue, is it? We're talking something else here. We're talking about me doing some kind of undercover number on you. And then you sussing it.'

'Too fucking right, mush. That's what they're all saying. That's what they're all telling me.'

'Then get on with it.' Winter nodded at West. 'Or piss off and let me get to bed.'

There was a long silence. West was staring down at the TV. The lions had given up on the antelope. Finally, Mackenzie turned away.

'Show him, Westie.'

With some reluctance West extracted an envelope from his pocket and tossed it towards Winter. Looking at it on the carpet, Winter knew exactly what was inside.

'Go on, mush. Open it.'

'Why?'

'Because I thought you might need a little reminder.'

Winter hesitated a moment longer, then shrugged and retrieved the envelope. Inside, as he'd expected, was a sheaf of photos. He flicked quickly through them. Mackenzie was watching his face, happy to be back in the driving seat.

'Are we kushti now? Only I took the liberty of

showing a couple of the best shots to Misty. And you know what she did? She laughed like a drain.' He took a step closer. When Winter offered the envelope back, he shook his head. He had his hand on Winter's arm now. He gave it a little squeeze. 'They're yours, Paul. I've got loads more. You OK with that? Only if you're not, I'd hate to have to go through all this again.'

He gazed at Winter a moment longer, then summoned West with a brisk nod. Winter was still rooted to the carpet, still holding the envelope, when he heard the front door click shut behind them. Then came the sound of footsteps disappearing down the corridor towards the lift.

Winter closed his eyes, felt blindly for the edge of the sofa, then changed his mind. The bathroom floor was still wet. He stood in front of the basin, eyeing his face in the mirror, then the trembling in his limbs swamped the rest of his body, and he just had time for his hands to find the cold rim of the lavatory bowl before it was too late.

Minutes later he struggled to his feet again, ignoring the trill of the phone.

8

Faraday and Barrie were driving up to Winchester. The meeting at HQ was due to start in twenty minutes time and Willard was extremely rough with anyone who turned up late. Barrie was behind the wheel, one eye on the rear-view mirror. His Rover was nearly as old as Faraday's Mondeo. At 95 mph, it felt less than happy.

Barrie glanced briefly across at Faraday.

'I talked to the Duty Inspector up at Bitterne this morning. He's had a couple of area cars out, just like we asked. Been round the whole patch, especially the more promising bits.'

'And?'

'Nothing. People just don't drive brand new Mercedes sports coupés in Thornhill Park. That's him speaking, not me.'

'Lock-ups? Someone's garage?'

'That's possible, I suppose, but the more I think about it, the more I'm sure the vehicle was nicked for resale, maybe a dealer, maybe a private buyer, someone already lined up. But are we really trying to put this same guy alongside Mallinder? I just don't see it.'

Faraday's attention was caught by a kestrel hovering over the scrubland at the edge of the motorway. A second later it was behind them.

150

'So how do we explain the CCTV sightings on Monday night and Tuesday morning?' he said at length. 'We're talking the same kid, as far as I can see. The one in the hoodie.'

'That's a supposition, Joe. There's no proof, no hard evidence, and even if there was I'm still not convinced.'

'No?'

'No.' He squeezed another five mph out of the Rover, and then crossed two traffic lanes, braking for the exit to Winchester. 'Say this kid, whoever he was, had been looking around Port Solent, doing a recce, sorting out what was on offer? Monday night, the night of the murder, he spends some time making himself a list. The Mercedes obviously figures on that list. He pre-sells, finds himself a buyer, maybe even lays hands on some keys from a bent dealer. Whatever. A couple of nights later he pays a return visit, has the car away in the middle of the night and flogs it before we have a chance to get anywhere near him. Who knows, maybe he even knew about Mallinder from the papers or the telly. There were shots of the house everywhere by Wednesday night and the Mercedes was in all of them. Nicking it would have been easy.'

Faraday nodded. They'd slowed now on the long approach to headquarters. Forty-five mph felt like walking speed.

'There's another possibility,' he said at length. 'There was something in the Mercedes that was important. Important enough to risk going back and nicking the car.'

'So why didn't they nick it when they did

151

Mallinder?' Barrie still wasn't convinced. 'Or are these guys just forgetful? This isn't amateur night, Joe. This is a class job.'

Faraday conceded the point with a nod. Then grabbed the door handle as Barrie lurched into the turn off the main road.

'So what happened to Mallinder's car keys?' He shot Barrie a look. 'Or is that another coincidence?'

★ ★ ★

The office of the Head of CID lay on the third floor of the big headquarters building. Willard was already in the chair at the head of the conference table. Faraday recognised the civvy who headed the Media Department, and offered a nod to the D/I in charge of forensics force-wide.

'Gentlemen . . . ?' Willard gestured at the two remaining seats. His physical bulk lent him an air of slight intimidation. He was loyal when it mattered but he never suffered fools and Faraday knew officers way above his own rank who'd quailed at the thought of taking him on. Neither was Willard a man without ambition. After a couple of years in charge of CID, he was already rumoured to have his eyes on an ACPO job.

Faraday and Barrie slipped into their respective chairs. As far as Faraday could tell, the meeting was already under way. The civvy from Media picked up his thread again. He'd been fending off a great deal of media interest from the national press over the Port Solent killing.

152

Jonathan Mallinder, it seemed, had friends in high places.

'How high?' It was Willard.

'As high as it gets. He was tucked up with New Labour. They'd approached him for a couple of sizeable donations and recently there'd been rumours that he was on their list to back one of Blair's City Academies.'

'That's serious money, isn't it?'

'Couple of million quid. For that you might end up with a peerage. Apparently Mallinder was keen.'

'Did we know about this?' Willard was looking at Barrie.

'No, sir. I don't believe we did.'

'Why on earth not?'

Barrie said he wasn't entirely sure. He'd authorised Mallinder's laptop for fast-track analysis but they were still waiting on the results. Production Orders had been served on the two banks that Mallinder had used but details of his various accounts had yet to arrive. Orange, meanwhile, were being unusually slow with his billing data.

'But what about intel? Who's driving that?'

'D/C Suttle.'

'Anyone with him?'

'Not at the moment, sir.'

'Get a D/S in there.' Willard was looking at Barrie again. 'Someone who knows what they're doing. This is ridiculous. The fucking red tops will be telling us who to arrest next.'

'With respect, sir — '

'With respect nothing, Joe. *Billhook*'s been

153

operational since Tuesday. It's now Friday. What else don't we know?'

He let the question hang in the air, then asked Barrie for an update on promising lines of enquiry. The Scenes of Crime report, as far as Willard could judge, had led nowhere.

'On the contrary, sir.' Barrie had got his second wind. 'It tells us a great deal.'

'Like how?'

'Like it gives us a very firm steer on MO. How many Pompey criminals could pull off a killing this efficient?'

'But that's my point exactly. Something like this, we need to be looking to London. That's where these people come from. That's where they've made their money. That's the kind of circles they move in, New Labour or otherwise. This is an intel job, Martin. It's got intel stamped all over it. We need to be talking to people in the Met, maybe the Fraud Squad, maybe even SOCA. Someone's called a debt in. Someone's a got a grudge. We need to nail down a motive here. And you're not going to find it in Fratton.' He paused. 'Or have I got this wrong?'

Barrie said nothing. The new Serious and Organised Crime Agency had taken over from the National Crime Squad, tackling class 'A' drugs and human trafficking. The Detective Superintendent glanced at Faraday, sitting beside him. They'd already discussed yesterday's interview with Fraser Gibbon, the estate agent.

Faraday summarised the new direction *Bill-hook* might take. Now, he suspected, wasn't the moment to speculate about teenage car thieves in deepest Thornhill Park. Willard, as ever, wanted a headline or two.

'So what are you saying, Joe?'

'I'm suggesting, sir, that we need to take a much closer look at Benskin. He and Mallinder worked hand in hand. According to Gibbon, something went badly wrong. One moment they were the golden couple, the name on everybody's lips, the next Mallinder's trying to carve out a new business career for himself on the south coast. Gibbon says Benskin may have known nothing about his plans to go solo but I find that extremely hard to believe.'

'And if he knew?'

'Then there might have been a big problem.'

'Big enough to justify . . . ' Willard's beautifully manicured nails tapped the *Billhook* file ' . . . something like this?'

'Possibly, sir. But we keep an open mind . . . ' he offered Willard a thin smile ' . . . as ever.'

'Martin?'

'I agree, sir. Joe and I have been wondering about Mallinder's missus. She's pregnant. Maybe the baby's Benskin's. These tight little business partnerships get very claustrophobic. It wouldn't be the first time. And if there was a financial problem on top of that, with Mallinder wanting his money out of the business, then you begin to see every reason why Benskin might be getting a bit edgy.'

'So where was he on Monday night?'

'At home, sir.' It was Faraday. 'He's got a place in Limehouse. Down by the river.'

'And he was there alone?'

'That's what he says.'

'No one to stand it up? No corroboration?'

'Only his PC. He claims he was on the internet until gone midnight, preparing for a meeting he had in Barcelona the following day. Then he sent a load of e-mails. He's quite happy for us to check it all out.'

'And what do you think?'

'I'd say he's probably telling the truth. But that's not the point. Benskin isn't short of a bob or two. What's the going rate these days? A hit as clean as this one? Ten grand? Fifteen? If Mallinder's really rocking the boat, and if the new baby was Benskin's in the first place, then that kind of money starts looking cheap.'

'OK . . . ' Willard opened the file and scribbled himself a note.

Barrie wanted to add something else. He was looking at the civvy from Media.

'If this New Labour thing is kosher,' he began, 'that could be a factor too. Maybe Benskin's a Tory. Or maybe, like the rest of us, he thinks politics is a waste of time. Having his partner making rash promises about a couple of million quid could be a problem . . . ' He spread his bony hands wide. 'No?'

'That suggests the money might be coming from the business.' The civvy was looking dubious. 'The way I'm hearing it, Mallinder had private means.'

'That I doubt.' Faraday shook his head. 'According to Gibbon, he was scraping the barrel. Selling his place in Wimbledon would have bought him something very respectable in

Old Portsmouth, but if he was suddenly living alone with a divorce on his hands he'd have been stretched. Gibbon says he was a bluffer.'

'Has to be.' Willard, for the first time, had a smile on his face. 'New Labour? Bunch of control-freak wankers.'

There was a ripple of laughter around the table. Willard had absolutely no patience with the bright-eyed Downing Street zealots who had turned the Home Office into a rod for every senior copper's back. Only now, after months of savage trench warfare, had the force managed to resist a shotgun marriage with neighbouring Thames Valley.

He began to muse afresh about the political angle. Faraday scented revenge in the air. Finally, he closed the file and addressed himself to Martin Barrie.

'*Billhook*'s intel cell is key to all this,' he said again. 'You need to sort out an extra face or two. Suttle's a good lad but he's young. Let me know who you come up with.'

★ ★ ★

Winter was on the train by ten o'clock. He checked carefully along the platform at the Harbour station seconds before the guard closed the doors, confirming that the heavy in jeans and a leather jacket had got on the train. He'd seen him before, months back, when Bazza had taken a table for the CID boxing benefit on South Parade Pier. That night, pissed, this same face had shed his tuxedo and threatened the referee

157

with a battering unless he reversed his decision against a young black lad from Stamshaw. The referee had told him to shut it and even Bazza had mustered the grace to look embarrassed, but the double chin and the savage grade one had lodged in Winter's brain. This morning, leaving Blake House, he'd clocked him on the promenade overlooking the harbour. Minutes later, as Winter plodded through the rain to the station, he'd still been twenty metres behind. Bazza, he realised, was taking no chances.

At Southampton Central Winter changed trains. The Bournemouth connection was coming down from Waterloo. According to the electronic boards, it was already fifteen minutes late. Easily time for a coffee.

Winter strolled into the buffet, eyeing the mirror behind the counter. The heavy was outside on the platform, buried in a copy of the *Daily Star*, nicely positioned to keep tabs on his target. Winter toyed with the idea of buying him a latte, striking up a conversation, reminiscing about the old days, but decided against it. Ten to one the guy had no sense of humour.

The Bournemouth train finally arrived. Winter boarded a carriage near the end, no longer bothering to check along the platform. In this situation it paid to trust the arrangements, and after this morning's conversation on the phone he didn't anticipate any glitches.

He settled peaceably into a seat by the window to watch the endless panorama of the docks unfold. He'd always had a sneaking affection for Southampton, something he was careful to keep

158

to himself, and to him the essence of the city lay here, in the huge cruise liners moored alongside, in the towering cranes and big slab-sided container ships. The containers themselves were stacked high beside the track, a solid wall of oblong boxes, and it fascinated him to think of each of them stuffed to the brim with hi-tech toasters and two-grand plasma screens, and all the other toys that kept the nation so content. The Asians had life cracked, he thought ruefully. Knock this stuff out for tuppence a shot and someone on the other side of the world will pay you a fortune for it.

The docks thinned. Then the train clattered over a bridge and after a last glimpse down Southampton Water they were heading for the New Forest. Winter sat back and closed his eyes, wondering what the next couple of hours would bring. He'd met this woman just once in his life, a month or so before Christmas, and he'd disliked her on sight. She was tiny, with a mop of ginger curls and a huge chest. She'd come down from the north, Lancashire somewhere, and was said to have ambitions way beyond D/I.

He'd heard that the regulars on Covert Ops avoided her like a bad smell, blanking her jokes and leaving her out of the coffee runs to the machine down the corridor. It didn't pay to be too leery when it came to working alongside a new guvnor but Winter gathered that they were in no danger of any kind of comeback because this woman was too thick to realise what they thought of her. She talked a good war, everyone said, but when the bullets started flying she was fucking useless. Given the importance of her role in this new life of his, Winter was less than reassured.

At Bournemouth he took his time waiting for a cab. When the queue had gone, he hailed a silver Peugeot, knowing that there were three more rides waiting on the rank. When the driver asked him where he wanted to go, he gave his new minder a decent chance to get into the car behind before fumbling in his pocket and producing the appointments card.

'Bournemouth Royal, mate,' he said, settling back.

The hospital was ten minutes away. The cab dropped Winter at the main entrance. He paid the driver and ambled in. The reception desk was busy. He joined the queue, aware of his minder lurking outside the League of Friends shop barely feet away. When Winter's turn came at the reception desk, he shot the woman a smile and asked for the Department of Oncology.

'Just a check-up in case it's come back, love,' he said loudly, tapping his head. 'At least that's what they're telling me.'

The department was on the third floor. Winter took the lift, no longer bothering to keep his minder in tow. The man had all the information he needed. Doubtless Bazza would be thrilled. Hospital visit, boss. Totally routine.

The door to the consultant's office was guarded by a secretary in a rather severe two-piece suit. She took Winter's name, consulted a typed list at her elbow and asked him to take a seat. Winter was halfway through

160

an article on stag weekends in Slovakia when a nurse appeared.

'This way, Mr Winter.'

Winter followed her back out into the corridor. There was no sign of his minder. The nurse paused at a door marked *Private*, knocked twice and stepped in. Winter followed her. D/I Gale Parsons was sitting behind a desk cluttered with medical journals. Give her a white jacket, Winter thought, and she could make a half-decent career out of this.

The nurse disappeared. Parsons nodded at the empty chair. She was extremely angry.

'The call you made this morning,' she said at once, 'was totally out of order. I've never been spoken to like that in my life. Not as a probationer, not as a new D/C and certainly not recently. Do you think an apology might be in order?'

'Fuck, no.'

Winter unbuttoned his jacket, spread his legs. He'd phoned her earlier, dialling the dedicated number. Normal procedure called for regular debriefs at a witness protection house in Lewisham, currently standing empty. Only in the direst emergency would Winter be permitted to insist on a meeting here, at the hospital.

Parsons was still demanding an apology. Winter told her she had to be joking.

'You think I enjoy that kind of language first thing in the morning?'

'I haven't a clue.'

'Well, let me mark your card. Nobody ever said this was going to be easy, least of all me, but part of our job is learning how to cope with pressure. And, by that test, I suspect you've got a problem.'

'You suspect right.'

'Good. At least we understand each other.' Parsons produced a briefcase and took out a notepad and a pen. 'Now I want you to explain it all to me again but this time I'd ask you to keep a civil tongue in your head.'

Winter went through the sequence of events. He'd been awake half the night, gazing up at the ceiling, re-running the exchange with Bazza in his head, trying to remember every last word, every tiny nuance, testing his own performance to see whether it really did hold water. Bazza, by the end, had seemed at least half-convinced that Riquelme was wrong. But that, as he knew only too well, meant absolutely nothing.

'So Mackenzie had drawn the obvious conclusion from all this? Is that what you're telling me?'

'Too bloody right.'

'Because he associated you with the Devon and Cornwall operation?'

'Of course.'

'And you're blaming us? Me?'

'Whoever.'

'But it wasn't us, Paul. And it certainly wasn't me. There are separate areas of responsibility here, as you very well understand. The principles are clear. As far as I can gather, everyone concerned acted within their separate jurisdictions. It was simply . . . ' she frowned, toying with her fountain pen ' . . . unfortunate.'

162

'*Unfortunate?* That they nearly bloody killed me? Listen. What it boils down to is this. Mackenzie's not into subtle. He doesn't understand about all that separate jurisdiction bollocks. To Bazza it's simple. If it looks like a duck, it *is* a fucking duck. I was in Cambados. Within a week or so a couple of kilos from that very same source go astray. It moves through Pompey. As far as Bazza's concerned, I *am* Pompey. And then some dickhead carrot-cruncher D/I calls a strike and half the dealers in Plymouth are on the phone to this bloke in Cambados, telling him they've been grassed up. Now this bloke's like Bazza. He doesn't believe in coincidences. Not for one second. And so he picks up the phone and gives Bazza an earful, and an hour or so later I find myself having to talk my way out of a serious battering. These blokes don't fuck around, love. I'm lucky we're not having this conversation in another hospital. Like the QA.'

'Of course. But I can only repea — '

'Repeat what you like. I'm just telling you someone should have kept an eye open, used their brain, seen it coming. And as far as I can gather, that someone should have been you.'

'How can you possibly justify that?'

'Because there has to be a system for these cross-border things. Somebody talks to somebody else. I've been there, I've done it myself. Go fishing in someone else's pond and you have to get permission, knock on a door or two, have a yak on the phone. Not at my level, Christ no, but somewhere in headquarters someone would have

163

known. And that someone should have told you.'

Winter's outburst changed the mood. Parsons sensed an opening, just a glimpse of somewhere they might beach this tiny boat of theirs before it capsized completely.

'You're right, Paul.' She was leaning forward now, blood pinking her face. 'And I understand exactly the way you feel, believe me. In fact in your position I'd probably be putting it a whole lot stronger. But you have to understand the realities here. This operation is ringfenced against practically everyone. There's only three of us in the loop, that's you, me and Mr Willard.'

'Then he should have flagged the Devon operation up.'

'He probably didn't know about it. Just like I didn't. You're right. Devon and Cornwall would have talked to Force Intelligence. They'd have made a courtesy call. But I doubt a whisper of that would have gone any higher.'

'Two *kilos*? Are you kidding?'

'They called a strike. They got a result. Not us, Paul — *them*.'

'So why didn't we know about this kind of weight?'

'Because, as I understand it, Devon and Cornwall had put in the legwork. And six months down the road, like I say, they scored a decent result.'

'And our blokes? You lot? Aren't you asking yourselves how come you never knew?'

'Of course we are. And believe me there's a big post-mortem going on. But that's after the event. Which doesn't really help you one bit, does it?'

Winter shook his head. The word 'post-mortem' didn't bear thinking about. It was his turn to lean forward. 'How much do you know about me?'

'I'm not with you.'

'My file. What's happened to me. Where I've been lately.'

'Are we talking medical history here? Brain tumours? Surgery abroad?'

'We are, boss. Listen to me. This is important. This is the way it happened, yeah? I've got a tumour that everyone in this fucking country says is inoperable. That's pretty much a death sentence in anyone's book but a good friend of mine finds this surgeon in Arizona and I walk out of that hospital with at least half a brain that's still functioning. That makes me grateful as well as lucky. So I go back to the job. This is last year now. I'm sitting in an office on Major Crimes for a while and I'm playing myself back in. I take a punt or two on a particular inquiry and one of those punts goes horribly wrong. I cross a line. I make some serious enemies. And that same Saturday night I find myself in some very bad company. Did you hear about that? Did anyone tell you what they did to me in the van?'

Parsons shook her head. She was really listening at last.

'Who's they?'

'Some mates of Bazza's. The way they saw it, I'd been completely out of order. Taken advantage.'

'So what did they do?'

'They lifted me off the street, they blindfolded

165

me, and they drove me round half the night. Then they stripped me naked, drove me to the top of Portsdown Hill, and chucked me out. And all this time they've been taking photos. Loads of photos. You want to know what that feels like? Fucking horrible.'

'You reported all this?'

'No way. For one thing these guys were too fucking clever to leave any evidence. For another, there were blokes in the job that would have paid a fortune for those photos. So I just kept my head down.'

'And hoped it would go away?'

'Yeah.'

'And did it?'

'Of course it didn't.' Winter frowned at the memory. 'There's a D/I called Faraday. You might have met him. He's an oddball but a decent copper, and fuck knows how, but he got the whole story out of me. Took it to Willard. Made a suggestion or two.'

'About what?'

'About ways they might turn the situation rather than just do me for not reporting what had happened. We all knew it had to be Bazza and we all knew he'd cash in those photos one day. The trick was to make it easy for him.'

Parsons nodded. 'So the DUI?' she said slowly. 'The night they pulled you in Albert Road?'

'All part of it. Willard thought I needed a legend so he dreamed one up. It was my job to sit and get pissed. Not hard. Then all I had to do was cross the road and get in the fucking motor.

The woollies didn't know of course. They all thought it was Christmas. They get a tip from someone who they think's been dying to shaft me. They drive round, park up, wait a couple of hours for me to get well and truly pissed, then they just do the business.'

'And you?'

'I get done. Kippered. Hung out to dry. Three times over the limit and I'm out on my arse.'

'So how did you feel about that?'

'Bitter as fuck. But that's all part of the legend too. Works a treat, doesn't it? The likes of Bazza can smell blood half a mile away. I was counting the days until the phone rang. And of course it did. Baz buys me a pint or two, commiserates about the sacking, and then he offers me a job. Why? Because I'm better connected than any other bastard detective in the city. Because I know where the bodies are buried. Because I know the way that coppers *think*. Bazza wants all that, or thinks he wants it, and he's still got the pictures so there's no way I'm going to say no.' Winter paused, nodding. 'That Willard's a clever bastard. Except he's just gone and nearly got me killed.'

'But you said yes to the original plan.'

'That's true. But you never expect things to go wrong, do you? Not *this* wrong. Not like last night.'

Winter sniffed, then sat back in his chair. To his surprise he felt a lot better. He gave Parsons a quizzical look.

'You're telling me you didn't know any of this?' he asked.

'I knew about the DUI, of course. And I knew a bit about other stuff you'd got up to, people's noses you'd put out of joint. And of course I knew about the target — '

'Mackenzie?'

'Yes. Plus the fact you had some kind of prior relationship with him. But the rest of it, the van, the photos . . . ' she shook her head. 'Need to know, I suppose. Happens all the time.'

'Yeah? So where does that leave little me? Given I'm still in one piece?'

Parsons took a long time to answer. At length she closed her notepad and put it back in the briefcase.

'To be honest, I'm not sure,' she said. 'I'm afraid you'll have to give me a little time on this one.'

★   ★   ★

Willard wound up the *Billhook* progress review after less than an hour. As everyone tidied their paperwork and got to their feet, he signalled for Faraday to stay behind. When the office had emptied he shut the door.

Faraday assumed he wanted to know something else about *Billhook* and braced himself for the inevitable inquisition. He was wrong.

'It's about Winter,' Willard said. 'I was wondering whether you'd seen him at all lately.'

'No, sir.' Faraday shook his head.

'Not at all? I thought you two were on speaking terms at last.'

'We worked together on *Coppice*. He was

168

effective. He did a good job. But I wouldn't say we were best mates.'

'But he doesn't do best mates.'

'No, sir. And neither do I. Which probably explains why our paths haven't crossed.'

Faraday held Willard's gaze. The last time he'd heard, Winter was having dealings with Bazza Mackenzie. Quite what lay behind the rumours was anybody's guess but Faraday had a shrewder idea than most that there was more to this supposed relationship than met the eye. Indeed, as the first person to hear the truth about Winter's abduction in the van, he'd sometimes wondered whether he might have been instrumental in whatever had happened next, a thought that made him feel extremely uncomfortable. He, after all, had been the one to take it to Willard with the suggestion that Mackenzie's leverage on Winter might somehow be turned to good account.

'So you know nothing?' Willard raised an eyebrow.

'No, sir.'

'Heard nothing?'

'No, sir.'

'But you'd let me know, eh? If anything comes your way?'

Faraday ducked his head. He wanted no part of this conversation. Finally, he looked up again.

'Of course, sir. Though I can't imagine it'll ever happen.'

9

Winter was back in Blake House by mid-afternoon. His phone was ringing within minutes. Bazza Mackenzie.

'The medics give you the all-clear then?' He was laughing.

Winter pretended to be surprised but he knew Mackenzie wasn't fooled for a second. This is becoming a game, he thought. If only.

'Did you phone last night by any chance?'

'Yeah, that was me.'

'What did you want?'

'Westie left his coat. I thought you could bring it round.'

Winter was looking at the coat now. First thing this morning he'd been tempted to chuck it in the harbour but he'd been late for the train. In a pocket he'd found a brass knuckleduster and a pair of heavy leather gloves. The consequences of getting last night wrong didn't bear contemplation.

'Bring it round where?'

'Our place. Sandown Road. We're having a bit of a party. Get a cab, mate. It's clearing up nicely.'

Winter was about to plead a prior engagement but the phone had gone dead. The invitation, he knew, had the force of an order. He slid open the

170

big glass door to the balcony and stepped out. Bazza was right. After this morning's rain the blanket of low cloud had lifted. Across the Solent he could see splashes of sunshine on the low swell of the Isle of Wight and there was a definite hint of warmth in the air.

He hung on for a moment, watching the sleek grey shape of a frigate pushing out through the Harbour narrows. A line of matelots stood at attention on the foredeck and he caught himself wondering how long they planned to be away. Just now, he thought, he'd have done anything for a sailor suit and a couple of months at sea.

He returned to the lounge and glanced at his watch. The meeting with his Covert Ops minder had lasted no more than twenty minutes. After agreeing what D/I Parsons termed 'the health and safety implications' of last night's encounter, he'd given her a brief outline of what Bazza had in mind for the Mackenzie Trophy. It was his job, he'd said, to make this spectacular happen. He hadn't any idea what he was going to do next but he'd squared a woman on the council and he suspected that the real key lay in the media coverage.

Parsons had written everything down and asked him when he might get the chance to nudge Mackenzie towards doing something silly. This, after all, was the whole point of the exercise, and on the face of it the sheer scale of the Trophy project might turn out to be a huge windfall. Mackenzie needed to take a risk or two. He needed some kind of incentive to abandon this new persona of his and cross the line back

171

into active criminality. Once he'd done that, and once they'd managed to evidence it, then the Proceeds of Crime Act would kick in and they'd be able — at last — to strip him of every penny of his precious fortune.

Winter had listened to this instruction with a heavy heart. Willard, only weeks ago, had said much the same thing. Get alongside him. Get your feet under his table. Make him trust you. And then bide your time until his guard finally drops. At that point, of course, Bazza's brother was still alive and no one had a clue how soon an opportunity for serious mischief might turn up, but sitting in the office at the hospital Winter had been only too aware how quickly Parsons had realised the potential of Bazza's latest wheeze. Properly managed, she'd told him, the Mackenzie Trophy could be the beginning of the end for the city's number-one criminal.

Properly *managed*? Winter had shaken his head, emphasising again the risks he was running, how clever these guys were, how shrewd. She'd nodded, agreed with him, done everything short of patting him on the head. He was doing fine. Just fine. It was a shame about the Devon and Cornwall job and she'd see to it that inter-departmental liaison procedures were tightened up, but in the meantime he was to press on with Operation *Custer* and take very great care not to compromise himself. For the second time she referred to the importance of health and safety, and Winter left the hospital with the phrase still ringing in his ears. This woman hadn't turned out to be quite the clown he'd been expecting but health and *safety*? Unbelievable.

Half an hour later a taxi dropped Winter in Sandown Road. Craneswater was Southsea's destination address for the city's shakers and movers. Broad tree-lined avenues led down to one of the quieter stretches of seafront and many of the handsome Edwardian villas enjoyed views across the Solent towards the Isle of Wight. Bazza had been in this kind of company for three years now, rubbing shoulders with captains of industry, professional high-flyers and a discreet circle of local friends he liked to dub his 'fellow businessmen'.

In social terms Craneswater was light years away from the Copnor terraces of Bazza's youth, but to the surprise of many in the city he seemed to have made the transition with effortless ease. His wife, Marie, hosted neighbourhood barbecues. His daughter, Esme, occasionally turned up for informal tennis tournaments on the courts at the bottom of the road. Bazza himself had even lent his new motor cruiser to an ex-navy commander who wanted to take his kids to Cowes for the weekend. Some day soon, thought Winter, he'll be joining the fucking Rotary Club.

Standing on the pavement, Winter was aware that the party was in full swing. Beyond the high garden wall he could hear laughter, music and the clink of glasses. Number 13 was the biggest house in the road, a beautifully proportioned Edwardian property in repointed brick with big double bays, tall sash windows

173

and a recently added balconette built into the roof. Quite how Bazza had managed to smuggle this feature through the planning process was anybody's guess, but Winter was brought to a halt by the sight of purple balloons and a huge banner hanging from the balconette's chromium and smoked-glass screen. *Happy Birthday, Marie*, went the greeting on the banner. *Forty Five Up and Still a Gem*. This, it turned out, was a birthday party. Why hadn't Bazza told him?

The electronic security gates were open. Winter squeezed past a line of SUVs in the drive and paused again to take stock. Beyond the swimming pool a grassy bank fell away to a sizeable lawn. Guests were milling around everywhere and there was a small army of kids mobbing a bouncy castle in the corner. Brett West was there too, obviously charged with keeping them from serious injury, and Winter stepped briefly inside the house to leave the coat on a chair by the front door. Back outside again he caught sight of Esme helping herself to a plateful of food from a spread that occupied a line of tables beside a flower bed, and he ducked his head as she turned to look for company. Then he felt a hand on his arm.

'Paul . . . Great you could make it, mate. Get one of these down you.'

It was Bazza. He had a bottle of Krug in one hand and three champagne flutes in the other. Winter helped himself to a glass, steadying it while his host did the honours.

'You never told me, Baz.' Winter was smiling

at a plump woman dressed as a priest. She was heading their way.

'Told you what?'

'That this was fancy dress.'

'It's not, mate. This is Caroline. She's our local vicar. Caroline . . . meet Paul Winter. Good friend of ours.'

Winter found himself shaking hands. Caroline, it seemed, was a regular visitor to Number 13.

'We're having a raffle later, a charity thing. Caroline's doing the honours. The way it works, Paul, is you stick something in the pot, anything, doesn't matter what, and then Caroline and I have a little auction. Worked a treat last time we did it, eh Caroline?'

Caroline nodded then made her excuses. She'd spotted the heart specialist who lived down the road. He was a mad keen jogger. She needed advice on preparing herself for the Great South Run. Bazza watched her make her way up towards the house.

'Fantastic woman.' Bazza was beaming. 'Salt of the fucking earth.'

He steered Winter through the mill of guests towards his wife. She spotted him coming and Winter had the distinct impression she'd been expecting this encounter. She was in conversation with a couple of other women and they stepped back as the two men arrived.

'You remember Paul?'

Marie nodded and Winter was surprised by the warmth of her smile. She was a tall, blonde woman who took some care to keep herself in shape and middle age had barely touched her

Scandinavian looks. The last time Winter had met her was a couple of years back, in the depths of winter, and on that occasion she'd scarcely spared him a word. Now, tanned and relaxed, she wanted to know how he was getting on. Winter grinned at the question. How much time did she have?

'All afternoon, Paul. Let's get you some food.'

Winter allowed himself to be led to the spread at the edge of the lawn. The other two women seemed to have disappeared. Marie piled a plate with rice and brochettes of scallops and lobster, and found a newly opened bottle of Krug to replenish Winter's glass.

'You're spoiling me.'

'You deserve it. Here, have a napkin.'

Something in her voice told Winter that Marie knew a great deal more than he might have expected. The thought of Bazza having a moment's regret about last night's episode was a joke but maybe she took a different view. Marie had always had a hand on Bazza's tiller. Indeed, she'd been largely responsible for bringing them to Craneswater.

'Great do.' Winter raised his glass. 'Happy birthday.'

She grinned and offered him a cheek to kiss. She smelled of sunshine and something wildly expensive.

'Are you happy?' she asked. It was a very big question. Winter didn't quite know what to say.

'How do you mean?'

'With Baz. With us.'

'Yeah.' Winter nodded. 'More or less.'

'Must be odd, though, mustn't it?'

'Yeah, a bit. Must be strange for you too.'

'Christ, no. Far from it. In fact I've been banging on at Baz for months. We're lopsided. We need someone like you on board. Have done for a while, if you want the truth.' Her eyes left his face. She was looking out across the lawn. 'Solicitors, accountants, professional people, they're two a penny in this town. In fact we've adopted so many it's becoming an embarrass-ment. They fight, you know. They're like puppies. You toss one the odd bone, tickle him under the ears, and suddenly they're all over you, the whole lot. Amazing, isn't it?' She laughed, turning back to Winter. 'Then someone like you comes along and it's all so simple again.'

'*Simple*? How does that work?'

'Because you speak our language. Because you understand the way we work, the way things really are. That's why you and Baz get on so well. Or hadn't you noticed?'

It was Winter's turn to laugh. Eighteen hours ago he'd been looking at a death sentence. Now this.

'That's very kind,' he said. 'I'm flattered.'

'No ... ' She beckoned him closer. 'I'm serious, Paul. You're practical. You've got contacts. You know how to handle yourself. We need all that, though I'm not sure Baz knows how important it might be.'

'Job contacts, you mean?'

'Of course. And a million others.' She paused. She had very blue eyes. 'You know whose idea this was? You joining the organisation?'

'No idea.'

'Mine, Paul. And because it was my idea it's also my job to make sure it works, to make sure you've got everything you need, to make sure you're *happy*. Can I ask you a straight question?'

Looking at her, Winter wondered whether she was taking the piss. To his alarm, he decided she wasn't.

'Go on.'

'My daughter. Esme. She can be difficult sometimes, a bit off-putting. Do you find that at all? Only it might become a bit of an issue, you two having to work together.'

Winter shrugged, said it wouldn't be a problem.

'But it might, Paul, it might. A lot of people get the impression Esme doesn't like them but it's just her manner, that's all. She was born awkward, that girl, and if you want the truth I blame it on us. We spoiled her to death. She had everything . . . the horse, the sports car, the lot. Maybe we should have spent more time with her, given her the right kind of attention, but love's a whole lot tougher than money, isn't it?'

It was a good phrase. Winter said he didn't know. He'd never had kids of his own.

'Do you wish you had?'

'Yeah.' He nodded, thinking suddenly of Jimmy Suttle. 'I do.'

'That's a shame then.' She sounded genuinely concerned. 'Baz says your wife died.'

'Yeah. It was a while ago. She had cancer.'

'And do you miss her?'

'Yeah. I do. We'd been together a long time.'

'Then I'm sorry.' Winter felt the warmth of her hand on his wrist. 'Because personally I couldn't think of anything worse.'

She held his eyes for a moment then stepped aside. Caroline, the vicar, was back with a cloth bag in her hand. She was after last-minute contributions. Winter was very definitely on her list.

Winter looked blank for a moment. Then he remembered the charity auction. His hand dived into his jacket pocket and he palmed the first thing he found into the bag. Caroline thanked him. Winter beamed back.

'My pleasure. When does it all kick off?'

The auction started barely minutes later. Bazza hoisted himself onto a wobbly chair and called the party to attention. The kids, scenting presents, abandoned the bouncy castle and gathered round. The vicar stood beside him, clutching her bag of goodies, while Bazza announced that all proceeds would be going to the 6.57 Old Lags Fund. There came a bellow of laughter from a group of overweight men beside the drinks table. Bazza silenced them with a look.

'Just a joke,' he said, trying to steady the chair. 'Excuse my friends.'

The auction began. First out of Caroline's bag was a pledge from a neighbour for a trip to London to see the Rodin exhibition. The bidding was less than brisk and after a protracted attempt to get it above thirty-five pounds, Bazza pronounced himself disappointed.

'Gotta do better than that,' he warned.

Next came two boxes of Beaujolais, deliverable in November, plus a meal for two in a local restaurant called Rosie's. This time Bazza managed to get to two-hundred and ninety pounds.

'Gone.' He clapped his hands. 'Gentleman over there in the gay shorts.'

The party erupted. The winning bid had come from a burly planning consultant famous for shagging other men's wives. Bazza reached down for another envelope. An evening with David 'Calamity' James, the new Pompey goalkeeper, came in for more derision. As did Bazza's own contribution, a weekend for two with a complimentary waterbed in the Royal Trafalgar. By now the auction had raised nearly a thousand pounds. A return flight to Barcelona plus a set of flamenco lessons took it comfortably over. The vicar felt around in her bag, frowned, extracted something shiny.

She examined it from several angles, then passed it up to Bazza. Bazza gave it a single glance. He scanned the faces below him, a grin on his face.

'Priceless,' he said, holding it up. 'One nearly new knuckleduster, barely used. What am I bid?'

The laughter, this time, was muted. Winter heard one of the kids ask what a knuckleduster was. Someone else offered a quid. Bazza dismissed the bid with a snort. Then he beckoned to a tall figure at the back of the crowd.

'A hundred quid to the bloke by the bouncy castle,' he said briskly. 'You got a problem with that, Westie? Only cash would be nice.'

★   ★   ★

D/S Brian Imber headed the Intelligence Cell at the Havant-based Crime Squad, working in a small, airless office eight miles north of the city. At Willard's insistence he'd driven down to Kingston Crescent to take charge of intelligence on Operation *Billhook*, joining D/C Suttle in the Major Crimes suite. Martin Barrie had also asked D/C Tracy Barber to be part of the intel team. With her Special Branch and MI5 contacts, her input might prove invaluable in assessing the strength of Mallinder's political interests.

Barrie had convened a meeting in his office to agree the new ground rules but this agenda had been overtaken by the arrival of a couple of dozen priority files, downloaded from Mallinder's laptop after hard-disk analysis. These had formed attachments to an e-mail addressed to Suttle, and by the time the meeting started he'd had a chance to print and read most of the material.

He spread the photocopied pages on the big conference table and asked everyone to help themselves, but first Martin Barrie wanted his preliminary thoughts on the files.

'As I see it, sir, they confirm what we'd assumed.'

'Which is?'

'That Mallinder was someone these people were after.'

New Labour, he said, were desperate for money. They were looking at a fourteen million quid deficit after the last election but were hamstrung by new laws on political contributions which they

181

themselves had drawn up. After 2002 every donation over £5,000 had to be made public. Most major donors expected something back for their money but were reluctant to see their names in print, especially if a largish cheque had eased them towards a knighthood or a peerage. Hence New Labour's sudden appetite for undeclarable loans.

'Where's this getting us?' Barrie was becoming impatient.

'I'm sorry, sir. This is background.'

'Suttle's right.' It was Imber. 'The Met are running an inquiry as we speak. If Mallinder was on their target list then we need to know why.'

Faraday smiled. He'd rarely worked with anyone as fearless or as conscientious as this man. Imber was someone who always spoke his mind. At fifty-four, all too sadly, he was rapidly approaching retirement.

Suttle was flicking quickly through the material he'd brought with him. After the 2002 election, he said, New Labour had chased the major donors, desperate to cover their overdraft. In the view of many accountants they were technically bankrupt. Only five and six-figure donations could get them out of the shit.

'And Mallinder?' Barrie again.

'He was on their target list. D/S Imber's right.'

'You can evidence that?'

'Absolutely. It's here in the files. They were bombarding him with invites, one-on-one meetings with senior party figures, a chance to sit at the top table.'

'And what happened?'

'It's not clear, sir. Mallinder was very reluctant to commit himself in print. The correspondence suggests he took up some of these invitations but nowhere is there any mention of a specific sum of money, not in respect to loans.'

'But they were still after him?'

'Yes. Presumably he did make them some kind of loan, probably quite modest, but that's only something we can confirm from his bank statements. What's probably more interesting is this.' He picked up another sheaf of photocopies. 'This is from a file he tagged CA01. CA, from what I can make out, stands for City Academy.'

He paused to let everyone else catch up. Heads bent to the paperwork. Barrie glanced up.

'City Academy?'

'Yes, sir. New Labour describes them as independent state schools. Basically it's a bid to get education out of the hands of local authorities. In areas where schools are failing Whitehall takes over.'

So far, he said, a number of these schools were up and running. They cost £25 million each and Downing Street were desperate to get local businessmen involved. For sponsorship of £2 million, a donor would end up with a substantial say in the management of the school.

'Philosophy, curriculum, uniform, the lot. Two million quid might sound like a fortune but you'd be amazed at the number of businessmen who've coughed up.'

'So what's in it for them?'

'Honours, sir. Apparently there's a rate card. £675k is supposed to buy you a CBE. For

183

£750k, you might get a knighthood. Put two and a half million in the pot and you could be looking at a seat in the House of Lords.'

'And Mallinder?'

'I've no idea, sir. Maybe he was after a peerage.'

'Through this City Academy scheme?'

'That's what it feels like. Nothing's spelled out of course, but Downing Street are desperate to hit their target, and that means setting up over a hundred new academies.'

'How many so far?'

'Twenty-seven. With another nineteen opening this month.'

'Ah . . . ' Barrie was smiling at last ' . . . so Mallinder was in the driving seat? Is that what you're saying?'

'I'm saying it's a buyer's market, sir. And when it came to this academy programme Mallinder certainly gave the impression he had the cash.'

'We're talking about a specific proposal?'

'As far as I can gather.'

'Where?'

'Here.' It was Imber again. He'd found the line in one of Mallinder's e-mails. A meeting with a New Labour apparatchik had evidently identified an opportunity in Portsmouth. In response, the same day Mallinder had described himself as 'extremely excited'.

'That was back in February.' Suttle confirmed. 'I'm not sure what's happened since.'

There was a brief silence around the table. Then Barrie congratulated Suttle on the speed with which he'd mastered this brief. Imber nodded in agreement and Tracy Barber shot the young D/C a smile of encouragement. Faraday was still studying the paperwork.

'There may be implications here . . . ' he said carefully ' . . . for the Tipner project.'

'In what respect?' Barrie asked.

'Mallinder's got his feet under the New Labour table. They need people like him. Whether Mallinder's bluffing or not, they want to believe he's got a lot of money. Now Mallinder's a real pro in situations like these. He plays both ends against the middle. By all accounts he's raised these kinds of negotiations to an art form. So what does he do?'

Faraday gazed round the table. Imber shook his head. He hadn't had a chance to study the *Billhook* file. He simply didn't know. Tracy Barber, embarrassed, began to play with her pen. Barrie hid behind a frown. Only Suttle voiced any kind of conclusion.

'He really *was* after the MoD land at Tipner.' He grinned across the table at Faraday. 'And he thought his New Labour friends were the ones to make that happen.'

★ ★ ★

Brett West, at Bazza's insistence, offered Winter a lift back to Gunwharf. The party was beginning to break up — lots of hugs, lots of drunken kisses, lots of knackered kids. Winter stood beside Westie's rusting Alfa Romeo, waiting for him to unlock the door. He could still smell Marie's perfume on his clothes. He'd even had a

185

half-civilised conversation with her daughter. All in all, much to his surprise he'd rather enjoyed the occasion.

'He wants us all to be mates, yeah?' Westie had finally let him in.

Winter didn't answer. He was watching Mackenzie at the kerbside doing a serious number on a pretty redhead he had noticed earlier and Winter found himself wondering about the rest of Bazza's love life.

'How's Mist these days?' he asked Westie.

'Nicely set up in Hayling Island. Ever seen that place of hers?'

'Yeah.' Winter nodded. 'I was over there last year. They were still putting the pool in.'

'Nice, eh? We all went over for the house-warming. Pissed the neighbours off big time. Baz was out of his head for once.'

Misty Gallagher was Mackenzie's mistress, a woman in her late forties with the face of a gypsy and the body of a goddess. A couple of years ago the relationship had run into severe turbulence after Bazza discovered competition in the shape of a local car dealer, but Mike Valentine was living abroad now and Misty was back on the payroll. Winter had always assumed that Marie knew about her husband's other relationship but after this afternoon he wasn't so certain. You see what you want to see, he thought. And the rest just happens.

They'd left Craneswater now, and West slowed late for the turn into Albert Road. He drove a car the way he handled everything else in life, with total disregard for the consequences.

'You owe me,' he grunted. 'That was fucking out of order.'

'The knuckleduster?' Winter laughed. 'Serves you bloody right.'

'I'm serious. That cost me a hundred quid. Say fifty in notes and we'll call it quits.'

'You have to be joking.'

'I'm not. You want to play games like that, maybe you should have stuck to the day job. Where I come from, man, you have to *earn* a little respect. Bazza might love you. Marie might be up your arse. But me? I still think you're fucking lucky not to be on crutches.'

They were in traffic, stuck behind a queue of cars at the lights. Winter nodded peaceably, smothered a yawn, then leaned over and pulled the keys from the ignition. His mouth was inches away from West's left ear.

'Listen, my friend,' he whispered. 'Fucking out of order is about right. Don't you ever, ever, pull a stroke like last night again. Not unless I deserve it. You understand me? You want to pass the message on?'

He waited a second longer for the traffic ahead to move, then he tossed the keys over his shoulder, opened the door, and stepped out. Minutes later, hunting for a cab, he could still hear the angry *parp-parp* of car horns in Albert Road.

⋆　⋆　⋆

Faraday was home by seven. Expecting to find J-J still in residence, he was surprised to learn

187

that his son had decamped and gone to London.

'He has some friends there?' Gabrielle was peeling potatoes.

'That's right. Quite a lot of friends.'

'OK. Then he's gone to see them. I took him to the station. Maybe he comes back next week. He's not sure.'

Faraday raised an eyebrow. Nothing J-J did surprised him any more but a tiny voice deep in his head prompted him to ask a question or two.

'You think I pissed him off?'

'*Comment?*'

'You think . . . ' he frowned, ' . . . him and me? You know? Father and son? *Ils ne sentent pas bien?*'

'Oh, no, *pas du tout*. He has to see some people. He told me it was very important. He had to see them this afternoon.'

'What sort of people?'

'Financial people. Money people.'

'Why?' Faraday couldn't help himself.

'I don't know. I think it's about . . . ' she smiled at him then shrugged ' . . . money.'

'The money from Russia?'

'Yes, maybe. He says he wants to go somewhere else too. I think he's going to fly there. Maybe tomorrow.'

'Fly where?'

'This place. He wrote it down for me. He said I could come too. They speak French there. I think maybe he needs, how do you say it . . . ?' She was still looking for the scrap of paper.

'An interpreter?'

'*Oui.* And maybe a voice. I said I'd ask you

188

but he didn't want that. He's nice, your son. He's unusual. *Il m'a beaucoup plu.*'

She gave up on the search and said J-J had been on the computer before he'd left. Maybe he'd made some notes. Maybe he'd left a clue.

Faraday followed her upstairs. The PC in his study was still on. The Google entry page hung on the screen and Faraday scrolled quickly through this morning's tally of hits. J-J had found his way to a number of banking sites, all of them advertising services in the Channel Islands. His final visit had been to the British Airways site, where he'd accessed information on flights to Jersey.

'*C'est celui-là.*' Gabrielle was pointing at the screen. 'He said the banks were in the main town.'

'St Helier?'

'*Oui.*'

'And you think that's where he's going tomorrow?'

'Yes.' She nodded. 'And I think there's more money. *Regarde* — '

She lifted a sheet of paper anchored by the binoculars Faraday kept beside the PC. Looking at it, Faraday recognised J-J's trademark scrawl. At the top of the page, he'd pencilled a figure, £35,000. Below it, another £28,000. Then, on the third line, £502,000. At the bottom he'd worked out the total — £565,000.

'And this is *his* money?' Faraday felt the first prickles of apprehension.

'*Je ne sais pas, cheri.*' Gabrielle kissed his temple. 'But he said not to worry.'

10

Faraday had been up since dawn, sitting in his study behind the big tripod, hunting for early-autumn visitors to the gleaming expanse of water beyond his study window. Recently he'd treated himself to a new scope, a Leica Televid. Eleven hundred pounds was a fortune in anyone's money but the optics were breathtaking and he'd cashed in an insurance policy, tucking away the balance to fund a decent trip abroad. A birding colleague at headquarters had recently returned from an expedition to the Florida Everglades, and his e-mailed descriptions of Crested Caracaras, together with a stack of photos of these awesome birds picking over alligator roadkill, had whetted Faraday's appetite.

Early autumn normally offered decent pickings from his perch up in the study. Swallows and house martins were readying themselves for the long flight south while the first arrivals from Siberia — flocks of brent geese — would be splashing down to feed on the soupy waters of the harbour. Recently, though, the seasons seemed to have got themselves into a muddle. Summers were lasting longer and longer, and if Faraday wanted evidence for global warming then all he had to do was look out of his window.

He settled the scope on a pair of turnstones pecking at a tangle of bladderwrack on the long brown flank of mud exposed by the falling tide, then tilted slowly up until he found the shag that sunned itself on a red buoy out in the harbour. This handsome little bird, smaller and blacker than Langstone's cormorants, roosted on the crumbling sea forts out in the Solent, and Faraday couldn't resist the thought that only the slow decay of Pompey's fortifications had brought it here in the first place. Maybe the shag should become the city's symbol, he thought. More apt, by far, than the current flagship.

Faraday's study was connected to his bedroom, and through the open door he could hear Gabrielle beginning to stir. Whatever the circumstances, she seemed to have an inner clock that woke her at this time in the morning. He checked his watch and smiled to himself. Quarter to eight. Spot on.

He padded downstairs to the kitchen and filled the kettle. By the time the tea was ready, he could hear her moving around overhead. Back in the bedroom with a tray of tea, he found her naked at the window with a pair of binoculars that had once belonged to his son. The blaze of morning sunshine threw her shadow across the polished floorboards. Faraday put the tray on the chest of drawers, stepped out of his jeans and slipped into bed. The sheets were still warm. He could smell the scent of mimosa she'd brought into this solitary life of his, and when she turned from the window he gestured at the space beside him.

They made love. Afterwards, the tea cold, Gabrielle curled her small, hard body round his. When something worried her, she had a habit of biting her lip. Just now she was close to drawing blood. Faraday gently lifted her head from his chest.

'What is it?'

She said she didn't know. He asked the question again, tried to put it a different way, tried to coax out whatever it was that had so suddenly come between them. But each time she shook her head, said she was being silly, *bête*, that he was to pay no attention, that she'd made fresh tea, maybe some toast, that they could make love again or go for a walk while the day was so young, anything.

Faraday shook his head. The last thing he wanted just now was tea.

'Is it us?' A tiny movement of his hand bridged the gap between them. 'This?'

'No.' She frowned then changed her mind. '*Oui.*'

'How?'

'Because . . . ' The frown had deepened. She shook her head.

'Tell me . . . ' Faraday drew her closer. 'Please.'

'I can't.'

'Why not?'

'Because . . . ' She suddenly struggled free, then propped herself on one elbow, gazing down at him. 'He went because of me. I know he did.'

'Who?'

'Your son. J-J.'

192

'That's nonsense.'

'*Pas du tout*. He hasn't seen you for so long. He wants you to himself. I shouldn't be here. I should go.'

Faraday tried to calm her down. He told her that J-J was a man now. She'd seen it. She'd said so herself. He was independent. He'd fled the nest. Did his own thing. A free spirit.

'*Vraiment?*' She wanted to believe it. He could see it in her face.

'*Oui.*' He gave her a hug, feeling her pressing into him.

'And you don't mind?' Her voice was muffled.

'What?'

'Me being here?'

'I love it.' He raised her face again and kissed her eyelids. '*Vraiment.*'

★ ★ ★

Later, mid-morning, they drove west. Barrie had declared a weekend break for the *Billhook* team and Faraday was determined to make the most of it. As the road swooped down towards Weymouth Bay, Gabrielle caught her first glimpse of the long grey hump that was the Isle of Portland. At the toe of the promontory, Faraday had explained, they'd find a lighthouse, and a perch on the rocky clifftop, and a perfect view of the boiling surf below. There'd be razorbills, and guillemots, and with luck they might even catch a glimpse of a distant gannet or two. Come back here in a month's time, he said, and the migration would have started, the sky

193

full of meadow pipits and siskins on passage heading south.

They parked within sight of the lighthouse. Gabrielle had prepared a modest picnic and they picked their way along the maze of clifftop paths until they found a sheltered corner. The wind was billowing up the cliff, carrying with it the scent of wild garlic, and Faraday indicated the line of distant breakers stitching across the tidal race that swept around the rocky headland. Gabrielle shielded her eyes against the sun, following his pointing finger, and when Faraday caught sight of a cormorant, low over the water, she laughed.

'It's hungry,' she said. 'It want a good meal. It's going to France.'

She'd made a salad of couscous with raisins and olives and a dice of tomatoes and shallots. She'd bought a fresh baguette from a baker en route and she poured generous mugfuls of a Spanish crianza she knew Faraday adored. Afterwards they lay on the spread of plaid blanket, eyes closed, listening to the grumble of surf on the rocks below.

'You never tell me about your work,' she murmured. 'Never.'

Faraday smiled to himself. It was true.

'Why would you want to know?'

'Because work makes people what they are. *Tu n'crois pas?*'

Faraday nodded. Of course he believed it. That was why he enjoyed days like this, turning his back on a world he found more and more incomprehensible.

He tried to put this into words and thought from her silence that she didn't understand. He was wrong.

'You're very . . . *sensible* . . . for a policeman.' Her hand found his. 'I've always thought that.'

Sensible, in French, meant sensitive. Another woman, long ago, had said something very similar. Except she'd used the word 'vulnerable'.

'Maybe you're right,' he said. 'Maybe I should be doing something else with my life.'

'Not at all. *Sensible* makes you a good policeman.'

'You think so?'

'*Absolument*. You take the time to look, to listen. Nobody does that any more. Not policemen. Not anybody. Everyone talks. *Tout le monde*. But nobody listens.'

Faraday nodded. She was right. He lay back, the sun hot on his face, his eyes closed, thinking about the clamour of voices in his working world, the snatched half-conversations, the desperate ongoing struggle to reduce the chaos of a crime scene to a motive and a name.

Lately, for whatever reason, the drumbeat of serious incidents on the Major Crimes beat seemed to have quickened. People were hurting each other more, taking advantage more, and there seemed no end to days when he'd find himself in conference round a table trying to think himself into the heads of total strangers, trying to understand why they inflicted such damage on each other and why they occasionally ended up dead. Mallinder was one example but there were dozens of other individuals whose

195

broken bodies he'd first glimpse on the mortuary slab, and whose broken lives would take weeks to piece together.

In this sense, he thought glumly, he'd become a kind of social pathologist. His real job was gathering evidence and making cases stick. That's what detectives did. But in the process it was impossible not to peer a little deeper, not to ask yourself exactly why society itself was dying the slowest and ugliest of deaths. The symptoms were everywhere. The selfishness. The greed. The short cuts. The constant trashing of family ties, of responsibility, of anything that smacked of a steady life decently lived.

This sense of disintegration, of things falling to pieces, had begun to preoccupy him, and as the jobs piled up he found himself more and more alarmed at the wider implications. Life, in his view, was becoming unreasoningly brutal. Much of it revolved around violence, and violence was like a hot wind, scorching everything in its path. People seemed to be tearing themselves and each other apart for no good reason. Often not for money. Often not for gain. But because the sheer act of violence had become as good an answer as any. But to what question? And for what purpose? For someone like himself, someone wedded to the comforting laws of cause and effect, to analysis, to the sweetness of reason, this was the stuff of madness. Look at life too hard through the prism of Major Crimes, he'd concluded, and you'd probably end up on the psychiatrist's couch.

He gave Gabrielle's hand a squeeze. She'd

given him back his sanity. With her cheerfulness and her sheer energy, she'd made him aware of another presence in the deeply shadowed recess that was his life. She was a fellow traveller. And like him, thank God, she had more than a passing interest in the view.

'*Chéri?*' She was bent over him. She was looking worried again. 'Are you OK?'

'I'm fine.'

'You were dreaming?'

'Yes.'

'*Un cauchemar?*' *Cauchemar* meant nightmare.

'No.' He found her hand again.

★ ★ ★

The invitation came in the early afternoon. Winter, returning from his weekend expedition to the supermarket, was standing in the sunshine outside Blake House watching the female cabbie unload his shopping from the boot. The mobile to his ear, he knew at once who it was. Add gravel to honey and you ended up with a voice like Misty Gallagher's.

'Mist, how are you?'

She said she'd been better but she'd spare him the details. It was a lovely day. From what she'd been hearing, Winter had at last decided to do something sensible with his life.

'We ought to celebrate,' she growled. 'Come over.'

Winter skipped lunch, sorted himself out a brand new short-sleeved shirt to go with his

Debenhams chinos and phoned for another cab. Pompey were playing at home and the queues of cars inbound on the motorway extended for mile after mile. They left the city and headed east. Within half an hour they'd crossed the bridge onto neighbouring Hayling Island and Winter was directing the cabbie into North Shore Road, a leafy avenue on the south-west corner of Hayling that featured regularly in the windows of the classier estate agents. This was where you settled if you had half a million quid to spare and fancied a bit of peace and quiet. Misty's spread, a gift from Bazza, was last on the left.

The last time Winter had been here, the property was at the mercy of a crew of Pompey builders Bazza kept on his books. At Misty's direction they were turning up from time to time to rip out most of the original features, swap wooden windows for UPVC and dig an enormous hole in the back garden for a twenty-metre pool. Another of Misty's projects had been an outdoor disco. The plans, which Winter had seen, called for banks of strobe lighting visible from the moon and a 75 kilowatt sound system, and at the time Winter remembered fearing for the neighbours' peace and quiet. Misty had never much liked silence.

She was waiting for him on the terrace at the back of the house. She was wearing a turquoise Prada T-shirt over a black bikini bottom and her face was largely hidden behind a pair of enormous FCUK shades. On the table beside her lounger was a radio tuned to Virgin FM. She'd made a promising start on a bottle of

Bacardi and said she felt a great deal better. Last night had been a bummer. She hadn't drunk that much malt since Bazza pushed the boat out at her warming party.

Winter bent to give her a peck on the cheek and helped himself to a chair at the table. Somebody must have been using the pool because there was a trail of wet footprints into the house.

'Yours, Mist?'

'You're joking. I've got company for the weekend. One of Baz's nephews.'

'Where is he?'

'Getting changed. You know something about kids these days? They have absolutely no idea of time. His game kicks off at three. It's now ten to.'

A blond youth in his late teens appeared from the depths of the house. He was wearing shorts and an Umbro top and borrowed Misty's vanity mirror to poke at the gel on his hair. Misty told him he was late.

'Got the keys have you?'

'They're still in the Porsche.'

'Cheers.' He gave Winter a nod. 'Be good.'

He danced down the steps beside the pool without a backward glance. Misty watched him with obvious affection.

'He's gay,' she said fondly. 'Though he doesn't know it yet.'

She told Winter to fetch more Coke from the kitchen. She also wanted the tanning oil and a fresh packet of Marlboro Lights. Winter returned with all three.

'What do you think then?' She lit a cigarette and gestured at the garden. Half an acre of lawn rolled down to a low stone wall. A gate in the wall led to a wooden pier. Beyond, shimmering in the heat, lay Langstone Harbour. On a windless day like this the water was mirror-smooth.

'Lovely, Mist.'

Winter narrowed his eyes against the glare of the sun. The Harbour was Hayling's moat against the encroachments of Pompey. Viewed from this distance, the high-rise blocks of Somerstown and Portsea were a soft blue-grey in the haze. They looked like battlements, Winter thought, or the kind of cut-out frieze a kid might paste onto a picture. Rearing above them, plainly visible, was the sleek whiteness of the Spinnaker Tower.

'There . . . '

Mist struggled upright on the lounger, following Winter's pointing finger.

'Where?'

'The one by itself, Mist. That's Faraday's place. Funny you should end up neighbours.'

The Bargemaster's House was no more than a speck across the water. Misty sank back then reached up for her glass. She wanted to know the gossip.

Winter tried to sort something out but knew he was struggling. One of the penalties of this new life of his was a social diary that rarely extended beyond appointments with the telly. Finally he remembered Suttle.

'Jimmy? How is he?'

'Fine. I saw him the other night. He's putting a deposit down on a place in Copnor. He got a bit of money after that job in Ashburton Road but he won't say how much. What's the going rate for a stabbing these days? Ten grand? A million?'

Misty laughed, then raised her glass. In general she had no time for the Filth but she'd always had a soft spot for Suttle.

'Good luck to him. Shame it never worked out with Trude.'

Trudy Gallagher was Misty's daughter, a looker in her late teens with her mother's appetite for a good time. She'd enjoyed a brief fling with Suttle some time ago, an act of trespass for which the young D/C had been duly punished. Bazza had always believed that he was Trudy's father. As it turned out he was wrong, but Bazza wasn't someone to let a paternity test get in the way of his family responsibilities and, thanks to Brett West, Suttle had ended up in hospital.

'You're telling me you had a drink with Jimmy?' Misty wanted to know more.

'I did, Mist. I did.'

'Isn't that crossing the line?'

'What line's that?'

'Us and them. There's rules, you know, not that you were ever fucking interested. Still, you want to be careful. Baz gets old fashioned about the wrong kind of company.'

Winter shrugged, all too aware where the conversation was going to lead. Odds on, it was Bazza who'd engineered this invitation of

Misty's. Get the old bastard over. Find out where he's really at.

Winter smothered a yawn. Very faintly, across the water, came the roar of the crowd at Fratton Park. The game must have just kicked off, he thought. He gave his ample stomach a pat, then looked down at the lounger.

'Are we eating, Mist? Or what?'

She'd readied a couple of Waitrose takeaways in the fridge. Winter did the honours, sorting out the plates and the cutlery, then waiting for the *ding-ding* of the microwave. Misty had already laid claim to the king prawn massala. The shepherd's pie, Winter thought glumly, was obviously his.

Back out in the sunshine Misty had shed her T-shirt and was straddling the lounger. Her tan was as flawless as the famous chest that had drawn Bazza in the first place, and she was about to coat herself with more coconut oil. She had her glass in one hand and the bottle of oil in the other. Always the optimist, Winter thought his moment had come.

'You OK there, Mist?' He put the plates on the table. 'Need any help?'

Misty ignored the offer. She abandoned her glass and began to oil her breasts. She wanted to know why Winter had finally said yes to Bazza. The word she used was 'surprised'.

'You know already, Mist. You don't need me to tell you.'

'Those pictures?'

'Yeah.'

'You're joking. You've got nothing to be

202

ashamed of, love. I've seen one even smaller than that.'

'Thanks.'

'So why the decision? Nobody does what you've done for a bunch of bloody snaps. Not in a grown-up town like this.'

'I fancied it.'

'Yeah, I can see that. But *why*?'

Winter gave the question some thought. These last few days he was beginning to get irritated by having to explain himself again and again but with Misty it was somehow different. He'd known her for years, and that knowledge had bred something close to respect. You underestimated Misty Gallagher at your peril, a mistake you only made once.

'Mist . . . ' he began.

She looked up, her attention caught by something new in his voice.

'Yeah?'

'If I was to tell you the truth, what would you say?'

'Are we talking secrets here?' She'd abandoned her breasts for a moment. 'Only this could be awkward. Me and Baz . . . you know.'

'Not secrets, Mist. Just the truth.'

'OK.' She nodded. She was looking puzzled. 'Go on then.'

Winter eyed the food a moment. He wanted to confide in her. He wanted to tell her how tough this whole thing was. He wanted to explain something of the confusion that boiled inside his aching head. Nothing to do with Covert Ops and ambitious D/Is eager to win a medal or two at

203

his expense. Nothing to do with the hideous complications of this double life of his. But something far simpler. Just who the fuck was he?

He tried the question out, unvoiced. Then he shook his head. He'd sound like an adolescent. He'd remind her of Bazza's gelled-up nephew with his giddy little ways.

'Those pictures . . . ' he began.

'What about them, love?'

'It was more than . . . you know . . . what you think. It was more than that.'

'I'm not with you. They were having a laugh, weren't they?'

'Yeah, sure . . . but it didn't feel that way.'

'No? You're telling me they scared you?'

'Yeah. Definitely. It wasn't the obvious. I didn't think I was in for a battering. They'd never have done anything, you know, really silly. I knew that. No . . . ' He shook his head. 'It was something else.'

'Like what?'

'I just felt . . . ' he frowned ' . . . exposed. Not in the naked way. Not freezing my bollocks off. Just . . . stripped bare.'

'You mean vulnerable.'

'Yeah, exactly, *vulnerable*.'

'And now?'

'The same. Exactly the same. And you know why? Because for once in my life I've no idea what happens next. Do you have any idea how scary that is, Mist? I'm a copper. I've made things happen. I've had my way with people. Apart from the tumour, I've bossed every single corner of my life since forever. Now all that's gone. Now someone else is in charge.'

'And who's that?'

'Good question, Mist. But it certainly isn't fucking me.'

He turned away, surprised and slightly embarrassed by the force of his feelings. She gazed at him a moment, then extended a hand.

'Help me up,' she said.

Winter did her bidding. The palm of her hand was slippery with oil. Then he felt her arms encircling his body, the moistness of her breasts pressing softly against his chest, her fingers cupping the back of his head. Everything smelled of coconut.

'I don't know what to say, Mist.'

'Say nothing, love.' Her mouth was close to his ear. 'But take advice from someone who knows, eh?'

'And what's that?'

'Don't fuck us about.'

11

MONDAY, 11 SEPTEMBER 2006. 10.01

Martin Barrie had fixed the appointment over the weekend. The Duty Officer in Downing Street had passed on his request and the bid for an interview had pinballed around the party machine until a special adviser in the Ministry of Education and Skills phoned him back. She was happy to talk to detectives from the *Billhook* squad about Jonathan Mallinder. She understood the interview was strictly for the purposes of background information. She'd had sight of the file and she wasn't anticipating a lengthy meeting. On the contrary, they might find themselves spending more time trying to fix themselves a decent coffee than discussing the degree of Mr Mallinder's political involvement.

Barrie had passed on the conversation more or less word for word but Faraday only remembered the reference to coffee when he and Suttle stepped into the pokey House of Commons office and saw the state of the percolator.

'I'll settle for tea, thanks,' he said, shedding his coat.

The special adviser had been camping in the office during the parliamentary recess and apologised again for the state of the place. Her name was Suzanne. She wore a permanent air of near-exhaustion and had a nervous habit of constantly referring to notes on her clipboard. Top of her priority list, thought Faraday, should have been a decent holiday.

Faraday wanted to confirm a timeline. Suttle's earlier analysis of e-mails from Mallinder's laptop had established correspondence dating back to 2003.

'That's right.' Suzanne had swapped the clipboard for a buff file with Mallinder's name in black Pentel across the top. 'Someone from membership contacted him in June that year. We were trawling for donations.'

'He was a member of the party?'

'Lapsed.' Her finger found an entry in the file. 'He joined before the 97 election, paid his subs until 2001, then sent us a letter saying he was holding off for a while. That's a pretty common story, I'm afraid. Talk to the Tories and you'll find they have exactly the same problem.'

'So why chase him for a donation? If he wasn't even a member?'

'Because someone passed on a tip. Said it might be worth the price of a stamp.'

'And who might that someone be?'

'I've no idea.'

The party's tap on Mallinder's shoulder was successful. In August 2003, he renewed his membership, wrote a cheque for a £4,000 donation, and accepted an invitation to attend a breakfast meeting with senior New Labour figures on the second morning of the annual conference, down in Bournemouth.

'Any idea who he talked to?'

'It doesn't say. He'd be one of at least a

hundred invited guests, maybe more. Normally we try and sprinkle the senior people around, get them to circulate, but it's not always easy.'

'How senior?'

'Cabinet level.' She forced a weary smile. 'If he was really lucky.'

'Secretary of State for Defence?' It was Suttle.

'It's possible. Or, failing him, one of the junior ministers. It really depends on everyone's schedule. Conference week can be mad.'

'But would there be a record?'

'I don't know. It's certainly not in here . . . ' She nodded down at the file.

Suttle made a note. Faraday wanted to know whether there'd have been other opportunities for Mallinder to bend a ministerial ear.

'Someone from the MoD, you mean? At conference?'

'Yes.'

'I doubt it.'

'What about back in London?'

'He could try. Just like everyone else.' Her eye strayed to the file again. 'Is there a particular issue you have in mind?'

Faraday didn't answer. Instead, he wanted to know about Mallinder's interest in City Academies. This time Suzanne was date-perfect.

'He approached us about a year ago, in August 2005. I gather he'd bumped into someone at a party. They'd been telling him about the Business Academy down in Bexley. He wanted to talk to somebody at the Ministry about the next tranche of projects.'

'So what happened?'

'I agreed to meet him.'

'*You did?*'

'Yes. I've been shadowing the Academies programme for a couple of years. I'm pretty much up to speed, certainly as far as this kind of contact was concerned. It was a very provisional enquiry. A fishing expedition, really.'

'And did you get the impression that Mallinder was serious?'

'In some respects, yes. But that really wasn't very helpful. He made all the right noises educationally. He was keen on coming up with a more balanced curriculum, for instance. I remember that very well. And he also ticked all the right boxes when it came to the community regeneration stuff. But when we got down to it, there turned out to be a problem.'

'Which was?'

'He didn't have the money.'

Suttle tried to hide a smile. Even Faraday looked faintly amused.

'Did this come as a surprise?' he asked. 'Don't you check out these individuals beforehand?'

'Of course we do, but detailed financial data isn't always easy to get hold of. In these situations we tend to rely on people's good faith, and most of the time that works. Mr Mallinder, I'm afraid, was an exception.'

Faraday recalled a key line from Suttle's intelligence analysis, high-lighted in yellow on the brief he'd e-mailed across.

'I understand there was another meeting back in February this year. By this time your colleagues appeared to be discussing a project in some detail. Down in Portsmouth.'

'That's right. I was involved in that too.'

'So what happened?'

'Mr Mallinder had laid hands on two and a half million pounds.'

'Where from?'

'I gather it was a bank loan. Secured on his business.'

'Did you see the paperwork?'

'Not personally.'

'But someone else did?'

'Of course. Otherwise we'd never have got that far. I think there was some talk of him making the party a loan to begin with, but for some reason that didn't work out so we started talking about the Academies programme.'

'And this project was going to happen?'

'We thought so, yes. In fact Portsmouth looked a prime candidate. At least one of the comprehensives down there had been a failing school and results across the board weren't wonderful.'

'I have a note that Mallinder described himself as 'excited'.'

'He was. That's right. In fact we all were. But then the Department started having second thoughts.'

'Why was that?'

'Because there turned out to be difficulties in Portsmouth. To put it bluntly, we had to back off.'

'And was Mallinder happy with that?'

'No, not at all.'

'So he withdrew his offer?'

'It lapsed.' The smile was weary. 'Just like his membership.'

Naturally, she said, they'd tried to table alternative projects in other cities across the country but Mallinder hadn't been interested. As far as he was concerned, it was Portsmouth or nothing.

'Do you know why?'

'I understand he was planning to move down there.'

'To live, you mean?'

'Yes. And under those circumstances I can understand the logic of his position. He said he wanted to be hands-on, which is of course what we try to encourage. The press just love knocking the Academy programme but the real driver, believe me, is the kids. They respond so well. In fact they *love* the idea. In education that kind of enthusiasm is hard to find. Especially at secondary level.'

Faraday had no interest in discussing the philosophy of education. He wanted to talk about the Ministry of Defence. Had Mallinder ever raised the issue of access?

'I'm not with you.'

'Did he ever ask for meetings with ministers or senior civil servants within the MoD?'

'Not to me, no.'

'He never mentioned the Estates Department?'

'No.'

'Did he ever ask anyone else, to your knowledge?'

'I've no idea. I work for the Dfes. Defence

211

isn't my field.' She was beginning to get visibly irritated. 'I don't see where any of this is going, Mr Faraday. What point are you trying to make?'

'I'm suggesting that Mallinder's money may have come with strings.'

'Strings?'

'Yes. That he may have wanted some kind of deal. He's a property developer. He's active in Portsmouth. The Ministry of Defence occupy a lot of land in the city. In the right hands some of that land could be extremely valuable. So here he is, suddenly offering you a large sum of money, and I'm simply wondering why. It's the kind of question we tend to ask ourselves. I'm afraid it comes with the job.'

'I'm sure.' She glanced at her watch. 'The rest of this morning is looking like a nightmare. This has been absolutely fascinating but I don't think there's anything else I can tell you. So . . . ' she forced a smile ' . . . are we through?'

★   ★   ★

Winter ducked out of Waterloo Station, deciding to walk the half-mile or so to the Savoy Hotel. Bazza had phoned him first thing in a state of some excitement. A woman called Katherine Brodie had been in touch by e-mail. She seemed to run some kind of media agency. She'd picked up rumours of a planned jet ski extravaganza somewhere on the south coast, and she'd be interested in further details. It would be a pleasure, she'd said, to buy Mr Mackenzie lunch.

'At the Savoy bloody Grill.' Bazza had been

laughing. 'And she's in the chair.'

Winter had never been to the Savoy. He'd logged on to the website, lingering over the virtual tour, and now he tried to spot the terrace overlooking the Thames as he crossed Hungerford Bridge. A maze of streets off the Strand led him to the front entrance. A uniformed concierge, sweating in the heat, directed him to the restaurant. At midday he was half an hour early so he found himself a perch in the neighbouring bar, shook open his copy of the *Daily Telegraph*, and turned his attention to the court reports.

'Mr Winter?'

Katherine Brodie was a lightly tanned woman in her mid-thirties. The grey two-piece suit gave her a slightly severe air but she had a warm smile and lips that Winter had last seen on a porn queen. Bazza, he knew at first glance, would love her.

They went through to the restaurant. A table for three awaited them beside the window. Winter settled himself into the chair with the best view and debated whether to stick to San Miguel or go for something else. Already he felt totally at home.

'I'm having a spritzer. You, Paul?'

Winter settled for a large gin and tonic. Mackenzie, he explained, would be joining them as soon as the last of his morning meetings permitted. With luck, there might still be some food left by then.

She smiled at his little joke and then sat back as Winter outlined their plans for the Mackenzie

Trophy. He'd got as far as the weekend of the race itself when she raised a query.

'I'm not quite clear, Paul. You're planning for an entry of maybe a couple of dozen. These are top riders from all over the world. You're meeting their travel expenses, providing accommodation, hospitality, engineering support, all that, as *well* as prize money and ancillary logistical costs? So just who's paying for all this?'

Winter had detected the faintest American accent. He said it was early days. Conversations were ongoing. Both sponsorship and media rights had yet to be finalised.

'Conversations with whom?'

'I'm afraid I can't reveal the details. As I'm sure you'll understand.'

'Of course. But you're close to some kind of deal?'

'Obviously.' Winter shot her a wolfish grin. 'You know how these negotiations go. Never shoot the rabbit till you see the whites of his eyes.' He'd no idea what had prompted this image. Neither, it was plain, did she.

'You say early days.' She smiled at him. 'It's September. You're talking June next year? That's a blink away. That's like tomorrow. Ambition's a wonderful thing, Paul. So is optimism. I not only applaud you, I wish you luck.'

Winter knew he was struggling. Bazza would have swamped the conversation by now, buried this delicious woman alive under a ton of bullshit.

'Let's talk about you,' Winter said. 'Tell me about yourself.'

She nodded and apologised at once for not explaining her interest earlier. She'd just returned from the States, she said, and was still decompressing after a couple of years running a sports consultancy out of a suite of offices in Southern California. She'd had lead input into a number of high-profile events, chiefly in the surfing and powerboat arenas. She'd dealt with major sponsors. She'd negotiated worldwide media rights, not just TV and sell-through DVD but print and magazine as well. The Mackenzie Trophy already sounded like a page lifted straight from her own C/V. The synergies were spooky.

Winter grinned. Synergies? He hadn't a clue what she was talking about.

'So how come you heard about us?'

'A friend in the jet ski world phoned me. He races super stocks. This guy's exceptionally well tuned in. He said he couldn't think of a comparable event and you know what? I suspect that's true.'

The waiter approached with the drinks. Her hand settled lightly on her glass. A Cartier watch. A single silver ring, third finger, right hand.

'Cheers.' Winter lifted his gin and tonic in a toast. 'Happy days.'

They touched glasses. The smile again.

'You know my problem?' she said. 'It's excitement. A project like this, it sells itself. The right quality sponsorship, the right media deals, the right marketing strategy, and you're looking at an event that'll turn into an instant classic.

215

Let's talk venue. Tell me about Portsmouth.'

At last Winter felt firm ground beneath his feet. He explained about the history of the place, all those wars, all that prize money, all those matelots sailing home in triumph after hammering the French. He described the Harbour, HMS *Victory*, world-class museums in every corner of the dockyard. Then he moved on to the venue itself, Spithead, the biggest stage in the world, a stretch of water tailor-made for an event like this.

To be honest, he said, Portsmouth had always raised a bit of a smile on anyone who really knew it. The place had always been full of character but a bit rough, a bit scuzzy. Lately, though, money had been flooding into the city. He told her about the glitzy new shopping developments, the harbourside apartment blocks, the marinas packed with ocean-going yachts. And now, he said, the council had found the bottle to fund the jewel in Pompey's crown, the Spinnaker Tower, five hundred feet of soaring concrete, a fantastic peg on which the city could finally hang its hat.

Winter was aware that these images were running away with him, that he should throttle back a little, but he realised as well that he didn't care. Maybe it was foolish to neck double gins on an empty stomach. Maybe he should have had a spot of breakfast before he left. Too bad.

He was still improvising plans for the project launch party — lashings of champagne in the viewing gallery at the top of the Spinnaker Tower, men in black on abseil ropes outside the tinted windows with boxes of Milk Tray for the ladies — when he became aware of Bazza

216

Mackenzie standing at his elbow. He'd heard the lot. Every single word.

'Brilliant, eh?' he couldn't take his eyes off Katherine Brodie. 'Took months to dream all that up.'

★   ★   ★

By half past two the lunch was over. Brodie had settled the bill, accepted a kiss on both cheeks from Bazza, and disappeared towards her waiting taxi. Bazza watched her leave the restaurant, turning heads as she picked her way between the tables. The expression on his face told Winter that the Mackenzie Trophy had just acquired a new recruit.

'She's perfect.' Bazza was signalling for another bottle of Chablis. 'Fucking wonderful.'

'We know nothing about her, Baz.'

'We don't? Those aren't eyes in your head? She wants us. She *needs* us. You can see it. You can practically *taste* how bloody eager she is. You're telling me we turn down an opportunity like this? She's got the contacts, Paul. She's got the knowledge. We need to start thinking pretty fucking hard about what we're going to do, and for my money she's the one to help us.'

Winter studied the card she'd left on the table. K-MAX had an office address in E17. Number 43a Lavender Road. She'd described it as a pit stop, handy for where she was living, a temporary arrangement to tide her over until she had a chance to sort out a sensible deal on something a little more central. On the back of the card she'd scribbled her mobile number. Any time, she'd told Bazza. Just call.

'Admit it, mush. She talked a good fucking war.'

Winter had to agree. On a speculative basis, for a percentage cut of the sponsorship money, she'd promised to scope the most promising media deals and report back. As Winter had suspected she'd seen through his bluster before Bazza's arrival, but by the time they were all tucking into the main course none of that seemed to matter. She'd taken a good look at them both, correctly concluded that they were out of their depth and offered to help.

In this respect alone her judgement had been absolutely faultless, and as she and Bazza bent ever closer, discussing the price of hospitality marquees and the need for a comprehensive insurance package, Winter had recognised all the hallmark talents of a seriously gifted negotiator. She'd played Bazza like the child he was. She'd taken this shiny new toy of his and put it on the topmost shelf of all. Only with her help would he ever be able to reach it.

And the ploy had worked. By the end of the meal Bazza was offering her free office accommodation at his seafront hotel and even a cash bonus if she'd concentrate her efforts exclusively on their project. Both of these offers she sensibly turned down, but this, of course, had simply spurred Bazza to make fresh efforts to lock her away, and as she rose to leave Winter had awarded her a silent round of applause. Two decades in the interview suite, using these very same skills, had given him an appreciation of exceptional talent. As a working detective, he'd concluded, this woman would be world class.

Another bottle of Chablis arrived. Bazza didn't wait for Winter's glass to be charged.

'Get on to her, mush.' He took a swallow of the Chablis. 'Talk to Ezzie. Tie her down to a fucking contract.'

★   ★   ★

The meeting at New Scotland Yard was scheduled for three o'clock. Faraday and Suttle signed for their passes at the front desk and made their way to the bank of lifts. The investigation into the funding of political parties was being run from a couple of offices on the fourth floor.

The cash-for-honours investigation was under the command of a Deputy Assistant Commissioner, and on the phone Faraday had got the impression that he'd be present at this afternoon's meeting. As it turned out, though, he'd been called away and Faraday and Suttle found themselves in the hands of a slim, impassive D/S with a taste for wildly patterned ties. He led them into a glass-walled cubicle at the end of the big open-plan office and departed for the coffee machine.

Faraday took a seat, steadying his briefcase on his lap. The cash-for-honours investigation, as far as he could gather, had been running for at least a year, triggered by the suspicion that New Labour apparatchiks were breaking the law that governed political donations. A couple of high-profile arrests had put the investigation onto the front page of every national newspaper and there were rumours that the investigation was about to knock on the Prime Minister's door. Jonathan Mallinder had evidently come to the attention of the detectives exploring the extent of possible corruption and Faraday had been promised a look at his file. It lay on the desk before him. It wasn't very thick.

The D/S returned, juggling three coffees. His name was Alex Kitson. He slipped into the chair behind the desk and apologised again for the absence of his boss. Scarcely a day went by without another crisis demanding his instant attention. Cash-for-honours, he said, had become the fox in the Westminster hen coop. There were chickens everywhere, and none of them had heads.

It was a nice image. Kitson's face was as deadpan as ever but there was a glint of amusement in his eyes. Or maybe satisfaction.

'Your Mr Mallinder . . . ' He reached for the file. 'Shame, really. What exactly happened?'

Faraday briefly outlined the facts. Mallinder had been the victim of an extremely professional killing. Forensics, for once, had failed to come up with a single piece of worthwhile evidence. Enquiries were ongoing, and a couple of leads might offer a way forward, but the key issue remained motive. Who'd want to organise a hit like this? And why?

Kitson nodded. Mallinder, he said, had been one of hundreds of names to come to the squad's attention. As far as straight donations were concerned he'd never qualified for interview because the only cheque he ever wrote had been comfortably below the declarable limit. But his more recent interest in the City Academy programme was rather different.

'You talked to him?'

'No.'

'Why not?'

'Because in the end there were no grounds for interview. But in a way it's more complex than that. When this thing kicked off, the focus was on the loans issue. Here you've got rich guys putting large sums of money in the pot. You have to declare donations like that and some of them don't want publicity. Neither does New Labour. And so those donations become loans. Loans aren't declarable, as long as they're genuine. That means a commercial rate of interest, and given the state of New Labour's finances, that's going to be at the high end, four or five per cent above base. Are they paying that rate? Very good question. And are these even loans at all? We wait to be convinced.'

'How does all this link to Mallinder?'

'Obliquely. Earlier this year he came up with two and a half million quid. That's a lot of money. Unlike other big donors, he was very picky about the terms. He wanted five per cent above base rate and he wanted a repayment schedule that gave him the right to demand the capital back at any time of his choosing. The New Labour people weren't at all keen. That's why they tried to steer him towards the City Academy programme.'

221

'And would that be a money loan?'

'No. A straight grant, a donation if you like, though the people at the Department of Education refer to it in terms of a stake. If you bung New Labour two and a half million quid for a new City Academy you become a stakeholder. You also move to the top of the list when it comes to honours though naturally they all say it's not that simple.'

'And Mallinder?'

'Mallinder was a strange bird. For a start, like I say, he seemed very nervous about his capital. He didn't want to lose it. In fact he wanted to be sure he could have it back just as soon as he needed it. That told us that the source of the money — his money — was a bit rocky.'

'But if he bought into a City Academy, he'd lose it all anyway. Isn't that the case?'

'Exactly. That's what we thought. And it's true. So that posed us a question. Just why would he suddenly become Mr Bountiful? Kiss goodbye to two and a half million quid?'

'Because they'd promised him something.'

'Maybe. Either that or he *thought* there was some kind of deal on offer.'

'Like what?'

Kitson abandoned the file. This was speculation now, by no means evidenced, but in his view there might be plausible grounds for thinking that Mallinder had got himself the inside track on estate negotiations with the Ministry of Defence. The negotiations related to land at Tipner on the edges of something called the Gateway Project.

'A kind of land-for-academy swap.' It was Suttle. He was grinning.

'Exactly.'

'And you're saying this isn't evidenced?'

'Not at all. But that doesn't mean Mallinder didn't think it *could* happen. There are two keys here. One is intent, Mallinder's intent. The other is the timeline.'

He returned to the file. Mallinder had come up with the money in February. Within weeks he was discussing the possibility of a City Academy in Portsmouth. A month later, in early May, the money had been abruptly withdrawn.

'But that was because there were difficulties in Portsmouth,' Faraday pointed out.

'That's true. But from Mallinder's point of view I suspect that turned out to be a blessing in disguise. It gave him cover. It got him off the hook.'

'I see . . . ' Faraday nodded. 'So why had he so suddenly withdrawn the offer?'

'Good question. What do you think?'

There was a moment or two of silence. Faraday could hear the distant clatter of a helicopter. Then Suttle cleared his throat.

'Either there was a problem with the money,' he said, 'or he finally realised the MoD thing was a non-starter. From what I understand there was never any prospect of land release.'

'You're right.' Kitson nodded. 'So what does that make Mallinder? Apart from wrong?'

'An optimist.' It was Faraday this time. 'But then that's been his MO from the start. This is the guy who never takes no for an answer. I can

223

imagine everyone telling him the MoD wouldn't budge an inch and him paying not the slightest attention. He knows the way money works. He's raised two and a half million quid. He regards it as an investment. The rest, from his point of view, is just conversation.'

'But it wasn't,' Suttle pointed out. 'It didn't work.'

'And so he withdrew. Cut his losses. That's typical too.' Faraday looked at Kitson. 'How did the New Labour people feel about all this?'

'He pissed them off. They won't say so but it's true. Not that any of this helps you guys at all.'

'Quite.' Faraday nodded. 'Or you either, come to that.'

For the first time Kitson smiled. Mallinder was off their list, sure, but they had plenty of other names in the frame. In fact they were spoiled for choice. He paused, glancing up at Faraday.

'So where do you go from here? You mind me asking?'

'Not at all.' Faraday drained the remains of his coffee. 'Ring me in a week's time and I'll let you know.'

* * *

Winter took the Central Line out to Snaresbrook. According to the A-Z, Lavender Road was only half a mile or so from the station. He strolled along in the sunshine, enjoying the warmth on his face.

Number 43a turned out to be an upstairs

corner unit in a sixties block of shops. Looking up from the pavement, Winter could see Venetian blinds in the two windows. One of the blinds had been damaged at the top and hung crookedly down. The other was stained a dirty brown colour. Water penetration, Winter thought. Crap windows with gaps round the edges and no one interested in sorting it out.

The shop beneath belonged to a greengrocer. Winter helped himself to an apple from the display on the pavement and stepped inside. He waited until the young Asian had finished serving. He paid for the apple, then asked about the place upstairs.

'You want?'

'No. But I have a friend who might. It's for rent?'

'Sure.'

'How much?'

'I dunno. Here. You make a call. The woman, she tells you.'

He knelt quickly, peering under the counter, and emerged with a business card. Ghitta Hira.

'She's a friend of yours? This lady?'

'Sure. You want anything else?' He gestured at the apple.

Winter said no. The entrance to the unit upstairs was at the back of the building. He followed the pavement round and pushed in through a broken gate. Paint was flaking from a flight of wooden stairs and there were scorch marks round the letter box in the door at the top. Winter took his time, testing his weight on the stairs. Then he bent to peer through the letter box. Mail lay scattered on the bare floor. There was a sour smell and the *plink-plink* of water dripping into a stainless steel sink.

He stood upright again, peering at the number on the business card. It took a while to answer. A woman's voice, Asian again.

Winter asked about 43a Lavender Road. He had a friend who was looking for office accommodation.

'He's too late, your friend.'

'It's gone?'

'Yes.'

'When?'

'This morning. It was very cheap.' Winter heard a baby crying in the background. 'I've got more, though. You want to see them?'

12

MONDAY, 11 SEPTEMBER 2006. 06.57

Jimmy Suttle was back at Kingston Crescent by seven o'clock. To his surprise, Major Crimes was buzzing. Phones were ringing everywhere and there was a knot of senior detectives deep in conversation at the far end of the long central corridor. Suttle stepped into the Intelligence Cell. Imber and Tracy Barber were still at their desks. Definitely something up.

'What's going on?'

Imber was talking to somebody on the phone. Tracy asked dryly about Suttle's day out in London.

'It was fine. What's the problem here?'

'You haven't heard?'

'No.' Suttle shook his head. 'So why don't you tell me?'

Imber was coming off the phone. He glanced up at Suttle then began punching in a fresh number.

'Someone tried to kill a government minister,' he said briefly. 'Just down the bloody road.'

* * *

Winter caught up with the news as soon as he got home. BBC News 24 had dropped every other story and were reporting live from the

227

scene of the incident. Winter recognised the distinctive logo of the Tesco Express on Goldsmith Avenue. The reporter was standing on the pavement in front of a loop of blue police tape. The road had been closed to traffic and Winter counted three SOC vans parked by the kerb. In the background a line of figures in baggy grey forensic suits were shuffling forward on their hands and knees, examining every inch of the tarmac.

The live pictures cut to footage shot an hour or so earlier. Some punter had evidently been taping trains from the bridge over Fratton Station. He'd heard what proved to be gunshots and he'd made it along Goldsmith Avenue in time to catch the traffic backed up around a distant Vauxhall saloon. People were standing on the pavement, staring at the car. The driver's door was open and one of the rear windows was smashed. The picture wobbled, swimming in and out of focus as the man holding the camera began to run again. Winter could hear the rasp of his breath on the soundtrack. When someone stepped in front of him, he pushed them aside.

Much closer now, a figure was visible in the back of the car. He was bent over something slumped on the rear seat. It dawned on Winter that this something was still alive. The driver extracted himself from the car, a phone pressed to his ear. Already, in the far distance, the wail of an ambulance siren.

The pictures cut again. Paramedics in green were carefully manhandling an inert body from the back of the Vauxhall. The head was swathed in what looked like a white towel and one of the paramedics was holding up a drip. Three traffic cars had arrived, using the clear lane on the other side of the road. There must have been fifty or sixty people by now, massed on the pavement, pressing forward for a better look, and Winter watched as the uniforms yelled at the crowd to get back.

The paramedics had eased the body onto a stretcher. They wheeled it quickly towards the waiting ambulance. The camera zoomed jerkily, closing on the stretcher, and Winter had time to make out a spreading crimson blotch on the towel before his view was blocked. Seconds later the ambulance was accelerating away, traffic cars fore and aft, blues and twos.

Back in the studio, the newscaster linked to another live update. The reporter was standing beside the approaches to the A & E Department at the Queen Alexandra Hospital. The minister was still in theatre undergoing emergency surgery. A spokesman for the hospital described his condition as critical. He'd suffered multiple gunshot wounds to the lower face and right shoulder. If he survived the next few hours, it was likely that he'd be transferred to a specialist neurological ward in Southampton.

Winter's phone began to ring. Stepping backwards, still watching the screen, he felt for the receiver. He knew already who it was.

'Baz,' he said. 'Are you watching what I'm watching?'

'Yeah.' Mackenzie was laughing. 'You're right, mate. Dodge fucking City.'

★ ★ ★

Willard had resisted the temptation to take charge and satisfied himself with a seat at the far end of the conference table. The meeting had just begun when Faraday slipped into the one remaining chair. Martin Barrie, as calm and methodical as Faraday had ever seen him, was confirming the precise sequence of events for those around the table who needed to get their bearings. He wanted no ambiguities, no deviation from the established facts.

The Under Secretary of State for Defence Procurement had arrived in Portsmouth by train. He'd been picked up at the station and driven to Whale Island where he'd shared a stand-up buffet with senior naval officers and an assortment of invited civilians before descending to the auditorium to deliver the keynote address at a day-long conference on the future shape of logistics integration across NATO. After the speech he'd stayed long enough on the platform to field perhaps a dozen questions. The conference had been sponsored by British Aerospace and he'd spent some minutes in conversation with a handful of their senior executives before leaving.

By now, said Barrie, it was nearly four o'clock. As a favour to one of Portsmouth's two MPs, the minister had agreed to make an appearance at a party to celebrate the hundredth birthday of a constituent who'd once served in the Royal Navy. The party was being held in a community hall in Milton and the MoD press office had

230

organised a photocall. The minister was driven across the city and arrived at about four fifteen. He'd accepted a cup of tea and a slice of birthday cake and chatted to the veteran and his family while a photographer circled, taking shots. Afterwards, still in the hall, there'd been a handful of media interviews — two TV crews and a reporter from Radio Solent — before the minister had said his goodbyes and departed.

The minister, together with a special adviser, was taking the train back to London. The station was barely ten minutes away. The driver knew the route.

Best estimate for the minister's departure from the community hall, said Barrie, was a minute or two before five o'clock. The treble nine calls — one from the driver, another seven from members of the public — had been logged at 17.03. Uniforms and D/Cs were still collecting witness statements but there was now a broad consensus on what had happened in Goldsmith Avenue.

The Vauxhall had been travelling west, towards Bradford Junction and the turn north to the Town Station. The car had come to a halt, trapped in a long queue of traffic. A motorcyclist had pulled up beside the rear offside door of the Vauxhall. The guy riding pillion had produced a handgun, firing down through the window at the minister. He'd taken the first bullet in the side of the face. The next one, as he tried to shield himself, had caught him in the upper shoulder. Two more shots had missed.

After that, according to a witness watching from the pavement outside Tesco Express, the

231

bike had roared away, cutting between two cars and making a left down Haslemere Road. House to house enquiries were ongoing to try and establish a precise route but so far there'd been no sign of the bike itself.

The RN driver had described it as a Kawasaki, colour blue. Neither he nor any other witness had a record of the registration. Nor were the physical descriptions of the two riders especially helpful. One was bigger than the other. They'd both been wearing leathers, gloves and full-face helmets with darkened visors. One witness thought she might have seen a black holdall strapped to the rack on the back of the bike. But she was by no means certain.

Barrie looked at the faces around the table.

'Anyone got anything to add?'

The silence was broken by Willard. He emphasised the need for steady, thorough, meticulous policework. What had happened in Goldsmith Avenue, thanks largely to the amateur video footage, was on TV screens across the world. The spotlight had fallen not simply on the city, but on the team still assembling to investigate.

Within the last hour the Chief had had one conversation with Downing Street and another with the Home Secretary. Jurisdiction over the coming days and weeks would remain with Hantspol but there was naturally a concern about resources. Willard himself would happily accept all the help on offer but he was adamant that the people around this table would be able to cope. The fact that a minister of the crown had been the target was, in a way, a distraction. If the minister didn't make it, then this would be a murder, just like any other. If he survived, then they'd still be putting a case together, assembling evidence, eliminating suspects, and finally — God willing — putting faces in the dock. This is what they did. This was what they were bloody good at. He wished them well and then he looked at his watch. As he stood up one of the D/Ss enquired about the command structure. The investigation already had an operational codeword, *Polygon*. Just who was in charge?

'Detective Superintendent Barrie.' Willard nodded at the thin figure at the head of the table. 'With D/I Faraday as deputy SIO.'

* * *

Winter kept the TV on for the rest of the evening, channel-hopping as the ripples of what had happened in Goldsmith Avenue spread wider and wider. By ten o'clock, in an extended news special, BBC One were openly speculating about the likelihood of terrorist involvement, al-Qaeda temporarily abandoning suicide bombings to open a new front in the war against the infidel.

Targeted assassinations, in the view of one studio pundit, offered an extremely effective weapon in a global village addicted to breaking news. Not only was the killing of a government defence minister guaranteed to seize worldwide attention, but because the bloodshed was so confined, the larger Muslim population might well be spared the backlash that came with random slaughter. More important still, the very efficiency of the act — four bullets in a rush-hour traffic jam and so far not a trace of the perpetrators — was a chilling reminder that militant Islam could reach into the very heart of Western democracies. No one is safe, went the message. A government complicit in the deaths of hundreds of thousands of Iraqis had very publicly been held to account. Those who live by the sword shall suffer the consequences.

This theory, to Winter, had its merits. The dodgier of the ragheads were obviously out of control and a stunt like this would certainly keep bums on seats for a day or two, but everything he knew about the local Muslim communities told him that the BBC's pundit was wrong. By and large, these were hard-working, conscientious families who kept their heads down and their noses clean. They ran restaurants, flogged saris and made sure their kids did their homework every night. A little bit of that, thought Winter, wouldn't go amiss on the city's white estates.

He changed channels to catch *Newsnight*, lingering to watch the amateur footage for the umpteenth time before diving into the kitchen for more ice cubes. If the al-Qaeda lot turned out to be genuinely in the frame, then why on earth kill the bloke responsible for defence *procurement*? Terrorists were supposed to be savvy. They'd surely go for someone with real blood on their hands — the top guy at the ministry or a senior general or the foreign secretary, or even Blair himself. But then, as the

234

paramedics raced the bleeding body towards the waiting ambulance, he thought about the level of protection these people must have, and how much easier it would be to choose a nice soft target, someone further down the ministerial pecking order. Earlier on he'd watched the unconscious figure on the trolley swapping small talk at some kind of birthday party. He'd seemed a nice enough guy. He had a smile for the ladies and the patience to listen to the usual drivel. Who'd ever expect to find someone like that on the end of an al-Qaeda bullet?

He shook his head, backing into the kitchen with his empty glass, trying to imagine the scene at Kingston Crescent. According to Channel Four, all police leave in the county had been cancelled and location reports had included shots of white Transit vans arriving on the motorway packed with reinforcements. Occasions like this, all too bloody rare, were truly special and Winter felt a physical ache at the knowledge that he could no longer be part of it all. With half the country breathing down your neck, the pressure would be awesome but there was nothing in the world to compare with the hot adrenalin rush of pushing the investigative machine to its limits. Informants to run down, arms to bend, calls to make, leads to pursue, doors to kick in, and never — for a second — any bollocks about overtime limits or the need for yet another fucking risk assessment. CID, he thought glumly, could so often be a pain in the arse but on a night like this the rule book would go out of the window.

He splashed Glenfiddich over the ice in his glass, resisting the temptation to pick up the phone and bell Jimmy Suttle. The boy would be working his arse off just now, with absolutely no time for some sad old buffer with his blanket and his Thermos and his seat in the stands. No, the war stories would come later, a pint or three in the Buckingham and maybe a curry in the place across the road afterwards.

The thought put a smile on Winter's face and he returned to the lounge to find Willard fending off a pack of reporters outside Force HQ in Winchester. Early enquiries, he said, had already thrown up a number of leads. A substantial squad of men and women would be chasing down every particle of information. Like everyone else in the world, he naturally hoped for an early breakthrough but not for a moment did he underestimate the size of the challenge they all faced. In reply to a shouted question about the gloves coming off, he paused.

'We work within the constraints of the law,' he said. 'You'd expect nothing else.'

Watching, Winter recognised the tone of voice, the subtlest hint of a smile. He was playing with these people. Beneath the gruff officialese he was letting them know that whatever it took, in whatever situation, he'd do it. Too right, thought Winter, wondering again about Gale Parsons.

★　★　★

By one in the morning Faraday knew it was time to leave. The last five hours had left him drained.

One meeting seemed to blur into the next, and with the ever-changing sequence of faces around Barrie's conference table came a never-ending series of interruptions — priority callers on the phone, apologetic knocks on the door, urgent messages delivered by hand.

Barrie himself, to the surprise of many, had remained totally unflustered in the eye of this storm, addressing one issue after another, calling for clarification over this point or that, seeking all the time to identify worthwhile investigative pathways forward as the sheer volume of incoming information threatened to overwhelm them.

The key task in these early hours, he kept reminding everybody, was concentration. They had to keep an open mind. They had to sift. They had to assess. And soon, once the focus became a little sharper, they had to eliminate. His one concession to Operation *Polygon*'s quickening drumbeat was an hourly break for a roll-up and a trip to the open window beside his desk, leaving others to sort out yet another round of coffees.

Past midnight, he called a halt. Only Faraday remained in his office. As the evening lengthened he'd compiled a list of developments. House-to-house checks by a small army of uniforms and D/Cs along the motorbike's presumed escape route had so far failed to raise anything of real significance. South of Goldsmith Avenue lay a warren of terraced streets, dozens of intersections, an endless choice of turns for a man in a hurry. Aggregate all those streets and you were looking at literally thousands of front doors.

Many of these people had been out at work or at the back of the house, and all of them were only too used to the howl of a passing motorbike. One pensioner at the northern end of Haslemere Road thought she might have spotted something through her net curtains. Another woman, much younger, reported seeing a blue motorbike with a pillion passenger making a left turn into Grayshott Road. She'd been on foot, wheeling her nipper back from the nursery, and it was only all the stuff on telly that had prompted her to make a call.

The bike, she said, had been going slowly. She'd had to stop on the kerb to let it make the turn. There'd been nothing at all to raise her suspicions. Asked for a description, she'd said the person on the pillion was much smaller than the driver. Also, she thought she remembered something distinctive on the forks that held the front wheel, a sticker or something, black and yellow. And, yes, there'd been a holdall strapped on the back panier rack.

The mention of Grayshott Road had at least been a lead. From here, the bike could have motored the half-mile or so to the Eastney Road. Directly north lay one of the major routes out of the city. At five fifteen, the Eastern Road was choked with rush-hour traffic and Barrie had ordered an appeal through the media for homebound drivers who might have spotted a blue Kawasaki. That appeal had produced nothing of any real value and neither — so far — had a trawl through the afternoon's CCTV tapes.

Within fifteen minutes of the shooting, traffic cars had been stationed alongside all three roads off the island, with others at the ferry terminals. That left a tiny chink in Pompey's wall but these roads were covered by cameras, and although there'd been dozens of motorbikes amongst the traffic, none of the CCTV sightings had precisely matched the target.

Other cameras monitored key roads and junctions across the city and Barrie had a team of four D/Cs combing through hours of pictures, while others sat beside the control room staff, monitoring live feeds as the evening went on.

Then, at dusk, had come a call from a woman who worked at The Orchards, a new psychiatric unit beside St James' Hospital. She, like everyone else, had been watching the coverage on television. Late in the afternoon, she said, she'd been looking out of the window and had seen a motorbike coming down the road that led to the unit. Beyond the turn into the car park lay the back gate to the hospital itself. The main gates were always padlocked but the side gate was open for staff on foot. Unusually, the bike had squeezed through the gate and then disappeared. At the time, she'd thought nothing of it. Only now, remembering the two leather-clad figures on the bike, did she start to wonder.

St James' Hospital was barely a mile from the scene of the hit. At Barrie's prompting, Faraday had sent a couple of D/Cs to interview the woman and dispatched a dozen uniforms to the hospital with instructions to comb the grounds. They'd been hard at it for three hours now but

239

by midnight there was still no trace of the blue Kawasaki. The conclusion, comfortable or otherwise, was only too clear.

The bike had been dumped somewhere else within the city, enabling the riders to make their escape at a time of their choosing. Shedding their leathers, they could have left by car, by public transport, even by ferry or hovercraft. They could be in London by now, or on the Isle of Wight, or even abroad. In the seven hours since the shooting, hundreds of flights had departed from Heathrow, Gatwick, Southampton and Bournemouth. The guys on the Kawasaki could be literally anywhere.

That left the bike itself. Alongside the house-to-house calls and revisits, Barrie had ordered a detailed street-by-street check on every garage, lock-up and patch of waste ground within a steadily expanding radius south of Goldsmith Avenue. The task was enormous but for once he could call on almost limitless manpower, and on the basis of progress reports from the Major Incident Room, he expected the south-east quadrant of the city to have been thoroughly checked within twenty-four hours. If nothing turned up, then he'd extend the search north and west, covering the whole of the island on which the city was built, but in truth he thought that unlikely. Already he sensed that these people had done their homework. There were simply too many CCTV cameras to risk any kind of breakout.

A professional hit. Almost certainly. Every fresh scrap of evidence — or lack of it

— suggested a carefully planned operation. The choice of time and place for the killing, the city in its usual state of rush-hour gridlock. The decision to use a motorbike, with near-perfect concealment inside a helmet and full leathers. Even the choice of weapon. According to the Scenes of Crime Co-ordinator, no spent cases had been recovered from the road. That meant the use of a revolver, rather than an automatic handgun, leaving only the bullets themselves, deformed lead slugs, to offer any kind of forensic lead. A couple had been dug out of the Vauxhall's upholstery. Of the other two, one had been removed from the minister's chest cavity after penetrating his shoulder, while the other was still lodged at the back of his skull, awaiting a second operation at the hands of the neurosurgeons in Southampton.

'How is he?' Barrie had almost forgotten about the victim.

'Still critical, sir.'

'And if he survives?'

'No one's saying. But an injury like that, full face, you'd expect impairment of function at the very least.'

Impairment of function was a horrible phrase and Faraday had only used it because someone else had, and because he was tired. The truth of the matter, he thought grimly, was far more graphic. This man had taken a bullet in the brain. If he was unlucky enough to survive, there'd be precious little function left.

'Poor bastard,' he said softly.

Barrie didn't appear to have heard him. He

wanted Faraday's thoughts on the intelligence picture. Brian Imber and Tracy Barber had spent the evening almost permanently on the phone, chasing their various contacts. Neither Special Branch nor the Serious and Organised Crime Agency could come up with any obvious candidates who might have wanted to kill the Under Secretary of State for Defence Procurement but the intelligence services were taking a very different view.

M15 were currently conducting dozens of surveillance operations on various groups of fundamentalist militants. A top secret report endorsed at the highest level in Thames House was ready for dispatch to Downing Street. The report, it seemed, carried a disturbing analysis of changing patterns in the terrorist threat and warned that UK-based fundamentalists appeared to be in the process of developing sophisticated cell structures very similar to the Provos at the height of the Troubles. Sooner or later one of these cells would mount an operation, and on the phone to Brian Imber a senior analyst had concluded that this was probably it.

The minister's visit had been flagged in various specialist defence magazines. The rush-hour certainty of near-gridlock in the city's traffic offered a perfect opportunity for a hit. The minister himself was unlikely to travel with armed protection. Four bullets at point-blank range would make headlines around the world.

Faraday, pressed for an opinion, thought the M15 view had some merit. The key weapon in the terrorist war was surprise. It was in the interests of these people to keep changing their MO. The lesson of 7/7, after all, was pretty plain. The intelligence services had known nothing about the London bombers, yet four of them had managed to kill fifty-three people.

'So you think Five might be right?'

'I think their analysis holds water. Until now, as far as I know, they've gone for suicide bombings. This is something different but that in itself may be significant. The best terrorist hits come out of nowhere.'

'Of course they do, Joe. But they're not giving us names, are they?'

'No, sir, not yet, but this is huge. Five will have the politicians all over them. The pressure will be enormous. And we should be aware of that too.'

'Of course.' Barrie frowned. He was as exhausted as Faraday. 'So we keep an open mind? Is that what you're saying?'

'I'm afraid so, sir. You wouldn't have it any other way.'

★ ★ ★

And he wouldn't. Faraday was sure about it. He made a start on tidying his desk, then gave up. One o'clock in the morning was far too late to worry about rogue paperwork. He reached for his briefcase, turned out the light, and stepped into the corridor. There was the trill of a telephone and a murmur of conversation from a nearby office. At the other end of the corridor, through the open door into the incident room, he could see the Outside Enquiries D/S locked

243

in conversation with one of the civilian indexers. Passing the Intelligence Cell, he paused. The lights were still on. He gave the door a gentle push, then peered round it. Jimmy Suttle was bent over a file on his desk, pen in hand. A pad at his elbow was covered in figures.

It took him a moment or two to realise he had company.

'Sir?'

'Bit late, isn't it?' Faraday nodded at the desk. 'What's keeping you?'

'Mallinder's bank details, sir.' Suttle stifled a yawn. 'I've only just got round to them.'

13

Winter sped north along the Meon Valley. The moment the cabbie had picked him up at Blake House, he'd insisted on a change of station on the radio. Virgin FM was fine for brain-dead thirty-somethings trying to kid themselves they were still young but on a day like today you very definitely needed Five Live.

Already, by the time they got to Fareham, he'd listened to Portsmouth South's venerable MP expressing his city's shock and grief at yesterday's events. Now, in a neat twist, someone had come up with the notion of talking to the football club's new owner, an ex-Israeli Army sniper of Russian extraction who presumably knew a thing or two about the application of extreme violence.

As it happened, the interview proved to be a non-starter, not least because Alexandre Gaydamak was unavailable, but Winter sat back, his briefcase on his knees, deeply satisfied that Pompey — both the city and the club — had finally earned its place in the sun. Not only had Goldsmith Avenue featured on TV screens worldwide but the Blues had just found themselves at the very top of the Premiership. Not one result, but two.

The Five Live presenter was taking phone-ins

245

on the wider implications of the Pompey hit.

Winter stationed his face in the rear-view mirror, catching the cabbie's attention. 'What do you think?'

'Dunno, mate, but the way this bloody government's carrying on, I say fair play to the geezer.'

'There were two of them.'

'Geezers then. Who cares? Bloody politicians, two a penny. Tell you something, though.'

'What's that?'

'It might make someone sort the fucking traffic out. Takes you forever to get anywhere down Pompey. Complete disgrace. Carry on the way we are, and this job won't be worth tuppence.'

Winter grinned, then leaned forward to listen to an item of breaking news. He didn't catch the details but he was sure it was in connection with the shooting.

'They've found that motorbike.' The cabbie was laughing. 'You'll never guess where.'

★ ★ ★

The breakthrough sent a ripple down the corridor at Major Crimes. Glen Thatcher, the Outside Enquiry D/S in the Incident Room, had lifted the phone to Faraday the moment he'd taken the call from the D/C on site.

'Blue Kawasaki, sir. Nine hundred cc. Black and yellow chequers on the front forks. We've got it down as nicked four days ago. Has to be the one. Has to be.'

'Where was it?'

'In some kind of derelict building — it's not clear from the report. Seems someone's poured paint stripper all over it.'

'But where?'

'St James, sir. In the hospital grounds. Turns out that woman from The Orchards was right.'

Faraday stared at the window. In the welter of enquiries last night, he'd almost forgotten about the call from the woman who'd spotted the two figures on the motorbike. St James was the city's psychiatric hospital, a substantial Victorian pile with extensive grounds. Many of the wards had been closed after the shift to community care but it still housed a sizeable group of long-stay patients. Oddly enough, it lay within half a mile of the Bargemaster's House. Faraday passed it daily en route to work.

He bent to the phone again. First things first.

'Have you talked to Scenes of Crime, Glen?'

'Yes, sir. I passed the word on. They're going to blitz it.'

'What about the hospital management?'

'The lads on site are talking to them now.'

Faraday nodded. The scene would need to be isolated. Then would come the interviews, dozens of them. The Outside Enquiry teams would need to quiz anyone in a position to see the long drive that threaded past The Orchards into the hospital grounds from Locksway Road. Many of these potential witnesses would presumably be inpatients and Faraday permitted himself a grim smile, imagining certain D/Cs on the squad trying to tease any sense from some of the St James' veterans. The guys on the Kawasaki had known exactly what they were about. Clever.

Glen Thatcher was still on the phone.

'Is there anything apart from the bike?' Faraday asked him. 'Leathers? Gloves? Helmets?'

'Not that anyone's told me, sir.'

'Fine. I'll pass this on to Mr Barrie. He's up at headquarters this morning.'

★　★　★

A bubbling pot of freshly made coffee was waiting for Winter by the time the cab dropped him at Esme's place. The smell greeted him as she opened the front door and she warmed the welcome still further by giving him a smile. There were toys all over the polished beechwood floor and Winter picked his way between an abandoned sit-on tractor and a yellow mini-slide as he followed her into the huge kitchen. She was wearing an apron and a pair of rubber gloves. The woman from the village who did the cleaning was down with flu.

Esme was as hooked by events in Pompey as Winter himself. She gestured up at a small portable TV wedged between a line of recipe books and a row of glass storage jars.

'Amazing, isn't it?'

She stripped off the gloves and poured the coffee while Winter helped himself to a stool to watch the TV. A junior government minister in the studio was acknowledging the need for enhanced security. Until now armed protection had been allocated on a strictly needs-must basis. After yesterday all that would change. He sounded, if anything, relieved.

'Has my dad talked to you this morning? Only he seems to have made a few calls last night and one of them was to a buddy of his in Dubai. This guy spent some time in Los Angeles. He's got part-shares in a couple of marinas and Dad wondered whether he'd come across this woman you both met.'

'And?'

'He says not. Dad thought it was odd, that's all.'

'Los Angeles is a big place.' Winter helped himself to another biscuit. 'There must be loads of people in her game.'

'Sure. He just wanted me to pass it on. He also asked me to draw up some kind of contract.' Her eyes strayed to the television. 'So what's your take on this lady?'

'She's a looker.'

'So I gather.'

'And she certainly talks the talk.'

'That's exactly what Dad said.' She shook her head. 'My poor bloody mother. Sometimes I wonder why she bothers. A decent lawyer and she could walk away with millions. She's still got it too. She could have any guy she wanted.'

'Maybe she loves him.'

'Yeah, I think you're right. You know what my mum once said to me? Before they were even married?'

'No.'

'She said she'd been mad for him ever since the day they first met.'

'So why didn't she marry him earlier?'

'Because that's not the way you play it with Dad. He knows exactly what he wants and he'll be all over you to get it so the trick is to hold off. I've done it myself. It works a treat. He's like a kid. The last word you should ever use is 'yes'.'

Winter grinned. The change in Esme's attitude was startling. She was treating him like one of the family. She seemed to trust him.

'Here. Have a look at this.' She passed across a stapled sheaf of A4 paper. 'It's just a draft. We can add or subtract as needs be. See what you think.'

Winter glanced through the contract. He was no lawyer but he supposed it made sense. At the end of the document, in the clause dealing with the fee payable for Katherine Brodie's exclusive services, there was a space left blank.

'How far is he prepared to go? Has he mentioned a figure?'

'Yes.'

'What is it?'

'Seven thousand a month.'

'A *month*? That's a fortune. Or at least for him it is.'

'Exactly. Dad doesn't make offers like that, not without due cause.' She glanced across at Winter again. 'That's why I thought we ought to ask a few questions first, find out a little more about this woman.'

'We?'

'You.' She offered him a cordless phone from the pocket of her apron. 'There's an extension out in the hall, if you'd prefer. Or you could use the study.'

'No problem.' Winter took the phone. 'This'll do fine.'

He still had the K-MAX card in his pocket. He dialled the mobile number on the back. It answered after two rings.

'Who is this?' It was Brodie. That faint hint of California in her voice.

Winter thanked her for the lunch. She said it was a pleasure. Then she asked what she could do for him.

'We need to meet again. Soon.'

'Of course. This afternoon some time? Round five, maybe? Or tomorrow? Your call.'

Winter covered the mouthpiece with his hand. He needed a lift to the station and a proper copy of the contract. Esme said yes to both. Winter went back on the line.

'Five o'clock's perfect,' he said.

'Fine, though it'll have to be somewhere central, I'm afraid. Why don't we say the Savoy again? We could have an early drink. That OK with you?'

★ ★ ★

With Barrie still stranded at Winchester, Faraday took temporary charge of *Polygon*. His first call went to one of the D/Cs who'd been dispatched to interview the registered owner of the Kawasaki. He lived in Southampton, and en route back to Portsmouth the D/C was explaining what had happened with the bike.

251

The owner, he said, was a third-year student at Southampton University. He had an evening job as a barman at a run-down pub on the edges of Sholing, a suburb on the city's eastern edge, and he'd left his bike in the car park all evening, walking out after closing time to find it gone. The bike had been locked up but someone had attacked the heavy-duty chain.

'CCTV?'

'Couple of cameras in the car park, boss, but apparently the recorder's on the blink.'

'No pictures, then?'

'No.'

Faraday wanted to know more about the pub. The state of the CCTV system might suggest someone with inside knowledge. How long had the recorder been down?

'The tenant says a fortnight, at least. You can safely double that.'

'What's the place like?'

'Crap. Full of low life. You'd have to be desperate to work there but apparently the money's OK. This is a guy who lives on fuck all, boss. I get the impression he can't afford to be choosy.'

'Did you statement him?'

'Yeah.'

Faraday thanked him and put the phone down.

Responsibility for the SOC teams lay with the Crime Scene Coordinator. A recent promotion had given Jerry Proctor the job and since this morning he'd been sharing an office down the corridor. He was a huge man with a wealth of sharp-end experience, and Faraday was extremely glad to have him on board. The SOC team had been at St James for a couple of hours now. Faraday wanted an update.

'They've done a preliminary trawl, boss. This is what we've got so far.'

A couple of keystrokes on Proctor's laptop raised a series of crime scene photos, pumped across from the hospital grounds within the last ten minutes. Faraday found a chair and wedged himself behind the desk, peering at the images. The first showed a long narrow road, edged on the right by a red-brick wall. Proctor's finger indicated a series of buildings on the left.

'This one's the Child Development Centre. Beyond that is The Orchards.'

The Orchards had only been open a couple of years, a handsome crescent-shaped building with a slightly Oriental roofline.

'It's a psychiatric unit,' Proctor explained. 'Takes all sorts. Two wards plus some single rooms.'

'And the other side of this wall?'

'Playing fields for the university.'

Faraday nodded. The next photos showed the gate that offered access to the hospital grounds. Beyond the gate was an acre or so of wasteland — a wilderness of shrubs, bushes and piles of plastic bags heaped against the same brick wall.

'The lads concentrated here first, poked around in the undergrowth, found nothing.'

'Then what?'

'They widened the search parameters. By midnight they'd been over the whole site, still nothing. The skipper in charge left a couple of blokes to keep an eye on things and started again at first light. A couple of hours later he got lucky.'

Faraday found himself looking at a two-storey building with a pitched red roof. Every window and door had been boarded up and the ruin was secured by a two and a half metre chain-link fence. According to Proctor, the building had once served as a self-contained ward, one of a number of villas in the hospital grounds. He keyed the next shot.

'Here.' He was pointing to a security gate set into the fence. 'One of the blokes was bright enough to get a groundsman along. This guy had a key to the padlock and you know what? It didn't fit.'

The team had called for a pair of bolt-cutters. They went through the padlock and took a good look at the exterior of the building. Out of sight of the path lay a side door. This too had been secured but this time the padlock was missing. Pushing inside, they'd found the blue Kawasaki. The bike featured in the next series of shots. SOC investigators, alerted by the search team, had brought in extra lighting and the bike was on its stand. The paint on the fuel tank had bubbled and close-ups showed damage to the seats and wiring.

'Turns out it wasn't paint stripper at all but acid, probably sulphuric. Nasty but bloody effective. It's going to take us a while to try and recover anything useful but I wouldn't hold your breath.'

Faraday nodded. This was more evidence, if he needed it, that these people were forensically aware. First the use of a revolver, minimising evidence at the scene. Then the careful selection of a place to dump the bike. Now a thorough dousing in sulphuric acid, effectively removing any possible traces of DNA. Seldom had he come across a job as meticulously planned as this.

'What about access?'

'The main entrance to the hospital is here, off Locksway Road.' The grid of thumbnails had been replaced by a full-screen map. 'There's a roundabout in front of the main building and a one-way system that takes you round the whole site. The bike was found here, on the eastern edge of the site. There's a building still in use in front of the derelict villa but coming in from the back you'd be home safe. No one to clock you. Nothing but rubbish and scrub.' Proctor's thick finger settled briefly on a carefully drawn rectangle close to the perimeter of the site. 'The access road they used leads straight to the villa.'

Faraday followed the thin black line. From the villa to Locksway Road, according to Proctor, was five hundred metres.

'So what are we saying?' He leaned back in the chair.

'My guess is this. They drive in along the access road past The Orchards, just like the woman said. They push the bike round the back. There's a rough path through the undergrowth.'

'Tyre tracks?'

'The lads have trampled most of it. We're still

looking.' He frowned, staring at the map. 'So when these guys get to the access gate round the back of the building, they do the padlock, push the bike in, do the second padlock on the door, then get the bike inside the building itself. Once you've got the door shut behind you, you can take your time.'

Faraday nodded. He remembered reports of the holdall on the back of the Kawasaki.

'They're carrying the acid?'

'Yeah.'

'They douse the bike? Get changed? Stuff the leathers and the helmets in the holdall? Leave?'

'Exactly.'

'Replacing the padlock on the gate in the fence?'

'Yeah. That way we'd assume the building was still secure.'

'Then what?'

'Then they've got options. They're in civvy kit now, just a couple of guys. The hospital's wide open. They could have been anybody.'

'But how do they leave?'

'Either back the way they came, which wouldn't be favourite.'

'Why not?'

'Too exposed. For my money they'd just walk through the hospital site and come out the back gate. There's a neat little estate just here . . . ' he indicated a tangle of roads north of the hospital grounds ' . . . plus a route that takes you out to Warren Avenue and away. They'd have pre-parked a car. Piece of piss.'

Faraday was still eyeing the map. 'What about

the playing fields? How high's the wall?'

'Two metres at least. And once you're over, there's a longish walk.'

'You're right. And it's overlooked.'

The playing fields backed on to Faraday's house. He gazed at the screen, lost for words. The thought that these two men might have been visible from his own back window was deeply ironic.

'They'd obviously done a recce, planned the whole thing out.' Proctor was clearly impressed. 'All in all, it was a beautiful piece of work. If our lad hadn't wondered about the gate in the fence, we'd still be looking.'

'Sure.' Faraday nodded. 'So how did they do the padlock?'

'Pad*locks*, boss, plural. Remember, there were two of them. Bolt cutters. Had to be. Just the way we did it.'

'But how do you manage cutters on a bike?'

'You'd slip them under your leathers. It's not something you'd want to make a habit of but it's perfectly do-able.'

'And afterwards?'

'You'd walk out with them.'

'You don't think they'd be too big for the holdall?'

'Yeah, definitely, but that wouldn't be a problem. You'd just carry them.'

'You're serious? Guys this organised. This *careful*?'

'Sure. It's a tiny risk.'

'No it isn't, Jerry. And you know why? Because these guys don't take risks.' Faraday nodded at the site map. 'We need a Polsa search, every square inch of those grounds. We're looking for the bolt cutters, and if we're really lucky we might find the padlocks he went through, though my guess is he'd have taken them with him.'

'Done, boss. Under way.'

'Excellent.' Faraday got to his feet. 'Then keep me briefed, eh?'

★   ★   ★

At Havant Station, Winter found himself on the same platform as D/S Dave Michaels. Barely weeks before Winter handed in his warrant card, Michaels had left Major Crimes to take up a new posting with the Serious Organised Crime Squad, which operated from a suite of offices at Havant Police Station. Michaels, an age ago, had been with the Met and he still carried with him a whiff of old-style coppering. He'd always shared Winter's appetite for laying artful traps and keeping occasionally dangerous company and had potted some decent villains in the process. With CID becoming daily more risk-averse, Michaels was one of the few ex-colleagues Winter would describe as a real thief-taker.

As the train approached, Winter debated whether or not to make himself known. In the event he needn't have bothered. Michaels, as ever, had spotted him first. He strolled down the platform, nursing a carry-out bag from the station buffet.

'Mr W . . . ' He was beaming. 'What a surprise.'

This time in the afternoon the train was virtually empty. They found a couple of seats either side of a table in a carriage towards the back. Michaels had always been direct to the point of bluntness. To Winter's relief, nothing had changed.

'How's Bazza then?'

'Fine.'

'What's he up to?'

Winter explained briefly about his brother's accident and Mackenzie's plans to mark his passing.

'That sounds almost legit. Where's the dodge?'

'I'm not sure there is one. You know Bazza. It's not money he's after any more, it's status. He wants people to give him a bit of respect. Plus he bores easily. Needs to do something with his time.'

Michaels nodded. He was a big man with a lifelong passion for sport. Like Bazza, he adored football and horse racing and the two men regularly bumped into each other at various venues. The last time he'd seen Mackenzie, he said, was at Glorious Goodwood barely a month ago, the day Kilburn came home in the Maiden Stakes.

'Twenty-five to one,' he said. 'And Bazza had £500 on. Always the same, isn't it? It's the guys with money who make money.'

Afterwards, in the bar, Mackenzie had bought a great deal of champagne.

'I took a couple of glasses off him. He was having a moan about some accountant fella from the Revenue who was always chasing him for paperwork. He thought we'd put him up to it. Pain in the arse, he said.'

'Had you?'

'Not to my knowledge. After *Tumbril* I said we couldn't afford him any more. He thought that was really funny. Kept telling his mates.'

Winter smiled, knowing it had to be true. A couple of years back Willard had mounted Operation *Tumbril*, a covert bid to bring Bazza Mackenzie to his knees. With Faraday at the helm, it had operated in conditions of extreme secrecy. Bazza, alas, had known of its existence from the start, and Dave Michaels was one of the coppers who hadn't been the least bit surprised when *Tumbril* retreated to lick its wounds.

'Complete waste of time.' He was demolishing a bacon roll. 'A year's work and what do you end up with? A six-figure bill and blokes all over the city thinking we'd lost it. The point was, they were right. We *had* fucking lost it. It's way too late to take down someone like Bazza. He's made his money. He's arm's length now. Plus he's protected by people who know what they're doing. Am I right? Of course I fucking am. And you know something else? You're one of them.'

'I am?'

'Of course you are. I'm not blaming you, mate. If we're thinking career move, you're playing a blinder. When was the last time you lost sleep over getting a RIPA through or having a ruck with the fucking budget manager? I bet you really miss all that bollocks.'

Winter sat back as the train whined up the long gradient towards the Buriton tunnel while

Michaels mused about his latest posting. His new squad at Havant had a target list of local criminals as long as your arm plus a decent budget to try and stitch them up. They could call on surveillance, test purchase, covert ops and a variety of elaborate scams, but a couple of months on this new job had made him wary of banking on success.

'It's never easy, Paul.' He wolfed the last of the roll. 'Some of the blokes we're targeting will roll over for a bunch of ripped-off iPods at a silly price, they're that stupid, but the good ones, the quality blokes, they always see us coming, always. And *they're* the ones we're really after. Still . . . ' he balled his paper napkin and dropped it in the bag, ' . . . you'd know about that, eh?'

Winter was beginning to wonder exactly where this conversation might lead. Michael's affable matiness had always disguised the sharpest of brains. He obviously knew that Winter was now working for Mackenzie's organisation. What else might he have picked up?

'Covert was never easy, skip,' Winter said. 'You talk to some of the blokes who go U/C and half of them are headcases.'

Michaels nodded.

'Too right,' he said. 'Spend your waking life pretending to be someone else and you end up not having a clue *who* you fucking are. I've seen it time and again. These poor bastards start out thinking they're Al Pacino but then it dawns on them they're well and truly fucked, bang in the middle of no-man's-land, totally on their tod. If they score any kind of result, then some other fucker grabs the credit. If it all kicks off and they end up hurt, no one bloody wants to know, absolutely *no one*. Watch my lips, mate. U/C sucks.'

The train was seconds away from the tunnel. Winter recognised the trees and scrub crowding in on both sides of the line. Then, without warning, they were plunged into the roaring darkness.

Winter could dimly make out Dave Michaels across the table. The whiteness of his teeth told him the Organised Crime D/S was grinning.

★   ★   ★

Martin Barrie was back in his office, briefing Faraday on developments at Headquarters. The word pressure, he said, didn't do the situation justice.

'The Chief evidently thinks the politicians are using us as a stick to beat the intelligence people. They're feeling badly let down. They're claiming the threat assessment just wasn't there. The word they're using is naked.'

'They're still thinking terrorist?'

'Absolutely. But I gather that's political too. They're looking to build the case for everything from ID cards to surveillance on Muslim communities and Goldsmith Avenue is a gift. The cynic in me says their best result would be no result at all.'

'Meaning?'

'We end up drawing a blank. That way they

can keep the pot boiling. The faceless enemy within. The need for constant vigilance. You know something? I never realised how many votes there are in fear. Scare ourselves shitless and these clowns will be in power for ever.'

'And the pressure?'

'It's coming from the Chief. Call him old fashioned, but he thinks we're investigating attempted murder. He says fairy tales are for politicians. I must say it's extremely refreshing.'

A knock on the door brought Jerry Proctor into the room. For once he had a smile on his face.

'You were right, boss.' He was looking at Faraday. 'They were under a bush, covered in leaves. I get the impression we were lucky to find them.'

'The bolt cutters?'

'Yeah. I had a call a couple of minutes ago.'

'Under a bush where exactly?' Faraday was trying to remember the site plan of the hospital grounds.

'About twenty metres from the back of the derelict villa. Dense undergrowth. Perfect spot.'

'He's coming back for them then.'

'Exactly. We've left it where it is for the time being. So ... ' he glanced across at Barrie, ' . . . what do you want us to do, boss? Your call.'

Faraday brought the Detective Superintendent up to speed. The bolt cutters might well yield DNA or fingerprints, though Faraday rather doubted it. Barrie was looking at Proctor.

'This location isn't overlooked?'

'I understand not, sir.'

'Then recover them. We'll need to mount

263

surveillance overnight. Anyone in the area, anyone, we want to know the reason why. Joe? You want to action that?'

'Yes, sir. There's something else, though.' Proctor had backed out of the office. 'This villa where they stashed the bike, I took a look at it this afternoon. It's derelict, fenced off. For what those guys needed, like Jerry said, the place is absolutely perfect.'

'So what does that tell us?' Barrie was scrolling through a long list of e-mails.

'It tells me, sir, that whoever chose the villa must have known about it beforehand. And to do that they must have had some connection with the hospital.'

Barrie's head lifted from his PC.

'You're saying these guys are loonies? You're telling me we're looking for a *patient*?'

'I doubt it. But maybe a member of staff, or a voluntary worker, or a relative on a visit. Or maybe someone who drops off supplies, laundry, whatever — someone who had a reason for being there, someone who'd have access to the grounds.'

'But not a terrorist?' Barrie, smiling now, reached for the phone.

★ ★ ★

Katherine Brodie was waiting in the American Bar by the time Winter made it to the Savoy. The ankle-length raincoat was spotted from the thin drizzle that curtained the view from the window, and the tan seemed to have faded a little since they'd last met.

'I've just arrived myself.' She shrugged away Winter's apologies for being a couple of minutes late. 'What are you having?'

'My shout. Spritzer again?'

The drinks were served at a table in the corner. Already the bar was beginning to fill, mainly women laden with booty from the pricier corners of Covent Garden, and Winter scanned the room, wondering just how many people could afford to cap an afternoon's shopping with seven-quid glasses of diluted white wine.

'How's your Mr Mackenzie?'

'Baz? He's fine. Sends his love.'

'Nice guy. Visionary too. I took the liberty of making a couple of enquiries.'

'Really? You should have Googled him.'

'I did. Neat site. I really liked it.'

Winter made a mental note to pass the compliment on. Bazza had persuaded a student lodger in one of his many houses to design him a website and had been so delighted with the results that he'd spared him a fortnight's rent.

'Did you see the hotel?'

'I took the virtual tour. The Nile Room? The Aboukir Bar? The Victory Banqueting Suite? We're talking serious history here.'

'Baz just loves all that. When he bought the place it was called the Royal Solent. He dumped the Solent and put Trafalgar on the end. Last year, you can imagine, he made a fortune. You remember the Fleet Review? The fireworks in the evening? The mock battle? All those TV pictures?'

'Yeah.' She nodded. 'They were brilliant. I

265

watched them with my mum. She's half blind. I had to describe what was going on, the fireworks especially, and you know something? With pictures that good you just run out of words.'

Winter nodded, looking at her. Then he raised his glass.

'But you were in California.' He smiled. 'Weren't you?'

The answering grin told Winter everything he needed to know. Too quick. Too bright. Too easy.

'I flew back for a while.'

'Decompressing?'

'To see my mum actually. She wasn't too well. I was in luck. I caught the Trafalgar celebrations. Hey . . . ' She frowned. 'You have a problem with any of this?'

'Yeah.' Winter nodded. 'I think I might. Tell me about 43a Lavender Road.'

'The office?'

'Yeah.'

'What do you want to know?'

'Just . . . ' Winter shrugged ' . . . the facts really. Is it furnished? Or did you have to kit it out yourself?'

She studied him for a long moment, the smile gone.

'You've been there,' she said at length. 'You've checked it out.'

'Of course I have.'

'So you'll know all about it already. The place is a dump. But it's also cheap. And starting any kind of business in this country, you have to watch the bottom line.'

'Me too.'

'What does that mean?'

'I *am* the bottom line.' He took a tiny sip of San Miguel. 'We've got a choice here. Either you tell me what's really going on or I walk through that door.' He nodded towards the lobby. 'And if that happens, believe me, you'll have some serious questions to answer.'

'I'm not hearing any of this.'

'No? I'm a detective, love. Or I was. And that makes me a nasty bastard when it comes to believing people. I'd say you've had to put this thing together in a very big hurry. I'd say you had a couple of days notice to sort out a half-decent legend. I'd say your bosses, your backup, whoever pulls your strings, need a kick up the arse. Given the short notice, you've done fucking well. Last time we were here you were world class, seriously.'

'And now?'

'Now we have a problem.'

'We?'

'Yeah.' The smile, this time, was weary. 'You and me.'

* * *

They left the Savoy. The rain was heavier now, dancing on the roofs of traffic-stalled cabs in the Strand. Winter shepherded Brodie through the press of commuters outside Charing Cross Station. There was a pub off St Martin's Lane where he'd feel a great deal more comfortable. He bought a pint of Guinness for himself, a glass of Stella for Brodie. They found two stools beside a mirror at the end of the bar.

'What's your real name?'

'It doesn't matter.'

'We'll stick to Brodie then?'

'Whatever.'

'OK.' Winter sucked at the Guinness, wiped his mouth with the back of his hand. 'So when did they call you in?'

'Friday afternoon. I was Duty D/S on call for U/C.'

'On call where?'

'It's irrelevant. You don't need to know.'

'But you're U/C trained?'

'The two-week course at Hendon. Passed with flying colours. What a fucking joke.'

'Is this your first job?'

'By no means.'

'So how come you blew it so easily?'

'To be honest I'm not entirely sure. It didn't help that I knew you're a cop, too.'

'Was.'

'No.' She shook her head. 'I don't buy that for a moment. I was there on Monday, remember. I was watching you. In a way you were funny, completely out of your fucking depth, but in another way you were looking out for yourself. You're right. People like us believe nothing. Scary, isn't it?'

Winter didn't answer. Instead, he wanted to know why this operation had been set up in such a hurry.

'There was a feeling you needed a bit of support.'

'Says who?'

'Work it out.'

'Gale Parsons? My minder?' Brodie looked at her hands, said nothing. 'Have you met her?'

'No.'

'She's not running you, then?'

'No. But I gather she was the one who said we had to get a foot in the door pretty damn fast. This Trophy thing needs a great deal of work. Within a week or so you'd have found someone on the media side. Then what do we do?'

'You leave it to me.' Winter raised an eyebrow. 'Don't you?'

'Very good question. And one I put myself.'

'The answer?'

'Same as before. You needed support.'

'Bollocks. You know the real reason better than I do. They don't trust me. They think I've gone over to the Dark Side. For real.'

'Yeah?'

'Yeah.'

'And have you?'

'That's irrelevant.' Winter was studying his empty glass. 'And it's your shout.'

★　★　★

After the pub Winter led the way to an Italian restaurant on the edges of Covent Garden. It was still early, and the place was nearly empty. They specialised in opera tapes, classic arias played slightly louder than was comfortable, giving Winter the chance to bury the conversation under the wail of successive divas. He wanted to know where *Custer* was proposing to go from here.

'We need to do deals,' he said. 'And they have to be kosher.'

'Sure. Of course.'

'So who sorts that out?'

'Me.'

'But you're a cop, love, not some hotshot media agent.'

'I know that. You know that. But there are media agents everywhere. I've spent most of the last forty-eight hours picking their brains. I've even got a list. I know who's good, who cuts the mustard, and I know who to avoid. All you need in this business is the right connections. The money takes care of everything else.'

'What money? Whose money?'

For the first time she laughed. It even sounded genuine. She put her hand over his, beckoned him closer.

'The money's in the event. The money *is* the event. I don't know how you guys ever managed it but you seem to have come up with something that barely needs selling at all. Didn't you ever wonder what made me so plausible back at the Savoy? The first time we met? It's because I wasn't lying. Talk to these guys like I've done and you'll come to the same conclusion. Bunch of crazy jet skiers? Hunkiest young guys in the world? Loads of stunt work? Loads of noise? All the Pompey bollocks? Never underestimate your audience, Paul. They'll *love* it.'

Winter looked at her. He'd crossed a frontier again. He was back on the same patch of turf. Trying to work out whether she was lying or not.

'You're taking the piss,' he said.

'You think so? Or you're not quite sure?'

He wasn't going to give her the satisfaction of an answer. Instead, he fumbled in his pocket and produced Esme's draft contract.

'Read it,' he said. 'Convince me you know what you're talking about.'

'No point. You know what happens in real life? I take it away. I show it to a lawyer. He suggests various changes. Then I come back to you. I think they call it negotiation.'

'Very funny.'

'What's this bit?' She'd got as far as the second page.

'That's Bazza's idea. He wants to offer you free office accommodation. Down at the Trafalgar. Probably a bedroom too, if you ask nicely.'

'Yeah?' She grinned. 'And what else?'

'You're a big girl, love. Handle it.'

'You think I can?'

'I don't think you've got an option. Not if this is ever going to work.' He glanced at his watch then reached for his coat. 'Shall I tell Bazza it's a yes? Only he's bound to ask.'

★   ★   ★

The minister died at five minutes past eight. His wife and two daughters were at his bedside in Southampton and the news was on the nation's screens within twenty minutes. The Prime Minister emerged from 10 Downing Street shortly afterwards and stepped before the waiting cameras to offer a heartfelt tribute to a valued colleague and a close personal friend. He died, he said, as he'd lived. In the service of democracy. An aide hovered in the background with an umbrella but the Prime Minister declined to use it.

In the Major Crimes suite at Kingston Crescent a full *Polygon* squad meet was in progress. A management assistant appeared at Barrie's elbow with a folded slip of paper. The Detective Superintendent announced the news and then called for a minute's silence as a mark of respect. Heads bowed around the room. Despite the recovery of the Kawasaki the inquiry wasn't going well and everyone knew it.

Afterwards, the meeting over, Faraday found himself intercepted by Jimmy Suttle. The young D/C wanted a private word. Faraday, with a to-do list that would take the rest of the evening to untangle, asked whether it could wait. Suttle shook his head.

'It's about Mallinder, sir. And I think it might be important.'

⋆   ⋆   ⋆

Faraday, with D/C Suttle in tow, found his office occupied by a DCI he hadn't seen for a couple of months. After nearly a year at Kingston Crescent, Perry Madison had been posted to the Major Crimes Team at Hulse Road in Southampton. A bluff, intense hill-walker with a very obvious contempt for the smaller courtesies of everyday life, his departure had been greeted with some relief.

Now, for whatever reason, he seemed to be back.

Madison, perched on the edge of Faraday's desk, was on the phone. Faraday waited for the conversation to come to an end. He felt like an intruder in his own office.

'Joe.' Madison extended a hand. 'One of the girls next door told me to help myself. Said you wouldn't mind.'

'Not at all, sir. Joining us, are you?'

Madison didn't reply. Martin Barrie had appeared at the open door. He told Madison he wanted a word. The DCI stepped past Faraday and disappeared. Faraday pushed the door shut with his foot and told Suttle to take a seat. The pile of messages on his desk appeared to have grown.

'This'll have to be quick, son.' He was still thinking about Madison. Detective Chief Inspectors didn't appear by accident. Especially in circumstances like these.

Suttle was talking about Mallinder's financial affairs. He had a number of accounts at Barclays, and the bank had sent him full details.

'I didn't have much time, sir. So I tried to concentrate on the period around February.'

Faraday was desperately trying to track back to the last conversation they'd had about Mallinder. Yesterday's meeting at Scotland Yard felt like another life.

'You remember he came up with the money? The two and a half million pounds?'

'Yes.'

'It turns out to have been a bank loan.'

'Secured on what?'

'That's the point, sir. I made time this morning to talk to the bank. Mallinder had put up some assets from the partnership as collateral. To do that he'd have needed Benskin's signature. The guy at the bank said the loan was only in place for a couple of months. Then it was repaid. In full.'

'And you're saying that's significant?'

'I think it might be, sir, yes.'

'Why?'

'Because Benskin had no time for all this stuff in Portsmouth, especially the Tipner project. He thought it was a waste of space. I talked to Tracy Barber about it this morning. I've even been over the tapes of the interview you both did with him. I *never liked it from the start. The place is a dump. Literally.* That's what he told us, word for word. So why would he be risking two and a half million quid of the firm's money to back something he thought was rubbish?'

'Have you seen the loan agreement?' Faraday was paying attention at last.

'No, sir. But I've asked for a copy.'

'You think . . . ' Faraday sank into his chair ' . . . he might have forged Benskin's signature? Kept the loan details to himself?'

'I guess it's possible.'

'But Benskin would find out, wouldn't he? In double-quick time?'

'Of course, sir. And then he'd want the money back.' Suttle smiled. 'In double-quick time.'

★ ★ ★

274

The summons to Barrie's office came minutes later. Faraday was still thinking about the implications of Mallinder's bank loan. Suttle had a point. The discovery that your business partner had been cheating you might have all kinds of consequences, especially if the stakes were as high as two and a half million pounds.

Barrie was on the phone when Faraday stepped into his office. At the other end of the room, at the head of the conference table, Willard was hunched over a spreadsheet. Beside him, talking on a mobile, was Perry Madison.

'Come in, Joe.' Barrie was off the phone. 'Join us.'

Faraday took a seat at the table. Willard barely looked up. Madison's cold eyes flicked from one face to another as Barrie joined them.

At length Willard folded the spreadsheet and offered Faraday a nod. Madison pocketed his mobile. Already Faraday sensed the direction events were about to take.

'Time is short, gentlemen.' It was Barrie again. 'We're now dealing with a murder inquiry but I don't think that comes as any surprise. It does, however, give us a problem. I raised it with Mr Willard this afternoon. Sir . . . ?'

'We're talking control and command, Joe.' Willard was giving Faraday his full attention now. 'We can't run both *Billhook* and *Polygon* out of the same incident room. It's obvious. It just doesn't work. The indexers are knackered already and it's going to get a whole lot worse. We could transfer *Billhook* to Hulse Road or Grosvenor House but they're both up to their necks with inquiries of their own.'

Faraday nodded. There were major incident rooms in both Southampton and Basingstoke. Either, had they been available, would have been an ideal home for *Billhook*.

'So what do we do, sir?'

'I'm transferring the Mallinder inquiry to the satellite MIR at Fareham. The techies are firing up the Holmes suite as we speak. You'll have a slightly reduced squad of D/Cs but full admin backup. Thanks to our friends in London, we're not short of resources but most of those are going to *Polygon*.'

Faraday was looking at Perry Madison. No wonder he'd been getting used to the feel of Faraday's desk.

'Joe?' It was Willard again. 'You understand what I'm saying?'

'Of course, sir. You're taking me off *Polygon*.'

'I am. I knew it would piss you off but I'm afraid I've got no choice. There's no way you and Martin can lead two inquiries. We'd simply end up hazarding both. You'll be SIO on *Billhook* until things settle down. If you need help, you know where to find me. OK?' He held Faraday's eyes for a moment then nodded at the door.

Faraday got to his feet, glancing at the faces round the table. He knew his disappointment was obvious but he was too exhausted to bother trying to hide it. He thought of saying something, maybe registering just the hint of a protest, but he knew it was pointless. In these situations you did what you were told. As he left the room Faraday paused a moment. Perry

Madison had just cracked a joke at his expense but nobody was laughing.

★ ★ ★

Winter found the message waiting for him on the answering machine when he got back from London. He'd agreed a procedure with D/I Parsons weeks ago, before he'd accepted Bazza's offer. If she urgently needed to get hold of him, she'd ring his home number. She'd pose as the BT operator. She'd asked if the fault on his line had been rectified. She'd quote his BT account number and ask for confirmation for her records. The last six digits would be the last six numbers of a dedicated mobile. The prefix he was to ring was 07961.

Winter replayed the message twice. Parsons, he thought, sounded twitchy. His finger still on the replay button, he looked round for a pencil and a scrap of paper. The rules had been clear. If a message like this arrived, it was imperative he got in touch. He played it a third time, trying to imagine what might have happened. The temptation was to ignore it. It was nearly midnight. The last thing he needed were yet more complications in this crazy life for which he seemed to have volunteered. Then he paused. She may have news that Winter couldn't afford to ignore. Not unless he fancied another conversation with Brett West.

He dialled the number and waited for Parsons to pick up. He couldn't remember whether they were supposed to continue the BT pantomime or not so when she finally lifted the phone he got straight to the point.

'Boss?' he said. 'You phoned.'

'I did. We need to meet.'

'*Again?*'

'Yes.'

'When?'

'Tomorrow, I'm afraid. You'll find an appointment for the Imaging Department on your laptop. Southampton General this time. Five in the afternoon. Be there, OK?'

14

Faraday was back in the Bargemaster's House in time for the eight o'clock news bulletin on Radio Solent. A brisk walk had taken him a couple of miles up the harbourside path. It was low tide and there was a small army of waders picking at the mud but for once he didn't spare them a second glance. Oblivious of the rain he strode on, determined to empty his mind of everything but the sweet kiss of the morning air. Just now, he told himself, life on Major Crimes was like a war. You hunkered down. You took your orders. And if those orders seriously pissed you off, then too bad. Two men were dead, for Christ' sake. Life could be a whole lot worse.

It didn't work. He sat at the kitchen table, listening to the Solent newscaster offering an overnight update in the hunt for the minister's killers. The BBC had a reporter who was practically in residence with the *Polygon* squad. Faraday had glimpsed her a number of times yesterday. She was young and pretty, and she knew how to play the more impressionable D/Cs. Faraday listened to her now, detecting the excitement in her voice, that special breathiness that came with the knowledge that you were at the very centre of events.

House-to-house teams, she said, had been out

279

since seven, trying to catch possible witnesses before they left for work, desperate for some fresh scrap of evidence. Yesterday, after the discovery of the motorbike used in the attack, the intelligence team had plotted the probable route taken by the killers, and now she tallied a list of streets, happy to add her voice to the chorus of other media appeals for information. If anyone had seen anything, she said, then here was the number to call.

There followed a brief interview with Martin Barrie. He sounded like he'd been up for most of the night and when the young reporter asked where the inquiry was heading next, he warned her that it was still early days. These things take time, he said. The offenders had clearly been well-prepared and at this stage in the investigation it would be unduly optimistic to expect them to make the kind of mistake that might lead to a breakthrough.

This thought clearly intrigued the reporter. She tried to press him further. How personal did a manhunt like this become? Were detectives tempted to give the killers a face? A physical presence? Or did the fact that they'd remained so invisible, so anonymous, become an irritation? Barrie paused. Faraday could imagine the pale skin stretched tight over the bones of his face and the thin fingers entwined around a pencil. Then he heard the rasping cough as the Detective Superintendent cleared his throat. 'With respect to your question, the answer's no.' He said at last. 'I'm afraid we deal in evidence. Not fiction.'

Faraday poured himself a second cup of tea. This was like listening to an account of a party to which he was no longer invited. He could picture Perry Madison at his desk, cranking up the *Polygon* machine for another day in the headlines. Last night, before leaving, Faraday had cleared his drawers of everything personal, as well as removing an armful of *Billhook* files, but something had made him leave his bird shots on the cork board over the filing cabinet. J-J's photos of gannets in the boiling swell off the Farne Islands were a statement of intent. They told anyone who might be interested that this leave of absence was strictly temporary. That just as soon as *Billhook* scored a result, he — Faraday — would return. And if *Polygon* was still active, then maybe he'd even get his office back.

Gabrielle appeared at the kitchen door. Preoccupied with the radio, Faraday hadn't heard her come downstairs. She was wearing an old T-shirt of his and not much else. She'd been asleep in bed last night when Faraday finally returned, and he'd taken care not to wake her.

Now, she slipped onto the chair beside him. He could feel the warmth of her body through the thin cotton.

'It goes OK?' She nodded at the radio.

Faraday got to his feet, furious at the strength of his own feelings.

'Dunno.' He shrugged. 'It's got nothing to do with me.'

★ ★ ★

Winter woke to find Bazza's face on the videophone.

'I've been down here for ever,' he yelled. 'I don't pay you to stay in fucking bed all day.'

Winter pressed the door release and glanced at his watch. Ten past eight. By the time he'd found his dressing gown and got to the door of the flat, Bazza was waiting in the hall.

'Well?'

'Well nothing. I might as well give you a key, Baz. Or why don't you move in? Take the spare room? Save yourself all those trips in the lift?' Still grumbling, Winter retreated to the kitchen.

'The lady. Our friend. What did she say?' Bazza was standing in the open doorway. His face was pinked with exercise and he seemed to be losing weight.

'She said yes, Baz.'

'To everything?'

'In principle, yes. She checked out that website of yours. The word she used was 'tasteful.' '

'What does that mean?'

'It means she's probably blind. You want tea or what?'

Winter made toast and jam. He'd been right about the exercise. Bazza had signed up for sessions at a local gym and been so impressed he'd just bought the place.

'They've got a special taster deal. Two free sessions to see how you get on. Can't fail. There's a big plasma screen in front of each place where you do the business. They call them exercise stations. You choose what you want to watch and they sort out the pictures.'

His neighbour, Bazza said, had fancied porn while the woman on the left had gone for a wildlife film about rockhopper penguins in Patagonia. Winter was mystified.

'What kind of bloke watches porn while he's working out?'

'It wasn't a bloke. It was a girl. Fat as you like. Told me she needed a bit of incentive. The state of her, I'm not surprised. Mess with that and you'd need a map to get out in one piece.'

He barked with laughter and spooned more marmalade onto his toast. Winter wanted to know what he'd been watching.

'Bridge on the River Kwai. As if I wasn't sweating to death already.'

'I thought you'd seen it before?' Winter remembered the DVD on a shelf at Sandown Road.

'I have, mush, every Christmas, without fail. It's a real classic, though, isn't it? That bit at the end when they do the bridge? I re-ran it three times this morning. My trainer thinks I'm weird. Blokes've got no fucking sense of history these days.'

The image of Bazza Mackenzie watching several hundred tons of locomotive plunging into a Thai river brightened Winter's morning. Esme was right. Her dad really was a kid.

'So you think Brodie'll be down?' Bazza was on the balcony now, giving a passing ferry a wave. 'Only I'll have to sort something out.'

'I'm sure she'll be down, Baz. She was talking to some media people yesterday. She thinks she might have a couple of names to run past us.'

'When?'

'This morning.' Winter looked pointedly at his watch. 'Though most people don't lift the phone before nine.'

★ ★ ★

Fareham was a once-sleepy market town ten miles west of Portsmouth. Good motorway and rail links had attracted a new breed of householder and the asking price for the rash of two-garage executive homes had reached dizzy heights. Nowadays, thought Faraday, Fareham was a place where you'd lay your head, raise your kids, and shop for chocolate biscotti from Sainsbury's at weekends.

The police station lay close to the busy main road south of the town centre. D/C Jimmy Suttle was already at the coffee machine by the time Faraday had negotiated a parking space and hauled an armful of paperwork out of the Mondeo's boot.

'Where, son?'

'Upstairs, boss. The duty Inspector's got us a nice office.'

'Us?'

'You and me.'

Faraday followed Suttle up two flights of stairs and along a corridor at the top. A largish office at the end served as a major incident room and a team of techies had just finished tweaking the computers. Faraday left the paperwork on the nearest desk and opened a window. The working space, though more modest than the MIR at

284

Kingston Crescent, was perfectly adequate for *Billhook*.

'And we are . . . ?'

'Over here, boss.'

A door at the end accessed a small, windowless room reeking of new paint. Two desks had been installed, one against the back wall, the other at right angles. Phones and computers, said Suttle, would be up and running by midday.

Faraday was eyeing the desks. At last, he was feeling better.

'What do you think, boss?'

'Put them face to face. Think you can cope with looking at me all day?'

'No problem.' Suttle began to haul one of the desks into position. 'My pleasure.'

For the time being, pending the arrival of a new team of civvy indexers, they moved next door to the Incident Room. At Faraday's request, Suttle was trying to get in touch with Stephen Benskin. Up early, the young D/C had been through the rest of the bank statements and was convinced it was time to press Benskin for a full account of his recent dealings with his dead partner. There was stuff here he simply didn't understand. Only Benskin himself would have the answers.

'He's en route to Southampton, boss.' Suttle was on the line to Benskin's secretary. 'Apparently he's got some meetings at a hotel over there.'

'Bell him on the mobile, then. Pin him down to a time and place.'

285

Suttle redialled. Within seconds he was talking again, his back turned to Faraday, his hand reaching for a pen.

'The Park Hotel.' He glanced over his shoulder. 'He says he's got half an hour to spare at twelve.'

'Twelve's fine. We'll meet him at the nick in the Civic Centre. Tell him to go to the front desk. And tell him he'll need more than half an hour.'

★ ★ ★

Mackenzie had gone by the time Katherine Brodie phoned. Winter was sitting in front of BBC News 24 with a bowl of porridge. The death of the minister was sinking steadily down the news order, kicked into touch by the return of the bodies of 14 dead RAF personnel from Afghanistan.

Winter steadied the bowl on his lap. Brodie had indeed been talking to some media people and one of them was extremely keen on a meeting.

'Who is he?'

'His name's Michael Lander. He's a freelance producer, good track record. He's made a bit of a name for himself with events afloat. Talk to anyone at Cowes. They all know him.'

Mention of Cowes unsettled Winter. What little he knew of the yachting fraternity told him that Bazza Mackenzie might come as a bit of a shock to someone of Michael Lander's pedigree.

'So what's he after, this bloke? A bit of rough?'

286

'Money.' Brodie was laughing. 'Like they all are.'

'And you're serious? He's kosher?'

'I'm not with you.'

'He does what it says on the label? You're not trying to bullshit me again?'

'Would I?' She was laughing again. 'He says he's got the inside track at Sky Sports. He does deals with them all the time and he thinks they'd really be up for something like this. What he needs now are proper costings. I've done some rough sums which might help. I'll bring them down.'

'Down?'

'Yeah. I've invited him to lunch. Maybe you could run it past Mackenzie. Royal Trafalgar? Half one? Something tells me it's Bazza's shout.'

* * *

Stephen Benskin was already waiting at the police station attached to Southampton's Civic Centre by the time Faraday and D/C Suttle arrived. An accident on the motorway had delayed them but Benskin wasn't interested in excuses.

'This is my solicitor.' He grunted. 'And her time's as expensive as mine.'

Wendy Pallister was a small, wiry, thin-faced woman with a slightly damp handshake. Busy on her mobile, she spared Faraday barely a glance.

Faraday had already phoned ahead to make arrangements with the duty Inspector. A civilian unlocked the access door to the main body of the

287

police station and led the party past a series of offices to the interview suite. Suttle's one attempt at small talk with Benskin had come to nothing. Pallister was still on the phone.

The interview room had recently been redecorated. The carpet tiles on the floor looked new and the smell of emulsion lingered in the stale air. Faraday gestured at the chairs around the single table. Benskin sat down first. At the very latest, he had to be away by a quarter to one.

Faraday said he'd do his best, then began to read the caution. Pallister cut short her phone call.

'My client has volunteered himself for interview. Are we to understand you suspect him of involvement in an offence?'

A heavy cold did nothing for her voice. Faraday glanced up.

'As you'll know, we've interviewed Mr Benskin before. Certain elements in that interview have caused us some concern. Mr Benskin is not under arrest. He can leave at any time.'

Pallister was about to protest but Benskin forestalled her. He wanted to get this thing over. He was perfectly happy to answer any of Faraday's questions. The last thing he needed was a third bite out of his working week.

'That OK with you, guys?' The coal-black eyes travelled from one face to another. 'You get this one for free. At 12.45, I'm out of here. Next time, you'll have to arrest me.'

Faraday read the caution again. By now, Suttle had unpacked his brief case. Back at Fareham, he'd spent an hour or so amalgamating downloads from Mallinder's laptop and financial data from his bank accounts into a detailed time-line. At a nod from Faraday, his finger found a specific date. 16th February 2006. His head came up.

'How much did you know about Mr Mallinder's political views?'

'I don't know what you're driving at.'

'I'm driving at nothing, Mr Benskin. I'm simply asking whether you ever, the pair of you, had any discussions about politics.'

'You mean how Jonno voted? Is that what you're after?' Suttle nodded. 'He voted New Labour. Does that make him a leftie these days? Christ knows.'

'But would you talk about it? Would you discuss the issues?'

'Not that I can remember, no.'

'Why's that?'

'Because we had better things to do with our time. Or I did, anyway.'

'Does politics interest you?'

'Not in the slightest. In my view, most of these people are on the make. Either it's money or . . . you know . . . advancement, their precious careers. How many of the New Labour lot have done anything practical with their lives? Very few. That's why most of them are so clueless.'

Suttle, poker-faced, returned to the file. The data again.

'On the 16th February, this year, Mr Mallinder raised a sum of money in the form of a bank loan. Did you know about that?'

'Remind me.'

'It was a big loan.'

'How much?'

'You really can't remember?'

'I asked you how much.'

'Two and a half million pounds.' Suttle extracted a sheet of paper from the pile at his elbow and slipped it across the desk. 'You were a co-signatory to that loan.'

'That's right. HSBC.' Benskin had barely glanced at the letter of agreement.

'Was this something you and Mallinder had discussed before?'

'Obviously.'

'So you knew what the loan was for?'

'Yes.'

'What was it for?'

For the first time, Benskin hesitated. He was irritated already and the solicitor's cautionary touch on his arm seemed to sour his mood even further. His eyes returned briefly to the letter, then he leaned forward across the desk, his weight on his elbows. Watching him, Faraday understood only too well why Mallinder had handled most of the negotiations. For Benskin, intimidation had become a habit.

'Listen . . . ', he began. ' . . . you're lucky I'm here. You're lucky I agreed to come. I don't have to go through all this shit.'

'You haven't answered the question, Mr Benskin. You're free to go, of course you are, but it might be simpler and quicker if we just established the facts of the matter.'

'The facts?' Benskin's laugh was savage. 'OK,

son, here are the facts. No, I didn't know about the loan. Or about the collateral. Or about the reasons Jonno wanted to lay hands on two and a half mill. And why didn't I know? Because he faked my signature. Easily done. More easily done than you might imagine.'

'The money went into his private account.'

'I expect you're right.'

'You didn't know?'

'Not then I didn't, not in February. It certainly didn't go into one of the business accounts, otherwise I'd have spotted it.'

'How about your financial controller?'

'We don't have a financial controller. We have a woman who looks after the books, and she's bloody good. We retain an accountant as well, of course, but only on a needs-must basis. Jonno was clever. He disguised it well.'

'So who spotted it? In the end?'

'The accountant. The loan was secured against a number of freeholds. A situation arose where we might have suddenly needed to liquidate a couple of those assets. The accountant discovered we couldn't.'

'Because they were collateral for the loan?'

'Exactly.'

'And when was that?'

'Some time in May.' Benskin nodded at Suttle's paperwork. 'It'll be down in your little list somewhere.'

Suttle nodded, then sat back in his chair. So far, thought Faraday, he hasn't put a foot wrong.

'Two and a half million pounds constitutes a serious fraud, doesn't it Mr Benskin?'

'It's a lot of money, sure.'

'So how did you feel when you found out?'

'I was extremely pissed-off. We had a conversation. Then he paid the money back. Plus interest.'

'Did he tell you why he wanted the money in the first place?'

'Yes.'

'And what was the reason?'

'First he said it was a loan to the New Labour lot. Then he changed that into a donation. There was going to be a school involved. Either way, he said it was going to help us get the inside track on the Tipner thing, you know, the dump. And once that happened, and we laid hands on acres and acres of extra land, right down by the water, then we'd make squillions of quid.'

'How would that work?'

'It wouldn't. I told him straight off. I said he was out of his mind. He seemed to think a whack of money into their war chest would buy him some civil servant in the Ministry of Defence. In fact to him it wasn't a donation at all. More like a business investment.' He studied his nails a moment, then shook his head. 'He could be naïve sometimes, Jonno. His worst bloody enemy, to tell you the truth.'

There was a long silence, broken at length by Faraday.

'So Mallinder, your partner, lied to you.'

'Obviously.'

'To the tune of two and a half million quid.'

'Yes. And you know why? Because there was no bloody way I'd ever have agreed that kind of loan in the first place. Bunging a bunch of politicians? You have to be joking. Jonno thought different. He genuinely expected to make on the deal. Big time. I don't doubt that for a moment.'

'But his judgement . . . ?

' . . . was crap.'

'And his honesty?'

'That shocked me. I can't pretend it didn't. I knew he could be . . . ' he frowned. ' . . . inventive when it suited us, like in a negotiation for instance. But this was the first time he'd tried it on me.'

'What does inventive mean?'

'It means . . . oh, come on, you know what it bloody means.'

'Tell me.'

The solicitor, this time, was firmer. She blew her nose then said that this line of questioning, in her view, was oppressive. Not simply that but potentially prejudicial. Benskin, once again, ignored her.

'It means he sometimes lied. Small lies. White lies. Evasions. Untruths. Whatever. Anything to put us in the driving seat. It mattered to Jonno that we won. It was going to be the same with the Tipner deal. He'd raised the cash. He'd made the investment. And sometime soon we'd buy the whole lot off the current developers, cash in the favour with New Labour, the MoD, whatever, access all that extra land, and walk away laughing. By then I'd probably have discovered about the bank loan but that didn't matter because by that time we'd both be seriously rich. It was bonkers but he believed it.'

'Unlike you.'

'Too bloody right.'

'So how did that affect the partnership afterwards?'

Benskin thought hard about the question. Faraday could see he knew exactly where it would lead. At length, he shrugged.

'I was pissed-off. Anyone would be.'

'So what did you do about it?'

'I told him I wanted the money back. Plus I said we had to tighten up. I meant in terms of accounting procedures. No way was that going to happen again.'

'And how did he react?'

'He agreed. Not that he had any choice in the matter. You're right. Technically, he'd committed fraud.'

Faraday permitted himself a smile. He could imagine the conversation only too well. No wonder, in the aftermath, Mallinder began to build himself a solo career.

Suttle wanted to know more about the collateral. Just what kind of freeholds secured a loan of this size?

'They were properties we'd acquired a while back. They belonged to a chain of hardware stores. Gullifant's.'

'Is this the same place as in Farnham?' Faraday remembered mention of an ironmongers the first time he and Tracy Barber had talked to Benskin.

'Yes.'

'And you're saying there was a chain of them?'

'Yes.'

'How many?'

'Thirteen.'

'And you bought the lot?'

'We bought the firm, yes.'

'And whose idea was that?'

'Jonno's.'

Mallinder, he said, had spent the best part of a fortnight driving across the south, visiting each store. All the premises were freehold, wholly owned by the Gullifant family. At least half of them had potential value in the event of major town-centre re-development, a fact seemingly lost on the company's management.

'So you bought the company?'

'Yes. It was complicated but . . . in essence . . . that's exactly what we did. And it turned out Jonno was right. As a going concern, Gullifant's was crap, but the freeholds — if we were clever — could be worth a fortune. In fact three of them we've sold already and you know what? We made back more than we paid for the firm in the first place. Maybe that's why Jonno thought he had some kind of right to use the rest as collateral. It was always going to be his baby.'

Faraday stirred. Time was moving on.

'Mallinder was spending more and more time down in Portsmouth,' he said carefully. 'You told us before you assumed it was the Tipner project. Now you say there was no chance of that ever happening. Especially once he'd paid back the loan. So what did you think he was really doing down there?'

It was a good question. For a second or two Faraday thought Benskin was about to draw a line under the interview, confer with his brief, bring proceedings to a halt, but he didn't.

'I think he was putting space between us,' he said. 'I think he was finding life in the office difficult to handle.'

'Because of you?'

'Because of what had happened. I'd be lying if I said things just carried on the same.'

'Did you trust him?'

'No. And I didn't trust his judgement, either. Not after that. Not after he'd gone off with two and a half million quid, right under my nose.'

'And he knew that? About you not trusting him?'

'Yeah. I think he did.'

'So what was he doing down in Portsmouth?'

'Looking for opportunities, bits and pieces, like he always did.'

'For the partnership? For the pair of you?'

'I've no idea.'

'But he's your partner, isn't he? He's fifty per cent of your working life, of your prospects, of who you are. If he decides to pack it in, what happens then?'

'We split the business, fifty/fifty. It's written down. It's in the agreement.'

'Had you discussed that?'

'No.'

'Had you discussed *anything*?'

'Not much.'

'Bit of a break-down, then?'

'It wasn't ideal, sure.'

'Bit of a threat?'

'I'm not with you.'

'You're not *with* me?' Faraday, with a smile on his lips, let the question die. Then he reached for Suttle's time-line. 'You've built the business between you. You've turned it into a real success. You're the perfect double-act. Then you realise that what makes your partner a brilliant negotiator might after all be a bit of a liability. Not only that, you realise as well that he might come knocking on your door wanting half of the business back. I've no idea what the partnership is worth, Mr Benskin, but I bet it's a lot of money. Half of a lot of money is still a lot of money. In that kind of situation you'd have a problem, wouldn't you? And problems, as we coppers like to say, need sorting out.' He offered Benskin a cold smile. 'Isn't that the case?'

★ ★ ★

The dining room at the Royal Trafalgar was Bazza's pride and joy. The Victory Banqueting Suite, as he preferred it to be known, occupied at least half the length of the first floor. It was a deep, handsome, high-ceilinged room and the tall picture windows, draped in red velour, offered a near-perfect view across Southsea Common to the milky blue wash of Spithead beyond.

This view, which featured heavily on Bazza's new website, was framed on the one side by the squat grey battlements of Southsea Castle and on the other by the tall stone pillar of the seafront war memorial. In his more expansive moods, Bazza liked to imagine these features as

297

personal bookends, explaining to his guests how chapter after chapter of British maritime history had played itself out on this unique stretch of water.

He'd conjure up the bulky figure of Henry VIII watching the capsize of his beloved *Mary Rose*. He'd point out where the *Monarch* had lay at anchor, awaiting the execution of the disgraced Admiral Byng. He'd describe, with some approval, the various dodges dreamed up by the stroppy matelots who'd organised the Spithead Mutiny. And finally, his party piece, he'd pray silence for the memory of Nelson's glorious three-deckers, putting to sea under full sail to give the French yet another hiding.

The fact that Pompey had so successfully elbowed its way into the history books gave Bazza enormous pleasure and when the brandies arrived and table talk turned to violence of a different kind, the city's apprentice hotelier was only too happy to add a footnote of his own. Just now, as Winter had half-expected, Bazza was at full throttle. No one had told him that Michael Lander was a Crystal Palace fan.

'Best firm in London, no question. Some of the happiest rucks of my life were against your lot. One time we were heading up north, Leeds away. Palace were showing for us at Waterloo as we got off the train. Classic, that was. Half nine in the morning, out by the taxi rank, hundreds of the bastards, really wanting some, the Old Bill nowhere. After that we had it at Elland Road, before and after the game, then on the way back, sweet as you like, Palace were showing again,

King's Cross this time, mob-handed. Four rucks in one day? Shit . . . ' He beamed across the table at Lander, using the salt and pepper pots to plot their various moves, one bunch of football hooligans ambushing another, real life pushed aside for a whole day of unrestrained mayhem. No wonder it was Pompey lads who manned the guns at Trafalgar, he said. Blokes in this city were bred to be violent. Imprinted in the genes.

Lander had looked, if anything, amused. He was tall and slightly stooped, with a mop of curly black hair lightly threaded with grey. He wore jeans and a faded denim shirt and talked in a soft drawl that Bazza undoubtedly regarded as posh. He'd come down on the train with Brodie and after the third bottle of Côte du Rhône he'd stepped across to the grand piano Bazza kept beside the tiny stage, taken a mock bow, and launched into a series of smoky jazz improvisations that had drawn a round of applause from even Bazza himself.

'I know that fucking tune,' he'd said on Lander's return, 'Give us a clue.'

'Rule Britannia.' Lander had laughed. 'Heavily disguised.'

'Yeah? To fox the fucking enemy, eh?'

Winter, watching, had raised a glass to Bazza's gleeful toast, still trying to work out whether Lander was another plant or not. Now, the meal over, he'd decided he wasn't. No copper he'd ever known could play the piano like that.

Winter glanced at his watch, aware that he needed to get to Southampton for his meet with Parsons. In terms of any kind of agenda, the

299

lunch had achieved very little. Brodie had tabled a list of basic costs, Lander had nailed down a rough outline of a running-order for the weekend, and there'd followed a spirited discussion of the kind of visual opportunities generated by an event like this.

Bazza himself had designed an oblong-shaped two mile course with a tight chicane on the landward leg. Pressed by Lander to describe exactly what it was he wanted to create, he'd settled on a Roman analogy.

'It's chariot racing afloat,' he'd said. 'Think Charlton Heston. Think Russell Crowe in a wet suit. You're sitting on the beach and these bastards are coming at you at a thousand miles an hour and suddenly there's two buoys, bang-bang, two markers like a gate, fifteen metres apart, maybe less, and it's chaos, collisions fucking everywhere, blokes in the water, big screens on the beach for the close-ups, brilliant, can't fail.'

At this, a smile of the deepest satisfaction had settled on Lander's face. Offshore racing starts at Cowes, he'd said, were very similar, millions of quids' worth of high-performance yachts all fighting for position at the start line, inches to spare, going about and going about, the snap of filling sails, the bellow of helmsmen calling for water, the clatter of choppers overhead.

Mention of helicopters had lit another fire under Bazza. He'd pushed the empty plates aside and described how he wanted live pictures beamed down to the big screens from aerial cameras, and tracking shots of the jet-skis from feet above the waves, and on-board cameras in the blokes' helmets, building a firestorm of live action he could unleash on the thousands of watching punters ashore. He knew what these people wanted, what people everywhere wanted. They wanted what the 6.57 had wanted. They wanted to be in the thick of it. But without the prospect of getting hurt. Or even wet.

Lander, with his sleepy grin, twirled a hand. The gesture had all the grace of a formal bow.

'It'll be a pleasure . . . ' he said ' . . . to lay it on.'

Quite how this was to happen was left to another day, to more meetings, but Winter knew that this didn't matter because the business on hand was of a different order completely. Bazza, in the end, was an animal. He had to sniff people out. He had to look them in the eye. He had to decide whether they were worth it or not, whether they were up for a laugh or two, whether their company would further brighten the already glittering prospect of the months to come. On every count, and seemingly without effort, Lander had won himself a big thumbs-up, and once Bazza had despatched him in a cab to the railway station, he pronounced himself a happy man.

'Dunno where you found him, Kath, but the guy's the business. Funny as fuck. And that stuff he played on the piano? Love the man to death.'

Brodie, reaching for her coat, was equally glad it had worked out. She'd also been thinking about the offer of free accommodation at the hotel and was happy to accept it. It made a great deal of sense, she said, to keep the people who matter under the same roof. Bazza shot Winter a wink. More good news.

Next door, in the lobby, Bazza drew Winter aside. Winter had already mentioned his hospital appointment in Southampton.

'How are you getting there?'

'Train. And then I'll cab it.'

'No need, mate. I'm going over to Southampton myself. I'll drop you off. Behave yourself, and you might even get a lift back, too.'

★ ★ ★

'You were good, son. He's not an easy man, Benskin, but you did well.'

It was early afternoon. Faraday, at the wheel of his Mondeo, had taken a detour en route back to Fareham. He'd talked to the duty Inspector at Southampton, sounded him out about despatching a small task force of D/Cs for house-to-house checks in Thornhill Park, and wanted to get a feel of the place before raising the actions with the Outside Enquiries D/S in the *Billhook* incident room.

Suttle was still thinking about Benskin.

'There's a problem, though, isn't there boss?'

'Tell me.'

'He could have said nothing. He could have left it to his brief. He could have brought the whole thing to a halt and walked out. But he didn't do any of that. Quite the reverse. We asked for an account and that's exactly what he gave us.'

302

'Not at the start he didn't. He told us he knew about the loan when in fact he didn't, not at the time. How honest was that?'

'But it was still a game at that stage, a negotiation if you like. Once he knew we'd done the homework, there was nowhere else for him to go.'

'My point exactly. And *you* did the homework.'

'Sure, but it turned out we were pushing at an open door. You remember what he said at the off? He wanted to get shot of us. And that's exactly the way he played it. He doesn't want to see us again, ever.'

'Of course he doesn't. But ask yourself why.'

'Because he's got better things to do with his life. And because, come the finish, he'd decided that Mallinder was a bit of a liability.'

'Quite.'

'But that doesn't put him in the frame for the killing, not in my book.'

'Why not?'

'Because he wouldn't want the hassle. Mallinder was already backing out of the partnership. Why not let events take care of themselves?'

'Maybe there was a financial problem. Maybe Mallinder taking his share of the business would leave a bloody great hole in the kitty.'

'Yeah, but even with Mallinder dead, he's still going to lose that same whack of money. It'll form part of his estate. It'll go to his widow.'

'And if Benskin's already tucked up with her?'

'Then it starts to sound half-way reasonable.

The baby's due in a couple of weeks. A DNA test might help sort it.'

Faraday nodded. Something very similar had occurred to him and even now he was still undecided about Benskin's real status in the enquiry. Mallinder's recklessness had certainly given the partnership a very big problem. The relationship between the two men had certainly soured. But was that enough to justify a killing? The prospect of losing half your business was one thing. Spending the rest of your life dreading the knock on the door, quite another.

At the end of the interview, with barely minutes left before Benskin's deadline expired, Faraday had raised the issue of Mallinder's private life. His wife was pregnant. There was evidence that Mallinder might be contemplating some kind of bachelor apartment existence on the south coast. Had Benskin been aware of tensions in the marriage?

Once again, Benskin had sensed immediately the real thrust of the question. On his feet, reaching for his briefcase, he'd looked down at the faces across the table. In these situations, as Faraday had come to recognise, he was rarely less than blunt.

'If you're asking me whether I was shagging Sally Mallinder, the answer's no. You get my drift, guys? You OK with that?'

Now, gazing at street after street of crumbling council-built semis, Faraday tallied the actions he'd pass on to the incident room. He wanted warrants for both Benskin's Canary Wharf apartment and the partnership offices in

Croydon. He wanted his PC and laptop seized, and he wanted sight of every last piece of paperwork on the Tipner project. He also told Suttle to sort out a production order on Benskin's bank accounts and a bid through TIU for billings on his various telephones.

These were obvious steps to take, and questions would doubtless be asked if he hadn't positively eliminated Benskin from the enquiry, but deep down he shared Suttle's doubts. After discovering the loan, Benskin had effectively washed his hands of Mallinder. He wanted him out of the partnership and out of his life. But that didn't make him a murderer. In the meantime, given the fact that the missing Mercedes remained a live lead, it made sense to take a hard look at Thornhill Park.

Suttle nodded in agreement. The estate was bigger than he'd thought. How wide did Faraday want to draw the search parameters? Just how many man-hours did he want to punt on the missing car? Faraday, in his mind, had already settled on a couple of days, enough to put the word around and maybe raise a cough or two. He was about to voice this thought when Suttle forestalled him.

'There's something else we need to look at, boss.'

'What's that?'

'Gullifant's.'

15

WEDNESDAY, 13 SEPTEMBER, 2006. 15.07

Winter had never met Paul Shreve. He was a big man in grease-stained jeans and a baggy leather jacket, not much given to conversation. He was standing at the foot of the hotel steps with a motor cycle helmet in one hand and a grubby Army surplus holdall in the other. When Bazza retrieved his Range Rover from the hotel car park, he clambered at once into the back. There was an obedience about him that reminded Winter of the family dog. In Bazza's empire, here was a foot soldier who definitely knew his place.

'Paulie? Best mechanic in town, bar none. Trust him with my life.'

They were heading north, towards the motorway. It had begun to rain, and Bazza slipped the Range Rover into the fast lane as they hit the dual carriageway out of town. Bazza was still bubbling after the lunch with Lander, demanding Winter's thoughts on exactly how many jet skis would give them the pictures they wanted, but Winter's mind was elsewhere. His hospital appointment was for 5 o'clock. Why were they setting off so early?

'We've got a call to make first. That's why I need Paulie. Bit of business to sort out.'

Mark, it turned out, had a sixteen year old son, also called Mark. Bazza's brother had abandoned the family years ago, decamping first to the Caribbean and then to Gibraltar before settling in Cambados. He'd never seen the kid, never kept up with him, and it had fallen to Bazza to try and help out as best he could.

Until very recently, he said, Chrissie and Mark Two had been living in an evil block of flats in Millbrook, an arsehole suburb near the docks. Mark Two had got himself in all kinds of shit with the Old Bill and Bazza, who'd given this situation a great deal of thought, had decided on two solutions. First off, Chrissie and Mark Two deserved somewhere half-decent to live. Secondly, the little tearaway needed something else in his life beyond shoplifting, Paki-bashing, and occasional car theft.

A new address had been easy. For a couple of hundred grand, Bazza had bought them a bungalow in a village on the edge of the New Forest. The place was a bit of a wreck but Chrissie was brilliant at schmoozing deals out of decent tradesmen and there was even a patch of garden at the back if she ever fancied keeping chickens. Mark Two, on the other hand, was a tougher nut to crack. This was a kid who was never going to handle school or college. He could barely read or write and his social skills were limited to street-level drug dealing. Bazza had asked around, getting nowhere, and in the end it was Marie, bless her, who'd come up with the answer.

Friends of her sister had a difficult sixteen year-old who'd turned to be mad about motorbike scrambling. He'd saved up for a machine and now competed every weekend. Bike scrambling, they said, was every parent's nightmare. It was noisy, muddy, and often extremely dangerous. Their errant son, of course, had loved it.

'So where are we going?'

'Millbrook. Same block of flats. Chrissie says there's a kid there living with his gran. Parents chucked him out.'

'And?'

'He's got a bike for sale, nearly brand new. He wants a silly price for it but a couple of hundred quid says he'll see sense.'

The Millbrook flats lay at the end of the spur motorway to Southampton docks, a gaunt Sixties tower block stuffed full, according to Bazza, with problem families. Rain had pooled on the cracked paving stones outside the main entrance and a spilling wheelie bin, abandoned in the middle of nowhere, was attracting a cloud of squalling seagulls.

Bazza parked beside a rusting Transit van and despatched Paulie to sort out the kid.

'Flat 76.' He said. 'Get him to bring the bike down.'

Winter was gazing up at the flats. The sheer size of the building reminded him of similar blocks in Pompey. Somerstown or Portsea, he thought. Grey lives, grey concrete, grey sky. No wonder half the population had settled for shit television and a freezerful of pizzas.

'Get the bike *down*?' he said. 'How does that work?'

'The little toerag keeps it in his gran's flat.

308

Round here you would though, wouldn't you?'

He gazed out at the line of graffiti on a nearby wall. The boy, he said, had bought the bike on hire purchase, signing in his gran's name. When she hadn't kept the payments up, the company wanted the bike back. The repo man was expected any day now. Hence the boy's desperation to sell it.

Winter was watching a young couple pushing a supermarket trolley through the rain towards the main entrance. The woman, no more than a girl, had draped her anorak over the shopping to keep it dry. Her Robbie Williams T-shirt was soaking and the baby cradled in her spare arm was fighting to get free.

'You know something, Paul?' Bazza had seen them too, 'This country's fucked. And you know why? Because it's all turned to ratshit. Families, schools, work, religion, it's all falling apart.'

'Yeah?' Winter was checking the time of his appointment. He'd left the consultant's letter Parsons had e-mailed on the dashboard. 'So when was the last time you went to church, Baz?'

'That's not the point. It's about faith, mush. You have to *believe*. It doesn't matter what you believe in, it's just gotta be there for you. In this country no one believes in anything anymore. But you know what? In my little gang, bad bastards though we are, we've always believed in *us*. And you know where that comes from? The 6.57. Because we were scrappers. Because we watched out for each other. A bit of that wouldn't do these people any harm.'

Paul the mechanic had reappeared. He was

pushing a scramble motorbike, thickly encrusted with dried mud. Winter watched as the mud began to soften and streak in the falling rain. Behind Paul trailed a thin, pale-faced youth in jeans and a black hoodie. He took a half-hearted kick at an empty Tennents Super Strength tin, and missed.

Paul hoisted the bike onto its stand and came across to the Land Rover. He had a handful of tools in the holdall. Bazza asked him about the bike.

'Looks alright. I don't think the kid's used it much. Couple of hundred miles on the clock, it's nearly brand new.'

He ducked back out into the rain and began to loosen the spark plug. The kid watched him a moment, hands dug in the pockets of his jeans, then wandered over to the Land Rover. Bazza had lowered the window on the driver's side.

'Alright?'

'Yeah.' He nodded across to the bike. 'Fifteen hundred quid. Cash.'

'Is that right?'

Bazza was still watching Paul. He'd removed the spark plug, sniffed it, and now he was screwing it back in. He straddled the machine, fiddled with the mixture, put on his helmet, then kicked the bike into life. Moments later, he was disappearing down the access road towards the big roundabout at the bottom.

Bazza turned back to the youth. 'Why aren't you at school then?'

'Binned it, didn't I.'

'Job?'

'No fucking chance. Not round here.'

'Help yer gran with her shopping?'

'She does it herself. Gets her out. You got the money, then? Only I'm getting fucking wet just standing here.'

Bazza ignored him. He spotted the appointments letter on the dashboard, read it, then turned to Winter.

'What's this one for?'

'A scan, Baz. It's supposed to be routine but they always tell you that.'

'You've still got a problem?'

'I get headaches.'

'Is that why you went to Bournemouth the other day?'

'Yeah.' Winter nodded. 'Nice of you to ask.'

'Pleasure, mate. Gotta keep tabs on the staff, know what I mean?'

He broke off, his attention caught by the chain-saw buzz of the returning bike. Paul stopped alongside the window, raising his visor.

'OK?'

'Fine, boss.' His voice was muffled. 'Newbridge, is it?'

'Yeah. Jasmine Cottage. It's a got a wonky gate and no one's taken the For Sale sign down. Chrissie's expecting you. I'll be along later.'

Paul nodded, gunned the engine, then made for the roundabout again. Bazza was digging in his pocket. Winter watched the roll of ten pound notes change hands.

'Yours.' Bazza said.

The youth began to peel off the notes, one by one. He did it twice. Then his head came up. He needed a shave, Winter thought. Either that or he was trying to grow a beard.

'You've given me two hundred,' he said. 'Where's the fucking rest?'

'That's it, mush. Good to know you can count.' He reached out, patting the youth on the cheek. 'Be nice to your gran now. And watch out for those repo blokes. Some of them can be a fucking nightmare.'

The window whirred shut and Winter heard a clunk as the youth aimed a kick at the departing Range Rover. Bazza hit the brakes. Seconds later Winter was watching him in the wing mirror, perfectly framed, as he threw the youth to the ground. He knelt on his chest, one hand tightening around the youth's scrawny throat, then he bent very low, his mouth inches from the boy's ear. The youth struggled to get free but Bazza wasn't having it. He kept talking. Slowly the youth's limbs went slack. Only when Bazza was on his feet again, adjusting his jacket, did signs of life return.

Back in the car, he shot Winter a look. The last couple of minutes had pinked his face.

'Way out of order.' He gunned the engine. 'Little twat.'

★　★　★

Back in Fareham, Faraday was glad to see the *Billhook* incident room in full working order. The indexers had arrived from Kingston Crescent and one of them was gridding a whiteboard in Pentel, ready for the Outside

Enquiries list of actions. Faraday conferred briefly with the D/S in charge, Glen Thatcher, briefing him on the Thornhill house-to-house operation. He wanted bodies on the ground by late afternoon, in time to catch working couples returning home. SOC photos of the Mercedes had been duplicated for each of the two-man teams. When the D/S asked about the interview with Benskin, Faraday pulled a face. There'd be follow-up checks to action in the London area but no one should be holding their breath.

From his desk in the office at the end of the room Faraday put in a call to Tracy Barber. The D/C was still part of the Intelligence Cell on Operation *Polygon* and Faraday wanted an update.

He caught a mumble of apology as Barber got up and closed the door. Then she was back on the phone.

'Not a lot,' she said, 'to be frank. We had a team in the hospital grounds all night to see if anyone showed for the bolt cutters.'

'And?'

'Nothing.'

'What about the cutters themselves?'

'Again nothing. No prints. No DNA. Clean as you like. The longer this goes on, the more we're looking at some kind of terrorist hit. These people knew exactly what they were about. Either they do it for a living or they've been to college, got a diploma, passed the exam.'

Faraday smiled. The sheer momentum of an inquiry like this would inevitably raise expectations. With so many bodies on the ground and so

313

much resource available, some kind of break-through became a foregone conclusion. In the absence of any real progress, therefore, the premium would be on speculation. Blaming a hit like this on the shadowy world of terrorism was a whole lot more comforting than the possibility that *Polygon* might be running out of steam.

'How's Madison?'

'Loud. I'd forgotten what a crap human being that man is.'

'And Mr Barrie?'

'Harassed. He tries not to show it, but if you know where to look all the signs are there. I was talking to one of the cleaners. She found him out in the car park, five o'clock in the morning. She's not absolutely certain but she thought he was skinning up.'

'Really?'

'Yeah. Either that or he's taken to smoking really long roll-ups. Not that anyone would blame the poor guy. Get this one wrong and he'll be on Traffic for the rest of his life.'

'What about the hospital? Anyone drawn up an interview list?'

'I'm looking at it now. Page five starts with the truckies who service the kitchens. There are . . . ' she began to count, ' . . . eight of them. Even with the bodies we've got, this is going to take a while. To tell you the truth, boss, I'm not sure — '

She broke off and Faraday heard Brian Imber's voice in the background. Moments later, he'd taken the phone.

'Joe? You still there?'

'I am. You sound knackered.'

'Too fucking right. Headless and chickens are two of my least favourite words. How about you?'

'Fine, Brian. Never better.'

'You've had another crack at Benskin?'

'This morning.'

'And?'

'I can't see it somehow.'

He talked it through, glad of the chance to run the interview past someone whose judgement he completely trusted. In the end, once you'd assembled all the available evidence, it often came down to something far more instinctive than hard facts.

'He's got the motivation, Brian. There's no question about that. And I'm assuming he'd have the money to buy himself a contract.'

'What about the wife? Mrs Mallinder?'

'He says there's nothing between them, never has been. Suttle's suggesting a DNA test on the baby. It's due any day now.'

'Good thinking. You might check the PM report too. I've no idea whether they test for vasectomies these days but if Mallinder had the snip that might be a pointer.'

Faraday scribbled himself a note. Why hadn't he thought of something so obvious? Imber wanted to know where *Billhook* went from here. Faraday told him about the house-to-house in Thornhill. In the absence of any other lead, it seemed as good a line of enquiry as any.

'I'm sure you're right, Joe. How's the boy doing?'

The boy, Faraday knew, was Jimmy Suttle. He could see him now, juggling two coffees as he picked his way back across the incident room. One of the indexers was a new face — young, raven-haired, pretty. Suttle grinned at her, spilling one of the coffees.

'He's fine, Brian. In fact he's bloody good.'

★ ★ ★

Mackenzie dropped Paul Winter at the main entrance to Southampton General. As Winter buttoned his car coat for the dash through the rain, Bazza leaned over.

'You want this, mush?' It was the consultant's letter.

'Thanks.' Winter folded it into his pocket, aware of Mackenzie still watching him. 'Should be through within the hour, fingers crossed.'

'No problem. Ring me on the mobile.'

Winter watched the Range Rover purr away. Working for Bazza Mackenzie had brought its own ration of surprises and one of them was how sane and thoughtful he could be. As a working copper, Winter had never associated either of these descriptions with the robber baron who'd built an empire from Pompey drug debts, but now he was beginning to realise that he might have had the man badly wrong. He pushed in through the big double doors, trying to rid himself of a growing sense of bewilderment.

D/I Gale Parsons was occupying an empty office attached to the Imaging Department. She came straight to the point.

'I've been talking to Mr Willard,' she said at once. 'To be frank, I found our last exchange somewhat disturbing. We have to make some decisions pretty damn fast. Hence my call last night.'

'Yeah?' Winter unbuttoned his car coat. 'So what did you tell him?'

'I told him exactly what you'd told me. He had the grace to say he was sorry about the cocaine seizure. You should have been warned. He regrets what happened. He asked me to pass that on.'

'Great. What else did he say?'

'I asked him about the deal the pair of you have. Deal was a word he didn't much like but I think he got my drift.' She glanced down at some notes on the pad at her elbow. 'I gather there's an informal agreement that you return to the job after *Custer* comes to an end.'

'That's right. That's what we agreed. Bazza goes down, along with half his firm, and yours truly is back in harness. He also mentioned some kind of special payment.'

'I see.' She reached for a pencil, pursed her lips. 'Do you mind if I ask you a personal question?'

'Not at all. Do I need a lawyer?'

'Of course you don't. I hope you trust me.'

'So what's the question?'

'It's very simple really.' She sat back in the chair. 'Why are you doing this?'

Winter took his time. The last couple of days he'd been asking himself exactly the same question.

317

'It's complicated,' he said at last. 'I was extremely pissed off with Mackenzie, that's the first thing, and I suppose I wanted some kind of . . . ' he shrugged ' . . . payback. I know I've made life difficult for him in the past but what happened in the van was way over the top. Then there was the challenge of the thing. I've been around a bit. I know you can't pot guys like Mackenzie by playing the white man. You have to break the rules. You have to get under their skins. You have to come at them from the direction they least expect. It's only that way you'll get any kind of result.'

'That's exactly what Mr Willard said.'

'I'm not surprised. He nicked it from me.'

Winter's answer put a smile on her face. She wanted to know more about the deal with Willard.

'There is no more. It was a handshake thing. Like I said last time, the DUI was a set-up. The least he owes me is my job back.'

'And you'd be happy with that?'

'Of course. How many other D/Cs in this town would have taken a scalp like Bazza's?'

'And what about . . . ah . . . repercussions?'

'I'm not with you.'

'People close to Mackenzie who might take offence. You think you can deal with that?'

'Of course. It's the rules of the game. If we've been smart enough to pot them, they're down for the consequences.'

'But you're winning these people's confidence. They trust you. They think you're genuinely bent.'

'That's true.'

'So afterwards . . . ' she was staring at the pencil ' . . . they might feel there's a debt to settle.'

Winter, at last, realised where this conversation was heading. He waited until her head came up. He wanted eye contact.

'This isn't about me at all, is it?' he said softly. 'This is about you. And Mr Willard.'

'There are issues, certainly, that we should be exploring.'

'Like?'

'This vulnerability of yours. Afterwards.'

'Sure. And yours too.'

'I'm not sure I'm following you.'

'Of course you are. I'm a copper. I accept an invitation to go U/C. I build myself a nice little legend. I'm old, I'm useless, I drink too much, and I'm slung out on my ear. Every Pompey villain knows me. There's no way I can pretend I've never been a cop. But that's the beauty of it. Half the city thinks I'm bent already. The fact that I end up on Bazza's books is old news. But then, hey presto, I lay hands on a little evidence or I lay a trap or two, enough to put Bazza away, plus some of his buddies, and there's a trial, and they all go down, and then months later yours truly, back in the job, gets himself a thorough smacking. Some little somerstown tyro trying to make a point. Probably half a dozen of them. Naturally, whether I'm dead or just laid out, there's an inquiry. Who dreamed up this little stunt? Who sanctioned it? Who monitored it? Who failed to anticipate what happened to poor old D/C Winter? And guess where the finger points . . . '

'Nice speech.' Parsons mimed applause. 'We ought to talk specifics.'

'Like?'

'Like Mr Willard's offer.'

'I'm not with you.'

'He believes that this business last week, the cocaine seizure, has changed the scenario. To put it bluntly, he believes you may be at risk.'

'I've been at risk from the start.'

'More at risk.'

'He wants to withdraw me? Abort the whole thing? Only that could be tricky. In fact that would leave me completely in the shit. What do I tell Bazza? That I've got a headache? That the money's crap? That I'm really a copper? Do me a favour, boss. This is like the cocaine thing all over again. In fact it's worse. Those guys know where I live. They'd nail me to the floor.'

'That's exactly the point.'

'What's the point?'

Parsons studied him for a long moment. Then she pushed the notepad to one side.

'I have to be frank. We've done a full risk assessment. It's late in the day, I admit, but at least we've got to grips with it.'

'Who's 'we'?'

'Myself and Mr Willard. There's no question of pulling you out, not at this point in the operation, not unless you insist, and of course that's *absolutely* your right, but whatever happens we're obliged to offer you resettlement.'

'You what?' Winter was staring at her now. '*Resettlement?*'

'Exactly. We'll make sure you have the whole

package, of course. New ID, new passport, new documentation, new address. Full pension.'

'*Pension?*'

'Yes.'

'Where?'

'You'd have a choice. Canada, New Zealand or Australia. We'd pay all relocation expenses plus we'd find you suitable accommodation until you'd had a chance to find your feet.'

'And then?'

'We'd contribute to the capital cost of a house or a flat, whatever you chose. There'd be adjustments, of course, depending on your own financial circumstances, once you'd sold your own place.' She reached for the pad again, and picked up the pencil. 'Gunwharf, isn't it?'

Winter ignored the question. He was still absorbing the implications of this bombshell.

'The full makeover then. A new me. Put out to grass.' The phrase made him laugh.

Parsons didn't see the joke. 'Absolutely.' She nodded. 'Mr Willard and I both agree it's an appropriate outcome.'

'And what if I say no?'

'Then we'd have to look at other pathways forward.'

'Like what?'

'Like a transfer to another force.'

'In the UK?'

'It's possible.'

'But not Pompey?'

'No.'

'So there's no way I can get back to the job? Like he promised?'

'I'm afraid not. Not the way things have panned out. It's for the best, Paul, believe me.'

There was a long silence. Winter could hear the clatter of a trolley in the corridor outside. At length Parsons adjusted the collar of the white coat she must have borrowed. Winter felt like asking her for an aspirin.

'I'm fucked,' he said softly.

'Paul, I'm not hearing this.'

'No?' He gazed at her, robbed of anything coherent to say. Two weeks undercover. A fortnight on the hardest job he'd ever been asked to sort out. Moments when he was certain they'd sussed him. Moments when he knew he'd be lucky to get away with a beating. And now this. Fucked. Rebottled. Relabelled. Stuffed on a plane and exported to the other side of the world. He shook his head. Looked away. There were tears in his eyes. He didn't want her to see them.

'Naturally, we don't expect a response immediately, certainly not this afternoon ... ' she glanced at her watch ' ... but we'd appreciate some kind of decision soon. Maybe in a couple of days. Would that be asking too much?'

Winter was still gazing into nowhere. There were two things he held precious in his life. One was the job. The other was Pompey. And here they were. Both gone. He tipped his head back a moment, gazing up at the ceiling. He had to get a grip. Now, above all, he had to makebelieve.

'I appreciate it, boss.' He gave her a smile. 'It's nice to know you've thought this thing through.'

He got to his feet and made for the door. Only when he'd opened it did she call him back.

'I'm glad you see it our way, Paul,' she said. 'Mr Willard, to be frank, had his doubts.'

★ ★ ★

Half an hour later, Bazza returned in the Range Rover. Shreve was in the back, reading a copy of *Exchange and Mart*. Winter hurried across to the kerb and climbed in. It wasn't until they'd left the one-way system that Bazza enquired about the scan.

'What did they find?'

'Sod all, Baz.' Winter felt unaccountably light-headed. 'And you know why? Because there's nothing fucking there.'

16

Jimmy Suttle, much to his embarrassment, was late for the breakfast meet. She was already waiting for him at the table at the back of the café. She must have been there a while because she'd nearly finished the *Guardian* quick crossword. She spared him a brief glance as he sank into the other chair.

'Disorder. Five letters.'

'Chaos.'

'Very good.' She pencilled the answer in. 'How are you?'

'Knackered.'

He'd known Lizzie Hodson, on and off, for the best part of a year. Small and baby-faced with a first-class honours degree in political science, she was a surprise addition to the *News* reportorial staff, but Suttle had always believed her when she said she loved the city, and her passion for the job itself had never been in dispute. Dogged, nosy and unforgiving, he'd often told her she'd make a great detective.

Now she carefully folded the paper and stowed it in her rucksack.

'So how much do you know?' she asked.

'The basics. A chain of ironmongers. A dozen or so shops across the south. Sold as a going concern three years ago. Collapsed soon afterwards. Does that sound about right?'

She nodded. He'd phoned her last night. Another contact at the *News* had mentioned an investigative piece she'd done on Gullifant's, the week the company went bust. He'd tried to access the feature from the *News* website but without success. Hence his offer to buy breakfast.

'Full fried? The works?' Suttle was studying the menu.

She shook her head. She'd had a bowl of muesli first thing. Another coffee would be good. No sugar.

'You mind if I . . . ?' He gestured at the menu. He was starving.

'Go ahead. Did you get the flat in the end?'

'Yeah. I exchanged last week.'

'The place in North End? The one you showed me?'

'Yeah. I held off for a bit because I thought I was in for a decent settlement after last year but in the end it was only four grand so the mortgage turned out bigger than I wanted.'

'How much?'

'You don't want to know.'

Suttle gave the woman behind the counter a wave. All-day breakfast. Pot of tea. Then he turned back to Hodson. They'd gone out a couple of times when he was still convalescing after getting himself stabbed and he'd shared his hopes of a big whack of money from the Criminal Injuries Compensation Board. At the time he'd enjoyed her company and been slightly disappointed at her reluctance to take the relationship any further. She was sharp and funny. More to the point, she cared a great deal about the job she did.

'You want to tell me about Gullifant's?' he queried. 'I know you're pushed for time.'

She nodded. Most days she had to be in the newsroom by half eight for the prospects meet but his morning she could stretch that by a quarter of an hour, max.

'This was a Pompey firm,' she said. 'Born and bred. The founder was a guy called Ernest Gullifant, sweet old thing by all accounts. I managed to lay hands on an old sepia shot of him outside the shop. Fratton Road. Number forty-three. It's a nail bar now.'

Gullifant's, she said, had been a hardware store. The business had stayed in the family for generation after generation. By the early eighties there were two other branches, one in Copnor, another in Southsea. They sold everything from paint and hanks of rope to electrical fittings and gardening equipment. Then, in 1983, control had passed to Simon Gullifant.

'He was young, barely out of his twenties. He was also the first of them to go to university. He was ambitious. He wanted to *grow* the business. He had big ideas. If you want to put your finger on where it all went wrong, it was probably then.'

Simon, she said, had raised capital by selling forty-five per cent of the shares in the company. This funded an expansion across the south. He opened a further ten hardware stores in towns like Farnham, Midhurst and Petworth, each of them badged with the Gullifant's guarantee of personal service.

'Bottom line, he was selling tradition. These were shops where someone looked after you. You could be as ditzy as you liked. You could be a clueless housewife or some brain-dead student but there'd be a bloke with lots of patience and a nice smile behind the counter who'd explain exactly what you needed. And location-wise they were accessible, right in the middle of town.'

'Sounds great. Where's the catch?'

'Timing. Retail was changing. Everyone was moving out to the trading estates.'

'But surely that's what this Gullifant guy had anticipated?'

'You're right, but pretty quickly he found out why. The big players were building these huge out-of-town retail sheds. They offered parking, convenience, coffee — all that stuff — plus they had huge buying power so they could afford to knock the merchandise out at killer prices. Simon Gullifant stuck at it for the best part of twenty years but, looking back, he never had a prayer.'

Year on year the losses mounted. An expensive advertising campaign failed to attract more punters. A couple of the worst-performing stores were closed. Thirty or so workers were made redundant. A vast hole appeared in the pension fund. And by 2002 an increasingly harassed Simon Gullifant — by now in his early fifties — was only too eager to listen to overtures from a Croydon-based development company.

'Benskin, Mallinder?'

327

'Exactly. These guys were sharp. They were tuned in. They recognised a car wreck when they saw one, but they'd done their homework and knew that some of the Gullifant's freeholds were potentially worth a fortune. Largely because they'd hold the key to town-centre redevelopments.'

Farnham, she said, was one example. Dorking was another. Suttle, eyeing his breakfast, wanted to know why Gullifant hadn't spotted this.

'He was tired, Jimmy. He'd had enough. He had a price in mind for the whole business, the whole chain, and if this Croydon bunch could meet it he'd be more than happy. He wanted to buy himself a yacht. He wanted to set his family up and sail away.'

'So what happened?'

'Benskin, Mallinder gave him more or less what he was after. Gullifant was happy as Larry, though in terms of what happened later it turned out to be a steal.'

'And the shops?'

'Here's the killer. Benskin, Mallinder had bought Gullifant's through a stand-alone company they'd created specially. They called it Redmayne. It was a condition of sale that they continue trading but they just ran it into the ground. Stock levels were all over the place. Service was crap. There was no budget for advertising or price reductions. Gullifant's just curled up and died.'

In 2005, she said, Redmayne went into receivership. Over the last two trading years, she said, they'd booked cumulative losses of nearly four million pounds. Survivors from the old Gullifant's workforce collected their P45s. Even worse, they learned that the company pension fund would be able to pay out barely fifteen per cent of their expected benefits.

'Some of these people had been with the firm all their working lives. A handful of them came from Pompey. The more I found out, the more I knew I was looking at a really substantial piece. Nothing sells like bad news, and if you'd been behind the counter at Gullifant's all your life, the news couldn't get worse. Here . . . ' She extracted an envelope from her rucksack and handed it across. Suttle found himself looking at a photocopy of the piece she'd written. The headline read *Thanks for Nothing*.

'So what about Benskin, Mallinder?'

'They cleaned up. They bought the freeholds from Redmayne and popped them in the bank. The sale of just three of them, when the moment was right, has covered their entire investment in Gullifant's. The rest will be bunce.' She laid a cold hand on Suttle's wrist. 'Capitalism in action, Jimmy. Never fails.'

'And the pension fund? That's not their responsibility?'

'It turns out not. This is a bit technical but their sense of timing was perfect. The rules changed on the first of April 2005. After that, Redmayne would have had a problem.'

'So when did they go bust?'

'March the 27th.' She smiled again. 'Neat, isn't it?'

Winter was treating himself to a mid-morning coffee. He'd been living in Gunwharf now for the best part of two years and from the huge choice of waterfront café-bars and restaurants, this was his favourite. The table in the sunshine beside the window. The waitress who took the trouble to give him a smile. The French pastries that came with his cappuccino. And above all the view.

He was gazing at it now, soaking it in. It was like a lotion, he'd decided. It made him tingle inside. It brought a smile to his face. It made him feel like the person he really wanted to be. Bottle a view like this, he told himself, and you'd make a fortune.

He was watching a pair of novice sailors in a dinghy, no more than kids really, trying to cheat the tide and make it through the Harbour mouth. They were on the far side of the channel, zigzagging out, heads up, desperate to keep the sail filled, oblivious of the churning wake of a passing ferry. The V of the wake spread and spread and the dinghy was broadside on when the kids found themselves suddenly enveloped.

The dinghy rolled, righted itself briefly, then a gust of wind caught the back of the sail and the boom swung savagely over. Winter found himself on his feet as the kids threw themselves across the tiny boat in an effort to avoid the capsize. It didn't work, and seconds later two tiny heads bobbed up alongside the upturned hull. The tide was stronger here, a river of water surging out towards the distant triangle of sea forts, and the dinghy was no more than a dot with a sail by the time they'd got the thing upright again.

Winter sank back into his seat, glad they were safe, acutely aware of the temptation to read too much into an incident like this. The irresistible drag of the tide. A sudden wave. A blast of wind when you least expected it. Then disaster, everything upside down, everything green and wet and cold. Shielding his eyes against the brightness of the morning sun, he tried to imagine how the lads were coping. Were they having a laugh? Were they frightened? Or, like him, were they readying themselves for the next blow?

He'd been awake for most of the night, trying to still his racing brain, trying to tease some kind of order into the chaos of the recent weeks, trying — above all — to get this bloody woman into perspective.

The lads on Covert Ops, he now realised, had got Gale Parsons completely wrong. This wasn't some novice D/I on the make. This wasn't some over-promoted graduate entrant with some vague idea of where she might be heading next. On the contrary, she had real grip. She'd sussed what modern policing was about and she'd made herself word-perfect on every line of the management manual. She'd even had the bottle to front up to Willard and tell him exactly where his wider responsibilities lay.

Winter could picture the confrontation only too well. The risks they were running on D/C

Winter's behalf. The chances of something going wrong and the likelihood of a post-mortem afterwards. Winter shook his head, reaching for the last of the *pain raisin*. Post-mortem was a phrase he was beginning to treat with a great deal of respect.

He looked out at the view again, hoping for a glimpse of the dinghy. In his heart he knew he couldn't do without this place, the busyness, the faces, the memories, the scams, the times he'd stood every fucking rule on its head and still emerged with a result. There was simply too much history here, his own and other people's, to even contemplate stuffing his life into a pile of cardboard boxes and legging it. Manchester or Leeds would be bad enough. Auckland or Winnipeg unthinkable. That's what you'd do if you lost your nerve. Or someone else did on your behalf.

His mobile began to chirp. He looked at it. He wasn't sure he liked the budgie ringtone.

'It's me. I just talked to our pianist friend. Mush, we've got a fucking problem.'

A smile warmed Winter's face. In real life, he thought, there was nothing that couldn't be sorted.

'What is it, Baz?'

'This jet ski business. The Trophy. All that. Turns out someone's got there first.'

'Like who?'

'Fucking *Scummers*. Can you believe that?'

'Horrible.'

'Where are you?'

'Gunwharf.' Winter named the café-bar.

'I'll be there in five. Double espresso. No sugar.'

He arrived minutes later, out of breath. He'd cut himself shaving and there was still a wisp of cotton wool scabbed on his chin. Winter had yet to order the coffee.

'Forget it. I'm pushed as it is. Listen . . . '

He outlined what little Lander had been able to tell him. The producer had talked to the people at Sky. The good news was that jet skis definitely did it for them. There was a big audience out there, no question about it, and Sky Sports would be happy to oblige. The bad news — and it couldn't be worse — was that a bunch of numpties from Southampton had already pitched something similar.

'Like what?'

'That's what we don't know. Lander thinks it's some kind of endurance race but he hasn't got any details. Either way, we're in the shit.'

'Why?' It seemed a sensible question. Bazza didn't agree.

'Because, fuckwit, there's only room for one player at this table. In case you hadn't realised, Southampton is only twenty miles down the fucking coast. That makes us next-door neighbours. There's never going to be room for *two* trophies.'

'Maybe they're taking a different angle.'

'Yeah, and maybe I'm the man in the fucking moon. Listen, mush, a jet ski's a jet ski whichever way you cut it. This thing's about pictures. That's what gets people creaming themselves. That's why the Trophy's going to be

333

such a huge draw. And that's why I'm not having a bunch of Scummers nicking off with it. This is family, right? And that was my brother we just buried. So ... ' he leaned low over the table, nodding at Winter's mobile ' ... you get on the blower and sort it out. If you need wheels, ask Brodie. She's over at the hotel, settling in. OK?'

★ ★ ★

Faraday was in conference with Jimmy Suttle when D/S Glen Thatcher appeared at the door of the tiny office.

'A word, boss?'

Faraday broke off. It was with regard to the Thornhill Park house-to-house over in Southampton. A D/C had just rung in. He and his oppo seemed to have scored a result at an address down near the edges of the estate. A woman recognised the Mercedes from the photo she'd been shown. It had been stored in a lock-up at the bottom of the road. She'd seen it a couple of times when the doors had been open, though yesterday she'd taken a peek through a crack between the doors and thought the lock-up was empty. She was positive it had been the same vehicle.

'How can she be?'

'Apparently she took the reg number.'

'Why?'

'You need to talk to the D/C yourself, sir.' He gave Faraday a number. 'It's Bev Yates.'

Faraday shot Suttle a glance and reached for the phone. Yates was one of the older D/Cs on the *Billhook* squad. Faraday had worked with him for years, both on division and Major Crimes. With his sullen good looks and chaotic love life he could occasionally be a handful but Faraday had never questioned his worth at the sharp end.

'Bev? It's Joe Faraday. Tell me about the Mercedes.'

'It's gone, boss. As of a couple of days ago.'

'I know that. Tell me the rest.'

'I'm not sure I can. We're still checking it out. I think it boils down to some kind of neighbourhood feud. It's been going on a while.'

The lock-up, he said, belonged to a family round the corner from the witness. According to her, they'd been a problem on the estate for years. There was a husband who was out of it most of the time, a fat mum who swore blind all her kids were angels, and then the kids themselves. Tearaways. All of them.

'How many?'

'She says eight.'

'*Eight?*'

'They're Irish.'

'I see. You've talked to these people?'

'Not yet, boss. I thought it was worth phoning in first. See how you wanted to play it.'

'Of course.'

'There's one other thing.'

'What's that?'

'Our witness is pointing a finger at a particular lad. She thinks he's the eldest. And she swears he's the one who laid hands on the Merc to begin with.'

'Nicked it, you mean?'

'She's keeping her fingers crossed.' Yates laughed. 'I think she's looking for payback here. When I told her we were coppers, she thought it was Christmas.'

★ ★ ★

Winter got Brodie to pick him up from Blake House. He'd been on the phone non-stop since Bazza's departure and had finally nailed down an address.

'Lee-on-Solent, love.' He slipped into the passenger seat. 'Bloke called Nigel Evans.'

Lee-on-the-Solent was a quiet residential suburb west of the city highly favoured by retired couples. The price of property kept the riff-raff at arm's length, and a couple of miles of promenade offered a front-row seat when the huge ocean-going liners from Southampton slipped down the Solent towards the open sea. Winter had always associated the place with invalid buggies and lavish bring-and-buys. The sight of a Harley-Davidson outside Nigel Evans's bungalow came as a bit of a surprise.

'You've talked to this guy?' Brodie asked.

'No.'

'Then how do we know . . . ?'

'Because he's the man they all go on about. Trust me, love. I used to be a copper.'

Evans turned out to be tall and skinny with shoulder-length hair and the need to listen to heavy metal at pain threshold. Once they were in the tiny living room Winter asked him to turn the music down. He'd never much liked Led Zeppelin.

'What's all this? Only I've got a living to make.'

Winter said he was interested in jet skis. He understood Evans was a bit of a force in the field.

'Force? That's a bit strong. I'm out on the water a lot, if that's what you mean, and yeah, I've got lots of mates who do the same thing.'

'Locally?'

'All over. Here. Abroad. Wherever. Why?'

'Because we might be able to help each other out.'

'*You're* a rider too?'

Winter didn't much like the tone of his voice. He said he wasn't. Then, without going into details, he outlined the plans for the Mackenzie Trophy. Mention of sponsorship and media interest at last got Evans's attention.

'Sit down.' He nodded at the only armchair. 'You want something to drink?'

Winter shook his head. He wanted to know about the Vectis Enduro.

'Who told you about that?'

'Doesn't matter. It's round the Isle of Wight, right?'

'Sure. We've been running it for a while now, four seasons. Get the right weather, bit of chop on the water, and it's massive. Eight hours in the saddle and you're lucky to move for days.'

'Are these stand-ups or sofas?' Winter stole a look at Brodie. This was ski-talk. Stand-ups were what they sounded like; sofas you sat down on.

She didn't look the least impressed.

'We get both,' Evans said. 'Doesn't matter which. So far it's been open entry — bit of a laugh, an outing basically, plus a ton of moolah for charity — but all that might have to change.'

'Why?'

'Because the telly fancies it. Sky to be precise. Couldn't believe our luck. A chance to be cowboys *and* TV stars? Bring it on . . . '

He explained that someone connected with the big Southampton Boat Show, a major backer, had a daughter who was mad for jet skis. She'd mentioned the Isle of Wight event to her dad, who'd instantly thought of tying it to the week of the Boat Show. The show already drew loads of media. If they talk up the Isle of Wight thing, turn it into a proper race, give it a fancy name, then there'd be even more TV crews knocking on Southampton's door.

'The Vectis Enduro?'

'Exactly. And you're looking at the guy who had to dream all that up. The rest of it, to be honest, isn't my bag, but jet skis, believe me, I can deliver. As many as you like. To whatever standard.'

'What's the rest of it? You mind me asking?'

'Not at all. We're talking profile, the media deals, sponsorship — all that shit.'

'And that's sorted?'

'More or less. There's a syndicate, Southampton businessmen mainly, rich bastards who've been involved a bit themselves. You know, nothing fancy, just roaring around impressing the ladies.'

'So who are they? These rich bastards?'

338

'You want names?'

'Yeah. And a couple of phone numbers if you're offering.'

'Why?'

'Because we might all end up in bed together — pool resources, get something really special going. There's a fancy word for it . . . ' Winter frowned. 'Kath?'

Brodie had been studying the framed colour shots on the wall. One of them featured Evans aboard a jet ski in mid-air. Upside down.

'Synergy,' she said drily. 'It's a business term.'

★   ★   ★

Faraday drove to Southampton. A detour to the CCTV control room in Port Solent had given him a black and white print from the surveillance camera in the car park, and before he talked to the owners of the lock-up on the Thornhill Park estate he wanted to show the shot to Yates's witness.

'That's him. Little squirt.' Her finger hovered over the youth in the grey hoodie. 'I'd recognise him anywhere.'

She was a severe-looking woman not far short of sixty. She wore a small gold crucifix round her neck and there was a fading picture of St Francis of Assisi on the wall above a fish tank. Half a lifetime living in Thornhill Park had done nothing for her sense of charity.

Faraday wanted to know more about the youth she'd ID'd from the picture. Did he have a name, for instance?

'Of course he has a name. Everyone has a name.'

'Do you know what it is?'

'No.'

'Can you describe him?'

'There.' She jabbed a finger at the photo again. 'Him. That one.'

'And what makes you think the car was stolen?'

'Your colleague asked me that earlier and you know what I told him? I said that everything is possible in God's kingdom, absolutely everything. But how in heaven's name would a hooligan like that end up with a Mercedes? Unless he'd helped himself? There's no other explanation, Inspector. Miracles, I'm afraid, have to serve a higher purpose.'

'Has he stolen before? To your knowledge?'

'Not from me, no. But you people are round all the time.'

'How do you know?'

'Because I've got eyes in my head. Because I've seen your cars outside their house. They're a disgrace, the whole lot of them, the whole *tribe*. They breed like rabbits. They have absolutely no sense of *responsibility*. There. I've said it. I'm sorry. But it's true.'

* * *

Bev Yates was waiting in an unmarked car across the road. He and another D/C had been checking nearby addresses, looking for corroboration of the woman's story. Two other witnesses had confirmed the presence of the Mercedes in the lock-up. One of them, a retired postman, had also seen the car leave.

'When?'

'A couple of nights ago. He was walking the dog.'

'Did he see who was at the wheel?'

'Yeah, the same kid. The description matches.'

'Does he have a name?'

'No, boss, but I do.'

Yates had phoned Jimmy Suttle for an electoral roll check on the address. Number 147 Tennyson Drive was occupied by a Mr and Mrs O'Keefe. Further PNC checks established that young Dermott, from the same address, had made two recent court appearances for shoplifting. In both cases the articles involved had been either food or household goods. Suttle, intrigued, had probed further. Household goods evidently included bleach, loo roll and tins of dog food. Listening to Yates, Faraday began to wonder who had drawn up the shopping list.

They walked round the corner. Number 147 was one half of a council semi. There was an abandoned cement mixer and a rusting bike in the tiny oblong of front garden, and closer inspection of the hedge revealed a couple of car tyres, both bald. At the back of the property a patch of beaten earth was scabbed with flattened curls of dogshit. Amongst them stood a line of sandcastles, each topped with a tiny flag. Might the Stars and Stripes be significant? Faraday didn't know.

Yates knocked at the door. A dog began to

bark. It sounded like a big dog. Then came a woman's voice and a yelp. Finally, the door opened.

'Mrs O'Keefe?' Yates showed her his warrant card.

'That's me.'

She was enormous, with a plump, contented face and a fringe of black curls escaping from a pink shower cap. She had milky white skin and a flawless complexion but her ample forearms were criss-crossed with crimson scars.

'Burns, love.' She knew they'd caught Faraday's attention. 'The amount of cooking I get through, you wouldn't be surprised now, would you?'

She had a strong Irish accent. Sight of the warrant card didn't appear to upset her in the slightest. She invited them in, filled the kettle and indicated the one intact chair in the chaos of the steamy kitchen.

'Help yourself, love,' she said to no one in particular.

Faraday had become aware of watching faces at the door. There were three of them, all toddlers. One, the boy, was wearing a red spotted pirate's scarf knotted round his tiny head. Faraday was trying to identify the smell. Cabbage, he decided.

Yates had his notebook out. He wanted to confirm the names of the people who lived here. Mrs O'Keefe obliged, spelling them out. Dermott, she said, had been the first of her brood.

'How old is he now?'

'Sixteen next birthday.'

'And where is he at the moment?'

'I haven't the faintest idea. The boy's a mystery to me.'

'He's not at school?'

'He doesn't like school.'

'Isn't that a problem?'

'Not to Dermott.'

'But don't the education people come looking for him?'

'All the time. Nice, they are. Helpful.'

'But you're telling me he lives here?'

'Sure he does. When it suits him.'

'But not at the moment? Is that what you're saying?'

'No, not since . . . ' She frowned, hunting in a cupboard. Faraday glimpsed a whole shelf of Tesco Own Choice beans and wondered whether they were spoils from one of Dermott's expeditions. Maybe he'd started life as a pirate too. 'Monday night,' she said at last.

Yates asked about the lock-up round the corner. Did that belong to her?

'Not me, love. My husband.'

'What does he use it for?'

'I've no idea. Ask him. He's upstairs.'

'Does he have a car at all?'

'God, no. On my money? You have to be joking.'

She was a dinner lady, she said. As if there weren't enough saucepans in her life.

'So the lock-up's empty most of the time?'

'I don't know. My husband's the one. Give him a shake. Save me the stairs. This time in the afternoon he ought to be getting up.'

Yates scribbled himself a note and then checked his watch. Nearly half past three.

'Does Dermott have access to a car?' It was Faraday this time.

'Of his own, do you mean?'

'Yes.'

'He doesn't, no, not that I'm aware.'

'Does he drive at all?'

'He does.'

'But he can't have a licence. He can't have passed the test. He's too young.'

'That I don't know.'

'But you're saying he still drives cars? Other people's cars?'

'Lord, yes. As often as he can. Loves it too. Just *loves* it.'

'And these cars, does he ever store them in the lock-up?'

'Well I suppose he might now, yes.' She passed the tea. 'Sugar?'

Faraday shook his head. He said he was interested in a particular car, a Mercedes.

'White thing? Flash? New-looking?'

'That's it.' Yates produced the photo. Mrs O'Keefe studied it a moment.

'Dermott's,' she said. 'Proud as you like of it.'

'And you say you've seen this car?'

'I have. Sure I have.'

'When?'

'When he brought it back. Last week? The week before?' She beamed at them both. 'Beautiful it was.'

'Do you know where he got it?'

344

'Not the faintest idea.'

'Did you ask?'

'Never.'

'It didn't bother you at all? Dermott having a car like that?'

'Not at all. Dermott leads the life he leads. Always has done, always will. But you know something? He's a good boy — a sweet nature, a heart of gold. He'll share anything that boy. I sometimes tell Father Joseph, he's not made for this world at all, not Dermott.'

'The car was reported stolen, Mrs O'Keefe. We think there might be grounds for suspecting Dermott did that.'

'Really? That would be a shocking thing now, wouldn't it?'

Her surprise seemed completely unfeigned and Faraday had the feeling that it was she, not Dermott, who lived in a world of her own. These days it was probably enough to put food on the table, give the dog an occasional belt and answer the door to a succession of concerned professionals, beginning with the educational welfare officer and ending with a string of coppers. The rest of it — the aggravation, the whispers, the anguished hand-wringing — was for the likes of the vengeful Christian round the corner.

Yates wanted an address for Dermott. She said she hadn't got one.

'He has friends? A job? You must have *some* idea.'

'He's never mentioned a job. As for friends . . . ' she poked a wisp of hair back inside the shower cap ' . . . I just wouldn't have the first notion. Who knows anything about Dermott? Not me, I'm afraid.'

'But you're his mother.'

'Sure, and proud of it.' She beamed at them both, that same big smile. 'In fact *extremely* proud of it.'

17

Winter sat with Brodie, parked on the crest of Portsdown Hill. A stiffish wind was gusting up the face of the hill and a young girl with blonde hair was flying a scarlet kite, making it swoop and soar against the pale blue of the sky. Brodie had been watching her for some time now. She'd once had a kite, she said, as a kid. Her brother had borrowed it without asking and the thing had ended up entangled in power lines, miles from home. That was the day she'd decided to become a copper. Not because she had any great convictions about law and order but because she was sick of being ignored.

'There, look.' Winter hadn't been listening. 'That's where it happened.'

He was pointing at a patch of scrubby turf a hundred metres down the hill. Earlier he'd described the night he'd been lifted by a bunch of young thugs in the badlands of Buckland. They'd pulled a bin liner over his head and driven round half the night before stripping him naked and dumping him.

Brodie had told him they were crazy to pull a stunt like that. Nearly as crazy as Winter himself for not reporting it.

'They just drove off?' She'd given up on the kite.

'Yeah.'

'So what did you do?'

'Legged it down the hill. I knew I had to find a call box. They'd nicked everything — mobe, cash, clothes, the lot.'

'And?'

'I got hold of a mate. He came and picked me up. Can you believe that? Tucked up in someone's front garden, waiting for him to arrive, stark fucking naked?' He shook his head. The memory still made him faintly nauseous.

'And you're sure it was Bazza organised all that?'

'Positive. He's still got the photos.'

'*Photos?*' She was beginning to understand.

'Loads of them. How would you feel? That kind of stuff going round?'

'Exposed.'

'Exactly.' Winter was brooding now, unable to tear his eyes away from the neat line of avenues below. He could still feel the dampness of the pavement under his naked feet, still remember his terror that some insomniac, at three in the morning, might catch a glimpse of an over-weight, middle-aged lunatic, not a stitch on, hurrying past. Total humiliation, he thought. And now the probability of worse to come.

'How did you get into this game?'

'I just told you. My brother nicked my kite.'

'I meant U/C.'

'Oh.' She shrugged. 'I suppose I must have fancied it. My marriage had just packed up. I didn't feel like being me for a while. I had a girlfriend who'd already qualified. It just seemed to make sense.'

'And do you like it?'

'Yeah, I do. You're working out of area, of course, and there's always the danger that you're going to get dicked around by people who don't know what they're doing, but by and large . . . yeah . . . it's OK.' She helped herself to another of Winter's toffees. 'What about you?'

Winter didn't answer for a while. He was thinking about his relationship with Gale Parsons. 'Dicked around' was a perfect description.

'It's different with me,' he said at last. 'I'm not U/C at all, not like you. There isn't a villain in this town doesn't know who I am.'

'I know, I've been thinking about that. It must make it hard for you.'

'Fucking impossible, if you want the truth.'

'So why did you do it?'

'Because I was asked to. And because I fancied it. At my age you've done pretty much everything. This was something new.'

'And you think it's working out?'

'Yeah.' He nodded. 'Too right it's working out.'

'You make it sound a problem.'

'Do I?' He glanced across at her, wondering whether to take the conversation any further, but decided it was a bad idea. Instead, he nodded at her mobile.

'Give him another ring. We're probably bottom of his list.'

Earlier, she'd belled the D/I in Basingstoke

who was running her. She had three names they'd culled from the conversation with Nigel Evans and she wanted the D/I to run them through PNC.

The D/I apologised for not getting back quicker. He'd pinged the names through the Police National Computer but raised no hits. A check on the force Records Management System had also drawn a blank. One of the names, though, had rung a bell with him. He'd served a spell on the Southampton Major Crimes team and had a feeling that the guy might be worth checking out. He told her what he could remember and wished her good luck.

Brodie returned the phone to her bag.

'Cesar Dobroslaw?' She enquired.

'Never heard of him.'

'He's Polish. Second generation. Runs some kind of import/export business. Lives in a huge pad at the back end of Chilworth.'

Winter was watching the girl with the kite. Chilworth was as close as Southampton got to Beverly Hills. He'd once made a bust there, following a load of Ecstasy tabs hand-delivered to a rave some fifteen-year-old had organised when her parents were away at their second home in Antibes. The swimming pool alone had been bigger than Winter's back garden.

'So why would this guy be suss?'

'We're not sure. There were rumours he was funding a girl trafficking racket. My guy says he'll chase up a couple of contacts, get back to me.'

'When?'

'Soon as.'

Winter eyed the bag of toffees. He liked Brodie. She was far less uptight than most of the female officers he knew, and she seemed tuned in to the more absurd aspects of the job, which made her rarer still. They sat together in a companionable silence. The city lay below them, bathed in autumn sunshine. Winter could see the force spotter plane, Boxer One, flying slow figures of eight over the clutter of Fratton rooftops.

At length Brodie frowned. 'What are we looking for here? Exactly? Only no one's really told me.'

'We're looking to put Bazza under pressure.'

'That's easy. We just leave him to it. That man lives for pressure. He loves it, thrives on it. Take pressure away and he'll be running on empty.'

'I meant real pressure.'

'Like?'

'Like serious competition from the Scummers. Bazza's a turf man. You've probably noticed. As far as he's concerned the Scummers should stay in their cage.'

'But we're talking jet skis, not turf.'

'It's the same thing, love. Or it is if you happen to be Bazza. As far as he's concerned, jet skis are now off-limits to everyone else. His brother died on one. That gives him sole rights. If it sounds barmy, that's because it is. But that's the way he works. Always has done. Always will.'

'So how do we handle it? Take advantage?'

'We keep pushing. This Southampton thing sounds like an open door to me. If some of the

351

money, the sponsorship, turns out to be dodgy then no one's going to be happier than Baz. He's a Pompey boy. He's spent half his life trying to screw the Scummers. If he's ever going to do something silly, something *really* silly, then this is it.'

'And that's enough?'

'As long as it's indictable, and as long as it's a lifestyle offence, sure. Favourite would be some kind of turf war. If we can nudge Baz towards this Polish guy, for instance, and if he was to lift some business off him — narcotics, girls — then we'd be laughing. We supply the evidence and the CPS take care of the rest of it. Baz is loaded. Twenty million quid and counting. There are blokes in our financial unit can't wait to nick it all off him. And as I understand it, under POCA, they can do just that.'

POCA was the Proceeds of Crime Act, a ferociously effective piece of legislation that Winter had given up trying to understand. So-called lifestyle offences included drug or people trafficking, money laundering and pimping.

Brodie was deep in thought. She'd never been to Portsmouth before and the last day or two she'd started asking some serious questions. She nodded down at the view.

'It's a fortress really, isn't it? Not a normal city at all.'

'You're right.' Winter turned in the seat, indicated the line of red-brick battlements along the crest of the hill. 'Some bloke built those in the nineteenth century. Same with the forts out on the water. Pompey was always up for a ruck. Nothing's changed since.'

'And Bazza?'

'Born to it. Bred to it. Couldn't be without it.'

'Without what?'

'Sticking it to the enemy.'

'But what happens when he runs out?'

'Of enemies?' Winter laughed. 'He won't, love. And you know why? Because there'll always be Scummers. Always. And that, deep down, makes blokes like Bazza very, very happy.'

'You like him really, don't you?' It was Brodie's turn to laugh.

'Bazza?' Winter sat back, suddenly reflective. 'Yeah, you're right, in a way I do.'

★ ★ ★

Willard descended on Faraday's office beside the *Billhook* incident room at half past five, fuming at the traffic outside. He'd left Kingston Crescent nearly an hour ago. This was no way to run a city.

'Happens all the time, sir. As you might remember.'

'Never as bad as this, Joe. Ever.'

Jimmy Suttle had beaten a discreet retreat. The Head of CID helped himself to the empty seat, then nodded at the open door. Faraday closed it.

'How's it going?'

Faraday couldn't make up his mind if this was simply a state visit. Willard liked to get around, press the flesh, put the fear of God up the

353

troops. Half an hour of motivational small talk, and he was normally gone.

'It's fine, sir. Cramped, but we make do.'

'Good. Progress?'

Faraday told him about the Mercedes over in Southampton, about the boy Dermott O'Keefe. The link to Port Solent was lawyer-proof. CCTV, witness statements, even his own mother. The fact that the car was nicked had to be down to O'Keefe.

'Of course, Joe. Of course. Good work. But where does that leave us with Mallinder?'

'We don't know, sir. Not yet.'

'Martin Barrie seems to think it might have been opportunistic. The boy saw the car, saw his chance and took it. No connection to Mallinder at all.'

'Mr Barrie may be right.' Faraday shrugged. 'But he's yet to explain the missing keys. Scenes of Crime looked everywhere. So did Mallinder's wife. The fact was, they'd gone. Are we seriously suggesting there were *two* break-ins that night? One to kill Mallinder? Another to nick his car keys?'

'It's possible. Anything's possible. You know that, Joe. All I'm asking for is a sequence of events, proved beyond reasonable doubt.'

Willard was enjoying this, Faraday could see it in his eyes. Nothing pleased him more than a round or two of devil's advocate, a game on which he seemed to have based his entire career. Faraday's next move was obvious to both of them.

'Then there's the CCTV. On the Monday

night the lad turns up alone in a nicked Escort. A different set of pictures puts him in the cinema, leaving a late-night showing with an older guy. Later, after Mallinder's probably dead, we can evidence two blokes leaving in that same car. It's odds-on that one of them is Dermott O'Keefe.'

'And the other?'

'Probably the older guy. The Escort is torched that same night in the New Forest. The next day we find Mallinder dead and the Mercedes keys missing. Two nights later, the Mercedes is nicked. And guess who's at the wheel.'

'OK, Joe.' Willard nodded. 'So we're looking at a really professional hit. Let's just assume it's your older guy. What on earth is he doing nicking the keys to the Mercedes? Taking a risk like that?'

'Maybe he didn't nick the keys. Maybe the kid did, Dermott.'

'And never told him?'

'Yes.'

'So what kind of relationship are we looking at here?'

'Good question, sir. And as soon as we find Dermott O'Keefe I hope I'll be able to give you an answer.'

Briefly, he outlined the steps he was taking to trace the youth. Willard remained unconvinced.

'But it still doesn't work, Joe, does it? We assume the hit is down to some kind of contract killer. You're suggesting he takes a *kid* along with him? Are you serious?'

Willard let the question hang between them.

Faraday reminded him that anything was possible. Then he changed the subject. He wanted to know about *Polygon*.

'It's a mess, Joe, to be frank. We're between a rock and a hard place. We're grinding away for a result, as ever. The lads are putting in the hours, we've got lines of enquiry running God knows where, but always there's a cop-out.'

'Terrorists?'

'Exactly. Don't get me wrong. It may turn out that our London friends are right. It may be that some al-Qaeda cell tossed a coin and decided that the Procurement Minister was due a head job, and why not Pompey, but somehow I still can't see it. This is home-grown, Joe. Not that it makes me popular in certain circles to say it.'

'You can evidence that?'

'Of course I bloody can't.'

'Then why . . . ?' Faraday left the sentence unfinished. It pleased him to be able to play Willard at his own game.

Willard shook his massive head. He had a limited sense of humour and it certainly didn't extend to letting D/Is wind him up. He unbuttoned his jacket. Shifted his weight in Suttle's chair. Lowered his voice.

'There's something else we need to talk about.'

'Sir?'

'Paul Winter. You know about the DUI charge? Albert Road?'

'Of course.'

'I imagine you probably guessed that there was more to that incident than met the eye. And

. . . ah . . . if you *did* guess, then you guessed right. Are you with me?'

Faraday shook his head. He didn't want to hear any of this.

'No, sir. I'm not.'

'Don't pretend to be obtuse, Joe. It doesn't suit you. The fact of the matter is that you were the one who came to me first with the tale about Winter's abduction. You remember that little incident?'

'Yes.'

'And you remember our little chat afterwards? Over at Hornet? When you suggested that I shouldn't be coming down on the man like a ton of bricks? That there might be another way? A subtler way? A *cleverer* way?'

'To do what, sir?'

'To turn this situation to our . . . ah . . . advantage.'

Faraday nodded. He could hardly do otherwise. Time and again he'd wondered why he hadn't simply let Winter take the rap for not reporting the incident in the van. Maybe it was down to a misplaced sense of loyalty. Or maybe he, too, cherished the thought of somehow snaring Bazza Mackenzie. The man was bound to make the most of the leverage he'd won. And there was no better detective than Winter to turn that leverage against him.

Willard was watching him carefully. Something's gone wrong, Faraday thought.

'This is absolutely in confidence, Joe. The DUI was a set-up. And Winter's been in play ever since.'

'You're telling me he's working for Mackenzie?'

'Yes.'

'But half the force know that.'

'Of course they do. And that's exactly the situation we wanted to create. What half the force *don't* know is that in reality he's still reporting to us.'

Faraday nodded. It was no surprise. In fact it was exactly what he'd tried to suggest the night Willard bought him supper at his bloody yacht club. My fault, he thought. Hence this conversation.

'So how's it going?'

'It's going well, Joe. It's complicated, as these things always are, but yes, I'd say it's going well.'

'But there's a problem?'

'Yes.'

'Concerning Winter?'

'Yes.' Willard was taking his time, choosing his words with extreme care. 'To be utterly frank, Joe, I'm not sure we trust him.'

'And you're telling me that's a surprise?'

'Of course it isn't. We always knew what the man's like. But there are elements in this situation that . . . how can I put it . . . are threatening to get out of control.'

'Is that what Winter's telling you?'

'Not at all. In fact Winter's telling us very little. Which is in itself a bit of a worry.'

'Who's handling him?'

'That's none of your business.'

'But you're telling me that Winter is?'

'Yes.' Willard smiled. 'To put it bluntly, we need a second opinion.'

* ★ ★

Until Bazza arrived it had been an extremely peaceable evening. Marie had rung Winter on the mobile, inviting him to supper. He was to come early. She had a couple of pictures she wanted to show him on the laptop, a couple of things she needed to discuss. Winter had showered, changed, dabbed on a little aftershave and taken a cab to Sandown Road.

Marie had readied a couple of large bottles of his favourite San Miguel. There was a bowl of cashew nuts and another of cheese and onion crisps in case he had an allergy. He'd followed her through to the den she used as a study and taken the offered seat at the desk. Her laptop was already fired up and Winter found himself looking at an aerial shot of a stretch of coastline. The sea was very blue, the strip of golden beach virtually empty, but inland a thicket of cranes loomed over a sprawl of unfinished buildings.

'It's a building site,' Winter murmured.

'You're right. It's a development we're calling La Playa Esmeralda. Just down the coast from Barcelona. Door to door, you could be there in six hours. Bazza once did it in four and a half but that was a cheat because he got a lift in a chopper from Barcelona.'

She fingered the touch pad. There were more shots, ground level this time. Winter was trying to count the individual buildings, trying to get some sense of the scale of the development, but Marie saved him the trouble.

'There's a medium-scale apartment block,

seventy-odd units, plus a little estate of low-rise with garages and a bit of garden, plus a couple of stand-alones up on the hill here with a bit of a view, and we've also got permission for a modest hotel if the thing takes off. That'll be here, overlooking the beach. What do you think?'

She'd produced a map. Winter followed her fingernail as she traced the outlines of this latest addition to Mackenzie's business empire.

'Looks fine. Did you design this lot from scratch?'

'No. The developer went bust a couple of months ago. It turned out he had no money. We've bought it off him.'

'Good price?'

'Excellent price. And with most of the infrastructure work already done. We had a surveyor down there last week. He's crawled over every last inch of the place — sewerage, water supplies, power feeds, foundations, the lot. There's oodles to do yet but that's nice too. We can add a few touches of our own. Here.'

She opened a file and showed Winter some artwork. These were artist's impressions rather than computer simulations but if the finished development retained even a hint of these surroundings — mature palm trees, extensive lawns, an artfully designed terrace overlooking the apartment block's pool — then a couple of hundred residents were in for a treat.

'Who thought all this up?'

'Me.'

'They're lovely.'

Marie was delighted. She gave him a peck on

the cheek, poured more beer.

'You'll be wondering why I'm showing you all this. The fact is I've been pestering Bazza all week.'

'About what?'

'You. We'll need someone down there, Paul. Not now, of course. But soonish. If you get the right firm, Spanish builders work at a thousand miles an hour. We'll be looking to have the first clients in by this time next year.'

'You want me to *sell* for you?' Winter's heart sank.

'God, no. We get kids to do that. They're ten a penny. No, what we're after is someone to keep an overall eye on the place. There'll be a general manager of course, but he'll be Spanish. We're not asking you to move out there permanently. I know you'd hate leaving this place. But what we need is a regular presence there, someone from the family, someone we trust.'

'Me?' Winter was astonished.

'You, Paul. And you know why it's a *really* great idea? Because security is the key. The kind of people who can afford the prices we're after are very security-conscious. They want to know they'll be safe down there. They want to know that there'll be no trouble from the locals. And they want to know that the younger element within the development, kids really, are going to behave themselves. This isn't Brits on the piss, Paul. With Playa Esmeralda we're selling peace of mind. It's people's quality of life that concerns us. And little me says you're the man to sort that out.'

Winter reached for his glass. The last time he'd been to Spain was years back, with Joannie, his late wife. On that occasion they'd ended up in a crap hotel in Torremolinos. The food was disgusting, the room looked onto an open-air discotheque, and on the third night of an August heatwave the air conditioning packed up. At the time he'd sworn never to set foot in Spain again. Now this.

'I'd have somewhere to live while I'm down there?'

'An apartment of your choice, Paul.'

'An office?'

'Of course. And a car. And whatever secretarial help you need. Bazza has a line into a local agency. Really nice girls.' She helped herself to a cashew nut. 'What do you think?'

Bazza himself appeared minutes later. He'd been held up by the last of a thousand meetings. He sounded, thought Winter, like an overstretched businessman at the end of a particularly heavy week. Which was exactly what he was.

Marie poured him a Coke with a slug of Bacardi. He took a sip, eyeing the laptop's screen.

'Nice, eh? Marie give you the tour?'

'She did, Baz, she did.'

'And what do you think?'

'I think it's great.'

'Fancy it, do you? San Miguel on tap? Bit of bronzy? Couple of hours in the office when you get bored?'

Without waiting for an answer, Bazza scooped up a pile of mail and began to sort through it.

Marie flashed Winter a smile and retreated to the kitchen. The scent of garlic hung in the air. Winter was starving already.

'Shit.' Bazza was frowning at a document. It looked like some kind of contract. He flipped through page after page, shaking his head, then glanced up.

'Tell me about the Scummers. Brodie says they're planning to race jet skis round the Isle of Wight. So who's behind all this? Who's paying the bills?'

'Still working on it, Baz.'

'You must have got some names.'

'A few, yes.'

'Who are they?'

Winter tallied a couple of Southampton garage owners. Bazza, buried again in his correspondence, said he hadn't heard of either. Then Winter paused, trying to get the pronunciation right.

'And some other bloke called Cesar?' he said. 'Cesar Dobroslaw?'

The name brought Bazza's head up. Winter had seen that expression before.

'Caesar? Polish bloke? Fat bastard? Ships in East European totty by the lorryload? Fuck me, Paul.' He grinned. 'This guy's seriously evil. Result or what?'

★ ★ ★

Troubled by his exchange with Willard, Faraday made his way home. It was late again, gone ten o'clock. In between conferences with members

363

of the *Billhook* team, he'd toyed with making a call to Winter, but in the end decided against it. For one thing, given the Mackenzie situation, he wouldn't welcome contact with a serving cop. For another, Faraday hadn't a clue what he was supposed to say. Willard, in his view, had launched this particular operation. Given his choice of U/C, Operation *Custer* was never going to be less than challenging. Surely it was now up to him, as SIO, to sort it out?

Faraday knew, of course, that this was whistling in the wind. The whole point of being Head of CID was that you *made* the rules. Rule number one with U/C operations was the absolute need for secrecy. Only a handful of individuals ever needed to be in the loop and extending that loop incurred considerable risks. But if Willard genuinely thought that *Custer* was in trouble, and that the only way forward lay in hazarding the operation's integrity still further, then so be it. Sooner or later, whatever his reservations, Faraday would have to pick up the phone. Not now though. Not until he'd worked out something sensible to say.

He swung the Mondeo into the cul-de-sac that led to the Barge-master's House. Gabrielle, for the last two days, had been in London. Faraday had talked to her a couple of times, glad to be part of a conversation that hadn't revolved round contract killers or errant teenage car thieves. She'd been meeting academic colleagues from the Department of Anthropology at Imperial College. These were people with whom she'd only ever had e-mail relationships and it had been great, she'd said, to be able to put faces to names. They'd been enthusiastic about her work with the Vietnamese hill tribes and promised full peer review of her new book in a number of leading journals. They'd also made a fuss of her, dragging her out to a highly recommended Thai restaurant in the depths of Bloomsbury.

Faraday found her in the kitchen, slicing a line of bird chillies. Barefoot on the cold lino, she broke off to kiss him. There was a saucepan of something wonderful bubbling on the stove and she'd readied a bottle of South African Pinotage for his return. After two days of snacking from the fridge, two days of no one to bounce off, Faraday realised how much she'd become a part of his life.

'I missed you,' he said, dumping his briefcase and finding himself a stool. 'How was it in London?'

'Good. Today I meet the professor. He was very kind, very *genereux*. One day I think he might offer me a job.'

'Congratulations. Would you want to work in England?'

'Me? Would *I* like to work in England?' She smiled, emptying the sliced chillies into the saucepan. 'Maybe that's not for me to answer.'

'No?' Faraday was tired. For once he didn't pick up the inflection in her voice. She glanced across at him, a little reproachful.

'It's for you, *chéri*. Would *you* like me to work in England?'

Faraday said he couldn't think of anything nicer. Except maybe moving to France.

365

'You're serious? *Toi? Un flic en France?*'

'Not a cop, no. Maybe a human being.'

The comment brought a smile to her face. She said he was famous. The famous Mr Faraday. Someone at the university had brought her a picture from the newspaper. She had it in her bag. Abandoning the stove, she stepped next door. Seconds later Faraday found himself looking at a black and white shot from the *Evening Standard*. A group of detectives were standing in Goldsmith Avenue. Behind them, beyond the barrier tape, the empty ministerial Rover.

'You, *chéri*.' She pointed him out. Faraday barely recognised the hunched, greying figure. He looked even older than he felt. 'Famous. Everyone in London is talking about it. *Célèbre*.'

'France.' Faraday reached up and kissed her again. 'Definitely.'

★ ★ ★

They ate an hour or so later. It was nearly midnight, and as soon as they'd finished Faraday had an irresistible urge to go outside and stand by the harbour. Driving home, he'd spotted the fullness of the moon away to the south-east. By now, with luck, it would be high water.

It was. He led Gabrielle by the hand. A line of wooden steps accessed the tiny ribbon of pebbly beach. Away in the darkness he could visualise the birds huddled in their roosts. Then came the long haunting call of a curlew. Gabrielle had her arms around him. He could smell her, feel the warmth of her body through the thin cotton of his shirt. Happiness, he thought, could be such a simple proposition.

They stood together for a long moment. Miles above, in the thin moonlight, the whine of a passing jet.

'I didn't tell you, *chéri* . . . ' She gave him a squeeze.

'*Quoi?*'

'J-J sent me a text. He's buying a house. In London.'

18

Robbed of sleep, Faraday finally slipped out of bed, groped for his dressing gown, and tiptoed out onto the landing. J-J's bedroom was at the far end. He switched on the light and closed the door behind him. His son, as usual, had left the room in chaos. The bed was unmade and a cup of cold tea lay beside the brimming ashtray on the window sill. There was a heap of dirty laundry behind the door and the contents of his rucksack spilled across the carpet. Days after J-J's departure, Faraday could still detect the bitter-sweet scent of marijuana.

Faraday surveyed the wreckage for a moment or two, uncertain where to begin. He hated having to do this, hated even the thought of prying into J-J's private life, but last night's news left him no option. If his son was sharing something as momentous as the purchase of a house with Gabrielle rather than his father, then there had to be something seriously awry.

He made a start on two pairs of jeans. From the pockets of one he disinterred a book of Russian matches, a couple of metro tickets, a handful of coins and the stump of a pencil. From the other came a ball of tissue, more coins, a scrap of paper with a scribbled name and phone number and a neat little fold-up map of central

368

Moscow. He put the phone number to one side and sorted quickly through the rest of the clothes. Socks, T-shirts, vests yielded nothing. Likewise two pairs of trainers and a sturdy pair of boots.

Faraday eyed the scatter of paperbacks beside the rucksack. The *Lonely Planet Guide to Russia*. A battered copy of a Martin Cruz Smith thriller. A brand new edition of *Crime and Punishment* that looked untouched. Three books of Manga. He flicked through each of these, holding them upside down, hoping for a letter, a note, maybe even a receipt — anything that might shed light on his son's sudden wealth. In one of the Manga books he found a couple of the postcards to which J-J had attributed his windfall. They both featured shots taken in a cemetery and Faraday studied them a moment. The images were stark, arresting, deeply unusual, but how many of these would you need to sell to earn yourself $70,000? He shook his head, knowing that J-J had been lying. But why?

He began to dig around in the rucksack. At the bottom was a litter of miscellaneous rubbish — more scraps of paper, a box of toothpicks, four packs of Russian condoms, two wafers of chewing gum, a single crusty sock. He emptied the contents onto the carpet, wondering why J-J could possibly need a dozen hairclips, when something else fell out of one of the rucksack's side pockets. It was a small digital camera in a soft leather pouch. He looked at it a moment. Inside the pouch, tucked beside the camera, was a memory card wrapped in cling film.

369

The camera was an Olympus. Faraday found the power button and turned it on. Prompts on the tiny screen took him through a couple of dozen stored shots, faces mainly, beaming at the camera. The venue seemed to be some kind of bar. Many of the shots featured J-J himself. He had a bottle in one hand while the other was draped round an assortment of friends. He looked drunk and happy. Faraday peered at the digital readout. 03.09.06/23.13. This must have been his leaving party, he thought, a chance for J-J's mates to say goodbye. Next day, thick-headed, this son of his would have been heading out to the airport.

The rest of the memory card was empty. Faraday stripped the cling film from the other card and loaded it into the camera. The first shot, from street level, showed a block of flats. Next came a railway station, somewhere out in the suburbs, with an electric train disgorging hundreds of commuters. Then, suddenly, Faraday found himself looking at a woman in early middle age. Naked, she was sitting on a bed with her back against a bolster. She had a full body, big breasts, and a smile that spoke of recent sex. One hand held a tumbler of something pale and fizzy. The other, between her splayed legs, was displaying her genitalia. Faraday gazed at the image. The detective in him was trying to fathom the link between the station and this moment of post-coital celebration. The father in him was starting to wonder what else J-J had got up to.

He flicked on through the memory card. Many of the shots were close-ups. The woman had scarlet nails and a dedicated sense of adventure. Whatever pleasure she derived from an empty bottle of vodka and a series of other implements was difficult to gauge because these shots rarely included her face, but she was clearly determined to leave J-J with a reminder of what he was missing once he got home. Towards the end of the card J-J must have put the camera on remote and lodged it elsewhere in the room because there were now two people on the bed, J-J on his knees, his thin white body arched back, while the woman took him in her mouth. Faraday was still trying to cope with the strangeness of seeing his son like this when he heard the door open behind him.

It was Gabrielle. She knelt beside him. Faraday felt her stiffen as made sense of the image on the tiny screen.

'*Merde* . . . ' she said softly.

★   ★   ★

Carisbrooke Road backed onto the south side of the football stadium at Fratton Park, a row of modest terraced houses with single bays on the ground floor. The curtains upstairs at number 14 were still pulled shut.

Suttle took a chance on Sam Taylor being in. At eight in the morning, he told himself, a man in his sixties who'd recently been made redundant was unlikely to be at work. He knocked again, listening for signs of life inside. He'd rung Lizzie Hodson for the address last night. He'd read her *News* feature piece on the collapse of Gullifant's, and Sam Taylor seemed to have been the most articulate of the victims quoted. He'd talked of pension rip-offs and the helplessness of the little man in situations like these, and according to Lizzie he'd appointed himself spokesman for the abandoned Gullifant's workforce. Ask him about the day they all got their P45s, she'd said. And give him my love.

At last Suttle heard footsteps. A shadow loomed behind the pebbled glass in the front door. The *News* photographer had pictured Taylor as a sturdy, big-boned man with steady eyes and a quiet smile. In barely six months he seemed to have aged a decade.

'Yeah?' He was wearing an old dressing gown. He needed a shave.

Suttle showed him his warrant card. He'd appreciate a moment or two of his time. It wouldn't take long.

'What's it about?'

'Gullifant's.'

Taylor invited him in. From upstairs somewhere came the sound of a bath being run. Then the clump of heavy footsteps overhead.

'My missus. She takes first turn. I jump in afterwards. You want tea?'

Suttle found himself in the kitchen. A cat eyed him briefly then disappeared through the flap in the back door. Taylor was plugging in the electric kettle. Shopper's Choice tea bags. Just one for the pot.

Suttle perched on a stool. There was a gruffness about Taylor that told him his time was limited. A bathful of hot water cost a fortune.

Best not to waste it.

'I got your name from Lizzie Hodson at the *News*, Mr Taylor.'

'Why's that?'

'Because I'm interested in what happened to Gullifant's.'

'Why's that?'

Suttle mentioned Mallinder. Just the sound of his name brought Taylor to a halt.

'That man deserved everything he got,' he said at once. 'And you can write that down if you want. I haven't a clue how it happened but I just hope to God that whoever did it took his time. Can you shoot someone slowly? I hope you can. And I hope the bastard suffered — excuse my French.' He gave the teapot a stir and filled a mug. 'Sugar?'

Suttle took the mug. He wanted to know about the local Gullifant's workforce. How many had been made redundant?

'In this town? Sixteen. That's nine full-timers and the rest just fillers-in. It's the full-timers that really copped it.'

'People like you?'

'That's right. Like I say, nine of us in Pompey, but across the whole company you're talking over a hundred, women too, not just blokes, and all of us out on our ears. Was it a surprise? No, of course it wasn't. We knew trade wasn't good, hadn't been for a while. But that was their fault, the new blokes, the management, Redmayne, whatever they called themselves. They just weren't interested. You could tell that from the start. Whatever you asked for, the answer was always no. Customers after a new line of paint? Forget it. Buy in extra stocks for spring? When everyone starts decorating? You're joking. New lead for the staff electric kettle? Make do with the old one. An attitude like that, we were bound to go under. The only surprise was it took so long.'

Suttle had a feeling Taylor had made this speech before but there was no mistaking the anger, and the bitterness.

'So what happened the day they went bust?'

'We all got a letter. Not even personal. Just 'Dear Sir', and even then they couldn't be arsed to get *that* right. Just imagine. You turn up to work, a Monday morning, and there's security van parked up outside with a couple of goons in uniforms in case anything kicks off, and then you walk in, just like normal, and there are all these letters waiting, envelopes with names on. You know how mine started? With my name on the envelope? Mr S. Taylor? It started 'Dear Madam'. They'd put the wrong one in. That's how much they cared about us.'

Many of the local blokes, he said, had been with Gullifant's all their working lives.

'They'd paid into the pension scheme. That's five per cent of everything they earned. You do the sums. Take me, for instance. I'm sixty-three. I joined Gullifant's out of the Navy, nineteen seventy-three. So for thirty-three years I'm paying my dues, keeping my nose clean, thinking it's all watertight, and then — bang — they say there's a problem with the pension fund, bloody great hole, not enough money, and you know what we get come the finish? Fifteen per cent of what we're due. *Fifteen per cent*. And that's if we're lucky. My missus got the calculator out. She reckoned I'd paid in tens of thousands come the finish. And what will I see of that? A pittance. Pathetic. Absolutely pathetic. Should never have been allowed. Not in a decent country.'

Suttle asked about redress. Surely there was some kind of right of appeal? Some kind of compensation fund?

'Yeah.' Taylor nodded. 'You'd think so, wouldn't you? Well let me tell you, son, there's bugger all you can do about it. You write to your local councillor. You phone up your MP. You get a letter in the paper. You make a fuss. We even got a petition going, not just us Gullifant's blokes but loads of others in the same boat. Thousands of signatures, *thousands* of them. And then what happens? You get a letter from some smartarse minister telling you there's all kinds of help available, this scheme, that scheme, but then you look a bit harder and it's never that simple. Either the money's not there at all, or if it is then it's nowhere near enough. My missus has got a file upstairs thick as your arm, all the letters she wrote, but what it boils down to is a queue. All you want is what you put in. But they've had it off you. It's gone. Just disappeared.'

'Who's they?'

'Bloody good question. I asked that myself. Tell you the truth, I'm *still* asking it. It's like a conjuring trick. You put all that money in and — puff — it just goes. Someone's had it. I know they have. Thieving bastards.'

'And what about Mallinder. Did you ever write to him?'

'Yeah. We went up to see him too, took a little deputation over to Croydon, tried to put our case. That Lizzie Hodson was very helpful. She was the one who got us all the information, all the stuff about Benskin, Mallinder, how they'd bought Gullifant's in the first place, then sold it, then bought the freeholds back. Makes you dizzy, doesn't it? Trying to keep up with these people?'

'So you met Mallinder?'

'Yeah. Charming bloke, couldn't be more sorry for us. Not his fault, though. Not the way he saw it. Market pressures, that's what he blamed it on. That and the way the hardware trade had changed. Me, I asked him why he'd bought Gullifant's in the first place in that case, and you know what he said? He said that every time a businessman made a decision he took a risk. That was the nature of the beast. Sounds brave, doesn't it? All that risk-taking? Except it turned out that the risk wasn't his at all, it was ours. Like I say, a conjuring trick.'

Upstairs Suttle could hear movement again. His wife's out of the bath, he thought.

'So what are you doing now? How do you make ends meet?'

'I've got a job. B&Q, just up the road. I do the afternoon shift. The money's not great but it's better than nothing.'

'Still in the hardware trade then?'

'Yeah, funny isn't it? A couple of the other

Gullifant's blokes are in there with me. Tell you the truth, B&Q couldn't wait to snap us up. It's not the same though, in fact it's not a shop at all, more a warehouse. Cheap, though, compared to the prices we used to charge.'

Suttle finished his tea. He'd asked for details on other members of the Gullifant's workforce and Taylor said he'd get something together for later in the day. Walking back up the narrow hall, Suttle wondered how big a blow the Gullifant's collapse had been for Taylor and his wife. These days even some occupational schemes would barely keep your head above water. How on earth could you survive on a state pension alone?

'Good question.' It was Taylor's wife. She was sitting on the stairs, a big woman in a grey tracksuit with a pair of pink fluffy slippers. 'Tell him, Sam.'

'Tell him what?'

'Tell him what we were going to do. Before this lot all happened.'

'Yeah . . . ?'

With some reluctance Taylor described their retirement plans. The cash element of the Gullifant's pension was going to pay off what they owed on the house with a bit to spare. They then planned to sell the house, invest the money in a little place in Spain, and live off the annuity plus the state pension.

'It's cheap, see, Spain. And nicer too. Quieter.'

'But can't you still do that?'

'No way.' He nodded in the direction of the stadium. 'This new chairman wants to move the club somewhere else. That means they'll tear

377

the old ground down and build loads of houses, flats, whatever. With all that going on, no one in their right mind would want a house like this. It's development again. Can't bloody win, can you?'

Suttle said he was sorry. He found a card and handed it across. With the door open he turned to say goodbye but Taylor beckoned him back.

'I don't want you to think I'm moaning,' he said. 'There are blokes worse off than me, much worse off. Did that lass from the *News* mention Frank Greetham at all?'

Suttle shook his head. He couldn't remember the name from Lizzie's article. Taylor was nodding at the notebook in Suttle's hand.

'Write it down,' he said. 'Frank Greetham. Lovely man. Lovely, lovely bloke. Been with Gullifant's all his working life.'

'Where do I get hold of him?'

'You don't, son. That's the whole point. He killed himself last month. I was going to give that Lizzie Hodson a ring but I never got round to it.'

* * *

Bazza had told Thom Pollard to make himself available. Winter found him in the locker room at the indoor tennis centre, a five-minute walk from Gunwharf. His hair still wet from the shower, he was pulling on a pair of tracksuit bottoms. Beside him, on the bench, was a list of names with pencilled notes beside each.

Winter glanced at it. In his late forties, Pollard had a reputation in the city for putting himself around. Fitter than most twenty-somethings, he

378

made a precarious living by mixing tennis lessons with fashion shoots and occasional appearances in various TV soap operas. Teenage girls got silly about him, often finding themselves in competition with their mothers for his attentions. Winter had always liked him. He was wry and funny, with a reckless streak that had always appealed to Bazza.

Pollard consulted the list. His first pupils were due on court at a quarter to ten. There was a café upstairs. Winter had half an hour of his undivided attention. After that he'd have to queue up, like everyone else.

Winter bought two coffees. Pollard was deep in the sports pages of the *Daily Telegraph*. The morning run had put colour in his face.

'This bloke Cesar . . . '

'You met him at all?' Pollard didn't look up. 'Never. So tell me.'

'Big bloke. Handy too. Used to box a bit, years ago. Nearly turned pro, or that's what he always says.'

Winter reached across and folded the newspaper. Pollard looked up, amused.

'Baz says you're on the payroll now.'

'He's right, son.' Winter nodded at the paper. 'So a bit of respect, eh?'

'Good money?'

'Not bad. Better than working my nuts off for the Men in Black.'

'Yeah, I heard about that. You want to be careful of policemen. Some of them are nasty bastards. Bent too, if you believe everything you hear.'

Winter ignored him. Bazza had mentioned Pollard giving private lessons to Dobroslaw's kids.

'That's right, I did, a couple of months back. One of them turned out to be good. The kid had real talent plus he wasn't quite so much of a dickhead as most of them. There were days on court when he even listened to me. Shame, really. If he'd stuck at it, he might have got somewhere.'

'So what happened?'

'I took him to Barcelona. There's a tennis school there. The standard's really high. I turn up with a handful of kids, plus their mums, and we put them through three days intensive coaching. It's just a taste of what they can expect if they want to be serious about the game but it sorts out the duffers — you know, the ones who've got an attitude problem.'

'And Cesar's boy?'

'Was bloody good.'

'So what was the problem?'

The café area was beginning to fill up. Pollard gestured Winter closer.

'The deal in Barcelona was this. The mums bugger off to some fancy hotel and go shopping for a couple of days while I sort the kids out. The accommodation's pretty rough but that's all part of it. There were three kids and me. We were dossing down in a Portakabin, basically. The first night I'm trying to get to sleep but the kids are pissing themselves laughing. In the end I've had enough so I put the light on. Turns out they've got this electronic thing, hand-held, some kind

380

of gizmo that gets you on to the Internet. And there they all are, perving on some porn site. Not the usual stuff but *really* heavy — women giving donkeys blow jobs, that kind of shit. Truly vile.'

Winter gazed at him. 'How old were these kids?'

'Eleven, twelve . . . ' Pollard scowled. 'Much too young for donkeys.'

'So what did you do?'

'I took the machine off them, told them to go to sleep. The machine belonged to Cesar's kid. Next day I got on the phone and had a word with his mum, told her what had gone down. And you know what? She just fucking shrugged. Nothing she could do about it. Just give him the thing back and let them get on with it. Kids will be kids. *Qué será* . . . '

Outraged, Pollard had phoned Cesar. Within half a day the kid and his mum had been on a plane to Gatwick.

'Did you see him afterwards? This Cesar?'

'Yeah. He called me over to his place in Southampton. Believe me, mate, this bloke's impressive. He lives like a king . . . big, big spread on the outskirts of Chilworth. Tennis court, swimming pool, stables, the lot. But he's still strict, hard as nails with his kids. Maybe it's the Catholic thing, Christ knows, but he thanked me for what I'd done and told me how he'd sorted the boy out, and I believed every word. Which is odd, really, isn't it? Given where the money comes from?'

Winter nodded. Brodie had got more details from the D/I who was running her. Dobroslaw had a successful import/export business, all totally legit, but on the side he was thought to be buying Belarussian girls on forged documents from an agent in London. These girls were lodged, four to a house, in premises in Southampton. With each of them servicing ten punters a day, Dobroslaw was looking at a take of around twenty grand a week from each house. Naturally, there wasn't a shred of proof to connect the Pole to any of this, but years of trying to nail Bazza on narcotics charges had taught Winter how money could buy the very best in terms of protection. The right financial advice, a clever brief, a series of offshore accounts, and you were home safe.

'So the kid's not playing tennis anymore?'

'Not to my knowledge. And that's just one of the things he's not doing. Like I say, the guy's really old-fashioned. Won't put up with any shit. Christ knows how he ever married that bimbo of a wife.'

'Right.' Winter glanced at his watch. 'Did he ever mention jet skis at all?'

'Jet skis?' Pollard shook his head. 'No. Why?'

Winter explained. The possibility of Cesar backing a big event drew a nod from Pollard.

'He'd do that,' he said at once. 'That's exactly what he'd do.'

Before it had all kicked off in Barcelona, Pollard had got to know Cesar's wife a little. Like her husband, she was from Poland. The Polish community in Southampton, she'd said, was enormous, and there was a lot of pressure to get to the top of the pecking order. What spoke loudest, of course, was money but what mattered as well was profile. You had to be *seen*. You had to be *recognised*. And the quickest way to acquire a sprinkle or two of that kind of stardust was to buy it.

'It's true about immigrants,' Pollard said. 'They just try harder. All that acceptance stuff matters. They want to end up more English than the English, and if spending a couple of bob on some dickhead race round the Isle of Wight does it for them, then so much the better. Cesar wants to join the club. He's got deep pockets. Because he's a businessman he'll call it an investment but actually it's a lot more than that. Like I say, it *matters* to him.'

Winter smiled. Bazza, in his own way, was doing exactly the same thing. He remembered the garden at Sandown Road, the guests flocking round for the raffle, the endless supply of Krug, Marie's extravagantly wrapped birthday presents heaped on a table in the lounge. The club, he thought. And all the countless benefits of membership.

'That's my lot.' Pollard was eyeing three adolescents beside the drinks machine. They'd abandoned their rackets on the floor and were debating how many cans of Pepsi they could afford.

Pollard got to his feet, glancing at his watch. Then he picked up the paper.

'You're going to have dealings with Cesar?'

'I expect so.'

'Then watch yourself. He's like all these alpha guys. Just hates to lose.'

* * *

Twenty-four hours of intense activity had failed to locate Dermott O'Keefe. Checks with the Education Department at Southampton Civic Centre confirmed that persistent truanting had brought him to the attention of the Youth Offending Team. Attempts to transfer him to a special school had come to nothing chiefly because no one could ever find the lad, but Suttle — at Faraday's prompting — had turned his attention to Social Services, and in the shape of a guy dealing with vulnerable young people, he thought he might have raised a lead.

Faraday, unusually preoccupied, had just returned from Kingston Crescent. Suttle had typed up a brief intelligence report on the Gullifant's collapse but Faraday scarcely glanced at it.

'So what are Social Services saying?'

'They want a meet, boss. The guy's name is Rick Bellinger. He's been carrying O'Keefe's file.'

'Does he know where he is?'

'He says not. But he still thinks it's worth getting together.'

'OK.' Faraday was unpacking the contents of his briefcase. 'Let me know how you get on.'

* * *

Suttle drove to Southampton. Rick Bellinger worked from a big, airy office on the first floor in the Civic Centre. He was dressed for a summer rave — jeans, T-shirt, sleeveless leather jerkin — and his shoulder length greying hair was in need of a wash. He hadn't shaved for a while either and confessed the weekend couldn't come too soon. The caseload lately, he said, had been crippling. Whatever else New Labour had achieved, it didn't pay to be a kid anymore.

They talked in a small, bare interview room. A nest of fluffy toys and a Coldplay poster were the only concessions to informality.

'I phoned the lad's mother just now. Strictly speaking, she needs to sign a form for this to happen but she seemed quite happy so I'll sort it out later. That OK with you?'

Suttle said fine. Dealing with kids, as he knew only too well, could be a nightmare. Bellinger looked like a refugee from the sixties. Guys that old sometimes took a more relaxed view of the paperwork.

O'Keefe's file lay on the desk. Bellinger didn't touch it. He wanted to know whether Suttle had ever met the lad. Suttle shook his head. If only.

'He's unusual,' Bellinger said. 'Most of the referrals we get, you can bet there's trouble at home. Broken families, step-parents who can't cope, various forms of substance abuse, domestic violence, whatever. Trouble's like sand. It obeys the laws of gravity. It trickles down through all that shit and it's the kids at the bottom of the pile who get dumped on.'

'But this Dermott's the oldest.'

'Exactly. And that's not where it ends either. I don't know whether you've been round to the house at all but chaos would be a polite word.

385

There are eight kids in that house and the old man's out of it most of the time, but in a funny way the whole thing works. So for once we're not talking a shit home life. Far from it.'

'So where's the problem?'

'Money. They're skint. Eight kids take a lot of looking after and I'm betting the old man's booze bill is astronomical. We made sure they're getting everything they're entitled to but even so it's really hand to mouth. Mum's the one who holds it all together.'

Suttle was trying to reconcile this account with the version he'd heard earlier. According to Faraday, young Dermott's mother had declared UDI. The fact that her oldest was breaking every law in the land didn't appear to concern her in the least. No school. No driving licence. No insurance. Regular court appearances. Someone else's £40K motor in the lock-up round the corner. Surely this was tolerance gone mad?

'She's overwhelmed,' Bellinger said at once. 'She's just got too much on her hands. As far as she's concerned, Dermott's a good wee boy, well-intentioned, and the rest of it is none of her business.'

'So why has Dermott gone off the rails?'

'Well . . . ' Bellinger smiled, ' . . . that's just it. In a way, he hasn't. If you analyse his behaviour, ask yourself why he's done each of these things, then you start getting a pattern.'

Both court appearances, he said, were down to shoplifting. In both cases he'd pleaded guilty and flatly denied he'd gone shopping with a list that his mother or someone else had drawn up. But the fact remained that few fifteen-year-olds stuffed loo roll, bleach and soap powder under their anoraks. They just couldn't be arsed.

'So what does that tell you?' asked Suttle.

'It tells me that the boy cares, that he *contributes*. In some societies he'd get a medal for what he's done.'

'And school?'

'Bored shitless, like more or less every other kid in the country. But bored shitless because as far as he's concerned there's no bloody prospect of learning anything. Listen to Dermott for half an hour and you start realising why kids get into university without knowing how to read and write properly. The only difference is that the Dermotts of this world aren't prepared to put up with it. When school showed no sign of ever getting better, he walked.'

'But why isn't he living at home then?'

'Same reason he didn't stick it at school.'

'Which is?'

'Chaos. No space. No space to think. No space to call his own. The house isn't big. Seven siblings is a lot of noise. Three tellies are three tellies too many. Ask the neighbours. Dermott's a kid who's been trying to pay his way for years. You know how old he was when he got his first paper round? Eleven. That impressed me. Four o'clock in the morning and here's this kid on this broken-down bike his dad's rescued off the tip pedalling around in the pitch black. I said to him, Dermott, that's outstanding. And you know what? He gave me this funny look, as if I was trying to patronise him, and then he said, Mister why do you think I took the job? Why do you think I kept it up? Year after year? And you know the answer? Because that was the only way he could get any space in his life. He wasn't abused. He wasn't unloved. He wasn't bullied. He wasn't even seriously disadvantaged. He was just desperate to get a bit of peace and quiet. See what I mean?'

With some reluctance Suttle nodded.

'And the Mercedes? You're telling me that's good karma? Nicking forty grand's worth of someone else's motor?'

Bellinger didn't know about the car. Suttle explained. They had CCTV evidence plus witness statements from the estate. At best, the lad was down for a serious theft. At worst, he could be up for something very nasty indeed. Like conspiracy to murder.

Bellinger was still thinking about the Mercedes. O'Keefe, he said, didn't move in criminal circles. He'd undoubtedly have nicked the car to sell on but he'd be pushed to get a decent deal. Some cowboy with a forecourt would have it off him for a couple of grand.

'But a couple of grand's a couple of grand.'

'Sure.'

'So where would that go?'

'His mum,' Bellinger laughed. 'I'd put money on it.'

At last, he opened the file. Suttle wanted to know about friends, older kids who might have access to a rented flat, relatives maybe with a house of their own — any lead that might give *Billhook* an address. Bellinger shook his head.

'Can't help you, I'm afraid. The lad's a bit of a loner. If there was someone he was especially close to, I'd probably know. However . . . ' He frowned, turning the pages of the file, hunting for something in particular. 'Ah, here we are.'

Much earlier in the summer, he said, Social Services had paid for Dermott to attend a four-day residential course in the New Forest. Bellinger had been dubious from the start about his suitability but the magistrates at his last hearing had made a point of recommending that he be included in the next tranche of candidates, and magistrates were bad people to cross in this respect.

'What kind of course?'

'Bottom line, it's about self-esteem, trying to turn kids' lives around, offering them all kinds of challenges within a carefully constructed dynamic. They wrap this stuff up in all kinds of psycho-bollocks but actually this one seems to work. Whatever 'work' means.'

'And Dermott?'

'Dermott was wrong for it. I said so from the start. He's never had a problem with self-esteem. Far from it. Here's a kid who knows exactly what he wants, what he needs and pretty much how to get it.'

'And what happened?'

'Well, he certainly turned up. That was a bit of a result, for starters. And he saw the thing through as well. In fact I've a feeling he was a bit of a star because they got him back for the Junior Leader programme. The reports we had back talked about his maturity and the way he coped with some of the stroppier kids. The people running the course liked him, definitely.'

'And Dermott himself? What did he think?'

'I've only seen him once since then.' Bellinger was checking the file again. 'That was last month. We were back in court so we didn't talk much about what had happened in the New Forest. I do remember one thing he said, though. It was the first time he'd been camping, out in the open air, and he loved it, couldn't get enough of it. The only problem was everyone else. Same pattern, you see? Young man who likes his own company.'

19

It was Bazza Mackenzie's idea to drive across to have a chat with Cesar Dobroslaw. Winter counselled patience, said it might be better to get a little more information before they jumped in, but patience wasn't a word for which Bazza had much time. Here was someone deeply dodgy who was in danger of planning a spoiler. It wasn't his fault that he didn't know about Mark's death or plans for the Mackenzie Trophy so Bazza owed him, at the very least, a bit of an update.

En route Winter was curious to find out whether Bazza regarded this man as a Scummer.

'Of course he is. He lives there, mush. He pays the fucking council tax. He's tainted. Just like they all are.'

'But he's Polish, Baz. Fair play.'

'Fair play, bollocks. A man settles in Scummerdom, puts his kids through their schools, buys his groceries from their supermarkets, what else could that possibly make him? Christ, I bet he's even got a *season ticket* at St. Mary's.' St. Mary's stadium was the home of Southampton Football Club. Rivalry between Pompey and the neighbouring city was at its most volatile on the pitch and on the terraces. Baz, Winter knew, viewed the hated Scummers as the devil's spawn. That made Dobroslaw a prime target.

'So what do we say to this guy?'

'We explain our interest. If the man's got an ounce of decency in his body, he'll back off.'

Electronically controlled gates and a sweep of gravel drive led to Dobroslaw's house. Winter had phoned ahead, asking for half an hour of his time, and the Pole had agreed at once. It seemed he'd heard of Bazza Mackenzie. It would be a pleasure to meet him.

Now, late afternoon, Winter climbed out of the Range Rover. The house belonged on the cover of one of the magazines he occasionally flicked through on visits to the dentist. On the outskirts of Chilworth, it was surrounded by fields. There were crows in the tall stand of trees beyond the treble garage, and the autumn sunshine, still warm, made the soft ochre brickwork of the old farmhouse glow. Mackenzie stood looking at it, lost for words. He'd always wanted a thatched roof over his head.

'Nice, eh?'

It was Dobroslaw. He was a big man, powerfully built. The trousers belonged to a business suit and he wore a blue and red striped tie with his crisp white shirt. He stood in the open doorway in his polished Gucci loafers, his weight balanced on the balls of his feet. The offered handshake was a crusher and, close-up, his big, flat face was mapped with tiny broken veins. A drinker, thought Winter. Like Mackenzie, this man has no patience.

From inside the house came the sound of

someone practising on a piano, playing the same phrase again and again. Then the playing stopped and Winter heard a low series of instructions followed, moments later, by the same sequence of notes, repeated and repeated.

'Chopin. My son is learning the piano. Not as easy as tennis. You guys want something to drink?' He had a deep voice, thickened with booze and cigarettes. The accent was still heavy. Not a Scummer at all, thought Winter.

Bazza was looking at an oil painting that dominated the low-ceilinged hall. The artist had caught a certain expression on the woman's face. She looked, if it were possible, both demure and alluring.

'Wicked,' he said. 'Who's that?'

'My wife.'

'She's beautiful.'

'I blame the artist. Too much praise and a woman, she becomes impossible. You find that at all?' He roared with laughter, not waiting for a reply but leading them into a sitting room at the back of the house.

The room was intimate yet imposing, softly lit by the spill of light from the shallow bay window. The window looked out onto a terrace. Beyond the swimming pool was a paddock. Bazza, Winter suspected, was counting the horses. There were five. Faintly, as Dobroslaw clumped from the room, came the growl of a distant tractor. Everything in the house, the garden, the view, smelled of money.

'Not bad, eh?' Bazza muttered. 'For a fucking Pole.'

393

Dobroslaw returned with a tray of drinks. The bottle of Bison Grass sat in a nest of ice cubes. Dobroslaw poured generous measures and proposed a toast.

'Na Zdrowie, gentlemen. To a long life.'

'Yeah.' Bazza raised his glass. 'And a good woman.'

The chilled vodka coiled in the pit of Winter's stomach. Already, he could sense this encounter getting out of hand. Dobroslaw, by virtue of his sheer presence, had taken charge. And Bazza wouldn't like that.

'So, gentlemen . . . ' Dobroslaw waved them onto the sofa ' . . . how can I help you?'

Bazza began to explain about his brother. Winter, who'd heard all this a thousand times, was watching Dobroslaw's face as he settled in the armchair. His eyes were narrow, almost slits, pouched with good living. His jet-black hair was swept straight back, no parting, and one of his ears had obviously suffered damage in the boxing ring. Listening to Mackenzie, he gave nothing away.

'So then . . . you have a trophy?'

'Yeah. For Mark. Respect, really. You got any brothers?'

'Three. All of them still in Poland. And four sisters. Two in Milwaukee, one in Florida, and one in the military. You notice that about women? Always braver. Always.'

Mackenzie wanted to know about Dobroslaw's own interest in jet skis. He understood he was backing a similar event.

'How can I? My brothers are alive.'

'I meant a race, mush.' Bazza was getting definitely edgy.

'Ah . . . the Enduro. A wonderful idea. Wonderful. You ever do jet ski? You should. Lots of fun.' The massive head nodded and he got to his feet, a single movement. More Bison Grass. Another toast.

'To your brother.' He lifted his glass. 'And to this race of yours.'

They swallowed the vodkas. Winter felt his eyes moistening. Bazza wiped his mouth with the back of his hand.

'But that's the point, mush.'

'Cesar.'

'Cesar. That's what I've come about. Your race and my race. We can't have two. Ain't on. Won't work.'

'Why ever not?' Both hands in the air, an expansive gesture, the best of friends.

'Because it won't. Tell him, Paul. Tell him why we've got to have a sort-out here.'

Winter began to explain about sponsorship, about the media coverage, about the size of the trough they'd be sharing. Everyone was telling him there was only so much exposure to go round. Two events on the same piece of ocean just didn't make sense. There was a long silence. Dobroslaw looked unimpressed. Winter wasn't even sure he believed it himself.

'But I don't understand,' Dobroslaw said at length. 'You come here to say no to my race? To tell me it can't happen? Is that what you're saying?'

He sounded reproachful, almost disappointed,

as if he'd expected something better. Bazza wasn't in the mood for this kind of negotiation. Neither was he used to talking to someone who'd probably tucked away the same kind of money.

'I'm not here to fanny around, mush. I'm just saying, that's all.'

'Saying what?'

'Saying that one of us has to back off. And it ain't going to be me.'

'Please . . . that sounds like a threat.'

'Not at all. Call it advice. Call it whatever you like. All I'm saying is our Mark deserves a bit of a send-off. And that's exactly what we're going to give him.'

'Then do it, my friend. Do it. Send me an invitation. I'll bring my family. We'll raise a glass. Wish him *szerokiej drogi*.'

'Wish him what?'

'God speed. Bon voyage.'

'Yeah, and half a dozen Hail Marys. Listen. There's something I haven't mentioned. My friend Paul here, you know what he used to do for a living? Until recently? Until *very* recently? He was a copper, CID, smart-arse detective, one of the best in Pompey, no *the* best in Pompey. And you know who he works for now? Me.'

'Congratulations.' The glass again, raised in Winter's direction. 'Happy retirement.'

'No, but think about it, mush. Think about all those mates he's got back in the job, think about all those conversations he might just be having. Business can be difficult. You're talking to someone who knows. The last thing you need is

396

that kind of aggravation.'

'What kind of aggravation?'

'Paul here passing on a tip or two, marking a few cards, maybe even suggesting his mates, his ex-mates, start taking an interest in all that Russian fanny you've got tucked up. Don't get me wrong, mush. It's nothing personal. I've got nothing against a man making a decent living, whichever way he wants to cut it. I just need a clear run for Mark. It's that simple. No hassle. No drama. Just a handshake.' He forced a smile. 'That sound reasonable?'

Dobroslaw was eyeing the bottle. Winter knew, with a terrible certainty, that Bazza had got this completely wrong. Either he was about to get the bottle over his head or they'd simply be slung out. In the event it was the latter.

The Pole was on his feet again. He said he had to pay the piano teacher. Then he was due at a meeting back in Southampton. After which he had to take the train for London. It had been a pleasure meeting Mr Mackenzie, being able to put a face to the reputation, and he was delighted to say that he hadn't been remotely disappointed. Bazza gazed up at him, confused.

'What does that mean?'

'It means, my friend, that we are — all of us — the prisoners of our past. Of who we are. Of where we come from. Of where we grow up. Me? I'm a stubborn old Pole. You?' He smiled, shepherding Mackenzie towards the hall.

Beside the front door he paused. Well over six foot, he towered over Mackenzie. Bazza still wanted a decision, a guarantee, an assurance that

Dobroslaw would back off, but the big Pole shook his head. That look of faint reproach again. He'd expected something better, something that Bazza had clearly failed to even comprehend. He extended a hand, which Bazza ignored. Then he smiled and patted him on the arm.

'Goodbye, Mr Mackenzie. And good luck with your little trophy.'

★   ★   ★

Bazza was incandescent. Winter had rarely seen him so angry. He'd trekked over there in good faith. He'd been nice to the man, polite. He'd never once suggested that only scum, *real* scum, make themselves a fortune from the bodies of country girls from the depths of God knows where. He'd said nothing about white slavery or pimping off helpless toms or any of the other stuff that bastard immigrant arsewipes seemed so good at. And for all that he'd got nothing. Absolutely fuck all. Except a virtual declaration of war.

'*Little* trophy? What's that about? Is this guy life-tired? Does he know what he's saying? Does he understand the way things work in Pompey? Or do we have to tell him?'

Winter thought it best to let the storm pass. It didn't. Back in Portsmouth, early evening, Bazza insisted on summoning a council of war.

A handful of his closest mates turned up, crowding into the den he used as an office, faces Winter recognised from the 6.57 days and from a thousand run-ins since. These were middle-aged men now, blokes Bazza had trusted all his life. One or two had drifted, with various measures of success, into full-time crime. Others ran garages or pubs. One had made a fortune in the scrap metal business. But all of them were bonded by a loyalty deeper and richer than words could properly express. They'd fought together on football terraces all over the country. They'd exported Pompey violence abroad, to shopping malls and café-bars, and — on one famous occasion — to a pre-season friendly in Honfleur. They'd had a laugh and made a bob or two and they still bumped into each other in pubs and clubs and certain restaurants. In the one-man corporate enterprise that had become Bazza's life, these individuals formed a shadowy but important non-executive board of directors. He didn't ask for their advice. They didn't have a vote. But — especially on occasions like these — he wanted their support.

And he got it. Each time a new face appeared Bazza would go through the afternoon's events again, and each time he did Winter sensed that the real issue became a little clearer. This wasn't about jet skis any more, or the Trophy, or even the fact that it was Mark's precious memory at stake. No, this was about insult, about restitution, about *respect*. No one was going to patronise Bazza Mackenzie. Least of all some Polish heavy with more money than manners.

Heads nodded round the room. There were growls of agreement when Bazza said that they had to hurt this man, attack his business empire where it was most vulnerable, take lots of money off him, expose him for what he really was. Honour called for a settling of accounts and if Dobroslaw was really up for a serious ruck then that was exactly what he was going to get.

At this point Westie arrived. He had an instinct for violence. He knew when trouble was brewing, when the scent of blood was in the air, and it was he who suggested an expedition to Southampton that very night, mob-handed. They'd seize Dobroslaw, bung him in the back of a van, beat the crap out of him, dump him somewhere visible, where no scummer cunt could miss him. The second bottle of Black Label was nearly empty by now and it was only a couple of the wiser heads who managed to prevent Bazza from strapping on his fighting boots and heading for the motorway. We need time, they said. We need to plan this thing. We need to be a bit clever.

There followed a detailed discussion of tactics. Some options were tabled, rubbished, dismissed. Others won general approval. By now there was absolutely no question that a kind of war had been declared, and Winter, watching, could only marvel at how easy it had been to put a match to the tinder that was Bazza Mackenzie. Willard had been right all along. The guy was like one of Pavlov's dogs. Create the right situation, feed in the right prompts, and this was someone who might easily self-destruct.

Marie sensed it too. Winter, ducking out to get himself a glass of water, found her in the kitchen. She wanted to know what was going on. She'd only just got back from a night out with some girlfriends. She'd counted the cars in the driveway, recognised the odd coat in the hall, been aware of the angry growl of voices from the den beyond the big lounge. She'd spent the last year or so trying to soften Bazza's rougher edges, trying to leaven their social life with a sprinkle of middle-class friends, trying to turn twenty million quid of narco-loot into a legitimate business that would keep her husband out of trouble. Now this.

'It's mad, love.' Winter could only agree. 'Baz has fallen out with a villain in Southampton. It happens that he makes his money from trafficked toms. There are blokes in there suggesting we bust all his brothels and set these women free. Can you imagine that? A bunch of tarts from Minsk? Wandering round some shopping centre in their py-jams? These people should join the Animal Liberation Front. It's the purest bollocks.'

Marie didn't see the funny side. She'd lived with Bazza for more than a decade. She'd seen him in these moods, knew what he could do when the red mist descended, knew how easily he could chuck away everything they'd managed to build together. The word she used was 'wanton'.

'He's like a kid,' she said. 'On the one hand he can be really clever, really shrewd, really cluey. People he respects, people who know stuff that he doesn't, he'll listen to. He'll take advice. He'll be patient. He'll see the advantage in some investment or other and realise that it's going to

401

take a couple of years at least for the thing to come good and he'll be quite happy about that. Then something happens, something like this, and it all goes out the window, the whole lot. Why? You tell me. Maybe it was the white powder. Maybe he went over the top when he was younger. He's just so . . . ' she found a glass for Winter ' . . . *volatile.*'

'But that's his charm, love. That's why you married him. That's why you're still here.'

'You think so?'

'Definitely. The day Baz puts his feet up is the day it'll all fall apart.'

'That won't happen.'

'I meant Baz putting his feet up.'

'I know you did. It's just not in his nature. Sometimes I wish it was. But you're right, Paul, life would get very dull.' She nodded towards the den. 'So what are we going to do?'

★   ★   ★

The session broke up past midnight. Marie, who'd retreated upstairs, returned to find Winter and her husband sitting alone in the lounge, watching a DVD of *Apocalyse Now* on the huge plasma screen. Martin Sheen was going slowly insane in the bedroom of a Saigon hotel. Bazza, noticing his wife at last, patted the sofa.

'Paul's told you about this bloke Cesar?'

'Yes.'

'He told you what happened this afternoon? Over at his place?'

'Yes.'

402

'Completely out of order. Total fucking liberty. We've got to sort it, love. Else it'll only get worse.'

'Why?' Marie at last sat down. 'What's any of this got to do with us?'

'*What?*' Bazza seized the remote. In his excitement he hit the wrong button. Instead of muting the sound, he turned Martin Sheen green. 'Shit.' This time he hit Pause. There was a moment of silence, broken by Marie.

'I'm asking you what's so important about this man. It's a difference of opinion, Baz. He doesn't agree with you. In the real world stuff like that happens all the time. You ride it. You ignore it. You get on with the rest of your life.'

'*Ignore* it? I'm not hearing this. The geezer knew exactly what he was doing. He'd probably written himself a fucking script. He'd probably spent half the afternoon rehearsing. He knew exactly what he was about. He wanted to wind me up. And you know something? He succeeded. Big time.'

'So leave it. Walk away. Spare him the satisfaction.'

'What satisfaction?'

'Of taking it any further.'

'You think he *wants* that?'

'I'm sure he does.'

'But you think he knows what he's in for? What we can do to him?'

'Of course he does.'

'Then he's a nutter.'

'You're probably right. Isn't that something to think about?'

403

Bazza was brooding. His hand found the remote. Martin Sheen came to life again. The scene cut to helicopters swooping down onto a jungle landing zone. Winter turned the volume down.

'There might be another way, Baz.'

'Yeah? What's that?'

'I go and have a talk to some mates. Like you mentioned this afternoon.'

'From the Filth, you mean?'

'Yeah.'

Winter began to think aloud. He could raise interest in Dobroslaw's organisation, feed in some intelligence, supply a few addresses, whet their investigative appetites. With a bit of a nudge, he said, the blokes in Major Crimes might organise a hit. It wouldn't happen tomorrow or even the day after, but if Bazza was really interested in settling accounts then an operation like this, properly mounted, could give the Pole all kinds of grief.

Bazza thought about it for a moment, then shook his head.

'Not the same,' he said. 'Not the same at all. You don't get it, mush, just like Marie doesn't get it. This is *personal*. This goes way back.'

'How can it? You never even met the guy until this afternoon.'

'That's not the point. He's a Scummer. He's taking the piss.'

'He's not a Scummer. He's a Pole.'

'Whatever.'

'And he's heavy, Baz. He'll have protection. You know how many Poles there are in

Southampton? Two hundred thousand. These people are tribal. They stick together. Do you really want that kind of war? That kind of aggravation? When everything else is going so sweetly?'

'Sweetly, bollocks. He insulted me. *Little* trophy? Arsehole . . . '

'Listen, Baz, what you've got to understand here is — '

'No mush, *you* listen. The guy's a disgrace. Plus he's an arsehole. I don't care how many friends he's got, how many bloody relatives. Two hundred grand? Three hundred grand? Half a million? Who cares, mush?' He was grinning now. 'We'll fucking have them all.'

* * *

Winter went home. It was late but the Friday-night traffic still clogged Albert Road. Winter sat in the back of the cab, eyeing a line of half-naked girlies weaving along the pavement, wondering what else he could possibly do. There'd been just a chance that Bazza might have swallowed the line about some kind of CID operation but in his heart of hearts Winter knew the plan was a non-starter. In the shape of today's developments, Willard was halfway to his dream result: not just Bazza Mackenzie on the verge of doing something extremely silly, but probably Dobroslaw as well. Not just one major criminal potted, but two. Would the Head of CID risk losing an outcome like that? Fat chance.

The traffic began to move again. Minutes later, thoroughly depressed, Winter was riding the lift at Blake House. Letting himself into the apartment, he saw the message waiting for him on the machine. It was Brodie. She wanted him to give her a ring.

Winter punched in her number. Since his last encounter with D/I Parsons, she seemed to have become the channel for passing updates back to Willard.

'Paul . . . ?'

'Me.' Winter could hear the blare of a television in the background.

'You went to Southampton? Checked the guy out?'

'Yes.'

'So what's happening?'

Winter hesitated a moment, staring at the blackness of the Harbour.

'Nothing,' he said at last.

'*Nothing?*'

'Zilch. Bazza was nice as pie. They both were. Babes in the Wood. Real love affair.'

'I'm not with you. You told me yesterday it was a turf thing. You said they'd be at it. Ferrets in a sack. Paul, you practically *guaranteed* it.'

'Yeah . . . well . . . ' Winter stifled a yawn ' . . . it turned out I was wrong.'

20

SATURDAY, 16 SEPTEMBER 2006. 07.56

Up early, Jimmy Suttle was on the road to the New Forest by eight o'clock. He'd cleared the trip with Faraday first thing, phoning him on the mobile. Rick Bellinger, the Southampton social worker, had recommended a visit to the Tile Barn activities centre. Positivo was leading a weekend residential for at-risk kids. This was the same outfit that had accommodated Dermott O'Keefe. Odds-on, some of the staff would know the lad.

Faraday, to Suttle's surprise, had registered barely a flicker of interest. Of course Suttle should go. The budget could wear the overtime and there might be some value in talking to other people about O'Keefe. He, in the meantime, was off to London. Suttle, assuming the visit was in connection with *Billhook*, had asked why.

'Family,' Faraday had grunted. 'I won't bore you with the details.'

Now, Suttle followed Bellinger's instructions. Tile Barn was bigger than he'd thought, a fourteen acre spread on the outskirts of Brockenhurst. He parked at reception and showed his warrant card to the woman behind the desk. He'd phoned the Positivo number last night and had been given a contact name for the weekend residential. Jane Plover.

407

'She's in the classroom right now. You might like to wander across. They're due for a coffee break in about half an hour. I'm sure you could talk then.'

The classroom was less than a minute away. Already, through the open windows, Suttle could hear the yelp of young voices. He paused outside the door. Through the big wired-glass panel he could see a couple of dozen kids. The desks had been pushed back against the walls and the kids had formed a big circle, all facing inward, hands interlinked. Various members of staff were patrolling the edges of the circle while a tiny woman with a savage haircut clambered onto a chair and clapped her hands. Some of the kids were giggling. Others looked lost. The woman on the chair shouted an instruction and the circle swayed and buckled while the kids tried to work out what to do.

Some kids pulled, others pushed. One girl fell over. But not once was there a break in the chain of hands. Back on her feet, the girl wanted to blow her nose. Suttle slipped into the classroom in time to hear the woman on the chair telling her to go ahead. As long as she didn't break the chain. The girl looked dumbstruck, then shrugged, ducking her head and wiping her nose on her neighbour's T-shirt. A boy across the circle shrieked with laughter, pointing at the girl.

'Snotface,' he yelled.

Everyone started laughing. Including the girl.

'You broke the circle,' she yelled back. 'Dickhead.'

By the time they stopped for coffee, the game was over. The challenge had been to reverse the circle, facing out rather than in, without breaking the ring of hands. A quarter of an hour of wrestling, fierce argument and general mayhem had come to an end with a whispered clue to the biggest of the kids. He and his neighbour had hoisted their linked hands, inviting the couple opposite to lead everyone else through. By now the circle had acquired a life of its own, sinuous, ever-changing, and the sight of twenty kids trying to squeeze each other through this tiny human arch had reduced everyone to helpless laughter. Which, according to Jane Plover, was the whole point of the exercise.

'These are kids who've never learned to help each other,' she explained to Suttle. 'Most of them are scared stiff of physical contact and even more frightened of making a fool of themselves. It's all down to laughter in the end. If you can make people laugh you can make them do anything.'

Suttle was impressed. The next game was under way, under someone else's supervision. A rubber gym mat had been cut into four squares. The classroom had become the Arctic Ocean. Kids crowded onto each of these tiny ice flows. The trick was to somehow manoeuvre the ice flows so they reformed the gym mat and thus made a bigger, safer ice flow. This demanded a great deal of synchronised shuffling on the polished wooden floor. The game was called Killer Whale. More teamwork. More hilarity.

'You mentioned Dermott O'Keefe on the phone.'

'That's right.'

'Is he in trouble again?'

'I'm afraid he might be.'

'Do you mind me asking why?'

'Not at all.'

Suttle restricted himself to the Mercedes. There was no absolute proof, he said, but there was strong evidence that Dermott had nicked it. More to the point, he seemed to have disappeared.

'That's strange. He was here only a couple of weekends ago. We run a Junior Leader programme. He did so well in the summer we invited him back.'

Dermott, she said, had taken everyone by surprise. His truanting record and steadily growing list of offences had prepared everyone for yet another teenage tearaway. Here was someone, on paper at least, who appeared to have turned his back on society. Yet in the flesh Dermott had been bright, quick-witted and only too happy to submerge himself in the general clamour. His interpersonal skills, she said, were exemplary. He had very few problems with the other kids. The only slight quirk in his character that anyone had spotted was a tendency to occasionally wander off.

'He likes his own company,' she said. 'But in his case we view that as a plus.'

Suttle remembered the social worker's story about the four a.m. paper round. His own space, he thought.

'And camping? The great outdoors?'

'He loved it. Absolutely adored it. He knew how to cook too, and believe me that's almost a first.'

Dermott, she said, had done equally well on the Junior Leader programme. Something in his life had bred a natural maturity and he wasn't afraid of taking responsibility. On the contrary, he appeared to thrive on it.

'Is the course ongoing? Does he have to come back?'

'Yes. The next stage is just before Christmas. We'll give him a bunch of kids to sort out and see how he copes.'

'So how do you get in touch with him?'

'At home. Through his mum. She's sweet.'

The coffee break was over. The kids were milling around. Jane had to get back to work. Suttle scribbled down her mobile number. Then he felt her hand on his arm.

'The person you should be talking to isn't me at all.'

'No?'

'No.' She shook her head. 'You need to get hold of Charlie. Charlie Freeth. He and Dermott were very tight.'

'And who's Charlie Freeth?'

'He's our boss. He's the one who heads all this up. In fact Positivo was his idea. And you know what he was before he saw the light?' She smiled. 'A cop.'

* * *

Faraday found it impossible to look his son in the eyes without thinking of the photos. He'd

411

found more of them on another memory card, equally explicit, same woman, different poses. He'd shared this discovery with Gabrielle, glad of a second opinion. Like him, she put the woman in her mid-forties. She wore an expensive-looking diamond ring on the third finger of her right hand. She occasionally affected a Gucci watch. So why was J-J, his errant son, his gleefully reckless offspring, bedding a middle-aged, possibly married woman? And how was this liaison tied to his purchase of a half-million pound house in fashionable W4?

The three of them were sitting in a café-bar on Chiswick High Road. The estate agent selling the property was virtually next door. Yesterday Faraday had sent his son a terse e-mail telling him they needed to meet. He'd texted his father back within the hour. The café-bar had been his idea.

J-J, not the least bit subdued, wanted to know what his dad thought of the property they'd just inspected. It was a Victorian terraced house, three streets back from the High Road. A recent refurb had opened out the ground floor, installed clever lighting, laid a beautifully finished oak floor and added an en-suite bathroom to the biggest of the bedrooms upstairs. The tiny back garden had been landscaped in brick with limestone insets and there was a barbecue for entertaining on hot summer nights. The whole area, said the agent, had recently become fashionable and there wasn't a car in the road more than a couple of years old. Number 17 was, of its kind, a gem. Hence, Faraday supposed, the asking price of £495,000.

'Where are you going to get the money?' he signed.

J-J's face was briefly darkened by a frown. He'd clearly been expecting this question. Equally clearly, thought Faraday, he hasn't had time to dream up an answer.

'No bullshit,' Faraday warned. 'Just tell me the truth. Are you trying to raise a mortgage? A loan of some kind? Is that why you went to Jersey?'

J-J shook his head. 'I opened an account.' He signed.

'In your name?'

'Two accounts. One in my name. One in someone else's.'

'Whose?'

'A friend.'

'A Russian friend?'

'Yes.'

'Who?'

He reached for the menu and gestured to Gabrielle. She produced a pen. On the back of the menu he scribbled two words. Faraday looked at them. The first he couldn't read. The second looked like Tarasov.

He was back in the bedroom again. The spread of her legs. The melting smile. How dexterous she was. How eager to please.

'This is a special friend?'

'Very.'

'How special?'

'We're very close. All three of us.'

'All *three* of you?' Faraday held up three

fingers, trying to make sure there was no ambiguity. For once in his life, talking to his son, he cursed the boy's muteness.

'That's right. Sergei is a businessman. He owns an oilfield. Part of an oilfield. He's very rich. He has a house in Moscow. Another in St Petersburg. Now he wants a house here.'

'And he's married? This Sergei?'

J-J nodded, reached for the pen again. His wife's name was Ludmilla.

'And she's a friend, too?

J-J nodded, giving nothing away. He'd met her, he signed, through the production company. When the location shoots were done, they'd brought the rushes back to Moscow and thrown a big party for everyone associated with the project. Sergei had been especially helpful. Away for the month in Siberia, he'd asked his wife to represent him.

'Nice lady?' Faraday enquired with a tiny raise of his eyebrow.

J-J nodded. Soon after the party she'd invited him and some others out to her house. It was a big house in a wealthy area. She had a couple of dogs but for once J-J hadn't been frightened. He'd been there a lot since. The husband, Sergei, had told him he was part of the family.

'And you're buying this house for these people? These friends of yours?'

'Yes.'

'They're going to live here full time?'

'No. Ludmilla will come for the shopping. Maybe Sergei too if he has time.'

'And you?'

'Me?' J-J placed a hand flat against his chest, beaming. 'I'll look after the place.'

* * *

After the café-bar they walked a little, heading back towards the Tube. Faraday hadn't the heart to ask about the postcards, and the windfall $70,000. He'd always thought this was a fantasy but he'd never dreamed it might be a cover for a far larger sum of money.

Whether or not, even now, he'd really got to the bottom of J-J's story remained to be seen, but what little he knew about the new Russia persuaded him that oil and gas exploitation, if you had a large enough stake, could easily fund the casual purchase of a house in Chiswick. The currency implications might be troublesome, and he shuddered to think of the tax bill his son might be unwittingly incurring, but both factors were insignificant against something far more troubling.

Years ago, on an extended visit to Normandy, J-J had got himself badly hurt over a relationship with a French social worker. That, too, had turned out to have been a threesome, though in this case the wounded party had been J-J. In Moscow, as far as Faraday could fathom, J-J had found himself in bed with someone else's wife. Had she made the running? Did the husband know? Did J-J know that the husband knew? Or was it more straightforward? Simply a routine betrayal by a bored, wealthy housewife? With the willing assistance of his eager son?

Faraday didn't know. In a minute or two they would be saying their goodbyes. J-J was staying with friends in Brixton. He had someone to meet this afternoon and a Polish movie he wanted to catch tonight. Faraday, meanwhile, was desperate to steer Gabrielle into a pub, sit her down, sink a beer or two, try and coax some sense from it all.

By the time they got to Stamford Brook Station it had started to rain. They ducked into the entrance while Gabrielle wrestled with her umbrella. Faraday had J-J's digital camera in his pocket. The picture card with the bedroom photos was still loaded and he'd selected a particularly explicit pose to appear the moment J-J powered it up. As a precautionary tap on the shoulder it was hardly subtle, but he'd never wanted his son to take him for a fool and he didn't intend to start now.

J-J gave him a hug. At the sight of the camera in his father's hand, his grin vanished.

'That's mine,' he signed.

'It is.' Faraday gave his thin body a final squeeze. 'Take very great care.'

* * *

Brodie's call took Winter by surprise. It was late afternoon. After his weekly visit to the supermarket Winter was contemplating a stroll round Old Portsmouth. He'd take the paper with him, have an early pint or two, try and work out exactly where this new life of his was really going to lead. Brodie spared him the trouble.

416

'We're going for a ride.' She said. 'I'll be round to pick you up.'

'Where are we off to?'

'Gosport.' She named a marina.

'This is about the Trophy?'

'Of course.' She laughed. 'Isn't everything?'

She arrived minutes later. The Gosport marinas were just across the water. Winter could see them from his balcony. No point going by car, he insisted. Nightmare round trip. Thirty miles there and back with traffic like you've never seen. We'll take the ferry and walk.

The ferry left from the station pontoon next to Gunwharf. Winter took her up to the top deck. A thin rain had cloaked the big busy spaces of the Harbour but Winter loved this crossing, the feeling of being briefly in amongst the constant churn of ferries and fishing boats, and slim grey warships nosing out towards the open sea. It was like stepping into the picture that greeted him every morning from his balcony. It brought the view to life.

'So who are we seeing?'

'Willard. Apparently he's got a boat in the marina over there. It's a navy place. Used to be called HMS *Hornet*. Don't ask me why but he's very keen to see us.'

'And you're telling me this is secure?'

'He seems to think so. I imagine we wouldn't be doing it otherwise.'

Winter shrugged, resigning himself to the next couple of hours. He could have been in the Pembroke by now, he thought glumly. He could have been reviving an old friendship or two, touching base with familiar faces, swapping gossip, getting peaceably drunk. Instead he was back in a world that seemed to offer nothing but the ever-growing likelihood of catastrophe.

'This U/C game, you're never off duty.' He glanced across at Brodie. 'You ever find that?'

★ ★ ★

The marina was tucked into the mouth of a creek behind the Harbour entrance, protected from wind and current by the defunct remains of the navy's nearby submarine base. Access to the pontoons was controlled by security personnel at the gatehouse. Willard was using the cover name Peterson. He'd left instructions for Winter and Brodie to join him in the clubhouse. The secretary's office lay on the same corridor that led to the bar. He didn't anticipate the meeting taking long.

The office was bigger than Winter had expected. Willard was sitting behind the desk reading a copy of *Navy News*. He was wearing a roll-neck sweater with oil stains on one sleeve and the anorak draped over the back of his chair was still wet. There was a teacup at his elbow and crumbs on the plate beside it.

He nodded at the two chairs readied beside the desk. He wanted to know about the Pole, Cesar Dobroslaw. A slight cold made him even gruffer than usual.

'Brodie tells me you and Mackenzie went across to Southampton to see him yesterday.'

'That's right, sir.'

418

'What happened?'

'Nothing. We talked. That was about it.'

'You're aware we have an interest in Dobroslaw?'

'Yes.'

'Does Mackenzie know that?'

'Mackenzie knows the man's a villain. He knows he deals in trafficked women. That would make him a target for us, obviously.'

'I understand Dobroslaw's backing this rival event. Is that true?'

'Yes, sir. He's put money in. He wouldn't say how much.'

'And Mackenzie's reaction?'

'He's keen the two events don't clash.'

'How keen?'

'He wants a clear run. For his brother's sake.'

'And Dobroslaw?'

'He sympathised. Poles are very tight with each other. Big on all that family stuff.'

'A meeting of minds then? Peace and love?'

'Absolutely. Much to Bazza's surprise.'

'Bazza?'

'Mackenzie, sir. We're mates these days.'

'So I gather.' Willard took a mouthful of tea. 'I have to be frank with you, Paul. We need to be very clear about where this operation is going.'

'Of course, sir.'

'My presumption has to do with Mackenzie. He's easily needled. Am I right?'

'Yes, sir.'

'So, given the right circumstances, we might find ourselves dealing with someone who'd lose control. Is that fair?'

'Yes, sir.'

'Brodie?'

'I agree, sir. Mackenzie's a firework. Point him in the right direction and anything could happen.'

'And Dobroslaw?' Willard was still talking to Brodie.

'I'd have said that was the right direction. In fact I'm sure it's the right direction. I was at the hotel yesterday evening, Mackenzie's place, the Trafalgar. People couldn't stop talking about it.'

'It?'

'Dobroslaw. What Mackenzie wanted to do to him. How he wanted to teach him a lesson or two. Break up his business empire and help himself.'

'And this was after yesterday's meet?'

'Has to be.'

'But you just told us fuck all happened.' Willard was looking at Winter again. 'Didn't you?'

Winter said nothing. He'd taken Brodie's question on the phone last night at face value. She'd asked about the meeting with Dobroslaw and he'd been careful to play the whole thing down. Now this.

'Well?' Willard wanted an answer.

Finally Winter stirred, shifting his weight in the chair. He said he had a question to ask. Not so much a question, more a statement of fact.

'Facts would be good.' Willard wasn't smiling. 'We like facts.'

'OK, sir. Fact number one. Of course Bazza is pissed off. Fact two, the Pole won't shift. Fact three, Bazza's liable to do something about it. Fact four, whatever he does will almost definitely be illegal. Presuming we arrest him, and presuming he's made some kind of criminal gain, that takes us, in the end, to court. So what happens then? Bazza will have sussed us. His brief will take us apart. Why? Because the whole thing, the whole situation, was a sting. We set it up. We set them at each other's throats. End of story. Case thrown out.'

'You're telling me you've lost faith in the operation?'

'I'm telling we're in danger of fucking up, sir. The last thing we need is a knock-back in court.'

'And you really think there's a danger of that?'

'I'm sure of it. Inciting Mackenzie to violence. Case closed.'

'But we haven't, have we? That's exactly what we haven't done. It wasn't us that killed Mackenzie's brother. It wasn't our idea to organise this jet ski thing. And neither did we have anything to do with the Pole's event. This has fallen into our laps. Take our interest away, our involvement, and these two guys would still be head to head. We're *lucky*, not complicit.'

'I don't agree, sir.'

'I can see that. But factually, Paul, you're wrong. And legally too. As I understand it, this situation has acquired momentum. The snow-ball's rolling down the hill. All we have to do is keep the bloody thing in sight. When it comes to the crunch we need to know when and where it's going to kick off and then the rest is down to us. Facts, Paul. Is that asking too much?'

Winter was robbed of a reply. Willard had thought this thing through. Was this a pep talk or a warning? Winter didn't know.

Brodie was looking at Winter. There was alarm in her face.

'You say Mackenzie will have sussed us. How would he do that?'

'Because we'd end up as witnesses,' Winter said.

'Sir?' She turned to Willard.

'Absolutely not.' Willard shook his head. 'And that's the beauty of the operation. Mackenzie and the Pole have a ruck. We let it run a bit and then nick them both. After that the pair of you gently disappear. You, Brodie, go back to ordinary duties while Paul here . . . ' Willard shot Winter a chilly smile ' . . . starts a whole new life.'

★   ★   ★

Winter took the call from Suttle when he was back on the harbour ferry heading for Portsmouth. Suttle had a name for him.

'What's that?'

'Bloke called Charlie Freeth. Thought you might know him.'

'You're right, I do. Or did. Why?'

'I need a bit of a steer. Are you in tonight?'

Winter checked his watch. Nearly seven. He'd have to bin the early pint.

'Make it eight o'clock,' he said.

Brodie glanced across. They'd barely said a word since leaving the marina and Winter felt no

422

inclination to put that right. She'd sussed last night that Winter was playing a game of his own and she'd promptly passed the message on. No wonder Willard had been so quick in demanding a meet.

'Friend?' Brodie nodded at the mobile.

'Yeah. Bloke in the job. Trust him with my life.'

★ ★ ★

Jimmy Suttle turned up early. He'd brought a bottle of wine with him and a couple of Elton John CDs his sister was chucking out. Winter already had them both but appreciated the gesture.

'Are we settling in or what?' Winter was looking at the wine.

'I'm driving. Help yourself.'

Winter opened the bottle. Suttle asked for a soft drink.

'In the kitchen, son. There's Coke in the bottom of the fridge. Bring a couple of glasses while you're at it.

Suttle did Winter's bidding, telling him about the circus that Operation *Polygon* had become. A small army of SB were camping out in Kingston Crescent, and as well as Special Branch there'd been regular state visits from a succession of high-ups in MI5. His own inquiry, *Billhook*, had been banished to the satellite MIR at Fareham nick but on balance he was glad to get out of Pompey. Sharing an office with Faraday, he said, was a bit of a novelty, but after

423

a couple of days he'd even warmed to that.

'How do you get on with him?'

'Fine. He's a funny bugger. If he didn't trust you, I get the feeling he'd make life bloody difficult. Put in the hours, keep your nose clean, and he pretty much leaves you to it.'

So far, Suttle hadn't said a word about Bazza Mackenzie, and for that Winter was grateful. Maybe the boy's decided I've retired, Winter thought. Maybe I've become someone he feels he ought to visit from time to time. Make sure I've got enough food in the fridge. Remind me to check the gas taps last thing at night. On the other hand, he'd mentioned a name on the phone.

'You're serious about Charlie Freeth?'

'Yeah. Absolutely.'

'How come?'

Suttle explained. Freeth had left the job a couple of years ago and moved into social work. According to a couple of other staff Suttle had managed to talk to at Positivo, the idea that had given birth to the organisation was his.

'They think he's bloody good. Sets the bar high, lashings of tough love, all that shit, but he's got loads of patience and apparently a lot of the kids really take to him. One of the women I talked to wanted to know what kind of copper he'd been. She said she just couldn't imagine Charlie in uniform.'

'I'm not surprised. Have you met him?'

'No, he's up north somewhere at the moment. What was he like?'

'As a copper?'

'Yeah.'

'He was good. He was a bit of a loner, not too many friends, but that's no handicap. I worked with him on a couple of jobs . . . must have been eight, ten years ago. We were both on division then. It was rubbish really, volume crime, kids nicking stereos out of motors, Portsea lads lifting giros off skagged-out junkies. Charlie got in amongst them, took a few scalps. He was a good listener, I remember that. I used to kid him about it. We'd be interviewing some dosser or other down the Bridewell on a Monday morning and Charlie would be in there with me, and the thing was he had this definite way about him. He knew exactly which buttons to press. It never failed. A couple of minutes with Charlie and these wasters were talking fit to bust.'

'Sounds like you.'

'Yeah? I'm flattered. But the difference is I always had the impression Charlie meant it. That was his only problem really. He let some of this stuff get to him and once that happens, as we all know, you're fucked. OK, if it's a good cause then maybe it's worth winding yourself up but most of these people were rubbish, real low life, total inadequates, yet Charlie still came out of that interview room banging on about the state of the world. The problem was, he always took things too seriously. In the end a job's just that. A job. We get these numpties to put themselves on the record. Then we lock them up. Charlie? He just couldn't see it.'

'What sort of age are we talking?'

'Now? He'd be late thirties. The week he

jacked it in, he'd just turned thirty-five. He was late entry so to make his twenty-two he needed another ten years or so. I remember him telling me he'd be gaga by then, probably sectioned.'

'He blamed that on the job?'

'Definitely. He saw the way it was all going. If the people upstairs wanted to turn him into a social worker, he said, then he'd spare them the fucking trouble.'

'But that's exactly what he became. More or less.'

'Exactly. None of us believed he was serious at the time. He'd been banging on for months about getting down to the roots of the problem. Most of the jobs that came our way were down to kids, you know, fifteen-to-nineteen-year-olds, often younger, and Charlie thought there were cleverer ways of sorting that stuff out without having to chase infant glue-sniffers round Somerstown or Buckland. He was probably right but coppers aren't built that way. They *love* chasing people round, you know they do. The rest of it, all the compassion bollocks, is dog-wank.'

Suttle smiled. He remembered the kids clinging to each other aboard the tiny squares of rubber matting. Maybe Freeth was right. Maybe Killer Whale was a shorter cut to a better society than a lungful of solvent fumes.

'He's gay? Freeth?'

'Shit, no. Jump anything. Often did.'

'Was he married?'

'Twice. Blew it both times.'

'Kids?'

'None that I ever knew of.'

'And do you ever see him now?'

'Never.' Winter reached for the bottle and poured himself more wine. 'But that's standard MO, isn't it? You leave the job and as far as everyone else is concerned you're halfway to the fucking grave. Bless you, son.' He raised his glass. 'Here's to Charlie Freeth.'

21

Revived, Suttle thought. Either a couple of days off or the new French girlfriend Faraday barely ever mentioned, or some exotic combination of both. Whatever the reason, the clouds seemed to have parted. There was a lightness in his step, a brightness in his eyes. He was even, for a brief moment or two, humming to himself.

'Good weekend, boss?'

'Excellent. We went up London, had a bit of a celebration, ended up at a concert on the Saturday night. There was a Palestinian singer Gabrielle wanted to see. She said she was really good and she was right. The woman was phenomenal. Reem Kelani. Incredible presence, almost operatic.' He dumped his briefcase on the desk and reached for the Policy Book. He wanted to know about Tile Barn, about Dermott O'Keefe, about developments regarding Stephen Benskin — about everything.

Suttle briefed him, aware of Faraday scribbling himself the odd note.

The warrants for Benskin's flat and the offices in Croydon had both been executed and Suttle had just received an angry e-mail from his solicitor to prove it. The seized paperwork and the expected billings records remained to be analysed but in the meantime he'd been chasing

428

another lead. When he mentioned Charlie Freeth, Faraday's head came up.

'There was a copper called Freeth.'

'That's right, boss.'

'Same bloke? Long spell in CID? Nearly made D/S?'

'Yeah. Though Winter never mentioned promotion.'

'You talked to Winter about Freeth?'

'Yes. He said he was good. Effective. Wanted to make a difference. I think he approved of the guy.'

'He would. Freeth was Winter with a conscience.' Faraday paused. 'And you say Freeth and the youngster were close?'

'That's what people tell me.'

'How close?'

'Hard to say, boss. It was Freeth who spotted O'Keefe's potential when he was sent on the course in the summer. It's Freeth who has the final say on who makes it onto the Junior Leader scheme. Everyone seems to think O'Keefe was a foregone conclusion. Partly because he was so switched on. Partly because he'd caught Freeth's eye.'

'What did they mean by that?'

'Nothing dodgy, boss. I asked the same question myself. Freeth's got a partner, a woman called Julie. She's a teacher. Apparently she helps out sometimes with the kids on the courses.'

'They live together? She and Freeth?'

'So I gather.'

'Where?'

'Here somewhere. I've got a number for her.

429

She says Freeth's away just now. Back tomorrow.'

'Good.' Faraday was deep in thought. 'We'll need an address. Sort it. Is Dawn Ellis around?'

'I'll check.'

Suttle left the room. Seconds later Ellis appeared at the door. Glen Thatcher, she said, had just given her a list of actions. Fingers crossed, she might be back by close of play.

'Forget it. I'll talk to Glen in a minute. You and I need to lay hands on the CCTV footage. The stuff with the hoodie kid. You seized the tapes?'

'Yes, sir. They're in the lock-up.'

'You've got a copy on VHS?'

'DVD.'

'Excellent.' Faraday peered over her shoulder, looking for Suttle. 'Phone Winter,' he told him. 'Make sure he's still at home.'

⋆ ⋆ ⋆

He was. Faraday pressed the buzzer on the entryphone, stationed his face in front of the video camera, waited for the lock to release on the big main door. Dawn Ellis, who'd never been to Blake House before, wanted to know where Winter had raised the money.

'He went half shares with that woman of his.' Faraday was still eyeing the camera. 'You remember Maddox?'

Ellis nodded. Maddox, a couple of years back, had been the talk of the upstairs bar at Kingston Crescent. Why on earth was an intelligent, well-connected, twenty-something hooker shacked up with the likes of Paul Winter? The answer, it turned out, was as complex as everything else in Winter's life, but by the time the relationship ended he'd won himself a brand new address.

'And he's really working for Mackenzie now?' They were waiting for the lift.

'As far as anyone knows, yes.'

'Our loss then.'

'I'm afraid so.'

Winter was waiting for them upstairs, the door to his flat open, the smell of burned toast in the air. The sight of Dawn Ellis put a big smile on his face. He gave her a buttery kiss.

'A deputation,' he said. 'Either that or you've come to fucking arrest me.'

Ellis was touring the big living room. She'd always had a soft spot for Winter, recognising just how effective he could be in situations most of her colleagues would have dismissed as impossible, and years of working alongside him had taught her a great deal. She paused beside the window.

'These curtains are crap, Paul,' she said. 'And so is the colour scheme. You need a good woman in your life. Magnolia's for wimps.'

'Help yourself, love. Come round any time. I'll give you a paint-brush.'

Faraday was on his knees beside the DVD player. Ellis gave him the disc and he posted it into the machine.

'What's all this then?' Winter was intrigued.

Faraday didn't answer. He began to skip

through the disc until he found the first of the traffic sequences that showed the Escort on the night of the murder. En route into Port Solent, the camera had only offered a rear view of the Escort. Hours later, leaving, there was a glimpse of two people in the front.

'There.' Faraday froze the image and pointed at the smudge behind the wheel. 'Who's that?'

Winter peered at the screen. The resolution was terrible.

'Haven't a clue,' he said.

'OK.' Faraday inched forward. The next sequence came from one of the motorway cameras, the quality infinitely better. Winter was on his knees now and Ellis had pulled the curtains to shut out the light. 'Same question,' Faraday said. 'We're interested in the driver.'

This time the quality of the image was infinitely better but both visors in the front of the Escort were down and only the lower half of each face was visible.

'Sorry.' Winter shook his head. 'Do I get a clue at all?'

'Afraid not. How about this one?'

Faraday asked Ellis to find the sequence from the car park at Port Solent. This had been recorded earlier on the Monday night, before the murder took place, but had come from a totally different control room.

Winter watched the two figures walking across the near-empty car park. The camera was mounted high, probably on a pole of some kind, and the angle only offered a quarter-profile from behind, but something caught Winter's attention.

Ellis froze the action as the two figures paused beside the Escort. At this distance details were indistinct.

'You're asking me about the big guy?'

'Yes.'

'Play it again.'

Ellis did so. Then a third time. Finally Winter nodded. The name was fresh in his mind.

'Charlie Freeth,' he said. 'Exactly the same build. Exactly that same slight roll when he walked. Yeah?' He looked up at Faraday. 'You spotted it too?'

*　*　*

Faraday was back at Fareham within the half-hour. He'd been tempted to accept Winter's offer of breakfast, mindful of Willard's instructions to sound the ex-D/C out, but he knew this wasn't the moment. Suttle was waiting in the office. He had an address for Freeth's partner but a couple of calls had failed to raise her.

'She'll be at school, boss. They normally knock off around three.' He paused. Ellis had just left the DVD on his desk. 'You showed this to Winter?'

'We did.'

'And?'

'He thinks it could be Charlie Freeth.'

'Shit.'

'Exactly.'

'So where does that take us?'

Suttle pushed his chair back from the desk, stretched his legs. He'd rarely met anyone as

433

unemotional as Faraday but Suttle was aware that even the D/I was finding it difficult to mask his gathering excitement. At last, after two weeks of largely fruitless effort, here was something that smacked of a breakthrough.

'Think about it, Jimmy. Here's a guy who's forensically aware. He knows what we look for at a crime scene. He knows the mistakes people make. No wonder he didn't put a foot wrong.'

Suttle was grinning. Faraday had never called him Jimmy before.

'Is Winter positive about the ID?'

'No. The image isn't good enough. But he's three quarters there so just think it through. It's odds-on that the kid in the hoodie is O'Keefe. It's definitely O'Keefe who comes back on the Wednesday night to pick up the car. Why? Because he's lifted the keys the night Mallinder got shot. That means he was inside the house. And *that* means Freeth was with him. Fits, doesn't it? Game, set and match?'

'Sure. Except this guy's *really* careful, so careful he doesn't leave a single clue. So if he's that bloody good, what's he doing letting O'Keefe come back for the car?'

'Maybe he didn't know. Maybe O'Keefe just spotted the keys on the Monday night and lifted them. His family's living on bugger all. A car like that buys a lot of groceries.'

Suttle was still thinking, still trying to testing Faraday's thesis, still trying to slot the pieces together.

'OK, boss. Let's say you're right. Let's say it was Freeth in the Escort, Freeth in the house.

434

Why on earth would he want to kill Mallinder?'

Faraday eyed him for a moment.

'Good question,' he said.

★   ★   ★

Lunch was Misty Gallagher's idea. She'd phoned Winter mid-morning. She had some shopping to do in Gunwharf. A Chinese at the Water Margin would make a nice break. Would Winter fancy joining her?

Winter agreed at once. Misty, like Bazza, never did anything without at least three ulterior motives. She obviously had something she needed to talk about. Just what was on her mind?

'It's Baz,' she said at once. She'd arrived late, heaping her bags round her chair and calling for a Bacardi and Coke. 'He'd turned up last night. I've never seen him like that before.'

'Like what before?'

'So upset. He was practically frothing at the mouth.'

It had been late, she said. She was still downstairs, playing online poker. She was about to call a guy in Vancouver when she heard a thump at the back door.

'That time of night it could only have been Baz, but he's got a key so I was starting to wonder. Then he obviously found it because the next thing I know he's walking mud all over my new carpet and telling me everything's turned to ratshit.'

'How come?'

'Some bloke in Southampton. Polish guy. He called him Caesar but that doesn't sound right. You know about any of this, Paul?'

Winter told her what had happened.

'And is that all? A little tiff about this *jet ski* race?'

'Baz thinks that's plenty. To be fair, Mist, it's not about the race any more, at least I don't think it is. He's just got everything out of proportion. You know the way he is. All he's got to do is *imagine* an insult. Maybe he needs a regular supply of enemies. Maybe that's it.'

'So there wasn't an insult?'

'The guy patronised him. I was there. I saw it happen. But it was no big deal. To tell you the truth, we should never have gone in the first place. Once we'd got past the door, we were doomed. The guy ate us alive. And we made it easy for him.'

'We?'

'Baz especially. He thinks the whole world's like Pompey. It isn't. You know that, I know that, but if it doesn't suit Baz to listen, then he won't. It's his way or nothing and if you have a ruck about it then he'll just batter you. I'm not talking violence. It needn't be physical. He'll just tell you the way he thinks it is. Twenty million quid says he must have done *something* right so maybe we're all out of order even talking about it.'

'That's crap, love. Of course we can talk about it.'

'Sure, but what do we *do*?'

'I don't know. Last night I tried everything.

436

Believe me, Paul, I know that man inside out. Every nook, every cranny. He's a pussycat, really. Tickle him in the right places and he'll roll over for you. I've done it a thousand times, never failed.'

'And last night?'

'Last night was hopeless. It took me a while to get there, to realise, but the truth is he's bloody unhappy. That's not Baz at all. Reckless, yes. Daft sometimes, definitely. But underneath he's a pretty well-adjusted guy. Something's got to him and I don't know what it is.'

'Mark?'

'Maybe. But they were never really close. You know that.'

'What then?'

'I haven't a clue. That's the whole point. Except . . . '

'Except what?'

'He mentioned a woman he seems to have taken on. In fact he mentioned her twice. Brodie?'

Winter nodded. Brodie was a media agent, he explained. Bazza's passport to the world of TV deals and five-page spreads in *Hello!* magazine.

'What's she like?'

'Very pretty. He fancies her, Mist. In fact he's installed her at the Trafalgar. She's got an office of her own in the basement.'

'And a bedroom upstairs? Surprise me.'

'I couldn't, Mist. You know the bloke he is. What he wants, he gets.'

'And she's come across? Be honest. Pretend I don't care.'

'I doubt it. I think she's too canny for that.'

'So she's giving him the bum's rush? Only that might not be a great career move.'

'I don't think career move would matter to her. The truth is Bazza's out of his depth with these people. Telly, the media, even the business with the Pole over in Southampton — it's a different world. Bazza doesn't speak the language. And that pisses him off.'

Misty was still interested in Brodie.

'He thinks there's something not quite right about her. He told me that.'

'What does he mean?'

'I've no idea. That's why I'm asking you, Paul.'

'Maybe he thinks she's a dyke.'

'No, love. That's not what he thinks.'

'What then?'

'You tell me.'

'I can't. Because I don't know.'

'Really?' She reached for his hand, gave it a little squeeze 'Baz can smell Filth. He's got a real nose for it. Have you ever noticed?'

'You're telling me . . . ?' Winter did his best to look shocked.

'I'm asking you, Paul. Asking you.'

'Then I don't know.'

'But you think she might be?'

'Anything's possible.'

'And if she was, would you ask yourself why you'd never noticed? The famous Paul Winter? Eyes like a hawk?'

Very slowly it was beginning to dawn on Winter that he wasn't talking to Misty Gallagher at all.

'He sent you, didn't he?'

'Who, love?'

'Bazza. He turned up last night and said his piece, and told you to pass it on.'

She gazed at him a moment, then shook her head. 'He didn't even have to, love. Like I said, we know each other inside out. I don't even have to guess anymore. I *know*.'

'Know what?'

'Know what to do. You're right, though. He fancies the knickers off this woman and being Bazza he's honest enough to treat me to the details. He's been listening in to a couple of her calls. Why? Because he wants to know more about her private life, who she's shagging, how often, what turns her on, all the usual crap. But what he hears makes him very, very uneasy. And just a little bit pissed off.'

'He thinks she's undercover?'

'He thinks she might be. And that, as you can imagine, Paul, is more than enough.'

'For what, Mist?'

'I've no idea, love. It's just a word in your ear.' She bent towards him, cupping his big face in her hands. Then she reached for the menu. 'Shall we order?'

* * *

By mid-afternoon Suttle found himself looking at Charlie Freeth's service record. He'd talked to the D/I in charge of Human Resources, keeping details to a minimum. Freeth had come to *Polygon*'s attention with regard to certain events.

439

D/I Faraday, as SIO, needed a feel for the career this man had made for himself. Within the hour, on the promise that Faraday would sign the accompanying Data Protection form, a twenty-six-page file arrived by e-mail.

Suttle hurried through it, looking for anything that might add to the profile he was trying to build. Freeth had joined up at the age of twenty-three. Within four years he'd finished his CID apprenticeship and was serving on division at Portsmouth North.

Suttle sped on, reading quickly through Freeth's annual assessments. His performance had won cautious applause from a series of D/Is. Freeth, wrote one, had 'an unusual empathy with certain kinds of offenders', a kinship which seemed to bear out exactly what Suttle had learned last night. *He was a good listener*, Winter had said. *He knew exactly which buttons to press.* Suttle smiled, his eye caught by another plaudit, more barbed this time. D/C Freeth, in the opinion of a different D/I, 'sometimes needed to be aware of the boundaries between sociology and the discharge of his professional responsibilities'. What exactly did that mean? Had Freeth strayed too far from the path beaten by countless fellow detectives? Had he put social theory in front of hard-earned experience? Had he, in short, gone soft?

Suttle noted the D/I's name in case he needed to make further checks. Then, two pages later, he paused. He read the entry twice, reached for his pad again, made a note of the date and the supervising officer. Then he picked up the phone. Faraday was down at Kingston Crescent, summoned by Barrie for a meeting. His terse response suggested this was a bad time to call.

'Apologies, boss, but I thought you ought to know.'

'Know what?'

'Freeth did the firearms course.' His eyes found the date again. 'Six months before he quit.'

★ ★ ★

Winter knew he was crazy to even make the call. They'll be listening, he told himself. They'll have wired her landline. They'll have a scanner tuned to her mobile. They'll have bodies outside the hotel, ready to tuck in behind her, stay close, watch, report back. He did it anyway. They had a code for exactly this situation, standard U/C protocol, the conversational equivalent of the panic button. The call connected to Brodie's messaging service.

'Kath? It's me. That bloke from London you thought you'd hooked? Turns out he wasn't interested.'

'Hooked' was the key word. 'Hooked' was the distress flare he'd fired in Brodie's direction. 'Hooked' told her that she'd probably been blown.

She phoned back within the hour, said it was a shame. There followed a minute or two of inconsequential conversation before she apologised for having to go and hung up.

Winter, back in Blake House, tried to imagine her in the basement office at the rear of the

Trafalgar. Bazza had made a special effort with a big desk he'd picked up in Albert Road together with a brand new mock-leather swivel chair with *Chief Executive* on the back. One of the kitchen porters had done a decent job with the white emulsion and Bazza had hung two prints of the Battle of the Nile to give the pokey little room a bit of class. Would Brodie, even now, be packing her attaché case and checking train times to London? Or might her nerve hold for a day or two while she tried to gauge the strength of the threat against her?

Winter didn't know, and tried to persuade himself that this threat, this suspicion, didn't necessarily extend to him. On the contrary, Bazza had evidently been impressed by Winter's attempts to argue him out of a ruck with Dobroslaw. Paul, he'd told Misty last night, had come on strong, tried to protect his interests, tried to argue him out of doing anything silly. No U/C in his right mind would have done that, Bazza had said, not if they were setting him up for a possible arrest.

Winter smiled, trying to picture this exchange. The problem with Willard, he thought, is the problem that has dogged U/C operations all along. We underestimate Bazza. We think he'll never suss what we're up to when all the time he's playing a far subtler game of his own. The thought warmed Winter and he toyed with putting in another call to Brodie. Sooner or later he was going to need a clear run, unencumbered, and for that he needed to be sure she was safe.

The trill of the mobile broke his concentration. It was Mackenzie. He needed Winter over at the hotel. When Winter said it was difficult, that he had another appointment lined up, Mackenzie cut him short.

'Five minutes,' he said. 'Just fucking be there.'

* * *

The girl at reception, obviously expecting Winter, directed him upstairs.

'Room 423.' She said, returning to her copy of *Heat*.

Winter took the lift to the fourth floor. Room 423 was at the end. Pausing outside, he could hear the low mumble of the TV. He knocked then went in. Bazza was sprawled on the bed, watching the horse racing. Brett West stood by the window, leaning against the fall of velvet curtain. The one chair in the room was occupied by Brodie.

'Lock it.' Bazza didn't take his eyes off the screen.

Winter secured the door. Brodie eyed him from the chair. If anything, she looked furious. Class act, Winter thought.

Bazza killed the sound on the TV, then announced that they had some sorting out to do. A couple of things hadn't been making much sense to him. He knew what treacherous bastards the Filth could be but he was a fair man and he needed a second opinion.

'That's you, mush.' He glanced up at Winter. 'In case you were wondering.'

443

'Delighted, Baz. So what's this about?'

'Her.' He nodded at Brodie. 'Westie's been on the phone. We're having a bit of difficulty tracing K-MAX. No one in Los Angeles seems to have heard of it. That makes people like me curious. Which is why Westie went up to town yesterday. Eh, son?'

'That's right, boss. I went to Snaresbrook, checked out the premises. The place is a shit heap. Belongs to a bunch of Pakis. No one's been there for weeks.'

'Kath?' Winter had decided on a tone of mild reproach.

'It's handy, Paul, and it's cheap. We've discussed all this. The fact is I never got round to doing anything about the place.'

'Sure.' Winter looked at Mackenzie. 'So what's the problem?'

'The problem, mush, is that no self-respecting agent would go near a dump like that. Westie says there isn't enough air freshener in the world to get rid of the smell. He's been in there. He got hold of the key. And you know something? Westie's someone I trust.'

Brodie began to protest. 'You move on. You trade up. It's a pit stop. And now I'm down here, I'll buy out of the lease anyway.'

'Who says you're staying?'

'Me.'

'Really?' Mackenzie found that amusing. 'I'll say one thing, Kath. You've got fucking bigger bollocks than I have. In your shoes I'd be bricking myself. Westie here does a party piece with a couple of Stanley knives taped together.

444

Thing is, a double cut like that is virtually unstitchable. Most of the time he practises on blokes. Don't get me wrong, love, but he's been dying to try it out on someone as pretty as you. Eh, Westie?'

'That's right, boss.'

'So tell her the rest.'

Westie was smiling now. He produced a small silver object, gaffer-taped at one end. He showed it to Brodie, enjoying his new role. Magician. Enforcer. Full-time nightmare.

'You know what this is, love?'

'No idea.' Brodie barely spared it a glance.

'It's a tracking device. Stick it under your motor and we know exactly where you are. Private dicks use them all the time. Rich blokes checking up on their wives. Works a treat.'

'Is that right?' Winter saw the first tiny flicker of doubt in her eyes.

'Yeah. So what were you doing on Saturday morning?'

'Saturday?' She frowned. 'I was at the hotel.'

'All morning?'

'No. I went shopping.'

'Where?'

'Southsea.'

'No, you didn't. You had the car out. Try again.'

'Pass. You tell me.'

'You were in Titchfield. You want the address? Seventy-seven Ingleside Avenue. And you know who lives there? This lady. Boss? You want to do the honours?'

Westie extracted three photos from a file and

445

passed them to Mackenzie. He studied the photos a moment, then offered them to Winter.

'Paul? You want to give us a name?'

Winter glanced at each of the photos. According to Bazza, Westie had shot them Saturday lunchtime after Brodie had driven back to Portsmouth. The woman in the bulky anorak lived at number 77 Ingleside Avenue. In the photos she was hurrying along a pavement beside a parade of shops. The anorak was blotched with rain and her head was down in two of the shots but the last one showed her face. It was unmistakable. Winter had known for days that this moment would come. And here it was.

'Her name's Gale Parsons,' he said. 'Last time I knew, she was a D/I on Covert Ops.'

'Spot on, Paul. Fucking result, mush.' He nodded at the door. 'You can piss off now.'

Winter shook his head. 'I'm afraid not, Baz.'

'Sorry?'

'I said I'm afraid not. Not until you tell me what happens next.'

'That's none of your business, mush.'

'I'm afraid it is.'

'Why's that?'

'Because in a situation like this you need some decent advice. Driving me round in a builder's van half the night is one thing. Lay a hand on this woman, no matter what you feel about her, and you'll be spending the next fifteen years keeping the bum bandits out of your arse.'

'Yeah? How's that?'

'Two reasons, Baz. One, I'll grass you up. And

two, you'll have walked straight into whatever hole these people have just dug you.'

'Grass me up? How come? You're with *us* now, mush. Different side of the fence. Different set of fucking rules.'

'You're off your head, Baz. What are you going to do? Let Westie slice her up? If you do that you'll have to have her killed. Got rid of. Dumped somewhere. If she's really a copper, you'll never hear the end of it. You know that. I know that. I signed up for a spot of free enterprise, not this garbage. Sadism's not my game, Baz. Never has been.'

'But you said grass, mush. That's the word you used.'

'Grass, shop, whatever. I'm saving you from a big mistake, Baz. We open the door, Brodie walks, and we all get on with our lives. Do you really need me to tell you that? Or are you back on the fucking powder?'

For a moment Winter thought he'd overplayed his hand. He could see the quickening pulse in Bazza's neck. Nothing would have pleased Westie more than a spot of recreational ultra-violence. He was on his toes now, the company Rottweiler scenting blood.

Brodie seemed to have lost interest. She was still in the chair, composed again. Her head was turned towards the window. She didn't even attempt to defend herself.

The silence stretched and stretched. Finally Bazza swung his legs off the bed and walked across to Brodie's chair. Briefly Winter toyed with opening the door himself, with summoning help, with bringing this whole charade to a halt. Then Bazza's hand settled on Brodie's jaw. He turned her face to his, bent low.

'You know what you should have done, love, don't you?'

'Sorry I disappointed you.' She had the coldest smile. 'But if you'd asked me again, I'd still have said no.'

'Shame. You don't know what you're missing.'

'All the boys say that.'

'I bet they fucking do. Except this one means it.' Her held her gaze for a long moment. Then his voice became a whisper. 'You've got ten minutes to get out of my life, love. If you're not gone by then I'll let Westie fill his boots. *Comprende?*'

She nodded and got to her feet. Winter unlocked the door, stepping aside to let her pass. The last he saw of her, she was heading for the lift at the end of the corridor. She didn't look back.

★   ★   ★

It was gone five o'clock when Jimmy Suttle finally managed to get through to Charlie Freeth's partner. Slightly out of breath, she was curious to know why a policeman wanted to talk to her. She had a stack of homework to sort out and the washing machine was still out of action so she was due a visit to the launderette.

'Can't it wait?' she said.

'I'm afraid not.'

'And you won't tell me what it's about?'

'We'd prefer to talk face to face.'

'We?'

'Myself and my boss, Miss . . . ' Suttle paused, realising he didn't know her surname.

'Greetham,' she said.

'*Greetham?* As in Frank Greetham?'

'That's right. You know about my dad?'

'Sure.' Suttle had caught Faraday's eye across the desk. 'Sure I do.'

22

Julie Greetham, Faraday sensed at once, had closed a door on the world. She peered into the late-afternoon sunshine, shielding her eyes against the glare. She was a slight, fine-boned woman in her midthirties. The cropped hair was already greying and there was something very defensive in the way she held herself, as if she'd recently pulled a muscle.

'You've come then?'

'I'm afraid so, Ms Greetham. Bad pennies.' Suttle, already, was doing his best to cheer her up. He senses it too, Faraday thought. The drawn, pale face. The flatness in the voice.

They followed her inside, down the narrow hall. The house was bigger than it looked from the street. A couple of steps led down to a long, dark room at the back with a kitchen at the far end. There was still a cereal bowl and a packet of Weetabix on the breakfast bar and when Faraday turned to close the door he found himself gazing at an enormous heap of laundry. On top was a pair of Calvin Klein boxers.

Suttle was inspecting a wallboard full of photos at the far end of the room. His eye was caught by a knot of kids wading across a stream. Some of these faces he'd seen before.

'Was this taken at Tile Barn?' He pointed to

450

another shot, three young girls mugging for the camera.

'Yeah.' Julie's face brightened for a moment. 'That was back in the spring. That one I took myself.'

'Is Dermott O'Keefe in any of these?'

'Dermott? Yes.'

She pointed out a thin-faced, frail-looking adolescent posed outside a two-man tent. The jeans were at least a size too big but the grey hoodie looked familiar and there was laughter in his eyes. Suttle asked whether he might borrow the shot. The school photo he'd acquired from O'Keefe's mother was three years out of date.

'Is that why you're here? Because of Dermott?'

'It's one of the reasons, yes. We're trying to find him. He seems to have gone to ground.'

'You say one of the reasons. What are the others?'

'Boss?'

Faraday had found himself a stool at the breakfast bar. This woman's father had committed suicide barely weeks ago. Frank Greetham had spent his working life with Gullifant's and the collapse of the firm had left him under enormous pressure. Half an hour ago, before they'd left the incident room, Suttle had been on to the Coroner, wanting the details, and the uniformed P/C who served as the Coroner's Officer had read him the contents of the note left on the dashboard of the Toyota in which Frank Greetham had killed himself. *By the time you read this I'll be dead, thank God.* He'd written. *If I was younger, and braver, I might have done something about it. People like you shouldn't be allowed.* Unusually in these circumstances, the note had an addressee. *Mr J. Mallinder.* If one was looking for a motive for the developer's murder, thought Faraday, then surely this was it: the family settling a debt or two, as if another death would offer some meagre compensation for the abrupt disappearance of a lifetime's savings.

'You live here alone, Ms Greetham?'

'No, I have a partner.'

'What's his name?'

'Charlie.'

'Surname?'

'Freeth.'

'And is he . . . ' Faraday frowned ' . . . upstairs? At work? Away somewhere?'

'He's away. Up north.'

'Where exactly?'

'I don't know. He didn't tell me.'

'So when do you expect him back?'

'I'm not sure. He mentioned tomorrow but it might be longer.'

'Why?'

'It just might. He changes his mind sometimes. That's not a crime, is it?'

'Not at all, Ms Greetham. Why would you think it could be?'

Faraday was looking at the heap of laundry. It was feasible that she hadn't done a wash for a couple of weeks. It was equally possible that there might be corners of the house concealing a hoard of other forensic clues. Traces of sulphuric acid. Fluff or hairs from Mallinder's house.

Maybe even the bloodied pillows from the dead man's bed.

'I'm afraid I'm going to have to ask you to come down to the Bridewell with us, Ms Greetham.'

'Why?'

'Because we need to ask some questions in connection with a major inquiry. We're investigating a murder, Ms Greetham. The victim's name was Jonathan Mallinder. He was killed in Port Solent a couple of weeks ago.' He paused. 'You'll know the name Mallinder.'

'Of course. It was in the note my dad left.'

'And you know he was murdered? Shot to death?'

'Yes.'

'Then I expect you'll appreciate our interest.'

She was doing her best to look blank. Neither Faraday nor Suttle were fooled. This might be simple, Faraday thought. Protestations of innocence. Followed by everything she knew.

'And what happens if I don't want to come?'

'I'm hoping that situation won't arise but I'm afraid we'll need to go through the house.' He produced a folded sheet of paper from his jacket. 'This is a Section 8 warrant, Ms Greetham. Under the Police and Criminal Evidence Act, it gives me the power to search these premises.'

'Who says?'

'The magistrate. His signature's on the bottom.'

'But why? Why the search?'

'Because of the contents of your father's note. And because of what happened to Mr

Mallinder.' He paused. 'Is the house yours?'

'It belonged to my father. He's left it to me but we're still waiting for probate.'

'We?'

'Me and Charlie.' She turned to Suttle, increasingly desperate. 'What's going on here? What am I supposed to have done?'

Suttle didn't answer. Faraday looked at his watch. Scenes of Crime were due any time now. Already there'd be a uniform on the gate.

'Shall we . . . ?'

* * *

It was nearly an hour before Faraday was prepared to begin the interview. Julie Greetham had declined the offer of the duty solicitor, preferring to phone her own brief. It was rare for Hillary Denton to make an appearance at the Bridewell. Most of the time she devoted herself to employment tribunals.

'She's represented me before,' Julie said by way of explanation. 'We've got to know each other a bit.'

Denton, when she arrived, wanted to check that her client hadn't been arrested.

'Absolutely not. She can leave whenever she likes. We simply need information. Your client may well be in a position to help.'

The interview began shortly after seven. Suttle quickly established the nature of Julie's relationship with Freeth. She'd met him a couple of years ago at a Youth Offending conference in Winchester. He'd been the voice behind a

PowerPoint presentation on Positivo. Afterwards, over a buffet lunch, they'd found themselves chatting. Later that month he'd phoned her in Pompey. They'd gone out a couple of times, argued fit to bust, laughed a good deal and got drunk. Listening, Faraday found it difficult to associate the picture she was painting with the tense, watchful figure across the table. Something's happened, he told himself. Something with which she can no longer cope.

'Were you living with your father at that point?' Suttle asked.

'Yes. I'd been married before but it didn't work out. Dad wasn't very well, even then, and it made sense for us all to . . . you know . . . muck in together.'

'All?'

'Me and Dad. Then Charlie.'

'So Charlie moved in with the pair of you?'

'Yes. He and Dad always got on really well. Dad had been with the paras for a bit when he was young. Charlie's a war freak. They had a lot in common.'

'Your dad had a long spell in the army?'

'No.' She shook her head. 'He broke a leg in a practice jump. It was a bad break and it never set properly. He was invalided out.'

'Did he get a disability pension?'

'Just a bit. A pittance really. Dad always worried about money. That's why he went into Gullifant's in the first place. Ever since I can remember, he was telling my mum what a safe job it was. He was good with his hands, Dad, always had been. He had lots of patience too, with the customers, spent loads of time with them. After it all collapsed, he got cards by the sackful. I think even he was amazed. Not that cards make any real difference. You can't live on fresh air, can you?'

Her dad, she said, had gone into what she called 'a dark place' after the news came through. It was a bad time anyway, because the anniversary of his wife's death was just round the corner and he'd never been able to cope with that, but the morning he'd brought the Gullifant's letter home was the day he began to give up.

'It happened during the holidays. Thank God I was at home. He was in a terrible state. I'd never seen a grown man cry before, never, least of all my own dad. I just felt so sorry for him. He knew that times were tough in the shop but I don't think it ever occurred to him that everything would go, every last penny. But then you don't, do you?'

His mates from work, she said, had been great, Sam Taylor in particular. Sam was the one who'd managed to keep his head above water, organise a protest, raise a petition, write letters to more or less anybody who might have been able to help. He'd sent her dad copies of all this correspondence but as door after door began to close, his mental state — already fragile — got worse and worse.

'We'd got him to the doctor by then. He diagnosed clinical depression. Dad hated medication. At first he refused point-blank to take any pills, told us he could cope by himself, but that simply wasn't true. In the end he took them as a favour to us, just to shut us up, but it was awful. They must have been really heavy. They turned him into a zombie. He wasn't my dad at all.'

Mention of pills prompted an intervention from Faraday. When, exactly, had it got to medication?

Julie thought hard about dates. She was looser now, more relaxed, far less defensive. The very act of telling the story, of satisfying the detectives' voracious appetite for detail, seemed to have touched a nerve. The least her father deserved, after all, were the right facts in the right order.

'That would have been June time. I remember the weather being brilliant. Charlie and I used to try and take him out every night. We'd go down to the seafront, to Old Portsmouth. There's a little quay down there, looking out over the Harbour mouth. There are seats and you can watch the sun go down over the water. There's lots going on, lots of boats, lots of movement, and I think I had this feeling that it might be a distraction for Dad, that it might help him, but I'm not sure it did. He just used to sit there, staring away into the distance, not saying a word. Charlie was getting angrier and angrier. I think it probably hit him harder than me, to tell you the truth. The fact that someone he knew, someone he loved, someone he *respected* so much had been reduced to this.'

'You say Charlie was getting angrier and angrier.'

'Yes.'

'Did he blame anyone?'

'I don't know. To be honest I'd just shut off by then. I think maybe he had too.'

Towards the end of July she and Charlie had thought of taking her father away for a holiday, Cornwall maybe, somewhere he'd always enjoyed when he was younger, but in the end Charlie's work had made that impossible so she'd decided not to go.

'That was a huge mistake. I should have taken him by myself, just me and Dad, but I didn't. I told myself he'd be too much of a handful and I thought he'd miss Charlie too, because he was back home most evenings. Then . . . ' she looked at her hands ' . . . that last letter arrived.'

'From who?'

'From Sam again. It was a photocopy, like the rest of the stuff he sent. Dad was much more stable by this time. He was taking different medication by this time and I think he'd convinced himself that the government were going to bail them all out. There was some sort of fund. Charlie's got the details.'

'And the letter?'

'It came from the Department of Work and Pensions. Some minion. I can't remember the name.'

'But what did it say?'

'Basically it said that there was no money.'

'None at all?'

'No, not in the sense that Dad wanted. According to the letter, demands on the fund had made things difficult. There'd be a possibility of some money in the end but that wouldn't be until 2008. It was pathetic really. All the fuss, all the hype, then it turns out there's nothing in the pot. Bastards.'

'So what happened?'

'Dad just folded up. It was the saddest thing I ever saw. He wouldn't speak to us, wouldn't eat, wouldn't go to bed, wouldn't sleep properly. He just spent all night in his chair downstairs with the cat. We tried to get through to him. We tried telling him not to give up. We said he'd be safe with us, that we'd look after him, make sure he never went short, but it was hopeless. You know what? In the end I don't think it was even the money. It was something else. Not the fact that this whole thing had happened but that it *could* happen. That's why he wrote the note, the one he left in the car. I'm convinced of it.'

Faraday nodded. *People like you shouldn't be allowed.*

'I understand your father killed himself in the garage. Is that right?'

'Yes. He did it in the middle of the night. It was Charlie's car. He'd rented a little lock-up round the back. Dad knew where the key was. He'd got it all sorted, a length of pipe, clamps, duct tape, the lot. Some of the stuff even came from Gullifant's. Horrible.'

'And Charlie?'

'He's never forgiven himself.'

'For what?'

'For not hiding the key.'

★   ★   ★

459

At Faraday's insistence they took a break. Suttle organised some coffees while Faraday made a couple of calls from a nearby office. When Suttle joined him, he was just putting the phone down.

'That was Tracy Barber,' he said. 'MI5 think they've got a line on a terrorist cell. There's evidence of some kind of recce, couple of guys, the week previous to the hit. Everyone's getting really excited. Stiffie time.'

'Yeah?' Suttle gave Faraday his coffee. What interested him more was Julie Greetham. 'What do you think, boss?'

'Me?' Faraday sat back in the chair, gazed up at the ceiling. 'I think the same as you, Jimmy. I think she knows everything. And I think it's bloody tragic.'

★   ★   ★

When the interview resumed, Faraday brought up the issue of Dermott O'Keefe. He wanted to know when the lad had first come to Freeth's attention.

'I can't tell you that. Charlie deals with dozens of kids, probably hundreds.'

'But when did you first become aware of him?'

'I didn't. Not in any special sense.'

'Charlie never brought him home?'

'Never. He never did that. Never mixed work and us.'

'But I thought you sometimes helped out? Over at Tile Barn?'

'I did. Occasionally. But that was different. That was their territory, not ours.'

'So you never met O'Keefe?'

'Of course I did. I showed him to you on the photo back at the house. But you're asking something else. You're asking if there was some kind of special thing going on there. And the answer is no.'

'And Charlie never talked about him?'

'No.'

'He never mentioned how much potential he had? He never talked about the lad making the Junior Leader course?'

'Yeah, OK, he did mention that. I remember now.'

'And what did he say?'

'He said the boy was outstanding.'

'So he *did* talk about him?'

'Yes, he did, a bit, once or twice. Now you ask.'

'So why pretend he didn't?'

Hillary Denton, sitting beside Julie, told her she didn't have to answer that question. Her client, she reminded Faraday, was here to deal in facts. The question he'd just asked was an accusation.

Faraday accepted the objection but said he wanted to be clear in his own head. Charlie had been impressed by Dermott O'Keefe. But there'd never been any suggestion that the relationship had ever been closer than that.

'Am I right?'

'Yes.'

'They'd never meet outside the confines of the course?'

'No.'

'You're sure about that?'

'Yes.'

Faraday nodded, scribbled himself a note. He wanted Julie to go over the last couple of weeks and to think very carefully before she answered. Julie glanced at her solicitor but said nothing.

'Does Charlie spend every night with you?'

'Yes. Except when he's doing residentials. Then he's with the kids.'

'Have there been any of these residentials since the beginning of this month?'

'No.'

'So he's been home every night? Is that what you're telling me?'

'Yes.'

'All night?'

'Yes.'

'You're absolutely sure about that?'

'Yes.'

Faraday sat back, signalling to Suttle to take over.

'Monday the fourth of September,' he said. 'A fortnight ago today. Can you remember what you were doing?'

'Why that particular date?'

'I'd be grateful if you could answer the question, Ms Greetham.'

'Is that when he got killed? Mallinder?'

'Yes.'

'And you think . . . ?'

'I think nothing, Ms Greetham. I'm simply asking you what you were doing on the night of the fourth. Like I say it was a Monday.'

She frowned, picked at her fingers. For the

first time Faraday noticed the scarlet blotches on the backs of her hands, on her wrists. Eczema, he thought. Often a nervous complaint.

'Mondays I go to yoga,' she said at last. 'I'm normally back by about nine. Charlie cooks. We eat after I get back.'

'And that Monday?'

'I'd have gone to yoga.'

'And afterwards? After the meal?'

'We'd talk a bit and then we'd go to bed.'

'So that's what happened?'

'Yes.'

'You're absolutely certain?'

'Yes.'

'OK.' Suttle glanced down at his notepad. 'So when did you find out about Mallinder?'

'I can't remember. I think it was the following day. It was in the *News*.'

'And what did you feel?'

'*Feel?*' Her laughter failed to mask the bitterness in her voice. 'How do you think we felt? We were delighted. We couldn't believe it. If anyone killed my dad it was that horrible man. And when we realised that someone had done it to him it was brilliant news, absolutely brilliant. In fact I couldn't believe it. I remember phoning Sam up, Sam Taylor. He thought it was brilliant too. Maybe you ought to arrest us all. Get it over and done with.'

'We haven't arrested you, Ms Greetham.' Suttle reminded her.

'No, but you'd like to, wouldn't you? That what all this is about. That's why you want to poke round the house. That's why you'll be

463

talking to Charlie. He was a policeman too. Did you know that?'

'Yes.'

'And do you really think a policeman, even an ex-policeman, is going to get himself involved in something like this? Knowing what he knows? Knowing the way you people work? Knowing about . . . ' she gestured at the bank of whirring audio cassettes, at the video camera mounted on the wall ' . . . all this?' She stared Suttle out, demanding an answer. When none came, she pushed her chair back and stood up. 'I know I shouldn't be saying this, I know it's irrelevant, but you've really upset me. Losing dad was bad enough. Now I'm supposed to have killed the bloke who took him away from us. That's what you're saying. You'll never admit it but that's what it boils down to. If you don't mind, I'd like to go home now. Is that OK with everyone?'

Home wasn't an option. Faraday brought the interview to a close, making a note on the tape of the time and the circumstances. The Scenes of Crime team, he told Julie, had already taken possession of number 72 Westbourne Road, and if she had nowhere else to go accommodation would be made available at the Travelodge on the seafront.

Julie stared at him. It hadn't occurred to her that she'd be locked out of her own house.

'You can't do this.'

'I'm afraid we can.'

'But what am I supposed to wear? Wash with? Who feeds the cat?'

Faraday assured her that the cat would be fine.

464

A WPC would accompany her back to collect whatever she'd need until the house was released.

'And when will that be?'

'It depends. These things take time. To be frank, it could be a while.'

'Like how long?'

'Three days? Maybe longer. We're treating your house as a crime scene, Ms Greetham. If you've nothing to hide, it'll simply be an inconvenience.' He paused. 'In the meantime there's something you might do for us.'

'What's that?'

'I expect you'll be talking to Charlie. Tell him we'd appreciate a word or two, the sooner the better.' He smiled at her. 'I'm sure he remembers the way these things work.'

★ ★ ★

Winter, still shaken, locked the door. Outside the apartment, somewhere in the depths of Gunwharf, he could hear the faint wail of a car alarm. He went into the living room, sank into the chair beside the window and stared out. From this angle he could see nothing but sky. The rain had stopped at last. If he could muster the strength to stand up, there might just be the makings of a decent sunset.

He lay back and closed his eyes. By the time he left the Trafalgar, Brodie had gone. No briefcase beside her desk in the basement office. No cashmere coat hung carefully on the hook behind the door. Not a single indication that she'd ever set foot in the place except the key to the Fiat Bazza had lent her. Looking at the key, Winter was reminded yet again of the reality of undercover work. You ghost yourself in, he thought. And one way or another, successful or otherwise, you ghost yourself out again. Was that really what he wanted? A phantom retirement in some godforsaken former colony? Having to hide under a pile of new ID? Having to kid himself, as the years slipped by, that he'd triumphed over evil and departed in a blaze of glory? Having to watch himself every step of the way through whatever remained of his life?

Already, deep down, he knew the answer. That's why he'd held off telling Brodie about the ruck with the Pole. That's why he'd done his level best to talk Bazza out of doing anything silly. Because, thanks to Parsons and then Willard, he'd finally sussed just where his real interests lay. If he somehow managed to pot Bazza, he'd be spending the rest of his days pretending to be someone else. And that, after this brief flirtation with a double life, just wasn't going to happen.

The phone rang within the half-hour. It was Willard. The call broke every rule in the book. He sounded extremely angry.

'I've just been talking to Brodie. She thinks you blew her cover.'

'She's right. I did. I also saved her life. Did she tell you that as well?'

'Don't fuck with me, Winter.'

'I'm not. That's the last thing I'm doing. Ask Parsons about Saturday morning. Ask her what was so important it couldn't wait until later. And ask her whether she saw a black guy with a long telephoto when she went shopping. Fucked is a good phrase. And just now I've had enough of it.'

'Do you know what you're saying?'

'Yeah. Brodie blew it. So did Parsons. And so, sir, have you.'

Winter put the phone down, surprised at how simple the truth could sometimes be. He'd made a decision. Taken a stand. He felt wonderful.

He picked up the phone again. Mackenzie answered in seconds.

'Baz? It's Paul. I owe you a bevvy. My pleasure.'

⋆　⋆　⋆

Faraday had rarely seen Willard so angry. He'd turned up at Kingston Crescent, nine o'clock in the evening, walking into Martin Barrie's office with barely a knock, hauling Faraday outside into the empty corridor, demanding to know what kind of sense, if any, he'd got out of Winter.

'I haven't, sir. We've been a bit preoccupied.'

'You haven't seen him? At *all*?'

'No.'

'Shit, Joe. I told you, I made a point of it — *talk* to the bloody man. What do I have to do? Send you a fucking *memo*?'

Faraday began to protest, then broke off. Barrie had appeared at his office door. He and Faraday had been having an important conversation. It might be nice to finish it.

'No problem, boss.' Faraday glanced at

Willard. 'This might interest you, sir, as well.'

Willard, with a visible effort, pulled himself together. They reassembled around the conference table in the Detective Superintendent's office. For Willard's benefit Faraday described once again the progress they'd made on the Mallinder killing. The prime suspects, he said, had to be Freeth and the lad O'Keefe.

'Freeth was a copper.' Willard pointed out. 'We're talking about the same bloke?'

'I'm afraid so, sir.'

'Evidence?'

Faraday went through it again. The CCTV. The faultless MO at the scene. The irresistible urge to avenge Frank Greetham's suicide. Not Stephen Benskin at all but an ex-cop with a great deal to get off his chest.

'Evidence?' Willard repeated.

'Scenes of Crime have been in the house since this afternoon, sir. They're taking the place apart. So far they've found nothing but it's early days.'

'And Freeth?'

'He's due back tomorrow. She'll be phoning him though. That might alter his plans.'

'You think he might not show?'

'I don't know. From what I can remember, Freeth was an arrogant sod, a real loner, a hard man to have on a team. Something tells me he thinks he's got this thing weighed up. He might even be looking forward to taking us on. Maybe we're another debt he's got to settle.'

'And what about the young lad? O'Keefe?'

'The way I see it, sir, he's the key. I think he

was there for the hit on Mallinder, I think he nicked the key to the Mercedes without telling Freeth, and I suspect he always intended to go back for the car later. Laying hands on it would be good from our point of view but finding O'Keefe would be much better. Once we've done that we can start taking this thing apart.'

A new photograph of the boy, he said, had gone to the Force Intelligence Bureau for circulation nationwide. By tomorrow, with luck, there wouldn't be a copper in the country unaware of his importance to Operation *Billhook*.

'Press? TV?'

'I left a message with Media Services this evening, sir. They've been copied on everything and the photo's also gone to them.'

Willard seemed placated. He even had the good grace to offer Barrie a mumbled apology. Barrie said times were difficult. They were all under pressure. He needed to know the latest from MI5.

'They've got a bunch of names and faces. Apparently we're talking a cell of four blokes, Provo-style. They seem pretty confident of the intelligence.'

'But why take out this particular minister?'

'For one thing he's defence-related. For another, it seems he's been taking a hard line in his constituency over the war. He refuses to apologise, refuses to entertain the idea of any kind of inquiry. Five say it takes fuck all to get these people going. If you can blow up a busload of total strangers, I suppose a head job on a government minister sounds almost rational.'

'And you think we should be running with this?'

'I've asked for sight of the evidence. You're SIO, Martin. It's your call.'

'But they're keen?'

'Very.'

'And the politicians?'

'They're irrelevant but since you ask then the answer is yes, they're keen too. Between you and me, the whole terrorist thing is getting out of hand. This government have been blowing smoke up our arses for years. Terrorism, Provo cells, state red alerts, liquid explosives on planes, it's just more of the same. There's nothing these people would like more than a bunch of al-Qaeda at the end of a strike that goes wrong. If we're left with nothing but bodies, who'll be counting?'

Faraday and Barrie exchanged looks. This was vintage Willard, patrolling his turf with a growl at anyone who dared trespass.

'So we do nothing premature, sir?'

'Absolutely not, Martin. It's boring, I know, but evidence is a word we should all regard as a friend. Especially now.'

★ ★ ★

Bazza and Paul Winter ended up in a small drinking club in the depths of Southsea. Winter had known of the place for years. It had once belonged to a pornographer with a mild drink problem. His stack of Scandinavian videos had been overtaken by hard core on the Internet and he'd wound up finding it easier to make a living with a late-night licence. His liver had exploded a couple of years later, and the last time Winter had seen him he was drifting towards a peaceful end in a hospice on the mainland. His wife used to arrive every Friday with a new copy of *Hustler*. It was, she'd told Winter, the least the poor man deserved.

Bazza had known him too.

'Top bloke,' he said. 'He sponsored us for shirts one season.'

'When he was still flogging porn?'

'Yeah. We had the name all over us. *Private View* the shop was called. One game a bloke called us all wankers. Didn't see the joke until afterwards.'

'After what, Baz?'

'After they got him out of hospital. Listen, Paul. That Brodie. I've been thinking.' He beckoned Winter closer. 'You were bang-on this afternoon, what you said, but there has to be some way, doesn't there?'

'Some way what?'

'Some way of sending these cunts a message. You know what *really* winds me up? The way they take us all for twats. As if we wouldn't spot her. As if we're *that* fucking blind.'

'So what do we do about it?'

'I'm not sure. That's why I'm asking. You're the one, Paul. You know the way these tossers think. What would really make their eyes water? Only it's a liberty, isn't it? Sending in a piece of fanny like that? Assuming none of us look

471

further than the end of our dicks?'

Winter laughed. He'd bought a second bottle of champagne, another forty quid that prompted Bazza to ask what the fuck they were celebrating.

'Nothing, Baz. Just this.' Winter had waved vaguely at the space between them. 'You get to an age, you know that?'

'Get to an age what, mush?' He was genuinely interested. Winter could see it in his eyes.

'An age when stuff starts sorting itself out. You're way too young, Baz, you won't have a clue what I'm talking about. And between you and me I'm far too pissed to explain. Except it's nothing but good news. Drink to that?'

They had. And the second bottle, with a wave of Winter's credit card, had given way to a third. Now, with the crowd at the bar beginning to thin, Bazza suggested an expedition to Misty Gallagher's.

'It's two in the fucking morning, Baz.'

'Doesn't matter. She's an owl that woman. Be a laugh.'

He ordered a cab. It was waiting at the kerb within minutes. At the top of the island, where the motorway divides, Bazza told the cabbie to take the left fork.

'Port Solent, mush.' He gave him an address.

The cabbie laughed. 'Lottery win, is it?'

'Fuck off.'

The escort agency lay in the genteel clutter of £400,000 houses fringing the marina. Telling the cabbie to wait, Bazza steered Winter up the front path. The woman who opened the door recognised Mackenzie at once.

'You should have phoned earlier, Baz. She's busy right now.'

'Doesn't matter, love. It's my mate here. We're talking an all-nighter. What have you got left?'

'Has he got a tongue in his head, your mate?' The woman was eyeing Winter. 'Only he can choose for himself, can't he?'

Inside, Winter found his way to an over-furnished lounge. Three girls were sprawled in various states of undress, watching a DVD. It was unbearably hot.

Bazza nodded at them. 'Freebie, mate. Call it a thank you. Help yourself.'

Winter took his time. All three girls ignored him. Finally, he chose a shapely blonde with dead eyes. She looked easily the oldest but even so could have been his daughter.

Bazza tapped her on the shoulder. 'You got a name, love?'

'Dawn.' She was chewing gum.

'Dawn, this is my mate Paul. I want you to be very nice to him. You listening to me?'

He disappeared from the room without waiting for an answer. Winter wanted more champagne. Badly. He nodded at the huge plasma screen.

'Like him do you, love? Tom Cruise?'

'It's Kevin Costner.'

'Costner then.'

'I think he's a wanker.'

'Really? Ever see *Top Gun*?'

'Top what?'

Bazza was back. He'd sorted a deal for the night and promised to have young Dawn back in time to get breakfast for her nipper.

'Nipper?' Winter was lost.

'Little girl. Dawn's mum stays over nights but she has to be at work by seven. Ain't that right, Dawn?'

Dawn wasn't paying attention. Bazza walked them all out to the cab. The three of them sat in the back with Dawn in the middle. Bazza had his arm round her. From time to time he nuzzled her ear and whispered something Winter couldn't catch. After a while she started to scratch herself.

Winter leaned across, poked Bazza on the knee.

'She's a junkie,' he said. 'I can tell.'

'No way, mush. I asked. It's just a habit. The girl gets nervous. Mist's got a fridge full of Moët. She'll warm up a treat.'

Misty was in bed when they arrived. Winter caught sight of her in one of the upstairs windows, trying to check out the noise at the gate. Bazza paid off the cabbie and found the key to the front door. By the time they were inside, Misty was halfway downstairs. The sight of Winter, the state of the man, put a smile on her face.

'Company, Mist. Paulie here's played a blinder. Thought he deserved a little prezzie. Say hello, Dawn. Pretend you're a fucking human being.'

Dawn ignored him. Misty, laughing now, took Winter by the hand.

'Are we up for a foursome?' she said to Mackenzie. 'Or what?'

'Piss off, Mist.' He grinned back at her. 'You're the prezzie.'

474

23

Winter surfaced to a cackle of laughter. For a moment he lay there, semi-conscious, neither asleep nor truly awake. The bed was enormous. It smelled musky with an edge of something sweet. The space beside him was still warm and when he summoned the courage to move his head on the pillow he found himself looking at the top of the bedside cabinet. Objects swum in and out of focus. Two empty champagne glasses. A paperback with a pink cover. An alarm radio. A bottle of body lotion. A packet of condoms. He blinked, told himself the thunder in his brain would go away, urged himself to resist the temptation to throw up, wondered where he'd find the nearest lavatory. There was an en suite through the half-open door beyond the wilderness of deep-pile carpet. He made it just in time.

Afterwards, forcing himself to his feet, he reached for the support of the big white basin. Then, very slowly, he soaped his face, rinsed his mouth and inspected his face in the mirror. Pale, jowly, thin on top, but still — somehow — intact. He held the gaze of this stranger for a moment or two, staring him out. The wink made him feel slightly better.

Misty was back in bed by the time he emerged

475

from the shower. She'd poured herself a cup of coffee from the cafetiere beside her and was leafing through a copy of the *Daily Mail*. Wrapped in her towelling robe, Winter eyed the front page. Police patrols had been stepped up around hundreds of mosques and churches after the Pope laid into Islam.

'How was I, Mist?' He was genuinely interested.

'You were fine. Nothing to worry about.'

'Just the once then?'

'Yeah. I like a man who can do it in his sleep. Saves me making conversation.'

'Are you up for another one?' He loosened the knot at his waist. 'Only I'm awake now.'

'No, love.' She finally emerged from behind the paper and patted the sheet beside her. 'You want a coffee?'

Winter stepped out of the robe and slipped in beside her. She was naked under the sheet and her body was warm to his touch. She caught his hand as he found her nipple. She had paracetamol if he needed it and she'd make him breakfast later to put something solid in his stomach. Winter frowned. He'd prefer a fuck.

'I know, love. But you can't.'

'Shame.'

'Yeah. But then we all get one go in life, don't we? Listen, Paul, you can have one look, just one, OK?'

She nodded at the sheet, an invitation for him to pull it back, but he shook his head.

'Where's Baz?'

'Gone. Took his little friend home half an hour

ago She had coffee too. I've put the mug in bleach.'

'Did she piss you off, turning up like that?'

'Nothing pisses me off, Paul. Be around Bazza as long as me, and you get used to the odd surprise. It's part of his charm. It's also his way of telling me never to take him for granted. He's subtler than you think, Bazza.'

'That was *subtle*?'

'This bit was.' She glanced across, then kissed him on the lips. 'He's never done that before.'

'Doesn't that worry you?'

'No. He knows I'm fond of you. It was a prezzie for me really.'

'Then we *can* fuck.'

'I said fond, Paul. Most of the men I've shagged in my life were animals. Why ruin a good friendship?'

Winter frowned. Maybe it was the hangover but he couldn't follow the logic. Neither would his erection go away. He lay on his back, tenting the sheet, trying to think of something plausible, something that would coax Misty to put aside her reservations and straddle him.

'Couple of minutes, Mist. That's all it'd take.'

'I know, love. I was there. That was me.'

'Baz needn't know.'

'It's not about Bazza. It's about me.'

'Shut your eyes then. If I'm that ugly.'

'That's unfair.'

'Good word, Mist.'

She eyed him for a moment. 'Have I upset you, love?' She sounded genuinely concerned.

'Yes.'

'Truly?'

'Yes.'

'OK then.' She exposed one breast before her hand slipped under the sheet. Winter felt the lightest scrape of her nails over the swell of his belly. Then a touch. Then another. Then a playful frolic underneath before her hand circled him for the briefest moment. 'There,' she said. 'All done.'

Winter, still groaning, turned over. Seconds later, he was asleep.

★   ★   ★

Faraday was in Westbourne Road by eight o'clock. Uniforms had guarded the house all night and the SOC team had resumed work an hour ago. Beyond the fluttering loop of police *No Entry* tape, a line of metal treading plates disappeared into the house. The senior of the two Crime Scene Investigators was a Geordie called Danny McPhee. He'd been with the force for less than a year but Faraday had already worked with him on a number of jobs and been impressed. He had the knack, all too rare, of coaxing a bigger picture from the smallest forensic detail. He also had the courage to back his own judgement.

Faraday summoned him with a call on the mobile. After a longish wait he stepped into the sunshine, pulling back the hood on his one piece suit and peeling off his thin latex gloves. When Faraday asked him how it was going, he shook his head.

'It isn't,' he said. 'Someone's been through every inch of that place. Either that or they've got a thing about disinfectant. It's spotless. Not a surface we can do anything with.'

They were moving through the house room by room, he said, prior to tearing the place apart. They were taping for hairs and fibres and looking for any evidence of blood or tissue that might have been carried back from Mallinder's bedroom. Each of the articles awaiting a visit to the launderette had been bagged and tagged, along with the filter on the broken washing machine, and all these items were already back at base awaiting a range of separate tests. Seven pairs of size 10 shoes had also been seized and scrapings from the soles would be subject to microscopic analysis. Organic material — grains as tiny as pollen — might supply a match against samples retrieved from Mallinder's front garden. On the other hand, he muttered with a shrug, all this painstaking work might take them absolutely nowhere.

'So what's your feeling?'

'My guess is we're stuffed. These people know what they're doing, or at least one of them does. Look at it this way, boss. This bloke's an ex-copper. He's been there, done it. If he's shot someone, he's going to bin the clothes and probably his shoes before he gets anywhere near going home. Same with the weapon. He used some kind of bag, is that right? No shell casings at the scene? This guy's anal. No way would he ever make it easy for us.'

'You're probably right. On the other hand, he

probably took a fifteen-year-old along. So what does that tell us?'

'Not my pay grade, boss. People do strange things. My oppo in there . . . ' he nodded towards the house ' . . . said this guy was always a bit of a head case. Knew it all. Control freak. Stroppy too. Wanted a medal for turning up.'

'He had a reputation,' Faraday conceded. 'And nobody was surprised when he jacked it in.'

'Strange though, a bloke like that. You'd think the last thing he'd do was end up with a bunch of kids. Don't they vet ex-coppers? Or do we get a free pass when it comes to all that risk-assessment bollocks?'

It was a good question, one that Faraday had asked Suttle to explore, and Faraday's interest was quickened by McPhee's description of the sheer number of photos around the house.

'Kids,' he said. 'Often with Freeth. Kids making camp, kids dressed up as pirates, kids on some kind of assault course. They're everywhere, even in the bedroom. Doesn't this bloke have children of his own? Or is he dropping her some kind of hint?'

He shook his head, picking at a scab on the back of his hand. When Faraday asked him for some kind of time frame on the search, he said at least another two days.

'Then there's the garden, boss.' He added. 'Better make that three.'

★   ★   ★

480

Winter was up and dressed by mid-morning. Of Misty there was no sign. He prowled around the big house, padding from room to room, waiting for his brain to kick out of neutral and catch up with the rest of his body. He couldn't remember a session as funny and satisfying as last night. As a welcome to this new life of his, he regarded it as extremely promising.

Back upstairs, in the creams and golds of Misty's boudoir, he stepped across to the window. It was a glorious day — bright sunshine, not a whisper of wind. There were ducks on the water and a couple of guys, further out, paddling their canoes towards the Harbour mouth. Crime bought this view, he thought. Crime bought the swimming pool, the speedboat moored to the tiny wooden jetty, the Moët racked in the cooler downstairs. Crime paid for the girlie last night and all the girlies to come. Was Winter the least bit disturbed by any of that? Did he anticipate sleepless nights trying to figure out why the bad guys jetted off to Dubai while the rest of the human race put up with crap television, traffic gridlock and arsehole kids? He thought not.

Misty kept a pair of binoculars hanging by a strap beside the window. Winter scanned the Harbour, adjusting the focus, briefly keeping track of a black bird with a long neck as it arrowed low across the water. Then he tilted up slightly, slowly easing south along the distant shoreline. After the greens and yellows of Milton Common and the odd figure walking a dog, he recognised the grey bulk of the tower block which housed students from the university.

Then, a nudge to the left, came the distinctive shape of Faraday's place. Upstairs, the big windows sparkled in the sun. Outside, in the garden, someone was hanging up a line of washing. At this distance it was impossible to be sure but Winter thought it must be a woman. Did Faraday pay someone local to come in and do his domestics? Or had that solitary life of his taken a turn for the better?

He didn't know, and the longer he thought about the question the more he realised he didn't care. Faraday had never been anything but a mystery to Winter. At first, on division, he'd despised him. Here was another time-server, he'd told himself. Here was someone else who'd played the system, who'd pleased the bosses, who'd flattered their sense of self-importance, who'd been canny and able enough to weather the promotion exams and wall themselves off from the world of real crime. With his office, and his PC, and his daily ruck with the budget manager, Faraday had become a pen-pusher, just like the rest of them.

But that hadn't been the case at all, and as Winter — through a series of largely self-inflicted accidents — had come to know the man better, he'd found himself developing something close to respect for this bearded loner, with his deaf son and his equally strange passion for watching birds. Faraday was shrewd. He never gave up. He was very much his own bloke, and deep down he had a decency and a stubborn sense of fairness for which Winter himself had reason to be grateful.

On a number of occasions, with a courage that Winter could only admire, he'd dug the wayward D/C out of the shit. The latest example, true, had led to Operation *Custer*, but Winter was sufficiently impressed by Faraday's track record as a copper to be sure that he wouldn't have made Willard's mistakes. The thing would have been tighter, better organised. And never, in a million years, would he have done anything as silly as threatening Winter with permanent exile. That way, as events had shown, you simply blew the operation out of the water. Not because your lead U/C wasn't up to the job but because he no longer saw the point. Better become one of Bazza's boys than some shuffling has-been in an Auckland suburb.

He was still watching the woman in Faraday's garden. She'd finished with the line of washing now, and she was standing at the front gate gazing out at the water. Maybe she can see me, Winter thought. Gladdened by the proposition, no matter how daft, he gave her a little wave then retrieved his mobile from his jacket.

Faraday's number was on the SIM card. When he answered, he'd clearly no idea who he was talking to.

'I'm driving,' he said. 'This better be quick.'

'And I'm looking at your house. Who's the lady in the white T-shirt?'

There was a brief moment of silence. Then Faraday got it.

'Winter?'

'Me, boss.'

'Where are you?'

483

'Hayling Island. Great pair of binoculars. What's her name then?'

Faraday ignored the question. Odd that Winter should put the call in.

'Why's that?'

'Because we're due a meet.'

'Who says?'

'Me.'

'My pleasure, boss. Let's say tonight. I'm buying.'

Faraday began to protest. It wasn't that kind of meet. He was up to his eyes in an inquiry. He had limited time. Winter let him finish.

'It's tonight or nothing, boss. Just give me a call when you're through.'

★   ★   ★

When Faraday finally got to the *Billhook* incident room, Suttle had just come off the phone. House-to-house enquiries in Westbourne Road had unearthed a young mother whose little girl attended the junior school at which Julie Greetham taught. It seemed that Julie had a lousy attendance record, so much so that the mother was getting fed up with her daughter's education forever being in the hands of a supply teacher or even a teaching assistant. There was no continuity, she said. It was the kids who were supposed to be always bunking off. Not the teachers.

Intrigued, Suttle had phoned the school secretary. She'd been extremely guarded but time and patience on the phone had finally given

Suttle the impression that Julie Greetham, from her employer's point of view, was a bit of a liability.

'In what way?' Faraday was scrolling through his e-mails.

'I'm reading between the lines here, boss, but I think she's a bit of a drama queen. She can be difficult. Stress is a bit of an issue, too. Apparently she claims she's got PFD.'

'What's that?'

'Professional Focus Deficit. What it boils down to is early burnout. You lose your grip, find you can't concentrate properly, then something snaps and it all gets on top of you.'

'Join the club. Has she had time off recently? This last month or so?'

'A couple of days, certainly. The secretary's sending me the dates.'

'And Freeth? O'Keefe?'

'Nothing so far. Freeth's in his Toyota. We've circulated details. It's just a question of time.'

Faraday nodded. By now the Toyota's registration would have been flagged to every ANPR camera controller in the country. Short of abandoning his car for the train, Freeth was a marked man.

Suttle was curious to know what Faraday wanted to do about Stephen Benskin. His phone billings had come through, and on receipt of a production order his bank were promising financial details within days.

'He still needs positive elimination. If you spot anything obvious, shout.'

'What about Mallinder's wife? She's due any

day now. Are we still interested in a paternity test?'

Faraday gave the question a moment's thought. Before he had time to make a decision, there came a knock at the door. It was Glen Thatcher, the D/S in charge of Outside Enquiries. He'd just got a call from a Duty Inspector with Gwent Constabulary. Charlie Freeth had been hauled over on the M4, travelling west. He was now in the back of a traffic car on the hard shoulder of the westbound carriageway eight miles from Newport. He was extremely pissed off at being stopped and was demanding to be allowed to continue his journey. What did *Billhook* want them to do with him?

'Newport? *Westbound?*' Faraday was frowning. 'He's supposed to be up north. He's supposed to be coming home.'

'I'm not sure that's the answer they're after, boss.'

'Tell them to arrest him, Glen. And he ought to be searched. The car as well. PACE-wise, what's best? We go up there or we ship him back here?'

'It makes little difference. Here would be best. The clock only starts when we put him in an interview suite.' He paused, still waiting at the door. 'I hate to be technical, boss, but what do we want him nicked for? Only they'll need to know.'

'Good point.' Faraday was grinning now, an increasingly rare event. 'Suspicion of murder.'

Thatcher backed out of the room. Suttle still

wanted a decision about Mallinder's wife and the imminent DNA test.

'Send her some flowers, Jimmy.' Faraday extracted a twenty pound note from his wallet and passed it across. 'Give her our love.'

★ ★ ★

Winter reported for duty at the Trafalgar in time for lunch. Mackenzie was in his office, demolishing a plate of sandwiches. The office occupied a sunny corner on the first floor with extensive views across Southsea Common to the startling blue of the Solent. Bazza, in a sentimental moment, had christened this room The Fratton End, and had added some trophy souvenirs to give it a bit of atmosphere.

A huge blow-up photo of fans celebrating last year's 4–1 thrashing of Southampton dominated one wall while a smaller framed shot of Alan Ball, Bazza's all-time favourite manager, had been positioned over his desk. Ballie, according to Bazza, could do no wrong. Forget the World Cup medal. Forget hundreds of appearances for Everton and Arsenal. Ballie was the man, in the dog days of the '97/'98 season, who had somehow engineered the greatest escape of all, clawing the club out of relegation with the miracle 3–1 away defeat of Bradford City. Bazza had been there that day, roaring for the Blues, half in love with one of the last teams not to be stuffed full of bloody foreigners. Steve Claridge, he'd often told Winter, was the real face of English football.

Bazza nodded Winter into the empty chair beside the desk. The sandwiches were corned beef with beetroot and French mustard. Winter helped himself. Mackenzie wanted to know about last night.

'How was it?'

'Crap, Baz. I went to sleep. No offence.'

'Shame. Maybe you needed a helping hand, mush. She's good that way, Mist. Heart of gold.'

He held Winter's gaze a moment longer than strictly necessary. He knows, Winter thought. She's been on to him since this morning, maybe even seen him. More to the point, he wants me to be aware of that.

'I'm blaming the bubbly, Baz.'

'You would, mush. But that's because you're getting too fucking old. Listen, we need to sort out our friend the Pole.'

'Why?' Winter's heart sank. He'd somehow assumed that talk of war was history. He was right. It was.

'We're gonna make a new start, Paul. It's silly, falling out . . . so there's something else I should be thanking you for. Last night was a loan, mind. So don't get ideas above your fucking station.'

'About what, Baz?'

'Mist. She's a lovely woman but absolutely no judgement when it comes to people she fancies. I told her you'd be useless but you know something? She wouldn't have it, not until she'd tried it out for herself. Nothing personal, mush, but from where I sit you're better off sticking to conversation. At least you make her bloody laugh, which is more than I do these days. OK, mush?' He extended a hand. 'Deal?'

Winter nodded, amused that Mackenzie needed to spell it out this way. Maybe he'd got it wrong about the paperwork. Maybe Bazza had a special form for situations like these. Sign on the dotted line. I promise not to shag Misty Gallagher.

'The Pole,' Winter reminded him.

Bazza bit into another sandwich. The time had definitely come to kiss and make up, he said. He'd be fucking useless in this situation, absolutely no self-control, so the task was to fall to Winter. He was to get the man's attention and negotiate a new deal.

'Like what?'

'Like we amalgamate. Like we join forces. I've worked it all out. I've even run it past Esme. She thinks it's a winner. In fact she thinks it's gold-plated. Can't fail.'

First we choose a key weekend in the summer, he said. Then we do the Trophy on the Saturday, with the Enduro to follow on the Sunday. Or maybe vice versa. Depends on the tides, on the logistics, on the small print. Either way it needs Dobroslaw's name on the dotted line with no more old bollocks about Scummers.

'That was your old bollocks, Baz.'

'I know. I was wrong. Again. But thinking about it, he's not a Scummer at all, is he? He's a fucking Pole. Something else, mush. That bloke we talked to about Sky Sports. The bloke who does the yachting at Cowes.'

'Michael Lander.'

'Yeah. Check him out. Properly. I wouldn't put

it past these bastards to try and smuggle another slimeball into the camp. What do you think?'

'I've no idea, Baz. I quite liked Brodie.'

'So did I, mush, so did I, but you know the way these things work. One arsehole introduces another and before you know where you are you've got the Filth all over you. That's another thing. You'll remember fuck all about last night, the state you were in, but I asked you to come up with something . . . ' he wiped his mouth with the back of a hand, ' . . . *fitting* for our friends in blue. I don't want to hurt anyone. I'm beyond all that. In fact if you want the truth I'm quite flattered by all the attention. But it's getting beyond a joke. It's also boring the shit out of me. So something to make their eyes water. Know what I mean?'

'Not really, Baz, but I'll try. Listen . . . this Lander. Assuming he's kosher, what then?'

'Use him. Wind him in on the deal. He was an amusing bloke, made me laugh. That stuff he played for us next door . . . ' He nodded towards the restaurant, ' . . . 'Jerusalem' all dressed up. Fucking classic.'

'It was 'Rule Britannia', Baz.' Winter reached for the last sandwich. 'There's a difference.'

★   ★   ★

Charlie Freeth was booked into the Bridewell at 16.04. The Custody Sergeant, who'd served on division with him in Aldershot, reminisced briefly about old times before starting the registration procedures on his PC.

490

'You'll be wanting a brief?'

'Duty'll be fine'

'You're sure?'

'Yeah.' Freeth yawned, losing interest. 'Whatever.'

Faraday arrived nearly an hour later, with Bev Yates and Dawn Ellis. Both D/Cs had been on the *Billhook* squad from the start and Faraday had enormous faith in the rapport they'd developed in the interview room over countless previous inquiries. They'd agreed a shape for the next few hours with the Tactical Interview Adviser, and Faraday had made time to run the strategy past Martin Barrie.

In essence, they were looking at a minimum of three four-hour sessions, with extensions beyond the twenty-four-hour PACE limit if they could stand it up. All they had to date in terms of evidence were the CCTV pictures, and these were far from conclusive, and the two big unknowns were Westbourne Road and Dermott O'Keefe. Forensic evidence from the house, or news that O'Keefe had resurfaced, would give Yates and Ellis a possibly decisive advantage in interview.

To this degree, as Martin Barrie had been the first to point out, Freeth's arrest might have been somewhat premature, but Faraday had strongly disagreed. At the time of his interception on the M4 Freeth had been going in the wrong direction, in the wrong part of the country. He might have been heading for an airport or a ferry. Alerted by his partner, he might have decided on flight rather than fight. A bird in the hand, he'd told the Detective Superintendent, was worth a great deal more than the chore of trying to trace a suspect who might, within a couple of days, have been anywhere.

D/C Yates had already conferenced briefly with the duty solicitor. Hartley Crewdson had built a successful practice from premises in the north of the city. A sharp legal brain married to a taste for impeccable suits had won him a degree of respect in the custody suite and he'd lost no time in reminding Yates that his client was due back at work in a couple of days time. Vulnerable kids might well be put at risk if the integrity of the Positivo programme was jeopardised. Yates parried this move with ease. If it turned out that Mr Freeth had a charge to answer, then the first to benefit would surely be those same kids.

Faraday was monitoring the interview from an adjoining room. Two video monitors gave him a choice of views of Charlie Freeth. Since leaving the job, the ex-cop seemed to have lost a bit of weight. His hair, on the other hand, was now shoulder length, gathered at the back into a ponytail. He was a rangy man, lean, tall, attractive to a certain kind of woman, and the expression on his face — sullen, dismissive — seemed calculated to sharpen that impact. On a billboard, thought Faraday, Charlie Freeth would probably be selling a brand of French cologne.

Yates began the interview. Quickly he established the facts of Freeth's relationship with Julie Greetham: where they'd met, when he'd moved into Westbourne Road, the presence of her father

492

in the house. From the start Freeth handled himself well. He was articulate, self-composed, a man keen to leave not a trace of ambiguity or doubt. He's thought about this moment for a long time, Faraday concluded.

Yates was asking about his relationship with Frank Greetham. Had the two men been close?

'Very. I'd say exceptionally. Frank was the father I'd never had. People say mixing the generations under one roof can be tricky. With Frank and myself that just wasn't true. The man was a fund of stories. He'd *done* stuff with his life. If you had the time to listen, he was the best company in the world.'

'And you found the time?'

'Always. We binned the TV early on, Jules and me. Actually, it broke and we just never replaced it. That makes for conversation. Believe me.'

Faraday scribbled himself a note. Danny McPhee, the CSI at Westbourne Road, had noted the absence of televisions in the house. Now Faraday understood why.

In response to another question, from Ellis this time, Freeth was describing Frank Greetham's working life. At the time Freeth had moved in with his daughter, Gullifant's was still a going concern.

'He lived for it. He took pride in it. They all did, all the people who worked in Frank's branch. We're talking half a dozen at the most. It wasn't a big place, but you'd go in there for some bits and pieces, screws, drill bits, whatever, and they bust a gut to make sure you got exactly what you wanted. Apparently Jules's mum used to make a little joke about it. There are two wives in this marriage, she used to say. Me and bloody Gullifant's.'

'So it mattered to him, the firm?'

'Enormously. After his wife went, it was Frank's whole life. Doing the job properly. Satisfying the customers. Enjoying the company of the people at work. That's what he lived for.'

'And you knew that?'

'Absolutely. The two things were inseparable. Frank was meticulous. It showed in everything he did. In the way he kept the house up. In the allotment he had. In his financial affairs. Everything.'

'Financial affairs?'

'His books. We're not talking anything complicated here. Frank was on PAYE. But he still kept a ledger, still recorded all the items he bought that might one day form some kind of claim. Receipts, too. Like I say, he was meticulous. And a lot of that came from Gullifant's. He was old style, Frank, old stock. And so was the shop.'

'And the new regime? Had that made a difference?'

'Of course it had. Looking back, the writing was on the wall. By the time I got to know Frank the new people had been in for a couple of years and the place was beginning to fall apart. Deep down I think Frank knew that, but people of his generation just never give in. They don't know how to. They soldier on. They do their best. If the boat's sinking, they try and plug the holes. From where I was sitting, believe me, that was an education. I loved the man, adored him. But that's because I *respected* him.'

Faraday, watching, found himself drawn in by the passion in Freeth's voice. This account of his, deeply personal, was beginning to shape itself into a sort of manifesto. D/C Freeth, to the best of his recollection, had stepped out of a job he'd come to hate. And in the shape of Frank Greetham, he seemed to have found a kind of salvation.

Yates sensed it too.

'You said he was like a father, Frank.'

'That's right.'

'What does that mean?'

'It means that I trusted him. And I suppose it means that I needed him.'

'Why?'

'Because he represented . . . ' He frowned, staring at Yates, taking his time. 'No, because he *was* somebody I'd never had in my life before. I was working with kids by now. We were getting Positivo together. And I saw it with them, too. Every life needs a direction. Life's a journey. You need to be sure about your bearings.'

'And Frank?'

'He gave me my bearings. Just the same way we try to do with the kids.'

'And how did he do that? Frank?'

'Because he *knew*. Because he'd been there. Blokes like Frank are like sticks of rock. They're honest through and through. Certain things have shaped their own lives. Obedience, for a start. And a sense that they're part of something much bigger than themselves. Frank came from a functional family. There were eight of them, here in Pompey. Strong mum, strong dad, bugger-all money. Then he joined the paras. Those organisations *worked*. And they produced blokes like Frank. Today?' Freeth lifted his hands, a gesture of contempt. 'You live in a bubble. You live for you. And you know the result? Kids, people, punters who haven't a fucking clue who they are.'

There was a brief silence. Yates was studying his notes. Ellis came to the rescue. Time to get the interview back on track.

'So it would be fair, would it, to suggest that you'd do anything for Frank Greetham?'

Faraday caught a flicker of concern on the solicitor's face. Crewdson raised a cautionary finger but Freeth ignored it.

'Absolutely anything.' The nod was vehement. 'And he knew that.'

⋆　⋆　⋆

Jimmy Suttle found Tracy Barber alone at her desk in the *Polygon* intelligence cell. At nearly eight in the evening, to Suttle's surprise, the Major Crimes suite at Kingston Crescent was virtually empty.

'Where is everyone? I thought this was the big one?'

'It is. We had a squad meet this evening, a major review. Most of the blokes are upstairs in the bar now, drowning their sorrows.'

'Sorrows?'

'Barrie monstered us. I never realised he could be so tough.'

496

Frustrated by the lack of progress, the Detective Superintendent had torn into the *Polygon* squad. He wanted detectives who thought on their feet, not plodders who went through the motions. He wanted people savvy enough to think outside the box, to suggest lines of enquiry no one else had dreamed worth pursuing. He wanted a bit of vision, a bit of originality. Above all, he wanted the first hint of some kind of breakthrough.

'The poor bloke's frustrated. That's the bottom line. You get the feeling that command has passed up the chain. It's not his baby anymore. There's just too much riding on the result.'

'You mean the right kind of result?'

'I mean a result that puts bodies in court. Or, failing that, a result that serves some other purpose.'

'Like what?'

'Like convincing the rest of us that all this terrorist stuff really matters.'

'And does it?' Suttle nodded at the pile of paperwork at Barber's elbow.

'Of course it does. We did no one any favours by going into Iraq and there are people out there who want to make us pay for it. Whether offing the Minister for Defence Procurement makes them feel any better, I don't know. It's difficult, Jimmy. These days you can dream up a useful motivation for any crime. Politicians do it all the time.'

Suttle nodded. He'd come to ask a favour.

'You know that list of hospital interviewees

you drew up? People who might have seen someone wandering around the grounds? Casing the shed where the Kawasaki ended up?'

'Yeah.'

'What's the status of the interviews?'

'They're done. Finished.'

'You've talked to everyone?'

'The people we could lay hands on, yes. The rest we'll get round to. If you're asking me if we turned up anything useful I'm afraid the answer's no.'

'Have you still got the list?'

'Of course.' She nodded at the paperwork on her desk. 'It might take a while to find, but yes.'

Suttle helped himself to a spare chair. Outside, down the corridor, he heard the door to the stairwell bang.

'Does this list include admissions?'

'It includes everything. Why?'

'I'm just curious.'

'I can see that, Jimmy, but tell me why.'

Suttle shook his head. He'd wait until she found her list. Then he'd be out of her hair.

'How's *Billhook*?' Barber was still sorting through the pile of paperwork.

'Fine. We've got a name in the frame. He's down at the Bridewell right now.' He smothered a yawn. 'Fuck all to throw at him, though.'

498

24

TUESDAY, 19 SEPTEMBER 2006. 20.34

It took a while for the cabbie to find the offices of Dial-a-Van. A stranger to this part of Southampton, Winter sat in the back of the Peugeot gazing out at the wasteland of retail estates, light industrial units and huge warehousing sheds that had spread north from the docks. He'd phoned Dobroslaw from Pompey in the late afternoon. He'd presented Mackenzie's compliments and asked for half an hour of the Pole's time. Dobroslaw, on the phone, had sounded surprised. Surprised and somewhat chilly. Four hours later Winter was still wondering why.

The cabbie slowed for an enormous articulated truck emerging from a fenced compound beside a meat packing factory. According to the address on the side of the cab the truck had come from Bratislava, and Winter sat back, aware of just how little he knew about commerce. There was money in this city. You could feel it, smell it. Pompey had always been martial, scraping a crust from foreign wars, but here in Southampton there were easier ways of earning a living.

Minutes earlier he'd eyed the line of container boats tied up beneath the huge yellow cranes. Trade, he thought. Trade and commerce and

499

blokes like Dobroslaw who made a fortune in what he'd doubtless call the service industry. Bazza, although supplying cocaine, had basically been in the same game. People wanted to get high. Blokes wanted to get laid. And you wouldn't stay poor very long if you saw to it that they got what they were after. That was the beauty of people like Bazza and the Pole. It was supply and demand. Get the sums right. Deliver a decent product. Crush the opposition. And you'd probably end up very, very rich.

Winter grinned to himself, immensely comforted by the simplicity of this equation. On the back of the white powder Bazza had erected a business empire. Dobroslaw was in the process of doing something very similar. From a small army of Russian toms had come the profits to finance an import/export business, a string of pizza parlours and now a van rental company. Earlier Winter had surfed his way to Dobroslaw's website. His fleet of second-hand Transits — vans and minibuses — were on offer at silly prices and were doubtless earning the Pole yet more dosh.

The way that bad money, criminal earnings, could so easily become a legitimate fortune had always fascinated Winter, and now he'd suddenly found himself part of that amazing conjuring trick. All day he'd been hunting for a word that would describe this new role of his. Was he Bazza's bagman? Or was he, in a more dignified sense, representing his new boss's best interests? Winter nodded to himself, preferring the latter description. He felt, in a word, ambassadorial.

Dial-a-Van operated from a pair of prefabs at the far end of a potholed compound beside the railway line. The lights were on in both. Winter got out of the cab, told the driver to be back in fifteen minutes and watched the lights of the Peugeot disappear towards the docks. An untidy line of rusting Transits stretched into the distance. Winter got to twenty, then gave up.

The first door he tried was locked. He walked to the other Portakabin, knocked twice, went in. Dobroslaw was hunched behind a desk at the far end, the phone to his ear. Winter had forgotten how big he was. He glanced up then put the phone down. Light from the lamp on the desk spilled onto the bare floor.

'Mr Winter, you're late. We wait an hour. Not good. Not polite.'

There was another man in the Portakabin, half hidden in the shadows. He was small and wiry with big hands seamed black with oil and grease. There was more oil on his jeans but the Nikes and the Saints Number 6 shirt looked brand new. It was an odd combination. Winter muttered an excuse. The train service was crap these days.

'You come by *train*?'

Winter nodded, wondering why he was bothering with this lie. The cabbie was on Bazza's books as well. A tenner to Southampton and back.

Dobroslaw was scribbling himself a note. Winter walked across, a smile on his face. The Pole studied the outstretched hand, then folded his massive arms.

'Cunt,' he said. 'And stupid too.'

'You what?' Winter wanted to talk jet skis, TV deals, money, fame.

'I said cunt.'

'Why?'

'You think I'm stupid?'

'Not at all.'

'You don't know?'

'Know what?'

Winter heard the scrape of a chair behind him. Then, without quite understanding how, he was sitting down. Dobroslaw was saying something in Polish to the man in the Nikes. Then his eyes found Winter again.

'You're either very brave or very stupid. I think probably stupid. Can you read, Mr Winter?'

Winter found himself looking at a copy of the *Southern Daily Echo* open at an inside page. There was a photograph of one of Dobroslaw's vans parked on the pavement outside the newspaper's offices. Inside, clearly visible, were half a dozen naked women. Some were blowing kisses to passers-by. Others were trying to cover themselves. One was showing the camera her arse. Across the top of the page ran the headline *From Russia With Love*.

'You really don't know?'

'No. Tell me.'

'A man comes here yesterday. Yesterday morning. He has money. He wants a van. No problem. We give him a van. He drives to a house I own. There are other men with him. They take all the girls. They take them naked. And they leave the van in the middle of the city.' He nodded down at the newspaper. 'A joke, you think?'

'You can describe him? This man?' Winter felt like a detective again.

'Very tall. Black.' Dobroslaw said something else in Polish. Seconds later Winter found himself looking at a photocopy of the booking form. Brett West.

'There's more.' Dobroslaw's hand settled lightly on the telephone. 'This afternoon I get a call. Bazza wants you to buy a newspaper, says the voice. Then nothing. Until you arrive. Have you come to apologise? Or are you here to share the joke?'

The word 'joke' triggered an explosion of pain in Winter's right ear. He rocked back in the chair, then toppled over, sprawling on the floor, looking up in time to try and shield himself from the blur of white Nike. The blow caught him high on the right shoulder. More pain. Then another pair of feet were visible, bigger, clad in black leather.

He brought his knees up, buried his head between his arms, waited for the worst to pass. It seemed to go on forever, blow after blow driving the breath from his body. It was years since he'd been in a serious ruck and the better part of a lifetime since he'd taken a beating like this. A couple of teeth went. He spat blood onto the floor, curled his body a little tighter, tried to trick his mind into thinking of something else. A savage kick to his lower body made him want to throw up. A second, and he was spewing on the floor. Pain tasted of bile. His eyes tight shut, he fought to concentrate on a single image. The view from his apartment. Misty. Anything. Then, quite suddenly, it was over.

Outside, dimly, he caught the clatter of a diesel engine. Dobroslaw was helping him to his feet. He seemed immensely strong. Winter's hand went to his mouth. His tongue explored something jagged where teeth had once been. Withdrawing his hand, he noticed it was covered in blood. A door opened. A face swam into focus. The cabbie, he thought vaguely.

'Tell Mr Bazza no more jokes, eh?' The voice was soft in his burning ear. 'Tell him next time we'll mean it.'

★   ★   ★

An hour and a half into the interview, Freeth's solicitor asked for a break. Yates and Ellis joined Faraday in the adjoining office. Faraday was looking nearly as glum as Yates.

'He's pissing all over us,' Yates said. 'This isn't an interview, it's a speech.'

Faraday could only agree. Every question, no matter how carefully phrased, seemed to lead back to the disgust that Freeth still felt on Frank Greetham's behalf. How a bunch of thieving bastards had bought the company and stripped out everything of value. How a decent pension fund had mysteriously emptied. How a bunch of guys who'd had this old-fashioned idea about customer service had suddenly found themselves jobless, potless and totally without prospects. So far, it was true, they were still in the opening phase of the interview. Freeth had yet to account for the CCTV pictures and for the evident closeness of his relationship with the missing O'Keefe. But the truth was that he was bossing the exchanges. In situations like these it was often difficult to persuade the interviewee to say anything at all. In Freeth's case they couldn't shut him up. He had a great deal to get off his chest. And this was as good an opportunity as any.

'Where next then, boss?'

'Dermott O'Keefe. Then make a start on Mallinder.'

Faraday's phone began to ring. It was Jimmy Suttle.

'I've just had a bell from the Duty Inspector at Fareham, boss. Gwent have been on to him. Apparently they've retrieved a phone number from Freeth's Toyota.'

The number, he said, had been found on a scrap of paper balled on the floor. It was a Fishguard number.

'You've tried it?'

'They did. That's why they phoned. The number takes you to a boarding house near the ferry port. Harbour View.'

Faraday reached for his pad. Fishguard was in west Wales. From Fishguard you could take a ferry to Ireland.

'The boy Dermott,' he said slowly. 'He's Irish.'

'Exactly.'

'You think Freeth was going to Fishguard?'

'More than possible, boss. I phoned the B & B. They'd had a call from a punter wanting a room for a maximum of three nights. He gave his name as Smith. It's their only call today.'

'Have they got an O'Keefe booked in?'

'No, I asked.'

'But you think Smith might be Freeth?'

'Almost certainly.'

'And you think he'd be waiting for the lad?'

'It's possible, boss. Either that or the boy's in Ireland already. In which case he might be waiting for Julie Greetham.'

Faraday nodded. A reunion with Julie made perfect sense but there'd been nothing in her interview to suggest she was planning a hasty exit from Pompey.

'OK.' Faraday glanced at his watch. Just gone nine. 'The Toyota's still with Gwent?'

'Yeah.'

'Get hold of Glen Thatcher. We need a couple of D/Cs over to Gwent. They're to take the Toyota to Fishguard and stake out the B & B. O'Keefe knows the car. He might just appear. It's a long shot, but to be frank, Jimmy, I'll take anything just now.'

The interview resumed at 21.14. After the half-time oranges, Freeth clearly sensed the game was going his way. When Ellis mentioned O'Keefe, asking why the boy was so special, he instantly turned the question on its head.

'We're the special ones,' he said. 'Not Dermott. He's a bright lad, no question about it. He's also much better adjusted than most of them. He's got a life. He sorts himself out. Family matters to him. But what he hasn't got is the kind of structure we supply, the kind of leadership challenges that come his way. It's water in the desert. The kid laps it up.'

'Does that make him unusual?'

'Yes. Very.'

'So how would you describe the relationship you both established?'

'*Relationship?* What are you assuming here?'

'We understand the pair of you are close.'

'Yeah? Care to tell me why?'

'Because people have told us so.'

'Like who?'

'I'm afraid I'm not at liberty to — '

'Then it's bollocks.' Freeth bent to his brief. 'Tell them, Hartley. Tell them this kind of stuff's out of order.'

Crewdson registered an objection. Yates stepped in. He wanted to know whether the relationship with O'Keefe existed at all.

'Dermott's a client. He's done well. He's on the leadership course. Do we talk? Have a laugh or two? Try and nail one or two things down? Of course we do. Do we have . . . ' Freeth smiled his dangerous smile ' . . . a *relationship?* The answer is no. Positivo has hundreds of clients. He's just one of them.'

'So you don't see him at all outside the course?'

'No.'

'Never?'

'No.'

Yates glanced at Ellis. Almost imperceptibly she nodded. Yates turned to Freeth again.

'How much did you know about Jonathan Mallinder? Before he was killed?'

'I knew that he'd signed a letter to the Gullifant's people. And I knew that a bunch of them had gone to see him.'

'Did you find out anything else about him? Did you Google him at all? Or Google the partnership?'

'Yes. Frank was in a state about the whole thing. I did whatever I could.'

'And what did you find out about Mr Mallinder?'

'I found out pretty much what I told you before. That these guys were asset stripping. That they were in it for the freeholds. That they'd make back their initial stake by selling a couple of the freeholds with planning permission, and then cash in on the rest when the time was right. None of this is rocket science. All you need is a heart of stone.'

'So your attitude to Mr Mallinder . . . ?'

'I loathed the man. In my view he deserved everything he got. If the nation's wealth depends on people like Mallinder we're better off living in mud huts. The man was a disgrace.'

Yates was smiling now. You'd never accuse Charlie Freeth of not speaking his mind.

'Last Monday week,' he began, 'that's Monday the fourth of September, can you remember where you were?'

'Here. In Pompey.'

'What were you doing?'

'I was at home at Westbourne Road. Monday evenings Jules goes to yoga. I cook.'

'And afterwards?'

'I can't remember. Bit of Radio Two probably.

Then bed. Kids are knackering, especially the kids we deal with. I'd just come off a residential weekend. I could have slept for a week.'

'You never left the house?'

'No.' He pretended bemusement. 'Why would I want to do that?'

'We have CCTV pictures that tie Dermott O'Keefe to Port Solent that night. He's with an adult. That adult looks like you. We have more pictures, three o'clock in the morning, that show him going back towards Southampton with the same adult. We think it was you, Mr Freeth.'

'You're sure about that? Only I was in bed. Asleep.' He held Yates' gaze a moment then bent forward. 'Listen, I know what you guys are driving at, I know what you think, what you suspect, but you're going to have to do a whole lot better than this to put me anywhere near Port Solent. Is that where the man lived? I've absolutely no idea. Did someone kill him there? That's what they were saying in the paper. Was it me? Absolutely not. Would I have been pleased to have done it? Absolutely fucking delighted. So a big round of applause for whoever pulled the trigger. But don't ask me to take the rap.'

'Trigger?' Ellis's question was barely audible.

'In the paper, love. The following day and the day after. They mentioned a gun and guns have triggers. Why were we so keen on reading all the coverage? Because we couldn't get enough of it. Does that make us vengeful? Yes . . . and extremely happy. Am I making myself clear here? Have we done with 'open account'? Do you want to get on to the 'challenge' phase next?'

Faraday winced. Yates was right. Freeth was totally in charge. Every in-depth interview began with an open account from the suspect. In classic CID theory the challenge phase would follow. But what was there left to challenge?

'You've admitted a debt to Frank Greetham . . . ' Yates said.

'I have. And gladly. He was a fine man.'

'You've been equally candid about Mallinder. Would it be fair to say he was someone you hated?'

'I loathed him. Despised him. Hate's too weak a word.'

'You had no regrets that he got killed?'

'None at all.'

'Would you have *liked* to have killed him?'

'I didn't say that.'

'Answer the question.'

'*Could* I have done it? Yes. *Did* I do it? No.'

'You knew Dermott O'Keefe?'

'Yes.'

'Dermott O'Keefe was at Port Solent on Monday night. With someone who looked a whole lot like you.'

'So you tell me. Except it wasn't me.'

'You were a police officer. You'd served with CID. You knew about crime scenes, about forensic procedures. You'd also done the firearms course. Is all that true?'

'Of course it is.'

'So.' Yates tossed his pen onto the desk. 'We have a classic kill. A totally cleaned-up crime scene. And a suspect who knows all about guns, all about CID work and — by his own admission

— thought Mallinder should be held responsible for the death of someone he loved. Is that all fair?'

'Absolutely.' The smile again. 'And your point is . . . ?'

★ ★ ★

Winter made his way slowly into the flat. The cabbie had offered to take him to Accident and Emergency for a check-up but Winter had said no. He wanted a large Scotch, a fistful of painkillers and a bit of a think. Now, he prepared a nest of cushions on the sofa and then limped into the kitchen to find a glass. Everything hurt. His ear. His mouth. His shoulder. His ribs. Even his buttocks where he'd tried to shield his groin. Thank Christ he'd managed to stay conscious.

He tipped Scotch into the glass and thought about ice from the fridge but decided that bending was too painful. A token splash of water from the tap three-quarters filled the glass and he held the countertop for support as he took a deep swallow.

A month ago, as a working copper, it would have taken a single phone call to rouse the cavalry. Dobroslaw and his grubby apprentice would have been inside by now, a holding cell each, tasting a little of their own medicine. Winter eyed his reflection in the kitchen window, glad that the shadowed image spared him the details. Sooner or later he'd have to clean himself up in the bathroom, swab his wounds in TCP and inspect the damage to his mouth, but for the time being all that could wait.

He took another mouthful of Scotch, topped up the glass then eased himself onto the sofa next door. His soiled jacket lay where he'd dropped it on the carpet and his hand explored the creases until he found his mobile. The temptation was to phone Bazza and demand to know what the fuck was going on, but he knew he had to straighten things out in his own head first. There was a possibility, just, that he'd been set up — that Bazza had planned this little prank, that sending him into the lion's den with an outraged Pole would be the ultimate test of his real loyalties. If Winter had been a plant all along, Bazza might reason, then this would surely flush him out.

It was a neat enough theory, and Bazza was certainly devious enough to have dreamed it up, but something told Winter it didn't hold water. For one thing he'd never have shared Misty with a working copper. And for another Winter himself was a reasonable judge of whether people were being sincere or not. Bazza liked him. There was a kinship between them that boiled down to something bigger than self-interest. In many respects, to Winter's amusement, they had a great deal in common.

So what else might explain a minibus full of naked Russian slappers in the middle of Southampton? Winter's favourite theory, the more he thought about it, was a dickhead piece of freelance mischief from Brett West. He'd been there in Sandown Road the night Bazza had summoned his council of war. He'd seen his boss

512

ranting about the Pole, demanding redress, insisting on a settling of accounts. And because Westie was a bit literal about these kind of things, taking Bazza at his word, he'd decided to seize the initiative himself. Nothing would please Bazza more, he might have told himself, than a full-page story from a Scummer rag in his scrapbook.

Winter lay back, closing his eyes, the warmth of the Scotch easing some of the pain. If he was right about Westie, then phoning Bazza would be the obvious course of action. Westie would get bollocked for acting out of turn, a thought which put a smile on Winter's face, but then Bazza was more than likely to take offence again at the Pole's lack of respect. He'd sent Winter across to Southampton in good faith. They had business to discuss. But instead of listening to Winter's proposals his newly recruited lieutenant had been subjected to a severe slapping. From Bazza's point of view this would be totally out of order, and even Winter himself, the victim, would have absolutely no say in what followed. Bazza would go to war and — irony of ironies — the likes of Willard would probably end up with the result they'd intended all along.

That, as Winter knew only too well, couldn't happen. Not if he was to make anything worthwhile of this new life of his. He was swallowing the rest of the Scotch, resigned to seeing this thing through by himself, when his mobile began to ring.

Caller ID was a blur. He put the mobe to his ear. Faraday.

'Bastard day,' he said at once. 'And it's bloody late.'

'Come round,' Winter replied. 'If you want to know about bastard days.'

★   ★   ★

Faraday was buzzing at the main entrance downstairs within half an hour. Winter limped slowly to the video entryphone in the hall. He opened his own front door and found his way to the bathroom. He was still swallowing four ibuprofen when Faraday appeared in the hall. One look at Winter's face told him everything. A truly bastard day.

'Shit,' he said. 'What happened?'

'Bit of an accident, boss.' Winter had trouble getting the words out. His tongue felt thick. Nothing worked properly.

'Accident my arse. Who did that?'

'Doesn't matter.'

'Mackenzie?'

'No.'

'Would you tell me if it was?'

'No. But it wasn't. Believe me.'

'Someone associated with Mackenzie?'

'Wrong again. It's a learning experience, boss. Thick old bastard like me, these things happen.'

'Learning experience?' He offered Winter a shoulder, then walked him slowly into the lounge. When he suggested a detour to the bathroom to clean up his face, Winter shook his head, sparking a thick wave of nausea.

'There, boss.' Winter was looking down at the

514

sofa. 'Gently, though, eh? You want a drink?' He nodded vaguely in the direction of the kitchen. 'Help yourself.'

With Winter settled on the sofa, Faraday found himself a can of Stella.

'You want to talk about it?' He tore off the ring-pull and took a deep swallow.

'This?' Winter's fingers briefly touched his swollen face. 'No, I don't. You do the talking, boss. I bet it's Willard, isn't it? Put you up to this?'

'Yes.' Faraday saw no point in denying it.

'And what did he say?'

'He asked me to find out what you were up to. Not in those words exactly but that's what he meant.'

'Right . . . Fair question.'

'So?'

'So?' Winter managed to summon the beginnings of a grin, then shrugged, 'Fuck knows,' he said at last. 'I used to be a copper, once. But I think he knows that.'

'He does. I think he's more interested in now. You don't have to tell me anything if you don't want to, in fact I'd prefer it if you didn't, but I get the impression he thinks you're a bit . . . ' Faraday frowned ' . . . out of control.'

'Then he'd be wrong. This is me, boss. This is who I am.'

'What does that mean?'

'You make a decision. Then you live with the consequences.'

'I don't doubt that. Not for a moment. He just needs to know what the decision was. If it's of

515

any interest, he thinks you were out of your head the last time he talked to you.'

'Quite the reverse, boss. He happened to catch me at the perfect moment.'

'And what did you say.'

'I told him to fuck off. Or that's what it boiled down to.'

'And you meant it?'

'Every word.'

'Why?'

'Because he'd let me down. Him and someone else. You know a D/I called Gale Parsons? Covert Ops?' Faraday nodded. 'I thought she was a clown to begin with. Then I thought she was incompetent. But in the end it turned out a whole lot worse. Like everyone else in the job, she just covers her arse. Get any kind of result for her and I'd end up in fucking New Zealand. How's that for incentivisation?' He groped blindly for the bottle. 'Maybe I got it right first time. Maybe she *is* a clown. Either way, though, all that bollocks is history. New life, boss.' He gestured at his face again. 'New prospects.'

Haltingly he told Faraday about the fuck-up over the Devon and Cornwall cocaine seizure. The stuff had come in from Cambados, two kilos of it, and no one had thought to warn Winter. As a result, he said, he'd been lucky not to have been hurt a whole lot earlier.

'And I mean hurt, boss. Really hurt. Not this. Not the way I am now.'

'So you've binned the job? For sure?'

'Yeah.'

'To work for Mackenzie?'

516

'Yeah. Does that sound odd to you? Be honest.'

Faraday took his time. He'd left the Bridewell nearly an hour ago. He'd seldom felt so empty, so exhausted, so utterly bereft of ideas.

'No,' he said. 'It doesn't.'

25

WEDNESDAY, 20 SEPTEMBER 2006. 07.12

Faraday awoke to a kiss. Gabrielle had curled herself around him, one leg flung over his belly, the moistness of her lips anointing the soft pockets of skin beneath his eyes. Now her busy tongue was exploring elsewhere.

Aroused, Faraday let her straddle him. Still half-asleep, he lay motionless, vaguely wondering whether the favour was his or hers. Then he was back in the interview suite again, watching Yates and Ellis on the video link getting absolutely nowhere.

Minutes later, his eyes closed, he felt the warmth of Gabrielle's breath on his ear.

'*Il ne reste que quinze jours.*'

She was right. In a couple of weeks she'd be back in Chartres.

'So?' He opened one eye.

'Maybe we can take a break. Go somewhere nice. You and me.'

'Like now?'

'*Oui. Pourquoi pas?*'

Faraday stared up at her, trying to mask his disbelief. After all the time they'd spent together, hadn't she understood anything about a copper's life? Wasn't she aware of the difficulty — the sheer impossibility — of trying to build a case, muster evidence, trap a man into a confession?

518

And afterwards, once charges had been laid, hadn't she realised the sheer weight of paperwork on which a conviction would depend?

For a second or two, while she waited for an answer, he toyed with putting all this into words, with just getting a little of the torment and frustration off his chest, but then he saw the expression on her face, an almost childlike disappointment, and instead he'd rolled over, closing his eyes again, too weary to bother with an explanation. Life, in the shape of *Billhook*, was ganging up on him. He had a killer under lock and key and absolutely no way of proving his guilt. So how, in God's name, was a holiday supposed to help?

Moments later, without a word, Gabrielle got out of bed. Faraday heard her soft footsteps cross the wooden floor, then the rustle of clothing as she quickly got dressed. He caught more footsteps, down the stairs this time, then the squeak of the lock of the front door as she left the house.

Faraday, up on one elbow now, was tempted to go to the bedroom window, to apologise, to tell her that somehow he'd find the time to fit in a couple of days away, but in his heart he knew it was hopeless. Gabrielle was the best thing that had happened to him in years. For a while he'd believed he could share his life with this wonderful nomad, that there'd be a way, but now he recognised the size of the gulf between them. The last person Gabrielle needed was a grouchy, morose, bad-tempered detective several months short of fifty. The truth was that the job, in the shape of Charlie Freeth, was robbing him of everything. Even hope.

Half an hour later, sitting at the kitchen table, Faraday did his best to temper a growing sense that events were slipping out of control. A night in the cells might soften a little of Freeth's arrogance. The two D/Cs in his Toyota might turn up something in Fishguard. Even this late in the day, with the PACE clock ticking, someone else on the *Billhook* squad might stumble over a promising lead. In this situation anything would be welcome, anything that would prevent him from having to release a man he knew to be guilty. That single fact, the near-certainty of Freeth walking free, had assumed an importance he'd rarely accorded to anything else in his professional life.

But why Freeth? And why now? He didn't know. Maybe it was because the man was an ex-copper. Maybe it was because he was demonstrating so clearly the real limitations of the investigative process. Think through the crime you wanted to commit. Pay scrupulous attention to detail. And there wouldn't be a detective in the world who could lay a finger on you. That's how tough people like Freeth could make this job of his, and the knowledge of his own helplessness simply deepened his gloom still further.

Could it get any worse? He knew it could. He thought of Winter, with his wrecked face and his broken teeth. Here was a detective unlike any other. He'd won countless victories, taken scalps by the hundred, potted decent villains with an artful nonchalance he'd made uniquely his own.

Faraday himself had certainly had his share of run-ins with Winter. He'd been frequently impossible to manage and had always offered the most elusive of moving targets. His open contempt for the bright new face of police work — transparency, partnership, delivery — had won him few friends in the upper levels of the hierarchy and his cavalier disregard for the rules had driven everyone else mad. But there was a germ of something profoundly reassuring inside Winter, a candle that twenty-plus years in the job had never been able to snuff out. For all his bent little ways, he'd always recognised the difference between right and wrong, between the good guys and the bad. That was a given. That was something on which you could depend. Until last night.

Shocked by the sight of the man, saddened by what he'd had to say, Faraday had taken the long route home to the Bargemaster's House, parking briefly on the seafront to stare out into the darkness. Even then, he'd known that this was the end of something impossible to measure. Winter had gone over to the enemy. Winter had cashed his chips and left the table with scarcely a backward glance. And he'd done it because at last he'd tumbled that the odds were against him. Now and probably forever.

Faraday shook his head, wondering how on earth he'd break this news to Willard. Winter, he suspected, had glimpsed for the first time the hardest of truths: that the job had become impossible, that his professional life had been, in the end, a failure. Then came the sound of footsteps as Gabrielle stepped back into the house. She was calling Faraday's name. And she was singing.

* * *

Jimmy Suttle stared at the name, not quite believing it. He'd got to the incident room early, knowing that if this hunch of his was right then the least he owed Faraday was a little extra ammunition for the morning session with Charlie Freeth. Extra ammunition? He checked again, aware of the hot stir of adrenalin flooding his body.

Between the sixteenth of June and the sixth of July, according to Tracy Barber's records, Frank Greetham had been an inpatient at The Orchards. He glanced at his watch, wondering whether to try and check out Greetham's medical records. The details of his GP would be on the Coroner's file. He could put a call through to the practice, try and elbow his way into the morning queue of patients, try and make a case for confirming this one single fact, but already he knew that it would be wasted effort. To access any medical data required, at the very least, a Court Order. The medical community was, at every level, fiercely protective when it came to patient confidentiality.

There had to be another way. He eyed the phone a moment, then checked back through his pocketbook. He still had Sam Taylor's number. Taylor's wife answered on the third ring. Suttle introduced himself and asked to talk to her husband.

'He's on the early shift at B&Q,' she said. 'Can I help at all?'

Suttle, about to say no, changed his mind.

'It's about Frank Greetham. I understand he was in The Orchards for a spell. During the summer.'

'That's right. Sam went to see him. Poor man, he was in a terrible state.'

'Why was he admitted? Do you happen to know?'

'Sam thought it was something to do with all the pills he was taking, but you ought to talk to him yourself. He'd know. He was very pally with Frank. He thought the world of him.'

He thought the world of him. Julie Greetham had used exactly the same phrase, describing the way Charlie felt about her father.

'When's he back? Sam?'

'Around two this afternoon. He comes home for a late lunch. You're bound to catch him then.'

Suttle thanked her and looked up to find Faraday at the open office door. He was talking to Glen Thatcher. According to the Outside Enquiries D/S, the two D/Cs had been in Fishguard for a couple of hours now, hoping Dermott O'Keefe might turn up. They'd found a parking space across the road from the boarding house and left a Positivo baseball cap on the dashboard. The cap had come from the boot of the Toyota. If O'Keefe was really heading for Fishguard prior to a ferry crossing, he'd know the car belonged to Freeth.

'So where are the lads?'

'In a café down the road. They've got line of sight on the Toyota. Turns out there was also a mobile in the boot, hidden under the spare wheel. Full marks to the blokes for finding it.'

'The mobile belongs to Freeth?'

'I'd have thought so. It seems to be brand new. There's nothing on the SIM card, no numbers stored. You just wonder why he bought it.'

'Where is it now? This mobile?'

'The blokes have got it.' He grinned. 'And it's switched on.'

Faraday's grunt appeared to suggest approval. He stepped into the office, shut the door behind him.

'Anything new?' He was looking at Barber's paperwork strewn across Suttle's desk.

Suttle told him about the psychiatric unit. At first he thought Faraday hadn't heard him properly. He'd sunk into his chair, letting his head fall back, staring up at the ceiling.

'Say that again,' he murmured.

'Frank Greetham was a patient in The Orchards for about three weeks. According to D/C Barber's notes, his visitors included his daughter and Charlie Freeth. They went to see him more or less every night. There's a note here about one of the nurses. Apparently she said that was unusual.'

'And this was a *Polygon* action?'

'Yes.'

'Did anyone follow it up?'

'Not that I can see.' Suttle nodded at the paperwork.

'Have you talked to Barber?'

'No, boss.'

'Do it. Now.'

Suttle lifted the phone. Tracy Barber was on another call. The third time he tried, the line was free. Suttle explained what he was after. Barber said she'd check with the incident room and call him back.

'Yeah. Quick as you can, Trace.'

The phone rang within minutes. According to an assistant in the incident room, neither Julie nor Freeth himself had been interviewed. They were both on the to-do list of actions.

Faraday was monitoring the conversation from the other side of the desk. The Orchards was next door to St James' Hospital.

'Ask her whether the hospital has CCTV. Ask her about the grounds. Ask her about the derelict villa where they found the bike.'

Suttle caught his eye, grinned, then relayed the question. A series of nods raised an answering smile from Faraday.

'The answer's yes, boss. There's nothing that covers the villa but there's yards of other footage. They've been through it all.'

'And?'

'She's got a list as long as your arm for people wandering around in the grounds. This kind of weather, everyone's at it. She says tracing them has been a nightmare.'

'But we know what Freeth looks like. We can check out the footage ourselves.'

'Of course, boss, but there's a problem. She's saying the tapes are wiped after a month. They don't go back as far as July.'

'Shit.'

'Exactly.'

Suttle mumbled a thank you to Barber and put the phone down. Faraday was looking at the ceiling again.

'Tracy sends her regards, boss,' Suttle said at last. 'And she wants to know what we're up to.'

'I bet.' Faraday reached across, helping himself to Barber's notes. 'So what possessed you to go through this lot?'

'Something in one of the statements that first day. It's been bothering me for a while.'

'Which first day?'

'The day the minister got shot. I didn't get to read it for a bit, and by that time we were being shipped up here, but it stuck with me, like it does sometimes.'

'And what was it?'

'It was the woman pushing her baby home from the nursery. You probably don't remember. She was about to cross a road. Greyshott Road. She'd stopped on the pavement to let a motorbike go past and she made a point of saying how small the bloke on the back was. I was struck by it. That's all. Some of the witnesses at the scene had said exactly the same.'

'So?'

'So I tucked it away, like you do. And then I began to think about the MO, how someone had thought this whole thing through — no shell casings at the scene, no CCTV footage, lying low the way they did, lots of local knowledge. What does that remind you of? Just a week beforehand?'

Faraday raised an eyebrow.

'You're telling me Freeth killed the minister? With O'Keefe on the back?'

'I'm saying it's possible, boss.'

'But why would he ever do that?'

'I've no idea. Except that he's got the skills. Think about it, boss. I wasn't there yesterday. I've no idea how he behaved in interview. But everything I know about this man tells me two things. Number one, he's incredibly meticulous, incredibly sorted, incredibly *good* at doing what he does. Number two, he knows it.'

'Right on both counts,' Faraday conceded. 'The man's arrogant. He can do no wrong. But this is old news. That's the way he was in the job. That's why no one was sorry when he jacked it in. And that's why we've probably got six hours before we have to let him go.'

'The Superintendent won't authorise an extension?'

'I can't see it. We need more evidence. This is terrific ... ' Faraday gestured at the notes ' ... and so is what lies behind it. But it's speculation, Jimmy. It's guesswork. The Superintendent's a hard bastard.' He glanced up at the clock on the wall. 'We need more.'

★   ★   ★

Winter did his best to fend Mackenzie off. The phone call came in at just gone nine. Bazza wanted to know how last night had turned out.

527

Had the Pole been happy to join forces? Had he seen the logic behind bringing the two events together? Might he even chuck a little money in the pot? Winter ran a hand over his battered face. He was still in bed, still trying to work out whether he could risk another couple of ibuprofen on top of the fistful he'd swallowed already. The bathroom cabinet seemed a bus ride away. Pain made you lazy.

'So what's the score?' Bazza wanted an answer.

'Early days, Baz,' Winter muttered, aware of the thickness in his voice.

'What?'

'I said early days. He wouldn't commit.'

'What's the matter with you, Paul? Forgotten to put your teeth in?'

'It's nothing. I just — '

'Bollocks, it's nothing. What have you been up to? You sound terrible, mush. You sound fucking *old.*'

'God forbid, Baz.' Winter tried to force a laugh. 'Me? Never better.'

'You're lying, mush. Stay there. You in bed or what?'

He didn't wait for an answer and Winter groaned, staring at the mobile, only too aware of where the next hour or so would probably lead.

Mackenzie, when he arrived, had brought Marie with him. Winter let them in. He'd managed to struggle his way into Maddox's dressing gown. Below the knee, his bare legs were purpled with bruising.

'Paul!'

Marie was in the bathroom within seconds, running water from the hot tap, filling the basin. She called for cotton wool. Soap was in the shower tray, TCP in the bathroom cabinet. She sat Winter on the loo then began to sponge his face. There was still blood crusted on his chin and cheeks. One eye had closed overnight and his swollen lips made it hard to keep his mouth closed.

'You need a dentist, Paul.' She was probing along the line of broken teeth. Through his one good eye Winter could see the concern on her face. She turned to Mackenzie.

'You didn't know about this?' It sounded like an accusation.

'Of course I didn't.'

'Paul?' She wanted to know what had happened.

'Little accident, love,' he muttered.

'Accident, bollocks.' It was Mackenzie. 'Tell me, mush. Tell me what happened.'

Winter shook his head. In moments of fitful sleep he'd dreamed about this very situation. Winter would hold his ground. Mackenzie would call for Westie. The whole thing would kick off again and Winter would end up without a face at all. Welcome to Bazzaland.

'A misunderstanding,' he managed at last. 'Nothing to get worked up about.'

'You walked into a lamp post? You fell out of the bath? You got hit by a meteor? What kind of what do you think I am? I ask you to go and see our new friend. Next thing I know you look like something out of the *Hammer House of Horror*. Our Polish mate's extremely heavy. Are we

529

talking some kind of connection here or am I just imagining it? Only this could be quite serious.'

'Yeah?' Winter managed a smile. 'You know something, Baz?'

'No. Fucking tell me.'

'That woman Brodie. I've worked it out. She'd have had a plan.' Winter had both eyes shut now while Marie swabbed his face with TCP. Mackenzie waited until she'd finished.

'What plan?'

'She'd have wanted to have provoked a war.' He gestured up at his face. 'Something like this.'

'So it *was* the Pole. Is that what you're telling me?'

'Yeah.' Winter nodded. 'Of course it was.'

Marie had left to put the kettle on. Bazza settled himself on the edge of the bath. He was like a kid. He was getting excited again. Winter could feel it. He explained about the minibus parked outside the newspaper offices. The thought of half a dozen naked Russian slappers put a grin on Bazza's face.

'Who organised that? You?'

'Westie.'

'No way.' Bazza shook his head. 'Westie wouldn't have the brain for it.'

'He did, Baz. I've seen the booking form.'

'Fuck me. Westie? A stunt like that? Amazing.' He was eyeing Winter's face again. 'So the Pole took it out on you, is that what you're saying?'

'Yeah, but that's not the point. The point, Baz, is this. You're safe on the van, they can't do you for that, but if you take it any further with the

Pole, do anything *really* silly, then Brodie will be in the medals.'

'I'm not with you.'

'They'll expect you to react. They'll be waiting. They'll mount a fucking huge investigation and then do you for GBH, conspiracy, perverting the course of justice — whatever. Then they'll go to town on the narcotics side of the business, turn something up, and once that happens they'll take it all off you, every last penny.'

'How do you know all this?'

'Because I do, Baz.' Winter's hand found Mackenzie's arm. He gave it a squeeze. 'Just trust me, eh?'

⋆   ⋆   ⋆

To Faraday's relief, the implications of Suttle's exchanges with Tracy Barber appeared not to have spread to Martin Barrie. The Detective Superintendent's call found Faraday at the Bridewell, preparing for the next interview with Freeth.

'How's it going, Joe?'

'It's not, sir.'

Faraday summarised yesterday's lack of progress. During the opening phase of the interview Freeth had blocked off every investigative avenue. He hadn't been at Port Solent on the night of the murder. He didn't keep company with Dermott O'Keefe. Only when it came to his feelings about Mallinder had Freeth opened up.

'Hatred? Bit strong, isn't it?' There was a hint of doubt in Barrie's voice.

'It was a boast, sir. And he knows it winds us up. He thinks he's got the result he wants — Mallinder dead — without the chore of having to stand trial. We know he did it. He knows he did it. And worst of all he knows we know he did it. In any other context I'd call it harassment. On his part.'

It was a poor joke but it drew a chuckle from Barrie.

'So what now, Joe?'

'We persevere. There are one or two angles we might be able to develop. We think he booked into a B & B at Fishguard under an assumed name, probably to link up with the lad O'Keefe. We haven't attacked him with that yet.'

'When does the clock stop?'

'Four 'o clock this afternoon. I've warned the Superintendent we might be troubling him for an extension but we'll need something else in the pot.'

'And have you got it?'

'No sir, not yet.'

★   ★   ★

D/C Jimmy Suttle was sitting in a management office in the B&Q Superstore. The retail park lay in the shadow of Fratton Park. Sam Taylor, quite literally, lived round the corner.

Summoned to the office by tannoy, he knocked at the door and stepped in. In his knee-length work coat, Suttle thought, he might

532

still have been the friendly face behind the counter at Gullifant's. The manager offered them both coffee and said there was no rush for Sam to get back to his section. Take as long as you need.

Suttle asked which section Sam was working on.

'Flatpacks.' He was looking worried. 'What's this about?'

'Frank Greetham. I was talking to your wife this morning. We need to know whether he was ever treated at St James.'

'Yes, he was in that new unit, The Orchards.' He paused, trying to recall the dates. 'June time, it was. A couple of weeks. Maybe more.'

'And you went to see him? Paid him a visit?'

'Twice. It's not a place you'd be keen on. The set-up is impressive and the staff do their best but . . . ' he shook his head ' . . . you wouldn't choose that kind of company.'

'Did Frank have other visitors? To your knowledge?'

'Yes. His daughter and that bloke of hers, Charlie, were there the time I went in the evening. I remember they wanted to take him out, give him a bit of fresh air. The weather was lovely, still hot that time in the evening, but the nurses wouldn't have it. I don't know whether they thought Julie was going to nick off with him but it was a shame. Banged up all day inside no wonder he was depressed, poor old sod.'

'Did you talk to the daughter at all? Or to Charlie?'

'Yes, we had a little natter.'

'And what impression did you get?'

'I'm not with you, son. What impression of what?'

'Of how they felt?'

'*Felt?*' He shrugged. 'They thought it was a terrible situation, just like everyone else did, and they were right, it was. How would you feel if your dad ended up in a psychiatric unit?'

'Do you think they were bitter at all?'

'Not bitter. Not that exactly. More angry. Especially the bloke, Charlie.'

'Angry how?'

'Angry at what had happened to Frank. Or at what had been *allowed* to happen. Like I said last time, Frank had a copy of all the correspondence. I'd made sure of that. And it turned out that this Charlie had been through it too. Intelligent bloke. Some of this stuff's really complicated. You should take a look through the file.'

Suttle nodded. It was a good idea. Getting Frank Greetham's paperwork out of the Copnor house might be complicated. SOC were still in possession of the scene and hated intrusions.

'You've still got all the correspondence?'

'Of course I have. Nip round the corner.' He checked his watch and got to his feet. 'Ask my missus. She knows where it is.'

*   *   *

Suttle was in Carisbrooke Road within minutes. Mrs Taylor was doing her washing. She led him upstairs to a tiny room at the back of the house that her husband used as an office.

'The stuff you want's in there.' She nodded at a stack of cardboard boxes on the floor. 'Help yourself.'

Suttle cleared himself a space on the table, wondering quite where to start. The first box was full of letters from Gullifant's staff, each carefully stapled to a typed reply. Suttle glanced through them. Some were bewildered, others outraged, but most of them voiced the same question: given the guarantees that had come with the pension scheme, how could a disaster like this ever have happened?

It was a good question, and as Suttle started on the contents of the second box he wondered how he himself would cope in a situation like this. Your employer insists you join the company pension scheme. Everyone tells you it's a very good idea, no risk at all. You assume they must be right, tuck away thousands of pounds for your old age, then wake up one morning to discover that it's all gone. By now you're looking forward to retirement. Yet suddenly, within the span of a single day, you find yourself facing the prospect of living the rest of your life on a dribble of money. No wonder Frank Greetham had turned his face to the wall.

So what exactly had happened? And how come no one appeared to be liable? Suttle helped himself to a handful of correspondence from the second box. This time Taylor himself had initiated the exchanges. He'd written, as far as Suttle could judge, to more or less everybody. There were letters to local councillors, to the

News, to his MP, to the editors of various specialist financial magazines, to the national press, to the secretary of the Institute of Actuaries, to the National Insurance Contributions Office. One of these letters had drawn a scribbled note of sympathy plus a copy of a press release from the office of the Parliamentary Ombudsman.

The government, according to Ann Abraham, had a unique responsibility for setting a policy framework with respect to pensions. People very reasonably put their faith in government information on the safety of various occupational schemes. Yet this information had proved to be inaccurate, incomplete, unclear and inconsistent. Taylor had highlighted the four words, adding a line of exclamation marks in the margin of the letter.

Suttle found another press release, downloaded from a website. This document addressed the issue of compensation. In response to massive pressure, the government had finally promised to set up a Financial Assistance Scheme. This scheme would be specifically designed to help the likes of Frank Greetham, employees in their fifties and sixties who'd found themselves penniless after the collapse of their company pension schemes. Some of these schemes were, in the parlance, 'contracted out' of the state pension scheme, which meant that victims would be denied even the minimum state pension. Suttle blinked. Was Frank expected to live on *nothing*?

He read on. The Financial Assistance Scheme,

after all the hype, had turned out to be a bitter disappointment. The Treasury had agreed to pay £400 million over twenty years, a sum expected to somehow compensate 65,000 people. So far, just four hundred victims had received money. Their average payment? Just £3,175.

Once again Sam Taylor had been busy with his highlighter, drawing attention to key statistics, and Suttle leafed quickly back, noting various names in case he ever needed expert witnesses in court. Then he turned to the next wad of letters. These were paper-clipped together and appeared to form a lengthy correspondence between Taylor and the Department for Work and Pensions. He was reading the first letter when his eye was caught by a reference to a House of Commons speech. The minister naturally regretted the plight that faced thousands of pensioners. Some of them indeed were his own constituents. But calculations had quantified the potential cost of full compensation at seventeen billion pounds and it would be improper for him, as a guardian of tax-payers' hard-earned money, to risk a sum of this size in mitigation of what, essentially, was a market failure. Suttle read the quote twice, trying to imagine what it might do to Sam Taylor's blood pressure. Here was a spokesman for the same government that had, in the words of the Parliamentary Ombudsman, been guilty of maladministration. The same government that had misled millions of pensioners. The same government that had begrudgingly chucked a few pennies in the direction of people like Frank Greetham.

Suttle reached for his pad again, making a note of the date of the speech then tracking back through the letter to check the name of the minister. Moments later he found it. He stared at the name, lifted his head, then checked a second time. No question about it. Not a shred of doubt.

He pushed the chair back, yelled down to Mrs Taylor from the tiny upstairs landing. There was a PC on Sam's desk. He wanted to know whether they were on broadband. The answer was yes.

'Do you mind if I get on the Internet a moment?'

'Of course not.' She'd come to the foot of the stairs. 'Help yourself, love.'

★ ★ ★

The morning's interview with Charlie Freeth offered just a glimmer of hope. For one thing, thought Faraday, his attitude seemed to have changed. The sullenness which Faraday had yesterday dismissed as a pose, now seemed unfeigned. Freeth was bored with answering these interminable questions, fed up with having to repeat himself again and again, insulted by the possibility that he might have left anything as unprofessional as a clue at the scene of this wholly deserved killing. Early on, within a minute of Yates cueing the audio and video tapes, he'd warned that time was short.

'I'm out of here at four 'o clock,' he'd said. 'As long as you guys are aware of that.'

The reminder had drawn an emphatic nod from Hartley Crewdson. Pre-interview, out in the corridor, he'd cornered Faraday, tapping his Rolex watch.

'I take it we're not expecting an extension to custody, Detective Inspector. Frankly, on yesterday's evidence, I'm amazed we're here at all.'

The comment had stung Faraday, not least because it contained a germ of truth, but now — with the clock approaching midday — Yates had set about probing the issue of the hospital.

'Frank was on medication from his doctor. Is that true?'

'Yes.'

'Strong medication?'

'I've no idea.' Freeth yawned. 'I wasn't taking it.'

'But medication that made a difference. To Frank.'

'Of course. He wouldn't take the tablets at first but in the end he did. If you want the truth, it turned him into a zombie.'

Yates nodded. He was taking his time.

'Julie told us he was at home at this point.'

'That's right. That's where he lived.'

'So he's sick. And he's under the doctor. And he's taking all this medication. And he's at home. Yes?'

'Yes.'

'Because that's where he wants to be?'

'Yes.'

'And that's where *you* want him to be.'

'Obviously.'

'So why do we suddenly find him in the

539

psychiatric unit at The Orchards?'

Faraday, his eyes locked on the video screens in the adjacent room, was aware of a flicker of something deep in Freeth's eyes. It could be surprise, irritation, concern — anything. But a reaction. Without doubt.

'The Orchards is the nuthouse,' Freeth said. 'That's where people in Frank's state end up. That's what happens. That's what Mallinder did to him.'

'But Julie never mentioned The Orchards. Neither have you.'

'You never asked me.'

'That's not my point, Mr Freeth. Yesterday we asked you for a full account of what happened in those few months between the collapse of Gullifant's and Frank's suicide. Not once did you mention The Orchards. Why's that?'

'I forgot. You blank off. Shit stuff like that . . . ' He shrugged. 'Whatever.'

'How long was Frank in there?'

'Couple of weeks? I forget.'

'Did you and Julie visit him at all?'

'Of course we did.'

'How often?'

'Often. As often as we could.'

'Every day?'

'Often.'

'And yet you never mentioned it, either of you. Why was that?'

'I just told you. I'd forgotten. It slipped my mind.'

'*Forgotten?* You loved Frank. You told us that. And you hated Mallinder for what he'd done to him, how he'd been responsible, as you saw it, for the state of the man. That mattered to you.'

'Of course it fucking mattered.'

Yates glanced at Ellis. He was smiling. For the first time the mask had slipped. At last, Faraday thought. At last.

'So it mattered to you. We accept that. We understand it. You're angry. You're outraged. You're telling us what Frank looked like, how he sat in the armchair all day, how pathetic it all was, how he'd become . . . ' he checked his notes ' . . . a complete zombie. Fair?'

'Absolutely.'

'Yet you couldn't remember him going into the psychiatric unit? That had slipped your mind?'

'He wasn't committed or anything. They were adjusting his medication. It was no big deal. He could have been out in a couple of days.'

'But he wasn't, was he? He was in there for three weeks. He was admitted on the sixteenth of June and discharged on the sixth of July. You're really telling me you'd forgotten all that? Paying him a visit? Day after day?'

Yates let the question hang in the air between them. Freeth looked at his solicitor. A tiny shake of the head. Crewdson's first.

'My client doesn't have to answer that question,' he said.

'OK.' Yates made a note then turned back to Freeth. 'Then let me ask you this. When you were at the unit, visiting Frank, did you spend the whole time on the ward with him, or did you ever have a wander round outside, get some air, nip into St James through that back gate, explore

541

the hospital grounds a bit?'

'Of course I did. Psychiatric units are depressing, even new ones like that. Half an hour or so and you need a bit of a break.'

'So what did you do?'

'I used to go for a wander, like you just said.'

'In the hospital grounds?'

'Yeah.'

Yates tried to press for more detail — Where, exactly, did Freeth used to walk? What did he see? What could he remember? — but at each of these questions Freeth simply shrugged. It had been a rough old time. They'd all been stressed out of their skulls. The last thing he was thinking about was his surroundings.

'Really?'

'Yeah, really. Next time you've got someone you love in the nuthouse, see how you cope. Sometimes you think you're going mad yourself. Just like the rest of those poor bastards . . .'

Faraday's phone began to ring. He glanced at the caller ID. Jimmy Suttle. He wanted to know how the interview was going.

'Better.' Faraday was still looking at Freeth on the monitor screen.

'Great.' Suttle sounded pleased with himself. 'I think we've got a motive, boss, assuming I'm right about the Goldsmith Avenue hit.'

'Yeah?' Faraday felt his pulse quickening. 'Like what?'

'Like revenge, again. There was a big government reshuffle on the ninth of May last year . . . and guess who used to be Minister of State for Pensions Reform?'

26

WEDNESDAY, 20 SEPTEMBER 2006. 14.38

Faraday called a halt in the interview suite just after half past two. Freeth's solicitor was demanding a conference with the Custody Officer over his clients' right to be released after twenty-four hours of detention, and Faraday had decided to gamble on an extension. But before making his case with the uniformed Superintendent, Faraday knew he owed Martin Barrie a conversation. The Detective Superintendent had been up at HQ all morning, his mobile switched off.

Barrie at first thought he was joking.

'You're telling me Freeth did the minister?'

'Not Freeth, not personally. He was driving. The way we see it, O'Keefe was the one on the back. He fired the shots.'

'A kid of *fifteen*? Jesus, Joe . . . '

'I'm saying it's possible. And I'm telling you that the minute we let Freeth go, we'll lose him.'

Barrie glanced at his watch. The PACE Superintendent for the Portsmouth OCU was Andy Secretan. According to Faraday, he was due to leave Kingston Crescent within the next half-hour.

'You think you've got a case?'

'I'll do my best.'

543

'And a twelve-hour extension? That'll be enough?'

'I've no idea, sir. If it isn't, you'll be the first to know. We're not talking low profile here. If Freeth was a suss terrorist, I'm not sure we'd be having this conversation.'

Barrie had the grace to laugh. Faraday was right. Under the new legislation, they could lock a suspected terrorist up for twenty-eight days before facing a custody review.

'Does revenge count as terrorism?' he mused. 'Maybe that's a line you could try on Secretan.'

★　★　★

Superintendent Andy Secretan occupied a spacious, sunny office in the same block that housed Major Crimes. As the city's senior cop, in charge of the Portsmouth OCU, he'd been in the post for three years, earning himself a solid reputation amongst coppers with a lifelong suspicion of senior rank. Secretan, it was commonly agreed, was a fair man. He'd got rid of the duffers, given praise where it was due and had refused a number of opportunities to showboat in the local press. To those who knew him well it came as no surprise to discover that mountaineering on the Isle of Syke was his favoured means of relaxation. This was a man who put a lot of faith in self-reliance. If the pitons gave way on the rock face and you fell to your death, the fault was entirely your own.

He waved Faraday into a chair beside his desk. He was a tall man, quietly spoken.

'I've just talked to Martin Barrie.' He nodded at the phone. 'You can assume I know the background.'

Faraday went quickly through the meagre evidence that had led to Freeth's arrest. Secretan wasn't impressed.

'That's on the thin side, Joe. What else have you got?'

'Freeth had access to Frank Greetham's file of correspondence on the Gullifant's' collapse. I just checked with SOC. D/C Suttle's up at the house now. He's telling me that the minister's name is ringed and underlined. At the time he was with the Department of Work and Pensions.'

'You think Freeth did that? Rather than Frank Greetham?'

'It's possible. We have a witness who says that Freeth was familiar with the file. Either way, it still gives Freeth a motive for killing the minister. He's nothing if not thorough.'

'But can you prove it?'

'Not yet, sir. We've seized the PC in the house but it's still awaiting hard-disk analysis. There may be Google searches, e-mails, all kinds of stuff.'

'That's in hand?'

'Yes, sir. Then there's the lad, Dermott O'Keefe.'

Faraday outlined the operation under way in Fishguard. So far, he admitted, there'd been no further reports from the two D/Cs.

'But you think another twelve hours might see you through?'

'I do, sir, yes. The last interview gave us

545

indications that Freeth isn't as sure of himself as he thought. It's reasonable to suppose that he was en route to Fishguard when we nicked him. He was carrying a passport. You can get a ferry to Ireland from Fishguard. Even if we bail him, I'm not sure we'll see him again.'

'This is an ex-copper, am I right? A D/C?'

'Yes.'

'And you're telling me he did the firearms course before he left us?'

'Yes.'

Secretan nodded. His face was grey with exhaustion. Pompey was his beat, his responsibility, and since Goldsmith Avenue he'd been working eighteen-hour days.

'OK.' He glanced at his watch. 'I've got Freeth's brief in the outer office. Give me a ring in ten minutes.'

⋆ ⋆ ⋆

Bill Prosper was one of three Coroner's Officers working out of a cluttered office in the wing of the city's Guildhall. Jimmy Suttle had never had dealings with the man but knew of his lifelong antipathy to Paul Winter. Now, early afternoon, he asked to see the file on Frank Greetham's suicide.

'Why's that?'

'Major Crimes inquiry. Operation *Billhook*. My guvnor's D/I Faraday. Phone him if you need to.'

Prosper ignored the invitation. He was a big, ponderous man, exactly the type, thought Suttle, to hold a grudge.

'How is he then?'

'Who?'

'Winter. I hear they drummed him out. Not before fucking time, son. I always said that man was a disgrace.'

'You think so?'

'I know so. I served with him in the early days. Bent as you like. Even then. What's the bloke's name again?'

'Greetham. Frank Arthur. He committed suicide seven weeks ago.'

Still grumbling to himself, Prosper made his way to a filing cabinet in the storeroom next door. Suttle was eyeing a spare desk beside the window. By the time Prosper returned he'd also spotted a curl of steam from the office kettle and was trying to figure out where they kept the Nescafe.

'Help yourself, son.' Prosper wasn't good at irony. 'That's exactly the kind of liberty Winter would have taken.'

Suttle carried the coffee to the spare desk and settled down with the file. What interested him most was the attending P/C's account of the morning he'd been dispatched to Westbourne Road. The call had come in at 07.32. Charlie Freeth and a distraught Julie Greetham had been waiting at the house.

The lock-up was a couple of streets away. All three of them had gone to the scene. Freeth had already broken a window at the back of the lock up to gain entry and managed to turn off the engine before beating a retreat. The lock-up was thick with carbon monoxide and he'd broken a

547

second window and waited for the fumes to clear before climbing in again.

He'd found Frank Greetham slumped over the wheel. His flesh was cold to the touch and in Freeth's opinion he'd been dead some time. Freeth had tried to open the front doors to the garage but Greetham had secured them with a chain and padlock. Unable to lay hands on a key, Freeth had finally managed to get the doors open. With the draught the fumes had cleared in minutes.

Suttle finished his coffee, reading carefully through the rest of the file, noting other witness statements — from Julie, from Freeth, from colleagues at work, from Greetham's GP — all of them testifying to a man whose faith in a decent life, decently led, had been tested to destruction by the events of the spring and early summer.

Somewhere amongst these bare, shocked accounts of Frank Greetham's death, Suttle had hoped to find a clue or two, some tiny morsel of evidence that might pin Charlie Freeth against the wall, but picturing the scene in the lock-up, tasting the fumes in the back of his throat, all he could summon was the conviction that no life should end like this. At the inquest the Coroner had recorded a verdict of Death by Suicide, adding a personal note of sympathy for those who had loved and cared for Frank Greetham. *A good man*, he'd written. *Sorely missed.* Too right, Suttle thought, getting to his feet.

Prosper's bulk occupied a desk on the other side of the office. He looked up at Suttle's approach. Suttle wanted to know what remained from the inquest in terms of hard evidence.

'Nothing.' Prosper nodded towards the property cupboard. 'Except the padlock and chain from the garage. You want a copy of that report?'

'Please.'

'The machine's over there. Help yourself.'

★   ★   ★

Faraday was in conference with Yates and Ellis when the call from the *Billhook* incident room found him at the Bridewell. It was D/S Glen Thatcher. He had a mobile number for one of the D/Cs in Fishguard. He needed to have a word with the guvnor. Urgently. Faraday wanted to know what it was about.

'It's complicated, boss. Best to talk to him yourself.'

Faraday rang the number. On the other end, in seconds, was D/C Phelps. At twenty-four, he was the youngest detective on the squad.

'We've got the nipper, boss. I'm looking at him now.'

'*What?*' Faraday got to his feet, turned his back on Yates and Ellis.

'He turned up just after lunch. He'd texted Freeth's mobile earlier and mentioned taking a boat for Ireland. We moved the Toyota down by the ferry port. Kid couldn't miss it.'

'He's secure?'

'Sure.' Phelps was laughing. 'He's sitting in the back. We've got the child locks on.'

'And what's he saying?'

'Not much so far. Except he's been in France for ten days.'

'*France?*'

'That's a roger, boss. I'm looking at his passport and tickets. He did the Poole-Cherbourg crossing on Saturday the ninth. Took the return trip last night, then caught an early train to Fishguard this morning, via Bristol. The paperwork's all here.'

Faraday shook his head. Couldn't be, he thought. Just couldn't be. The hit on the minister had been on Monday the eleventh. No way could Dermott O'Keefe have been on the back of the Kawasaki.

'Have you searched him at all? The boy?'

'Certainly have, boss. We've got an address and a phone number in County Kilkenny. You want to have a guess at the name?'

'O'Keefe?'

'Spot-on. And guess what else we found. This one's for the jackpot.'

'Pass.'

'Nearly three thousand quid.' The laughter again. 'In notes.'

★   ★   ★

Martin Barrie called the conference for six o'clock. Willard had driven down from Winchester. Jerry Proctor, the Crime Scene Co-ordinator, had spent the afternoon reviewing the forensic harvest from both major inquiries. The D/S in charge of *Polygon* Outside Enquiries was sitting beside D/S Glen Thatcher, who'd come over from the Fareham MCT, while Faraday occupied a chair near the end of the table. This shotgun marriage of *Billhook* and *Polygon*, an event Barrie had privately likened to the moment when two atoms triggered a chain reaction, was the last thing any of these men had expected, and even now Faraday sensed a deep reluctance to accept that the terrorist fantasy might be over.

Willard was the first to put this thought into words. Not that he didn't want to believe it but because he knew the strength of the case they'd have to make. A great deal of political weight lay behind MI5's conviction that the minister had been killed by a new strain of the al-Qaeda virus. The news that he had in fact been shot at the hands of an avenging ex-cop would come as a bit of a shock.

'We have to be a thousand per cent on this if D/I Faraday's to be proved right.' Willard was looking from face to face. 'Joe?'

Faraday summarised the afternoon's developments in Fishguard. The efforts of the two D/Cs, coupled with Faraday's shrewdness in anticipating O'Keefe's reappearance, earned a modest round of applause. Faraday himself, while flattered, knew exactly what was coming next.

'So O'Keefe's off the plot.' It was Willard again. 'Passport *and* tickets? Alibis don't come better than that.'

Faraday conceded that O'Keefe couldn't have been riding pillion. In a way, he said, the news had come as a bit of a relief.

'I know things are bad,' he said. 'I know there

are kids in Brixton running round with point forty-five Magnums. But the thought that a fifteen-year-old might have killed a government minister . . . ' He shook his head.

'Quite.' Jerry Proctor was studying his hands. 'And the kid's not even voting age.'

A ripple of laughter ran round the table. It didn't extend as far as Willard.

'So what's Plan B, Joe? Who else would you put on the back of that bike?'

'Julie Greetham.'

'Who?'

'Julie Greetham. She's Frank's daughter. She and Freeth are partners. They live in Frank's old house. She's small, thin, exactly the right build.'

'I thought she was a teacher, Joe?' It was Martin Barrie this time.

'She is.'

'So how come she's got time to fit all this in?'

'She wasn't at school on the Monday. We checked this afternoon. She's got a pretty dodgy attendance record as it is and Monday she logged as another sickie. If we're talking opportunity, she had all day to sort herself out. Freeth wasn't at Positivo, either. He had the whole of last week off. Julie's motive? She's just lost her dad. Her partner's put together this cast-iron case against the minister. He has a file full of correspondence. He has findings from the Parliamentary Ombudsman. Accusations of maladministration. Plus promises of compensation that turn out to be completely empty. From her point of view, or maybe the minister's, it couldn't be worse. Freeth does some research. Finds out the bloke's due down here. Gets himself a bike. Sets up the hit. This is the guy they think killed her dad. So who better to pull the trigger?'

It sounded, Faraday thought, entirely plausible. Willard was more interested in evidence. He looked down the table at the Crime Scene Co-ordinator.

'Jerry?'

'I think it's a great theory.' He smiled at Faraday. 'From where I'm sitting, I just wish I could stand it up.'

Mallinder's place at Port Solent, he said, had yielded nothing of any forensic value. Only the missing Mercedes keys had helped inch *Billhook* forward. As for Westbourne Road, his blokes were nearly through. They'd crawled over every room, subjected countless items to painstaking analysis, lifted floorboards, turned out the roof space, even dredged the waste trap beneath the washing machine and the pipe that ran to the main sewer in case it might yield anything worthwhile. This afternoon, aware that time was tight, he'd put in extra bodies to dig out the back garden, but again there'd been no sign of recent disturbance or hidden goodies. There was a box or two of seized paperwork to go through, but if it ever came to a court case, he said, he'd be making the briefest ever appearance in the witness box.

'Joe?' Willard wanted a reaction.

'It's a question of MO, sir. Both scenes were

553

cleaned up. Not just cleaned up but virtually clue-free. My betting is we'll find the same with the PC hard disk and probably the billings information. Freeth is a man who doesn't make mistakes and both scenes prove it. This is the dog that didn't bark in the night.'

'Terrific, Joe.' Willard mimed applause. 'So how do we put that to a jury?'

'We don't, sir. We wait. We attack him with today's developments. We tell him we've got a couple of hostages. O'Keefe for one. His girlfriend for another. For my money she's on a nicking, and this time we've got her for twenty-four hours. That woman's unstable. You can feel it. More importantly, Freeth knows it too. That means he can't be sure anymore. He doesn't know what we're up to. He's no longer in control.'

'And you really think that's enough?'

'No. Hand on heart of course I'm not sure. But there's another question you haven't asked me yet.'

'And what's that?'

'Do I think he did it? Do I think he killed Mallinder? And do I think he drove the bike in Goldsmith Avenue? In every case, sir . . . ' he reached for his pen and clipped it inside his jacket. ' . . . the answer is yes.'

        ★   ★   ★

Julie Greetham was arrested at the Travelodge at six thirty-five. On the point of returning home to Westbourne Road, she found herself in the back

554

of an unmarked CID Skoda, furious at this latest assault on her liberty. At the Bridewell, after registration by the Custody Sergeant, Faraday arranged for her to be walked past Freeth, on the way to a holding cell of her own. The turnkey reported that neither party said a word to each other.

Forty minutes later she was led to the interview suite. For continuity's sake Faraday had decided that he and D/C Suttle would be asking the questions. Suttle had done well in the previous interview and his performance since then had left Faraday deeply impressed. Not for the first time it occurred to him that this young D/C had learned most of his tradecraft from Paul Winter.

Hillary Denton, once again, was sitting beside Julie Greetham. Before he'd even finished the preliminaries, he sensed the strategy she was going to run. She's seen what I've seen, he thought. She's realised that this client of hers is liable to self-destruct.

Faraday invited Julie to go back to Monday the eleventh of September. Monday was a school day. According to the secretary, Julie had phoned in sick. How did she account for that?

'No comment.'

'Were you really sick?'

'No comment.'

'Julie . . . Ms Greetham, suspicion of murder is a very serious allegation. It might help you to answer these questions.'

'I don't think so.'

Denton shot her a warning look. There was a

script here, just two words long, and this was no time to rip it up.

Faraday glanced at Suttle, gestured for him to take over.

'Julie . . . ' Suttle leaned forward, lowering his voice ' . . . I don't think anyone's blaming you here.'

'They're not?'

'No. You loved your dad. That's not a crime.'

'I know. So why am I here?'

'Because we need to find out what happened.'

'What happened when?'

'On that Monday. When you didn't go to school.' He paused, waiting for an answer. When nothing happened, he leaned forward again. 'Charlie was off as well, wasn't he?'

'No comment.'

'It's a fact, Julie. We've checked.'

'Then you know.'

'Was he in the house with you?'

'No comment.'

'Did you spend the day together?'

'No comment.'

'Did you love your dad?'

'That's unfair.'

The interview hit the buffers. Hoping to lower her defences, Suttle had simply hardened her faltering resolve. She was angry now, refusing point-blank to help them in any way, and after twenty minutes Faraday called a halt to the pantomime. If these twin investigations ever ended up in court then Julie's silence would do her no favours whatsoever, but Faraday could tell from Hillary Denton's smile that she

556

believed this prospect to be remote. A day's absence from the chalk face was hardly proof of political assassination.

$$\star \quad \star \quad \star$$

It was now ten minutes past eight. Superintendent Secretan had authorised a further twelve hours of custody as far as Charlie Freeth was concerned but the PACE extension expired at 04.07 in the morning. To make a double murder charge stick with the CPS, Faraday knew he needed some form of confession and he only had one interview session to do it. So far, despite a wobble over Frank Greetham's stay in St James, Freeth showed no signs of caving in.

He was readying Yates and Ellis for the coming session. Suttle had organised more coffees. They sat around the table in the bare interview room beneath the cold gaze of the video cameras, aware of the ticking of the clock.

Faraday had been in touch with D/C Phelps again. They were bringing O'Keefe back from Fishguard, arrested on suspicion of vehicle theft. With luck, they should be back at Fareham within a couple of hours. Given O'Keefe's age, interviews would have to be handled by specialist officers from the Child Protection Unit. It was a cumbersome process and nothing in the lad's behaviour to date had led Faraday to expect any kind of easy breakthrough. His only concession to the D/Cs in Fishguard had been an acknowledgement that he'd texted Freeth's mobile. Beyond that, he was refusing to say anything.

'Doesn't matter, though.' Faraday was still optimistic. 'It may be enough for Freeth to realise that we've got the lad. The boarding-house reservation would put him on the ferry. The mobile in the boot proves he hasn't thought of everything. The guy's not quite as sharp as he thinks he is. That may be enough.'

'Enough for what, boss?' Ellis was never less than sceptical. 'You really think he's going to cough the lot? This is a guy who knows what we're up against, understands the hoops we have to jump through. We might have shaken him a bit over the hospital but he knows it doesn't take us anywhere really dangerous. The bloke goes for a walk in the grounds of a psychiatric hospital. So what are we doing him for? *Trespass?*'

'Dawn's right.' Yates threw his pen onto the table. 'We're a million miles from court. You've got to hand it to the guy. If he was sitting here now he'd be creaming himself.'

'Maybe arresting him was a bit premature.' Ellis stole a glance at Faraday. 'No offence, boss.'

'You're wrong.' Faraday shook his head. 'If Gwent hadn't nicked him, he'd be away by now. Ireland for starters. Then wherever they fancied.'

'*They?* We're sure about *they?*'

'I am. I don't think it's anything dodgy. But yes, these two are a team. Freeth trusts the boy, rates him. It was probably O'Keefe who nicked the Escort in the first place. That's why Freeth needed him at Port Solent. They could happily torch the car afterwards and no one would be any the wiser.'

'Except we clocked them on CCTV.'

'Sure.' Faraday nodded. 'But even then they were aware. The hoodie? The sun visors down in the middle of the night? I keep telling you. This guy's walked the course. He's been there. He's done our job. He *knows*.'

'What about the Kawasaki?' It was Suttle. 'You're thinking the kid nicked that as well?'

'I think he knew where to find it. The bike belonged to a uni student doing bar work in the evening. The pub is just down the road from Townhill Park, O'Keefe's place. He'd have seen it there most nights. Funnily enough, it was nicked the night before the lad pushed off to France.'

'It was locked up?' Suttle was trying to recall the details.

'Chained.'

'Bolt cutters?'

'Had to be.'

Faraday caught the expression on his face.

'What's the matter?'

'The guy who owned it.' Suttle had produced a pen. 'Can you remember his name?'

'No.'

'But he put a claim in for the bike?'

'Must have done. He definitely reported it because that's how we got to know in the first place. He'd have been after a crime number. Presumably for the insurance people.'

'And this was when?'

'The Friday before the hit.' Faraday frowned,

counting backwards. 'That makes it the eighth.'

'And the pub?'

'It's in Sholing.'

'I meant the name, boss.'

'Christ, now you're asking.' He shut his eyes a moment. 'The Wheatsheaf? Something like that . . . '

Suttle glanced at his watch then got to his feet. Faraday stared up at him.

'Where are you going?'

'I need to make a couple of calls, boss.' He was already at the door. 'Talk amongst yourselves, guys.'

27

Winter wasn't at all sure about letting Westie in. A day on the sofa watching World War Two DVDs had left him feeling remarkably painfree and he'd been toying with a re-run of *The Cruel Sea* when he'd heard a buzz from the videophone. Getting himself to the front door was still a bit of a test and one look at the big black face peering up at the camera made him wonder whether it had been worth the effort.

'What do you want, Westie?'

Grinning, West held up a bunch of flowers, then a big bag of Werther's Originals, before stripping the tissue paper from a bottle of what looked like Black Label.

'It's a litre, mate,' he said. 'In case you were wondering.'

Winter, with some reluctance, let him in. By the time Westie closed the door to the flat behind him, Winter was back on the sofa.

'Man . . . ' Westie was looking at Winter's face. 'The Pole did that?'

'Him and his oppo, yeah. It's worse than it looks. And you should see the state of them.'

'You're kidding me.'

'I am. If you want the full story, they kicked the shit out of me. And you know why? Because you, my friend, didn't — '

561

'Yeah, yeah, yeah . . . ' Westie put the flowers down and wandered into the kitchen in search of a glass. He hadn't come here for a lecture. Winter, up on one elbow, told him to look in the cupboard over the sink.

'Nice pad.' Westie was back, bending to charge Winter's glass. 'Man, I've come to apologise.'

'Because Bazza insisted?'

'Because I got you wrong. No one insists. Not with me. Not even Mr M.'

'Wrong?' In spite of himself, Winter was intrigued. He'd never associated Brett West with contrition. 'Wrong how?'

'Wrong because I still had you down as Filth. I didn't buy all the bitterness shit for a second. What does it take to put yourself a couple of times over the limit and then get nicked? Fuck all. The drink drive charge was a stunt. It was a fairy tale. It was Mr Paul fucking Winter blowing smoke up our arse. I don't know who dreamed all that up but I told Mr M he was crazy even giving you the time of day. The guy's still Filth, I told him. He talks a good war. He's coming on as your best fucking mate. But give it a month or two and you'll wake one morning and find his mates all over you. That's how these cunts work. And Mr W's the biggest cunt of all. Suck you in and spit you out. Good fucking luck.' He grinned, patted Winter on the arm. 'Turns out I was wrong.'

Winter was trying to look relieved. It wasn't hard.

'Good of you to say so, Westie.' He raised his glass. 'So why did it take so long?'

'Because it turns out you've got a very good friend. And if she says you're kosher even I'm going to sit up and take notice.'

'Mist?'

'The one and only.' He touched his glass to Winter's. 'And in my book that makes you the luckiest cunt on God's earth. Am I jealous? Yeah, too right. Am I sorry about the Pole? No, not really. Do I still think you're Filth? No, I don't. And you know why? Because you stuck it to that woman Brodie. I was watching, man. I was watching *really* hard. That was your test, man. If you'd flunked it in that hotel room, Mr M was going to give me a free hand. But you didn't hesitate. Not a flicker. You blew it for her and you did it without a clue about what was coming next. Cool as you like. I admired that, man. And I admired you standing up to Mr M. That was quality. That was *real* class. No way were you still Filth. So, Mr W . . . ' he drained his own glass and picked up the Black Label ' . . . are we doing this bottle, or what?'

* * *

The interview with Charlie Freeth began at 20.47, delayed while Faraday took a phone call from Suttle and then conferenced with Yates and Ellis. Settling himself in front of the video screens, Faraday was glad to see that Yates still had a smile on his face.

The preliminaries over, Yates gestured to Ellis. Ladies first. Help yourself.

'Dermott O'Keefe, Mr Freeth. You told us that

you have no dealings with the lad outside Positivo.'

'That's right.'

'You never see him?'

'No.'

'You have no contact with him?'

'None.'

'You never talk to him on the phone?'

'Never.'

Ellis glanced at Yates. Yates leaned across the desk.

'How many mobiles do you have, Mr Freeth?'

'One. You seized it.'

'Do you own a red Toyota Avensis? Registration LB17 GHD?'

'You know I do.'

'That's a yes, then.'

Freeth nodded, said nothing. He'd hunched a little in his chair. Yates read out the phone number retrieved from the scrap of paper in the Toyota.

'Do you recognise that number, Mr Freeth?'

'No. Should I?'

'It's a boarding house in Fishguard. It's called Harbour View. It's where you might stay if you were thinking of taking a ferry to Ireland.'

'Really?'

'Yes. Are you telling me you didn't know that?'

'Why should I?'

'Because we think you booked a room there. In the name of Smith. As you do.'

'Nice one.' He seemed to relax a little. 'And you think I've got plans to leave the country? You think that's why I was carrying my passport?

Maybe you should check the ferry bookings.'

'Good idea. Except this time of year you wouldn't need a booking. Six sailings a day from Fishguard? You'd just turn up and drive on.'

'Yeah . . . ' Freeth smiled. 'Except I didn't, did I?'

'No. Because you got a pull on the motorway.' Yates paused, studied his notepad. 'We had a good look at your car, Mr Freeth, and guess what we found in the boot?'

'No idea.'

'A mobile. And guess who texted you this morning?'

'Pass.'

'Dermott O'Keefe. Young Dermott. The lad you never talk to out of hours. He wanted to make sure you were there. He wanted to make sure you were waiting. Just the way you'd planned it.'

'Waiting where?'

'Fishguard.'

'*Fishguard*?' Freeth laughed. 'But I wasn't in Fishguard. I was here. That was me down the corridor. Talk to the Custody skipper. He keeps a log.'

'Sure. Of course he does. Of course you weren't there. But your car was. And so were a couple of our blokes. Clever, eh? Not something you'd necessarily expected?'

Freeth raised an eyebrow, then sat back and studied his hands. He doesn't want to believe it, Faraday thought. This wasn't in the plan at all.

Yates explained about O'Keefe finding the empty car.

'He walked straight to it, Mr Freeth. Are you telling me that was some kind of coincidence?'

Freeth said nothing. His head was down. When he looked up again, his eyes were glittering.

'No comment,' he said softly.

For the second time the man with all the answers was robbed of a reply. First the hospital, Faraday thought. Now this.

'Young Dermott's back in Fareham . . .' Yates glanced at his watch. ' . . . about now. We've arrested him for car theft but there's something that still bugs us. Maybe you can help us out here. The pair of you do Mallinder's place. We think you shot the man. We think you did a bloody good job. But why on earth did you let the lad nick the car keys?'

Hartley Crewdson began to protest. Freeth silenced him with a look.

'That's pathetic,' he said softly. 'And you know it.'

'Explain.'

'No comment.' Freeth shook his head.

There was a long silence. Watching, Faraday realised just how shrewd he'd been in the choice of Yates for this interview. The two men were of similar age, similar temperament. They'd never known each other well, never worked together, but one had stayed in the job while the other hadn't. As a result, by some strange chemistry the exchange had become intensely personal. Dawn Ellis knew it too. She'd crossed her arms, waiting.

'Here's another puzzler . . . ' Yates was

566

pretending bewilderment. 'That house of yours is squeaky clean. So clean we're thinking of putting it in for an award. But there's a problem with the paperwork. Why didn't you tell us you were moving?'

'Moving?'

'Yeah. The SOC lads have played a blinder. There isn't a floor-board they haven't lifted. But you know what they told us tonight? After we started asking the right questions? They said they'd found house details, agents' particulars, and you know where this place is? In County Kilkenny.' Yates grinned at him. 'Strange that. Given the address we lifted off young Dermott.'

'No comment.'

'No comment, you can't think of an answer? Or no comment, you can't be arsed?'

'No comment.'

'Shame.' Yates flipped a page in his notebook. 'Let's stick with the boy a moment. He had three grand in his pocket. Where did that kind of money come from?'

'No comment.'

'We think he sold the Mercedes. Not a great price but then I expect some hookey dealer saw him off. Unless the rest went to his mum of course. Do you know Mrs O'Keefe?'

'No comment.'

'Fine woman. And Dermott's a good lad too, if half what we hear is right. But then you'd know that, wouldn't you? Enrolling him on the Junior Leader programme? Trusting him the way you did? Having him along for the ride on the Mallinder job?'

This time Freeth said nothing. His eyes held Yates's gaze then he half-turned towards Crewdson before changing his mind.

'You guys are crap,' he said. 'If this is the best you can do, then no wonder we're all in the shit.'

'In the shit? How does that work?' Yates let the question dangle between them but Freeth shook his head, refusing to take the bait. At length Yates pushed his chair back, abandoning his pad. He was enjoying this. He wanted to take his time. 'Let's go back to Frank Greetham, Charlie. Let's just take a look at why you'd want to settle a debt or two.'

His briefcase lay on the floor beside his chair. He produced a file of correspondence and began to leaf through it. Freeth barely spared it a glance.

'This lot came from Sam Taylor, Charlie. Someone's been making notes in the margin and we think that someone is you. Someone's also been paying a lot of attention to the Minister of State for Pensions Reform. Here . . . ' Yates's finger hovered over a name ringed in scarlet Pentel, 'You want to take a look?'

Freeth shook his head.

'Anyone could have done that.' He nodded at the file. 'The way I remember it, the job used to be about evidence. Not this bollocks.'

'Evidence, Charlie?' Yates's smile was broader. 'Let's talk about the morning Frank died. Tell me exactly what happened. Pretend I know nothing.'

Freeth gazed at him a moment, weighing the question, looking for traps. Then he began to describe the sequence of events that had led him to the garage round the back, and to the realisation that Frank Greetham was sitting in the car with the engine running.

'Was the garage locked?'

'Yeah. From the inside.'

'So you broke a window. Am I right?'

'Yeah.'

'Waited for the fumes to clear?'

'Yeah.'

'Then dived in and turned the engine off?'

'Exactly.'

'So what happened after that?'

'I got out again. The place still stank. Frank was obviously dead. There was sod all I could do for him.'

'And later? Once you needed a decent draught through the place?'

'I got the front doors open.'

'And how did you do that?'

Freeth hesitated. Yates asked the question again. When Freeth didn't answer, he produced another document from the briefcase.

'This is a copy of the Coroner's Report, Charlie. You gave the Coroner's Officer a statement. You told him that the doors had been secured with a length of chain and a padlock. You had to break the chain to get the doors open. How did you do that?'

Freeth was eyeing the report.

'With a pair of bolt cutters,' he said at length.

'Bolt cutters,' Yates repeated. 'And where did you find them?'

'In the garage. They belonged to Frank.'

'Indeed. And he'd had them a long time, hadn't he? So long, there were little tiny nicks on the blades. You know about forensics, Charlie. You know what they can do with blow-ups in the laboratory, electron microscopes, metallurgical analysis, cut-patterns, all that bollocks.' He paused. 'Do I hear a yes? Am I getting warmer?'

Freeth said nothing. When Crewdson protested that this line of questioning was oppressive, Yates returned to the report.

'The Coroner still has the chain from the garage,' he said. 'We'll be submitting it for laboratory analysis.'

'So?' Freeth shrugged.

'We'll also be submitting a pair of bolt cutters we recovered from the grounds at St James' Hospital. Along with a chain that secured the Kawasaki you nicked from outside a pub in Sholing. That's the Kawasaki you used for the hit in Goldsmith Avenue.'

'The defence minister?' Freeth seemed to be losing interest. 'You think I did that too?'

'We do, Charlie, we do. And you know why we've got that chain? Because you left it outside the pub and the bloke who owned the Kawasaki hung on to it. And you know why he did that? Because he's making an insurance claim.' Yates tapped the file. 'Evidence, Charlie, sweet as you like. Two chains. Two sets of those nice forensic lab reports. Both of them admissible in court. And both of them tying you to the hit on the minister. We're not greedy, Charlie. One conviction for murder will do us nicely though a cough on the Mallinder job would make our day.

You're a careful man, Charlie. You like things neat and tidy. Best to get it off your chest, eh? Before we start on Julie.'

There was a long silence. In the adjacent room Faraday heard the scrape of the door opening and looked round to find Suttle stepping in from the corridor. He'd just had another conversation with the SOC boys. Amongst the seized paperwork they'd located a receipt for the bolt cutters. Frank Greetham had bought them with a special staff discount from Gullifant's in April 1992. No wonder the blades had been in a state.

'How are we doing?' Suttle nodded at the monitor screens.

'Fine. Take a seat. The next bit might be interesting.'

Freeth was refusing to say anything. It was Dawn Ellis's turn to put the questions. She wanted to know more about Freeth's interest in moving house.

'I have the SOC log here, Mr Freeth.' She ducked her head. 'Like Bev explained, they seized some paperwork of yours this afternoon. It seems you were negotiating to buy a property in . . . ' she looked up. ' . . . Tullaghaught?'

'That's right.'

'Did you intend to live there?'

'We do, yes.'

'Permanently?'

'Yes.'

'So what about Positivo? All your work with kids?'

'It's over. Done.'

'How come?'

'It's a funding issue. The way things are these days, I'd be spending all my time raising money. That's not why I set the thing up. Not at all. Julie feels the same way. Education's a joke in this country. She can't wait to be shot of it.'

'Just the two of you then? In Tullaghaught?'

'Yeah.'

'No Dermott?'

'I don't know what you're talking about.'

'But you do, Mr Freeth, you do. We can evidence your interest in the boy. We can evidence the meet you'd set up in Fishguard. We can prove your intention to move to Ireland, to set up home, to start a new life. Are you really telling me there wasn't room for young Dermott in all that?'

Freeth was staring at the wall, refusing to take this line of questioning any further. Faraday noticed the whiteness of his knuckles on the table. Yates was much closer.

'You never had kids of your own Charlie,' he murmured. 'How come?'

Freeth's eyes found Yates. Then Ellis.

'You wouldn't,' he said at length. 'Not in this world, you wouldn't. Not in this fucking country, the way it is, the way it's heading. We've lost it, totally blown it, and if we're talking evidence I can give you a hundred names, a thousand, and all of them kids. Kids from broken homes. Kids from the wrong side of the tracks. Kids who never asked to be born. Kids who find themselves up to their necks in the fucking swamp we've made for them. No order. No routine. No direction. Not the first bloody clue who they are. And you know why they end up that way? Because we've failed them. Totally. Because we're gutless. Because we've let ourselves become obsessed by money, and gain, and all the other shit. Because we've given up on decency and graft, and listening to each other, and trying to make an honest living. Because we lie on our backs and spread our legs and let a queue of arseholes have their way. Kids know that. They see it every day. And that's important because the people who get *really* fucked are them, not us. In our sad little lives we think we can take care of it. Kids can't. Won't. And you know what? I'm not sure I blame them.'

There was a long silence. Suttle, watching, mimed applause. Then Ellis bent forward.

'Arseholes like Mallinder?' she queried. 'Arseholes like the minister who wouldn't do right by Frank?'

Freeth looked her in the eye. A ghost of a smile came and went.

'No comment,' he said softly.

★   ★   ★

Yates called a halt to the interview at 22.26. By now it was clear that Freeth's cooperation was at an end. He was still denying every charge and refused point-blank to budge beyond a muttered 'No comment' when pressed for more information. His body language, though, told Faraday that he knew the game was probably up. This was a man who understood the slow, methodical assembly of evidence. He could measure the point beyond which the sheer weight of a case would persuade a jury. And as Freeth got wearily to his feet Faraday sensed that already he was preparing himself for the years to come. Being an ex-copper in a Cat A prison would never be easy.

Back at Kingston Crescent the lights were still burning in the Major Crimes Suite. Faraday had kept Martin Barrie abreast of developments during the evening. PACE regulations stipulated that Freeth should be freed by four in the morning. Now was the time to decide whether or not to formally charge him.

Barrie was in his office attending to a stack of paperwork. DCI Perry Madison sat at the conference table talking on his mobile. Barrie waved Faraday into a chair.

'Well . . . ?'

Faraday summed up the case against Freeth. As far as *Polygon* was concerned, he'd established both motive and opportunity. Freeth had made no secret of his contempt for the political system that had, as he saw it, put Frank Greetham in his grave. The current Minister for Defence Procurement, in his former office, carried responsibility for Frank's suicide, and Freeth, with his knowledge of firearms, was well qualified to settle that debt. His driving licence qualified him to ride a motorbike. He knew Pompey inside out. He was forensically aware. And when it came to an alibi for Monday the eleventh of September, he was relying, once again, on his partner. He'd spent the day at home with Julie. She'd been off school with a migraine. It happened a lot.

'So where did he keep the bike?'

'We don't know, sir. It could have been that garage of his. It could have been anywhere.'

'And you really think it was his partner on the back?'

'I think it's highly likely. We'll be talking to her tomorrow morning.'

'And the bolt cutters?

'We'll be submitting the two chains for analysis. I'd suggest another extension but I'm not sure that'll do the trick.'

Application to the Magistrates Court would keep Freeth in custody for another thirty-six hours. A second application, a further twenty-four hours. But the labs might need longer than a couple of days to come up with a positive match between the two severed links.

Given a forensic result on the chains, Barrie was worried about tying the bolt cutters to Freeth. Faraday was more bullish.

'We can evidence the fact they were in his garage. He admits it himself. He's never mentioned any kind of break-in, so we can assume no one nicked them. That leaves either him or Julie in the frame. They were both regular visitors to The Orchards. He admits walking in the hospital grounds. He'd have seen the derelict villa. He'd have noticed the padlock on the gate in the fence. He was looking for somewhere to stash the bike. For his purposes the villa was perfect. All he needed to deal with was the padlock on the gate in the fence.'

'And earlier? When the bike was stolen?'

'The same. In my view young Dermott had seen the bike outside the pub. He knew it was chained up. Their CCTV had been on the blink for weeks. All it took was Freeth and a pair of bolt cutters.'

'He was taking a risk, though, wasn't he? Going through two chains? With the same bolt cutters?'

'He was, you're right, but the bigger risk was walking out of the hospital grounds with the bolt cutters. That's why he left them hidden to collect later, probably that night. What he didn't anticipate was how quickly we'd be on to the hospital. With our blokes around there was no way he'd risk going back.'

'Indeed, Joe . . . ' Barrie was smiling. 'And on your initiative, as I recall.'

Faraday nodded. The bolt cutters had indeed been the key to Freeth's door but the real honours, he said, should go to D/C Suttle. It was he who'd spotted the possibility of a link and had chased up the evidence, he who'd badgered the Coroner's Officer and pinned down the owner of the Kawasaki.

Barrie nodded, scribbling himself a note. He especially liked Faraday's use of the word 'link'. Then he looked up again.

'So what are you recommending?'

'We charge him, sir. We obviously won't be able to interview him after that but he's gone No Comment anyway. It's a pride thing. He's just never going to make it easy for us.'

'And his partner? Greetham's daughter?'

'I've a feeling she may come across. She's not

that stable. There's O'Keefe as well, when we tackle the Mallinder hit. In my book the lad knows everything and if we press the right buttons, if we make it easy for him, I suspect he'll tell us. Freeth wasn't quite as bulletproof as he thought. Passionate, yes. Bitter, definitely. But there's something else there, too.'

'Like what?'

'Like a kind of madness. This is a guy who was always thin-skinned. He lets stuff get to him. He was that way in the job and he's been that way ever since. What happened to Frank was the tipping point. He just couldn't let it go. He worked out what he wanted to do, decided on a course of action, and after that the rest of the world just passed him by. No one sane does what he did.'

'That's what we say about terrorists, Joe.'

'It's true.' Faraday nodded, struck by the comparison. 'So maybe Freeth did it for the cause.'

'What cause?'

'His cause. Decency. Honour. Everything Frank Greetham represented.'

'And Mallinder?'

'Freeth punished him. Fatally. For what he did to Frank.'

'So do we charge Freeth for that, too?'

'In my book, sir, yes.'

Perry Madison had finished his mobile conversation. Barrie told the DCI to bring another chair over but he shook his head. Briefly, Faraday brought him up to speed. The news that the *Billhook* squad had very probably nailed

577

Polygon's target as well was clearly a major irritation. Faraday fought the temptation to salt the wound. At the very least, by tomorrow, he wanted his office back.

'So what are we saying, Joe? What are we putting this down to? The guy's some kind of vigilante? Or just plain crazy?'

'Neither, Perry. It's payback. It's a settling of accounts. It's revenge. Mr Barrie's right. In a way it's a terrorist thing. The guys he killed were the enemy. Live by the sword . . . ' Faraday's hand chopped briefly down. 'Die by the sword.'

Afterwards

Nearly a week later, after a visit to the dentist, Winter took a cab back to Gunwharf to find a message on his answering machine. It was Marie. She had a little treat in mind. Winter was to pack a bag, enough for a week or so, and be ready by five o'clock. The family, she said, had decided that their newest recruit deserved a bit of sunshine. The word she used was 'therapeutic'. Spain, Winter thought, listening to the message for a second time. Probably the Playa Esmerelda.

Bazza arrived at five fifteen. After days of avoiding the bathroom mirror, Winter had decided that his face was definitely on the mend. The swelling had gone down, the lividness of the bruising had begun to fade, and the dentist had made a decent start on capping his broken teeth. Bazza agreed.

'You look brilliant, mush. Good as new. Allow me . . . '

He carried Winter's bag to the waiting cab. A white envelope lay on the back seat. Bazza told him not to lose it.

'What is it?'

'Moolah. With our compliments.' He gave Winter's arm a squeeze. 'When you get to Gatwick, go to the Emirates desk. They're expecting you. And have a good time, mush, eh?'

Winter settled back, feeling the thickness of

the envelope. He'd been wrong. Emirates didn't go anywhere near Spain. He tore the envelope open and counted the notes. Sixty pink ones. He grinned at the cabbie, then looked out at the pale faces in the rush hour traffic, at the straggle of brain-dead students wandering across the road, at a couple of Somerstown toe-rags, two-up on a nicked bike, carving a path through the shuffling army of pedestrians on the pavement. Three grand, he thought, and a week in the sunshine. Easy.

A girl on the Emirates desk at Gatwick gave him another envelope. Inside was a first-class ticket to Dubai and instructions to look out for a limo driver once he was through immigration. The flight was a blur of champagne. By the time the big jet touched down, Winter was asleep.

From the airport, at two in the morning, the limo took him along the corniche. Sprawled in the back, Winter stared out at the inky blackness of the Gulf spiked with the lights of fishing boats. Then the motorway swung inland through the city centre and he gazed up at the gleaming tower blocks, trying to tell himself that this fantasy was real.

The Burj Al Arab stood on an island of its own, linked to the mainland by a causeway. From a distance Winter was reminded of the Spinnaker Tower — the same billowing concrete, the same white bones. Closer, he shook his head at the chorus line of water sculptures — yellows and greens and the deepest reds — that danced around the hotel. Without the Pole, he thought, I'd have seen nothing of this. He rubbed his face,

remembering the roughness of the bare Portakabin floor, thinking of Westie's little jape and
wondering whether a beating like that had, in the
end, been worth it.

At the kerbside, briefly, he was overwhelmed
by the moistness and warmth of the night air.
Then he was back in the air-conditioned chill of
the hotel itself. The atrium soared above him. At
reception the most beautiful woman he'd ever
seen in his life took his details. A flunkey stooped
to carry his bag. A pair of heavy lift doors
opened. Then came a thickness of carpet he'd
never thought possible and the briefest moment
at the door of his suite while the flunkey inserted
Winter's entry card.

Inside the lighting was dim. The bed looked
like an altar. There were drapes on the wall
behind it, the deepest blue. The flunkey
disappeared with a whispered goodnight, leaving
Winter inspecting an empty bottle of champagne
upended in a bucket of melting ice. He frowned.
His eyes returned to the bed. He could make out
a shape now, someone moving, a head, a glimpse
of a bare shoulder, then a sudden expanse of
white sheet as a hand threw back the coverlet.
Winter took a step forward, then stopped again,
recognising the swell of her breasts, knowing that
he'd finally lost it.

'Mist,' he said.

★ ★ ★

It was nearly a week before Faraday was able to
take a step back from *Billhook* and *Polygon*.

581

Charlie Freeth was formally charged with the murder of the defence minister and refused bail pending preparation of his case. From the remand wing at Winchester Prison came news that he'd assaulted another prisoner in the showers but further rumours about his mental state proved harder to check out. His partner, meanwhile, after a day in the interview suite, had made a full confession.

The attack on the minister, she said, had been Freeth's idea, an unmissable opportunity to avenge her father's death, and she'd willingly agreed to carry the gun and pull the trigger. A day with the revolver in one of the remoter parts of the New Forest had given her the basics, and when the time came she'd marvelled at how simple it had all been. She'd aimed four bullets at the face behind the glass, point-blank range, and nobody had lifted a finger.

Challenged over the Mallinder killing, Julie Greetham was less forthcoming. Yes, she and Charlie were planning a new life in Ireland. Yes, they'd wanted young Dermott along. And yes, she'd taken an intense pleasure in reading about Mallinder's death. But whether Charlie had done it, hand on heart, she couldn't say.

This, to Faraday, sounded unlikely, but a single interview with Dermott O'Keefe brought *Billhook* to a successful end. Faraday had plotted a strategy with the specially trained P/C who'd be talking to O'Keefe, somewhat surprised at the man's willingness to stretch the juvenile interviewing guidelines. The best line of attack, they'd both agreed, lay through O'Keefe's enormous family. Any threat to them might concentrate the lad's mind.

And so it proved. O'Keefe himself, much as his social worker had described, turned out to be a slight youth, obviously bright, with an openness Faraday had never associated with adolescence. Given an assurance that they'd leave his mum alone, he volunteered a full account of the night he and Freeth had waited in Port Solent.

The movie, he said, had been crap. The wait in the car park went on forever. Only at three in the morning had they driven to Mallinder's place. Freeth had forced the front door. Standing in the hall, looking at the car keys, O'Keefe had heard the soft *phutt* of the silenced automatic. Charlie had emerged with two pillows, one soaked in blood. They'd driven to the New Forest, drenched the pillows and the insides of the Escort with petrol, and burned the lot. Weeks later, he was still amazed how fierce the fire had been. A scorcher, he said, with a grin on his face.

At this point the D/C enquired whether he'd felt comfortable being party to a murder. The question stopped O'Keefe in his tracks but in the end, after some thought, he simply nodded.

'Charlie told me the bloke was an arsehole,' he said. 'And I believed him.'

Released on bail, O'Keefe now faced charges of vehicle theft and conspiracy to murder, though Barrie agreed on a plea to the judge for leniency on account of the lad's cooperation. Given the latter, Freeth now faced a second full-blown murder charge.

Back in his office at Kingston Crescent, much to DCI Madison's disgust, Faraday found himself preparing the CPS files for both *Billhook* and *Polygon*. A private word with Willard had earned D/C Suttle warm praise for his intelligence work on both operations and when the Head of CID dropped by to confirm the lad's return to full duties, his attention was caught by a postcard pinned to Faraday's corkboard.

'Where's that?'

Faraday glanced up. The postcard, surrounded by a litter of bird shots, showed three women enjoying exotic cocktails beside an enormous swimming pool. The sky was as blue as the water and in the background, rearing into the sky, was the full-bellied shape of a building that at first sight defied description. *The best hotel in the world*, ran the caption across the bottom, *Welcome to the Burj Al Arab*.

'It's from Winter. He sent it from Dubai.'

'Do you mind?'

Without waiting for an answer, Willard unpinned the card and turned it over. Faraday knew Winter's inscription by heart: *42 degrees. Krug on tap. And a woman who can't keep her hands off me. Where the fuck did I go wrong?*

Willard spent a moment or two digesting this message before tearing the card in two. Faraday watched the pieces flutter into the bin.

'The man's a disgrace,' Willard grunted. 'Can't you find something better to look at?'

Faraday held his gaze for a moment, then pulled his drawer open and began to rummage for the Sellotape.

We do hope that you have enjoyed reading this large print book.

Did you know that all of our titles are available for purchase?

We publish a wide range of high quality large print books including:
Romances, Mysteries, Classics
General Fiction
Non Fiction and Westerns

Special interest titles available in large print are:
The Little Oxford Dictionary
Music Book
Song Book
Hymn Book
Service Book

Also available from us courtesy of Oxford University Press:
Young Readers' Dictionary
(large print edition)
Young Readers' Thesaurus
(large print edition)

For further information or a free brochure, please contact us at:
Ulverscroft Large Print Books Ltd.,
The Green, Bradgate Road, Anstey,
Leicester, LE7 7FU, England.
Tel: (00 44) **0116 236 4325**
Fax: (00 44) **0116 234 0205**

ONE UNDER

Graham Hurley

Buriton Tunnel, just north of Havant. A body is torn apart under the wheels of the first morning train to leave Portsmouth for London. The body was naked and chained to the rails. Was this a brutal murder or a grotesquely calculated suicide? DI Joe Faraday must try to unravel this most gruesome of crime scenes. DC Paul Winter lands the task of searching through the missing persons list in an attempt to identify the dead man - and in the process comes across another missing man, someone who stepped out of his ordered life with no hint of leaving. Can Faraday and Winter untangle two tales of emotion and thwarted love?

BLOOD AND HONEY

Graham Hurley

The discovery of a headless body in the sea beneath cliffs on the Isle of Wight is Detective Inspector Joe Faraday's latest investigation. The disappearance of a violent-tempered delivery driver, who has fallen foul of the owner of a local nursing home, gives an important lead. Meanwhile, Detective Constable Winter's life is in crisis as he becomes involved with a prostitute at the centre of an investigation of a powerful local businessman. His difficulties are compounded by a series of worryingly debilitating and vicious migraines. Faraday and Winter must deal with the legacy of violence inflicted by people and society: a world where terrifying pressures combine to create unlikely killers and even more unlikely saviours.

DEADLIGHT

Graham Hurley

When Prison Officer Sean Coughlin is found brutally murdered, Detective Inspector Joe Faraday is called in to drive the investigation. Newly appointed to Portsmouth's elite Major Incident Team, Faraday begins to build a disturbing picture of the dead man's life. With few friends, and many enemies, Coughlin appears to be a murder waiting to happen. But as the inquiry begins to probe the prison officer's naval service, Faraday becomes uncomfortably aware that the investigative trail leads backwards to the Falklands War. Coughlin served aboard a naval frigate, bombed and sunk in San Carlos Water. Nineteen lives were lost to enemy action, a tragedy which may — two decades later — mask another murder.